Other Ace Books by Sharon Shinn

ARCHANGEL
JOVAH'S ANGEL
THE ALLELUIA FILES
ANGELICA

WRAPT IN CRYSTAL
THE SHAPE-CHANGER'S WIFE
HEART OF GOLD
SUMMERS AT CASTLE AUBURN
JENNA STARBORN

SHARON SHINN

ACE BOOKS, NEW YORK

An Ace Book
Published by The Berkley Publishing Group
A division of Penguin Group (USA) Inc.
375 Hudson Street
New York, New York 10014

This is an original publication of The Berkley Publishing Group.

This is a work of fiction. Names, characters, places, and incidents either are the product of
the author's imagination or are used fictitiously, and any resemblance to actual persons, living
or dead, business establishments, events, or locales is entirely coincidental.

Copyright © 2004 by Sharon Shinn.

All rights reserved.
This book, or parts thereof, may not be reproduced in any form without permission.
The scanning, uploading, and distribution of this book via the Internet or via any other
means without the permission of the publisher is illegal and punishable by law. Please pur-
chase only authorized electronic editions, and do not participate in or encourage electronic
piracy of copyrighted materials. Your support of the author's rights is appreciated.
ACE and the "A" design are trademarks belonging to Penguin Group (USA) Inc.

First edition: March 2004

Library of Congress Cataloging-in-Publication Data

Shinn, Sharon.
    Angel-seeker / Sharon Shinn.— 1st ed.
        p.   cm.
    ISBN 0-441-01134-9
    1. Life on other planets—Fiction.   2. Angels—Fiction.   3. Women—Fiction.   I. Title.

PS3569.H499A84   2004
813'.54—dc22

                                                                            2003066274

PRINTED IN THE UNITED STATES OF AMERICA

10   9   8   7   6   5   4   3   2   1

For four fabulous friends:

Linda—two tickets to Italy, free; two hotel rooms in Rome, free, quality time spent together at CDG airport, priceless.

Rhonda—funny, funky, forthright, fearless. Even if I'm famous, I'll always have lunch with you.

Connie—whose courage in setting personal goals has made me think about setting some of my own.

Laurie—who loves people more than I do, popular culture a little less, and words just as much. What else is there to talk about?

SAMARIA

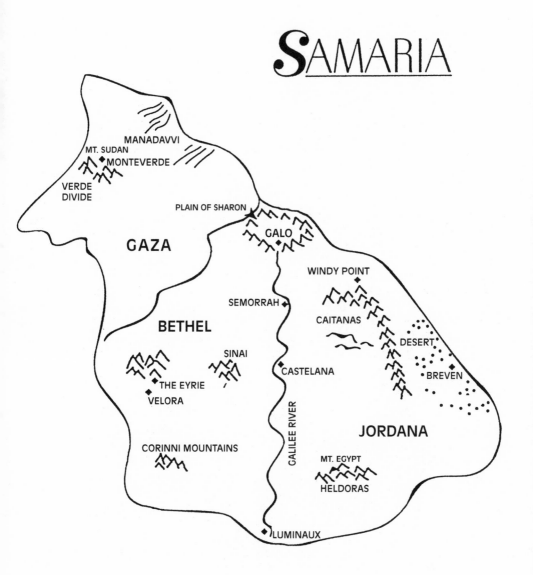

MANADAVVI

MT. SUDAN
MONTEVERDE
VERDE
DIVIDE

PLAIN OF SHARON

GALO

GAZA

WINDY POINT

SEMORRAH

CAITANAS

DESERT

BETHEL

SINAI

THE EYRIE
VELORA

CASTELANA

BREVEN

JORDANA

CORINNI MOUNTAINS

GALILEE RIVER

MT. EGYPT
HELDORAS

LUMINAUX

ANGEL-SEEKER

CHAPTER ONE

It was still dark when Elizabeth rose, moving silently through the sleeping house. In the kitchen she stirred up the fire and lit a few candles—the cheap ones, the ones that were good enough for the hired help but that wouldn't be tolerated in any of the grand rooms where the family dwelled. In a few minutes, she had the water boiling, the bread kneaded, and the porridge heating on the stove. The sun was beginning to make a sullen appearance over the horizon. By the look of the sky, heavy with fat-bellied clouds, this day would be as dreary as the one before, and the one before that.

And the one before that.

The field hands tramped in, their feet noisy but their mouths mostly silent, and settled themselves around the table. Elizabeth served them with a cool dispassion, nodding if one of them looked up and caught her eye but making no effort to converse or smile. Most of them had learned long ago that she wasn't your average farm cook, willing to flirt with a handsome new hand, softened by wheedling, happy to put together a special meal or a late dinner just because some brawny but brainless man grinned at her. Most of them had tried flirting with her anyway, because there weren't many diversions here on the sprawling farm. The nearest collection of buildings that called itself a town was a half-day's ride, and to get anywhere remotely interesting, like Semorrah or Luminaux, took a full three days and a knapsack of provisions. But they had soon learned, if they wanted dalliance, they were better off saddling up and riding across the low Jordana foothills and into the Blue City.

Elizabeth herself hadn't been to Luminaux in six months or more. The first few years she'd been at James's farm, she had pined for the gaiety of that most beautiful and luxurious of cities, and she had taken whatever opportunities arose to travel there for a brief holiday. But she had no money, so she just felt bitter and envious as she strolled through the azure streets, staring into the shop windows; and she had no true joy in her heart, so the constant thrum and backbeat of the music pouring out of the cabarets did not lift her spirits or make her smile. Luminaux just reminded her of what she had lost or what she would never attain, and so it was best for her if she did not return to Luminaux. She would stay, instead, mired forever on this limitless farm in the unexciting foothills of southern Jordana, and wish her life away.

"I'd take some more of that bread, if you've got any," one of the hands said in a neutral voice. Elizabeth nodded and cut another slice from the loaf.

"Anyone else?" she asked. A few murmurs of assent, so she continued cutting till the bread was gone.

"And some tea. Thanks," said another man.

"Looks like another wet day," someone observed.

"Damn hot for this time of year," the first speaker grumbled. "Should have cooled off a bit by now."

"Winter'll come soon enough, and you'll be wishing for weather this warm."

She let them talk around her, not listening until they asked for something she could supply, scarcely noticing as they finished their meals and filed out past her. Personally, she did not care if it was hot or cold or wet or dry or summer or winter or day or night. It was all the same: dismal, dull, pointless.

She had been made for a life much better than this. She had been born for finer things. Sometimes she still lay awake at night, eyes wide open in the dark, fists clenched to her sides, unable to believe she had come to this.

"Elizabeth?" The use of her name caught her off guard. She had turned to the oven to set the fresh loaves in to bake, and she'd thought she was alone in the kitchen. In fact, one man remained, a rangy, seedy field worker who'd been at the farm about three months. He hadn't entirely learned the lesson about flirting with the cook, for he still gave her a warm, private smile from time to time as if to remind her of some stolen kiss or illicit midnight tryst. His name was Bennie. She supposed it was short for Benjamin, but no one called him by the more elegant name. Bennie. As if she would ever consider someone with a name like that.

"What is it?" she asked somewhat warily, crossing her arms over her chest to underscore her unapproachability.

He smiled anyway and leaned back against the table as if prepared to perch there and gossip awhile. "His lordship's asked me to take a little trip tomorrow," Bennie said. James was hardly a lord, not like the wealthy merchants in the river cities; sometimes the field hands called him that as a joke, because James was so pretentious. "Thought you might want to come."

Elizabeth could feel her features tighten in distaste. "I don't believe it would be appropriate for me to travel under your escort," she said repressively.

He grinned. "Put that in plain language. You mean, you wouldn't be caught dead riding anywhere with me?"

His hair was black and unkempt, though it fell over his forehead with a sort of roguish charm. He was thin and wiry, but tall, and his demeanor suggested he had always had good luck with women. Not this woman. Elizabeth drew herself a little farther away. "I don't have any time off coming to me," she said. "Angeletta doesn't like it when I'm gone from the kitchen. So. Thank you, but I can't."

"Don't you even want to know where I'm going?" he coaxed.

"Luminaux, I suppose."

He shook his head. "Better."

For a moment she was tempted. "Semorrah?" The fabulous river city of white spires and soaring architecture was the most beautiful spot in Samaria, as far as Elizabeth was concerned, and she had not been there in nearly five years. But no. She would be even more unhappy there than she would be in Luminaux.

Bennie was smiling more widely and shaking his head more emphatically. "Not Semorrah, either. Even better."

She couldn't think of any place better than Semorrah. "I can't guess, then. Probably someplace I wouldn't want to go."

He cocked his head to one side. "Cedar Hills," he said.

She felt her hands fall limply to her sides and her mouth grow loose with desire. Cedar Hills. The angel hold still under construction in central Jordana. It was rumored to be a place of great sweetness and charm—not as artistically rich as Luminaux or as beautiful as Semorrah, but filled with life and laughter and music and hope.

And with angels. Overrun with angels. The most magnificent creatures in the world.

Elizabeth had only met an angel once in her life, when she was a little girl, when her mother had taken her to Semorrah to be fitted for a dress for some cousin's wedding. They had stayed in the house of a river lord who was friends with Elizabeth's father, and they had found that an angel was among the houseguests. He had been exceptionally tall, with thick golden hair and a sonorous voice, but all Elizabeth could really focus on were his wings. They trailed behind him wherever he walked like a commanding, ghostly presence, glowing with a life and sentience of their own. She had been consumed by a desire to sneak up behind him and run her fingers across their silky surfaces, but of course her mother had made sure she did no such thing. Touch an angel's wings, indeed! Such presumption was not allowed. The angel had been gracious, though; he had spoken courteously to her mother and kindly to Elizabeth herself, bending down from his great height to look her solemnly in the eyes. It had been the most terrifying and spectacular moment of her life to that point.

She still had not experienced anything to rival the moment an angel pronounced her name.

"Elizabeth?" Bennie said again.

She shook her head to clear away something—memories, or regrets, or the accumulated misery of the past five years. "Yes. I heard you. Cedar Hills."

"Wouldn't you like to go? Surely you can find some reason that will satisfy her ladyship. Something you need in Cedar Hills that can't be found anywhere else."

"I don't—what's in Cedar Hills that can't be found in Luminaux? She'll never agree to let me go."

He raised an eyebrow. "But you'd like to?"

She opened her mouth and then shut it. Acting like a stupid girl, seduced by promises, and in front of Bennie, of all people. "I would love to see Cedar Hills," she said in a voice that she tried to make frosty and dignified. "But I feel certain I won't be able to accompany you there tomorrow."

He shrugged and straightened up. "Well, if you change your mind before tomorrow morning, just let me know."

"When are you leaving?" she couldn't help asking.

"First light or before. In fact, if you could make me up a packet of food tonight, and just leave it here on the table for me, I'd be most obliged."

"How long will the trip take?"

"Three days, I imagine. Longer if the weather's bad."

"What are you going to be doing in Cedar Hills?"

He grinned at her. "Supplying food to the hold. Isn't that nice? His lordship negotiated a deal with Nathan over the summer. So I imagine I'll be heading off to Cedar Hills pretty often, once the whole harvest is in. Me or someone else, that is."

She felt her heart skip a beat. "So if I don't go with you tomorrow, I could go some other time. Maybe. If Angeletta doesn't mind."

"Well, you could," he said impudently, "if the offer was still open."

She felt herself flush. "Yes, well, I—of course, if you didn't want company I wouldn't—"

Now he laughed. "But I'd probably take you any time you decided to go. Pretty boring trip for a man alone."

"I don't know that my company would make it any more tolerable," she said in an icy voice.

He laughed again. "Oh, I don't think you're so cold as you'd like us all to think," he said cheerfully. "You're just unhappy. Tell you a few jokes, make you laugh, I think you'd warm up soon enough."

She was both furious and disgusted, but she didn't want to show either emotion. She didn't want him to rescind the offer, even though she couldn't think of a single way for her to accept it. Angeletta would never let her traipse off to Cedar Hills for a pleasure jaunt! To be gone a week or more, for no reason except that her heart craved beauty! There would be no way to explain it. No way to convince

Angeletta that Elizabeth *needed* to go to Cedar Hills, required it the way everyone else required a certain amount of food and water, and a healthy exposure to sun. Even if Elizabeth could come up with a good enough reason, she thought it would take more than a day to convince Angeletta to let her go and to find someone else to cover the kitchen while Elizabeth was gone.

Still, she might think of something. She might come up with a plan. She did not want to alienate Bennie at this juncture, in case he might be of use to her in the future.

So she contented herself with saying, with a touch of rue, "I'm not a lighthearted young girl. I don't think jokes and smiles will really have that great an effect."

He leaned a little closer, still smiling but with a certain kindness in his face. "No, you're not a lighthearted *girl,*" he repeated softly. "But you're still a young woman. You can't be more than twenty-five."

She gave a hollow laugh. He was right by a few months; she had had an unremarked birthday in the spring. "You think so? I feel like I'm about a hundred."

"That's what a hard life will do to you," he said with easy sympathy. "Look at me! I look about fifty, but I'm barely thirty."

He was grinning again, and she knew this for a lie. He was probably a year or two past fifty, in fact, and looked every day of it. But the lines around his eyes didn't seem as if they'd come from years of suppressed anger and want. In fact, he didn't appear as if he'd worried about much of anything during those fifty years, just moved amiably from event to event without much care for where each experience might take him. *That* was a skill she could envy, as long as she was envying everything else.

"I'm sorry your life has been difficult," she said, because she couldn't think of anything else to say.

"Not as difficult as yours, I'd wager," he said, turning and heading toward the door. "You can tell me about it tomorrow on the way."

"But I won't be able to go with you tomorrow," she called after him, a note of wistfulness in her voice.

He stopped with his hand on the door and grinned at her. "Oh," he said, "I think you will."

*   *   *

Elizabeth spent the whole rest of the day trying to think of a way to join Bennie on the trip to Cedar Hills. Every excuse she came up with sounded preposterous, even to her ears, and she couldn't imagine trying to use one to convince Angeletta. She needed more time. She needed better ideas.

She needed to be answerable to anybody but Angeletta.

If her circumstances had been even a little less dire when she had arrived at James's place five years ago, Angeletta would not have been the bane of her existence. For the farm wife was the worst kind of social schemer, a transplanted Manadavvi woman who clearly thought she had come down in the world by marrying a Jordana landowner, no matter how rich. Angeletta had set about making the property a showplace, renovating the large but rather plain house, furnishing it with Luminaux treasures, and throwing grand parties once a year that were attended by all the Jordana elite. Angeletta's stated goal was to work her way into the social strata of Cedar Hills, to be welcomed there by the host, Nathan, and his wife, Magdalena. Hence, no doubt, James's deal to supply produce to the angel hold. Quite possibly there were other negotiations in the works.

Angeletta had not been the kind of woman to welcome into her household an orphan girl whose parents were distantly related to her husband. She thought James's antecedents were questionable enough without having to explain away the presence of an awkward and destitute young relative. It didn't matter to her that Elizabeth's parents had been wealthy people of some standing before her father had lost everything in a series of bad investments with the Jansai. It didn't matter to her that Elizabeth didn't have another soul in the world to care for her. It didn't matter to her that Elizabeth was homeless, motherless, fatherless, penniless. Angeletta would not treat her as a daughter or a sister or a cousin. Angeletta would take her in as a servant—and James, after a few halfhearted arguments, had agreed.

Elizabeth hated Angeletta with all her heart, but she despised her cousin James. Weak-willed, stupid, vain, and ambitious, he was a man who had given over his whole life into his wife's control. Once Elizabeth had been relegated to the role of hired help, James went out of his way to avoid her, never coming to the kitchen, never lingering in the dining room or any public room where Elizabeth might come on him by chance. He had given her a place to stay and some certainty that it would be hers for life, but he had not given her a *home*. He had given her nothing she could really value.

For the first year of her tenure at the farm, Elizabeth had comforted herself with the belief that everything would change soon. One of her mother's friends would remember her existence, would invite her to come live in her gracious Semorran home. Her father's niece would track her down in Jordana and swoop upon the farmhouse, calling out, "For shame!" when she saw how Elizabeth had been treated. Or—an even better dream—one of the rich landholders who attended Angeletta's parties would bring his handsome son along, and the bored young man would wander out into the gardens, where Elizabeth would be resting after a long day of working in the kitchen to prepare the day's feast. He would sit beside her, and tell her stories, and catch sight of her features in the moonlight, and be struck dumb by her charm and beauty. . . .

But none of these things had happened, not in any of the years that Elizabeth had been hidden away in this green, gentle prison. She had lost all hope of being rescued. She had begun to wonder what she could do to rescue herself.

More than once it had occurred to her that she could hire herself out as a cook somewhere else—on a nearby ranch, for instance, or even in one of the hotels in Semorrah or Luminaux. She had learned how to cook for twenty or more people at a time, and—though she hated to do it—she could work as hard as anyone. Angeletta paid her virtually no wage, considering her room and board to be salary enough, and Elizabeth was pretty certain she could earn something far more satisfying at almost any venue.

But she did not want to be a cook. She did not want to be a servant of any kind. She wanted to be a titled lady, or a pampered wife, or even just an indulged young daughter in someone's house. Why should she have to work at all? Why had Jovah been so cruel to her?

She had not missed her father at all when he died, drowned in an unfortunate boating accident in the waters between Semorrah and the Bethel coast. He had not been around the house that much; he was a remote and somewhat severe figure in her life. But her mother's death had hit her hard, for they had always had the closest of relationships. They had already moved from the big house, the house she had grown up in, to the small house, the one that was too tiny to afford any privacy and that was too close to the neighboring butcher shop to ever smell entirely clean. Elizabeth had already been unhappy and petulant, unable to understand *why* they had no money, *why* they could not afford silk shawls and fancy candies, *why* she could not see her friends from Castelana and Velora. Coming home one afternoon to find her mother feverish and delirious in her small bedroom had been the greatest shock of Elizabeth's life. But even then, she had not known what terrible changes that illness had portended. If she had, she sometimes thought, she would have crawled in under those hot sheets next to her mother's restless body and hoped to contract whatever fatal disease had struck her mother down. She would rather have died than live the way she was living now.

But if she could get to Cedar Hills . . .

Moving through the kitchen without conscious volition, scarcely aware of what she was doing, Elizabeth cleaned the dishes and wiped down the table and rolled out another loaf of bread. But her thoughts were not on her work. If she could get to Cedar Hills . . .

There was no possible excuse she could fashion that would be good enough for Angeletta. But what if she did not tell Angeletta she was going? What if she merely left? Could Angeletta turn her away at the door when she returned? Wouldn't James, contemptible creature that he was, insist that Elizabeth be readmitted to the house? She was, after all, a blood relation; he would not let her starve in the ditches of southern Jordana.

Elizabeth's hands paused in the act of mixing dough. What if she left the house without the intention of returning?

Methodically, her hands resumed their motions, but her mind was racing elsewhere. She had a little money set by—not much, but enough to live on for a few weeks, she was sure. She could take every coin and copper with her on this journey. She could get a job in Cedar Hills, she knew she could. She would cook, or do laundry, or watch children, or anything else that was offered. She would take a job in Cedar Hills, and she would discover a way to meet an angel. . . .

At this point in her meditations, Elizabeth shivered. Even she was a little aghast at the direction her thoughts were taking. Angels were rare, mystical, divine creatures that should be admired from afar; they were the great winged messengers that carried the hopes and prayers of humans to the ears of the god Jovah. They were shaped like men and women, true, and they lived among humans on the earth, but they were not to be viewed as mortals were, or treated as human in any way.

Still, angels had to mate with humans in order to reproduce. Everybody knew that. So angels needed humans—for some things, at least, at some times in their lives.

Elizabeth set aside the shaped loaf and began to pour more ingredients into her metal bowl. A mortal woman who bore an angel child was welcomed into the hold forever. She could live there while her child was raised, and after—for as long as she liked. Perhaps she might be lucky enough to bear more than one angel child, and so become especially treasured by these divine beings.

Perhaps she would be lucky enough to actually spark true love in the heart of an angel.

Elizabeth was not stupid. She knew all about the wretched women who lived near the three holds, attempting to ensnare and seduce an angelic consort. No one had anything flattering to say about these desperate creatures, these angel-seekers, as they were called. Yet everyone forgot how manipulative and pathetic they seemed as soon as they produced those tiny winged shapes from their wombs. Anyone might mock an angel-seeker, but everyone cherished the mother of an angel. Such a woman would be honored till the end of her days.

I will go to Cedar Hills, Elizabeth thought. *And I will find an angel who will fall in love with me. And everything will be different then.*

CHAPTER TWO

It was still dark as Elizabeth moved silently through the kitchen. Three loaves of bread, some strips of dried meat, apples, jugs of water—they all took up more space than she expected, and she had to fill two baskets instead of the one she was intending. Her own clothing had taken up two dilapidated bags instead of one, but she hadn't wanted to leave behind anything precious. She had to take it all with her now, because she was never coming back to this place.

She heard the wagon pull up to the kitchen door, the creak of wood and metal, the complaining whicker of the horses, Bennie's soft voice raised in admonition. A few moments later he pushed open the door and stepped inside, his body dark and strangely elongated in the insufficient light of two candles.

He nodded at the baskets on the table. "I see you're coming with me, then," he said. "More there than one man could eat in two weeks on the road."

"Yes," Elizabeth said, and didn't embroider her answer.

He glanced around. "You'll have your own bag somewhere. Where is it? I'll toss it in the wagon."

Soundlessly, she pointed at the two frayed pieces of luggage. He laughed so loudly she had to make a shushing sound.

"You must plan to change your clothes more often than I do while we're traveling," he said cheerfully, bending over to pick them up.

"I didn't know what I might need," she said sulkily. "I just thought—I'd bring everything."

"Fine by me," he said, and went out through the door again.

Elizabeth glanced around the kitchen once more to see if there was anything she'd forgotten. The extra loaves of bread were cooling on the window shelf—a start on breakfast for the hungry field hands who would be arriving within the half hour. She'd also prepared an egg and sausage dish in advance. It would be cold by the time the workers arrived, but they'd eat it anyway without complaining, and go on out into the fields without rousing the rest of the house. Not till James and Angeletta came downstairs an hour or two later would anyone realize, or care, that the cook was no longer in the kitchen.

She picked up both baskets and went out.

It was cooler than she'd expected, but that was just fine; she was wearing her wool jacket, because it was too bulky to pack and she didn't want to leave it behind. The sky was just beginning to lighten in the east, though it looked more as if the black was shredding wearily away than that any gold was pouring enthusiastically over the horizon. The air smelled as clean as winter snow.

"Just hand those to me and climb on in, if you can make it by yourself," Bennie directed, and Elizabeth passed over the baskets. She clambered up to the high driver's seat, grateful to find it padded, and settled herself as best she could. The two horses hitched to the wagon did not even turn their heads to check out her fresh weight and what it might mean for their labors over the next three days.

In a few minutes, Bennie vaulted in beside her and gathered up the reins. He gave her a sly smile that she made no effort to return.

"Got everything? Then I suppose we're off," he said and clucked to the horses.

The first hour passed agreeably enough. A consumptive sun rose reluctantly to spread their way with light, and soon it was hot enough to make Elizabeth take off her jacket. Bennie talked casually and incessantly, but for some reason he did not annoy her. His voice was soothing, almost, as it skipped over topics ranging from corn harvesting to travel through the mountains during the rainy season. She didn't pay much attention, but it was impossible not to gather certain facts about his life and his attitudes. He had traveled a great deal, it seemed, and lived just about everywhere: Luminaux, Castelana, even the Jansai city of Breven, where very few strangers were welcome. He didn't care much for farmwork and didn't think he'd stay for long at the farm. He'd been considering heading over to the Eyrie, the angel hold in northern Bethel, and seeing if he could pick up any work in the neighboring city of Velora. Or he might fall in with an Edori tribe and travel for awhile with them.

"Edori!" Elizabeth exclaimed, her attention finally caught. "You have friends among the Edori?"

He shrugged and grinned. "Everyone has friends among the Edori if they give it even a little bit of effort," he said. "Friendliest creatures in the world."

"We used to have an Edori slave who worked with me in the kitchen," Elizabeth said. "Angeletta had to free her, though, once Gabriel said no one could have slaves anymore."

"Well, the Archangel Gabriel is one sanctimonious and haughty son of a bitch, but I do agree with him about the Edori," Bennie said comfortably.

Elizabeth was shocked to hear anyone speak so slightingly of the Archangel, but what she commented on was his remark about the Edori. "But everyone kept Edori slaves when I was a little girl," she said. "Even my mother."

He glanced down at her with a little smile. "And that makes it right? You might have felt differently about the idea of slavery if the Jansai were scooping up redheaded girls with big green eyes."

"My hair isn't red, it's auburn," she said, so annoyed that she turned her head away and ended the conversation. It wasn't as if she'd said she approved of slavery; it was just that she'd never thought about it. She scarcely could recall the Edori woman whom her mother had owned before they grew too poor to keep her, but Angeletta's Edori slave was a more recent memory. She had been quiet, kind, and unhappy, and she and Elizabeth had managed to work together courteously without forming any kind of real bond. Nonetheless, Elizabeth had missed her when she was freed. At times, the Edori voice had been the only friendly one she had heard for days at a stretch.

But all that would change, and change soon. She was on her way to Cedar Hills now.

Bennie was talking again, but she didn't listen. Instead, she squirmed on her seat, trying to find a more comfortable position, and let her eyelids close. A working girl never got enough rest. In about five minutes, she was fast asleep.

That first day, they stopped three times to have a meal or, as Bennie said, "relieve ourselves of accumulated distresses." By noon, the day had warmed considerably, though the sun never did burn away the lumpy clouds, and the air around them felt thick and muggy. Elizabeth was listless, drugged by the motion of the cart, the heaviness of the air, and the monotony of the journey.

It was close to nightfall by the time they came across a small town at the crossroads of two fairly major roads. A market town, no doubt, bustling and overfull on trading days, but quiet enough now. Bennie turned the wagon down what looked to be the largest street and carefully negotiated the uneven surface.

"Got a voucher for a room at a place called Bart's Tavern," Bennie told her. "His lordship has traded with this Bartholomew for years, so they tell me back on the farm. Keep your eye out, because I don't have any idea where it might be. Maybe I should have turned on that little street back there."

Elizabeth dutifully straightened on the bench and watched the buildings march past. Most of them looked like small homes or grocers' stalls, but she supposed any one of them could have doubled as a tavern if its guests didn't care much for roomy accommodations. She had never stayed in such a place, of course. When she had traveled with her mother, they had slept at the homes of friends or in the most elegant hotels of Velora and Luminaux. The few times she had made the trip into Luminaux in Angeletta's company, they had also stayed at the finest inns on the road between the ranch and the Blue City. Angeletta had been condescending about it, but she had allowed Elizabeth to sleep on a cot in her own room, as she was unwilling to pay for separate accommodations for Elizabeth, and of course Elizabeth had no money of her own.

She sat bolt upright on the bench and experienced a moment of complete revulsion.

"Ah. There it is. Small enough sign, wouldn't you say, not like they must be expecting a lot of business. Don't see a stable out back—well, damnation. I suppose we'd better carry in all our bags and then I'll take the horses back to the stables at the edge of town. You can stay here and settle everything in."

Elizabeth turned to him, mute with dismay.

"What?" he said, pulling the horses to a halt in front of a reasonably well-kept three-story building. "Did you see someone you know? Feel a sudden pain? You don't like this place? I have to tell you, I didn't see any better options as we were driving through town."

"I don't think—I can't—"

He waited a moment in kind patience. "You don't want to stop here for the night?" he said. "We could drive on, but I'm dead beat, and I don't know where the next inn might be found. I suppose we could do better, but I don't mind saying, we could do much worse."

"I can't pay for a room," she said baldly.

Bennie burst out laughing. "No, of course you can't. I'd be surprised if you could pay to buy yourself a glass of ale. I've got the voucher. We'll share the room."

She was both embarrassed and furious—unable to believe she had been so stupid as to put herself in this position. She was even more angry when her voice quavered as she spoke, though she tried hard to keep its tones cold. "I know I have appeared to be very shameless, coming away with you like this, but I did not intend—I'm not the kind of woman—"

He still sounded reprehensibly amused. "You don't want to buy a bed with your body?" he said. "I never thought you would. Jovah kiss you, child, you're young enough to be my daughter."

Her eyes lifted quickly to his face. "Then I can safely believe you will not expect—"

"I'm not saying I'd turn you away if you were willing," he said. He flung up a hand to signal a middle-aged man who stepped through the doorway, an inquiring look on his face. "Daughter's age or no. But I never thought I was going to get any more than your conversation on the journey. So you can worry about other things, as long as you're set on worrying."

It was a struggle to say the words, but he deserved them. "Thank you."

Bennie swung himself down from the wagon. "Don't mention it! Hello, my man, are you Bart? I've a voucher here from James Overman. I believe it will secure me a room for the night—"

In a remarkably short period of time, Elizabeth and all their luggage had been escorted to a room on the second floor. She inspected it while Bennie went off to settle the horses for the night. The floor was uneven but clean, the roof was low, the bed was wide and rather hard. She sat gingerly on one edge of the mattress and wondered if Bart would bring them a cot. Or if she would have to curl up on the floor, perhaps on top of this quilt. Nothing would induce her to sleep on the bed beside Bennie, no matter how innocent his intentions.

She had washed her face and combed her hair when Bennie reappeared, a thick comforter folded over his arm. "Not so bad," he approved, looking quickly around the room. "Not that we're likely to get too attached to it in any case, since we'll be gone by morning. Bart gave me something to make up my own bed," he added, and proceeded to lay out the comforter on the floor.

"You can have the bed," Elizabeth offered, coming quickly to her feet. "I'll sleep on the floor."

"Ha," he said. "I will take one of those pillows, though."

She tossed one to him. "I will. Really."

He turned to face her. "I might not look like a proud man," he said, "but I've got more pride than that. Are you hungry? They've got a public room downstairs, and the food smells mighty good. Our voucher covers the price of a meal, too. His lordship must be shipping some awfully fine produce to Bartholomew."

It didn't seem worth arguing about anymore. Elizabeth nodded, picked up a shawl in case it was chilly in the public room, and followed Bennie out the door.

The next two days followed much the same pattern. Bennie drove the wagon and talked, Elizabeth sat beside him and either listened or dreamed. Once in a while, impelled by boredom or curiosity, she asked him a few questions and listened to his answers, but he didn't seem to care if she participated in the conversations or not. The weather neither worsened nor improved, which Bennie said was a blessing. Elizabeth wrinkled her nose.

"A blessing? It's cold in the mornings and hot enough to make me sweat in the afternoon, and we've seen nothing but ugly clouds for three days in a row."

"Yes, but trust me, you'd rather not be traveling in straight sunlight. You're both hot *and* half-blind by the time you arrive at your destination. And if you'd ever traveled in rain, well, all I can say is, you wouldn't be complaining now."

She had taken off her jacket well before lunchtime, and now, in the full heat of late afternoon, she was rolling up her shirtsleeves. "You're right. I wouldn't want to travel in rain," she said.

He handed her the reins. "Here, just hold to these a moment. That looks good," he said, and proceeded to roll up his own sleeves all the way to the shoulders of his shirt. "Thank you, lady," he said, taking back the reins.

She couldn't help glancing over at him, at the crystal knob in his right arm that had been exposed by the elimination of the sleeve. On the seedy Bennie, even the divine crystal looked rakish and unkempt.

"You've got a Kiss," she observed.

He glanced down at the implant as if he'd never noticed it before. "I do, at that. I suppose you've got one as well?"

She turned slightly on the seat, so he could see the identical feature set into her own right arm. Even in the spare sunlight, the glasslike node took on a certain luminescence, sparkling with refraction. "Yes. My mother says I wasn't even a day old before they took me to the priest to have it installed. I never thought it did me much good, though."

Bennie grinned. "What good is it supposed to do you? They say that Jovah uses it to track your movements, so I suppose it means he's watched over me all these years, but I have to say I haven't really been aware of him looking down at me at any particular moment."

"Yes, but that's not all a Kiss does," Elizabeth said.

He looked down at her again, his face amused. "Ah. Some secret romantic ability, I'm guessing."

She flushed in irritation and answered a little sulkily. "It's not a secret. They say when you meet your true love for the first time, the Kiss in your arm flares with light. That's how you know you're meant to be together."

Bennie eyed the acorn-sized nodule nestled in his flesh. "That I did not know," he said. "So all these years I've been wasting my time with women who didn't cause my Kiss to light up like a wedding celebration? Although, I have to say, I've enjoyed some of those liaisons, Kiss or no, and I'm not so sure I would have been willing to pass them up."

She looked away. "I'm sure you made the choices that were right for you."

"And has this phenomenon ever happened to you?" he asked.

"Of course not," she said with dignity. "Or I would still be with the man the god had selected for me."

He laughed. "You know, I consider myself a god-fearing man. I try to live a good life. I try to be harmless. I try to do a kind deed from time to time. I say a prayer to Jovah when I'm afraid or grateful. I've even traveled out to see the Gloria once or twice, because it's a fine thing to watch all the angels of Samaria gather together and sing to their god. But I can't say that I believe Jovah is all that interested in what goes on in my life on a daily basis. I don't think he cares who I love. I don't think it matters to him at all."

"You're wrong," Elizabeth said. "Jovah cares about all of us."

He glanced down at her, and for a moment she could read the words trembling in his mouth: *Then why hasn't he taken better care of you?* But he did not say them. He just clucked to the horses and urged them to move at a little faster pace. "Glad to hear it," he said at last. "We could all use a little extra care."

They arrived at Cedar Hills late on that third day. Elizabeth had been dozing in the wagon but woke up when they pulled within sight of the angel hold laid out on one of the open plains of central Jordana.

At first she was disappointed. Cedar Hills looked like nothing so much as an extremely prosperous market town. Its collection of buildings appeared to encompass schools and shops and expensive homes spread over a dozen acres of unexceptional lowland. It was pretty enough, with patches of green scattered throughout the central area, and a few quite detailed fountains creating a sense of light and motion, but it did not look extraordinary. It did not look like a place angels would view from their great soaring heights and choose to settle in.

"Are you sure this is it?" Elizabeth asked.

Bennie laughed. "What were you expecting?"

She waved her hands. "Something more—magnificent. Something high and remote, on a great mountain."

"You've got to go to the Eyrie for that," Bennie replied, unimpressed. "It's high on a mountain, and you can't get to it unless an angel carries you up from Velora. Used to be, Windy Point was even worse, but it's gone now. Sheered away from the mountain when Gabriel called down a thunderbolt."

"Yes, I know. . . ." she said absently, still looking around her. Well, of course Windy Point was gone. That was why Cedar Hills had been built in the first place, because Gabriel had destroyed the hold of the evil Archangel Raphael. Elizabeth remembered how shocked Angeletta had been when they heard the news about the annihilation of Windy Point. It had been Angeletta's dream to be invited to that remote, inhospitable mountain stronghold, and now it had disappeared from the earth.

And in its place we have this? Elizabeth thought with some disappointment. Each of the three provinces had to have its own angel compound, so Gabriel and his brother, Nathan, had chosen this location to build a new hold in Jordana. Gone the majesty and the mystery of a mountain retreat! Anyone could get to Cedar Hills, any carter with a load of produce, any farmer with a complaint about his taxes.

Any angel-seeker with no dowry but hope and audacity.

"But where do the angels live?" she demanded. "I don't see any place grand enough for them."

"I don't know where they *live*, precisely," Bennie murmured, pointing upward, "but I see one flying even now."

Elizabeth quickly lifted her head to see, and her breath caught in her throat. Above them, but lazily descending, an angel shape made a fantastical pattern against the sky. The heretofore disobliging sun chose this moment to shine a little more brightly, outlining the graceful, impossible wings, the straight, muscular body, the halo of yellow hair. The angel lifted his wings with a slow, effortless motion, then lowered them as nonchalantly as a girl would lower her comb after unsnarling her tangled hair. He spiraled down like the embodiment of grace. The instant his feet touched the ground, he paused a moment, as if remembering what it felt like to be earthbound again, then strode forward a few paces. Within moments, he had disappeared inside a dark brick building and was lost to their sight.

Elizabeth turned to Bennie, her eyes so wide she thought she might be able to see the whole world at once. "An angel," she breathed.

"That's the major product here in Cedar Hills," he agreed.

"I'm so glad I came here."

CHAPTER THREE

Obadiah flew from the Eyrie to Cedar Hills in two days, cursing himself the whole way.

He had been glad enough to accept this commission from Gabriel, glad enough to leave the Eyrie, but he had been stupid enough to want to say good-bye to Rachel. And he was not sure he could fly fast enough or far enough to outdistance his regrets.

He had managed to be gone from the Eyrie much of the time over the past eighteen months, a time of slow rebuilding throughout Samaria. Everything had changed since that terrible and wonderful Gloria, when power had shifted from Raphael to Gabriel and the god had brought down Mount Galo in a ferocious display of power. Nearly a third of the angels in all Samaria had been destroyed that day—as well as dozens of merchants, Jansai, landholders, and power mongers of the three provinces—and help was needed everywhere. Obadiah had always been the first one to volunteer to join the task force in Semorrah, the angel council at Monteverde, the merchants' convocation in Luminaux. He had made himself useful. He had kept himself occupied.

It still had been hard to overlook how deeply Rachel had fallen in love with her husband, after all those months of seeming to despise him. And Obadiah was glad of that, truly he was. He admired the Archangel Gabriel more than he admired any man living or dead. Gabriel deserved a strong and passionate wife. It was just that Obadiah had this *tendre* for the angelica, a tenderness and an affection that couldn't be subdued and wouldn't go away. It was hard for Obadiah not to hate Gabriel just a little when he felt such longing for Rachel.

And Rachel, damn her, knew it.

Gabriel, Obadiah supposed, did not.

The Archangel had called Obadiah to his room a week ago to talk over the troubles in Breven. Even sitting relaxed in a specially fashioned chair, Gabriel appeared to be standing bolt upright on some high mountaintop, watching the landscape below him with an unwavering attention. The events of the past two years showed on Gabriel's austere face. His black hair had silvered at the temples; his fierce blue eyes were accented with lines at the far corners. But there was no weariness in Gabriel. There was no abatement of intensity. He still had the force and conviction of a righteous man who had become the personal confidante of the god.

"You sent for me?" Obadiah asked, stepping inside the room.

Gabriel nodded. "Please. Sit down. I'm facing a problem."

He had faced nothing but problems since becoming Archangel, Obadiah reflected, but none of them had proved stronger than his will. "Well, if it's something you can't handle without my help, it must be dreadful indeed," Obadiah joked, settling himself in an opposite chair.

Gabriel smiled only faintly at that. "It's Breven," he said without preamble. "Or, actually, all the Jansai, but Breven is where the discontent is the greatest."

Obadiah nodded, waiting for more information. The Jansai were a nomadic, opportunistic people who traveled the length and breadth of Samaria, selling goods and services. They were the lifeblood of Samarian commerce, but they were not entirely trustworthy, and Gabriel had always had an uneasy relationship with them. Raphael had made friends with the Jansai, had turned his back on their misdeeds, and encouraged them as they began a systematic enslavement of the Edori people.

Several Jansai leaders had perished with Raphael when Jovah leveled Mount Galo, but that wasn't the only hardship to occur among the Jansai since Gabriel had taken over as Archangel. By freeing all the Edori, Gabriel had completely destroyed the Jansai's most lucrative source of income. Breven, the haphazard and ramshackle city in eastern Jordana that all the wandering Jansai occasionally called home, was in deep financial distress. The Jansai caravans that had always criss-crossed Samaria, selling every staple and luxury produced in the three provinces, had grown tattered and unreliable. It was no wonder, thought Obadiah, that the Jansai were exhibiting discontent.

"Do you know Uriah? He stepped forward to take Malachi's place when Malachi was lost at Galo," Gabriel said.

"Middle-aged, heavyset, small eyes, snarling manner," Obadiah said lightly. "I know him."

Gabriel snorted. "You have just described the whole Jansai race," the Archangel said caustically. "But that's him. He has sent me a letter full of threats."

Obadiah's brows rose. "Threatening *you?* With what? What does he think he could do to harm you?"

Gabriel shook his head. "Not me personally. The welfare of the realm. He is offering to withhold the caravans from all commerce, to prove to me—and, I suppose, everyone—how necessary the Jansai are to our survival. Worse than that, he is threatening to turn the Jansai into vandals, sending the caravans out, but with malicious intent, to small country farms and isolated holdings."

Obadiah pursed his lips in a soundless whistle. "Vicious, but ulti-mately unproductive," he decided. "How will that solve the Jansai woes? It will just make people hate them more."

Gabriel gave him a wintry smile. "He feels no tactic is too des-perate to gain attention for the Jansai plight," he said. "Though I agree with you that this particular ploy would seem to be counter-productive."

"Well, he must want a concession from you that would prompt him to stay his hand," Obadiah said.

Gabriel nodded. "Oh yes. Freighting privileges and exclusive rights to ferry certain products. Tax incentives. The basic negotiating tools of business."

Obadiah grinned. "He must have found himself a Manadavvi advisor." The Manadavvi, wealthiest of all the Samarian people, lived on fertile land in northern Gaza and were constantly badgering the sitting Archangel for economic privileges.

"I wouldn't be surprised," Gabriel said. "The problem is, most of their demands are impossible."

"Can you give in on one or two of them?" Obadiah asked. "Just to avert calamity?"

"I hope so," Gabriel said. "That's what I need you for."

"Me? I'll help in any way I can, angelo, you know that, but I don't particularly have a head for business negotiations."

"No, but I'm not sure that's what's required," Gabriel said. "I think what is required more than anything is a knack for appearing interested in what the other man is saying. Even when you are not, in fact, interested. It is a skill I do not possess in the slightest."

Obadiah grinned again. "I would not contradict the Archangel," he said. "But Nathan—he's always been something of a diplomat—"

"Nathan has all he can do to oversee the building of Cedar Hills and the general well-being of Jordana," Gabriel said. "We are stretched too thin—all the angel holds—there are not enough of us to sing the basic prayers for rain and sun. I need Nathan to do the job he has been doing so well for the past year and a half. I need him to be leading the host at Cedar Hills. I do not need him mired in fruitless negotiations with the Jansai and leaving the rest of the province to languish."

"I'll be happy to go, Gabriel, but I don't know that I can promise exceptional results. If Uriah won't listen to reason—"

"I don't think he wants to listen to you at all," Gabriel interrupted. "He wants *us* to listen to him. I'm sure you'll have any number of conferences with him and his slimy friends, and they'll want you to drink some evil-tasting, badly made wine, and sympathize with their troubles, and tell them I am the most hard-hearted, intractable person you've ever met, man *or* angel, and make them feel as if they are not being overlooked in the great scheme of Samarian life. I think that may be all that is called for. At any rate, if any real negotiating is to be done, you know I will want to approve the terms. I will authorize you to make certain deals, but if anything develops outside those parameters, you will have to consult with me before agreeing to anything. So your negotiating skills do not need to be particularly developed. Only your charm. And everyone knows you have an abundance of that."

"My poor talents are yours to command," Obadiah murmured.

Gabriel raised his hands with an abrupt, decisive motion. "So when can you leave? What must you take with you?"

Obadiah straightened in his chair, raising his eyebrows a little at the tone. "I can be packed in a few moments, if you want me to be on my way immediately," he said.

Gabriel nodded, but he was frowning. "I do not think—going into this task you must realize—this is not something that will be accomplished overnight," the Archangel said, seeming to have an unaccustomed inability to find the right words. "It is not merely a matter of packing an overnight bag."

Now Obadiah was frowning, too, trying to get at whatever lay behind Gabriel's words. "No, I understand that," he said. "But you think it will take me longer than a few weeks? I should pack for a stay of some months?"

"It could very well be a lifetime commission," Gabriel said.

"Dealing with the Jansai?" Obadiah said, startled.

"Relocating to Cedar Hills," Gabriel amended. The Archangel hesitated, then shook his head. "Or perhaps not a lifetime assignment. But one that may last more than a year or so. All the holds are under great strain, but the situation is worst in Cedar Hills. At least in Monteverde, and here, Ariel and I have loyal supporters among the landed gentry. We have lived with our angels our whole lives, we know who can be trusted to carry out a petition, and who might bear a little extra watching. We have our systems in place. Poor Nathan is trying to learn it all at once—how to be a leader, how to deploy his forces, who his allies might be among the landowners of Jordana—and all the while he's trying to finish construction of the hold. I have complete confidence that Nathan can handle all these daunting tasks at once, but I would like to give him all the help I can." Gabriel's blue eyes stabbed in Obadiah's direction. "I would like to give him you. Not just for your help in the Breven matter. But for a long time. Because I trust you almost as much as I trust my brother."

"High praise, Gabriel. Thank you," Obadiah said.

Gabriel was still watching him. "It is a lot to ask, I know. And I will not command or insist. But if you would be willing to do this for me—"

"Happy to do it," Obadiah interrupted, leaning forward. "Gabriel, I will always do any task you place before me. And I will gladly undertake this one. But I may need a day or so to pack."

"And make your farewells," Gabriel said. "Though of course we will expect to see you often back at the Eyrie."

So perhaps Gabriel did know, after all.

It took Obadiah three days to arrange to move his life from the Eyrie to Cedar Hills. He had not thought of himself as a particularly acquisitive man, but when he looked around his bedchamber, it seemed overfull of items he would just as soon not leave behind. His casual clothes, his formal clothes, his flying leathers—summer shoes, winter boots—a favorite chair, some artwork, a rug that Rachel had helped him pick out in the Velora market, and a tapestry that Rachel had woven for him with her own hands. His books, his music, his jewelry . . .

His jewelry. For a long time, he stood in the center of his room and examined the sapphire-and-silver bracelet on his left wrist. Every angel wore just such a bracelet, ornamented with the patterns and the gems that marked the wearer for who he was and where he hailed from. All the angels of the Eyrie wore sapphires, whether set in gold or silver; the arrangement of the stones differed from piece to piece. Obadiah's family pattern consisted of oblong stones set in alternating positions, one horizontal, one vertical, in an unbroken circle around the bracelet.

If he were to relocate permanently to Cedar Hills, must he discard this piece and commission a bracelet set with rubies? An angel would flash his bracelet at any inn, tavern, or shop from one end of Samaria to another, so that the merchant knew which hold to charge for his goods and services. But Obadiah's expenses would fall to Cedar Hills now. He supposed he must, after all, have a new bracelet fashioned to mark him for his new place in life.

He did not allow himself a moment to feel saddened by this realization but headed immediately out the door. He must fly down to Velora and hire someone to cart his belongings to Jordana. It was clear he had accumulated way too much to be able to carry everything himself.

*　　*　　*

"When do you leave?" Rachel asked.

"Tomorrow."

"Tomorrow! And you're just telling me now?"

"I thought Gabriel might have—"

"He did, of course, Gabriel tells me everything, but he didn't say you were leaving so soon."

Despite the really quite sizable lump of grief that was causing his heart to labor hard, Obadiah grinned at her. The angelica was an expressive, combative, stubborn, outspoken, and dangerous woman who really did not need the additional enhancement of masses of golden hair to make her wholly irresistible. Well, irresistible to Obadiah. There were plenty of people, at the Eyrie and elsewhere, who were not so fond of the Archangel's unpredictable wife.

"Everything in my room is packed up and on its way across the Galilee River," Obadiah said. "I don't even have a sheet to sleep on except what I've borrowed from Hannah. I think I'd rather be at Cedar Hills awaiting my possessions than here, simply missing them."

"That's not the point," Rachel said coldly. "The point is, you could have let me know yesterday or the day before that today would be your last day here."

"Well, perhaps I put it off because I did not want to say good-bye. I never like sad things, you know."

"No, you're a delightful man who scatters happiness all around him, and it's really not fair that Cedar Hills gets to have you. We need a little joy at the Eyrie, too."

"But the Eyrie has you," he could not resist saying, the note in his voice teasing. "How much more joy could it endure?"

She gave him an exasperated look, and then both of them laughed. They were best friends, in a way. They understood each other as well as if they had known each other forever, instead of only for a couple of years. Obadiah could always charm her from a sullen mood, and she could always cast him into despair; he supposed that was the definition of a close relationship.

"You want to go, don't you?" she asked suddenly.

"Angela?" he said carefully. "Why would that be?"

She shook her head impatiently. "Because it is difficult here for you.

I know that. Although I can't deny that sometimes I like to think it is difficult for you, because I know why." A quick mischievous look, and then she was pouting again. "But it's still not fair. You'll go to Cedar Hills and cheer up Magdalena when she's gloomy and help Nathan when he's overwhelmed, and be best friend to all those Monteverde angels, and everyone will love you, and who are we left with? Eva and Ishi. I think if you come back to visit you'll find us all depressed. I think we need you more than Nathan does."

This speech, remarkably, made Obadiah feel better than he had in three days. She would miss him, at any rate. He had known she would, but it was good to hear her say it. "I wish my ability to spread joy was as great as you imply, angela," he said. "But I actually think my presence at Cedar Hills won't really change anybody's attitude very much."

"But you want to go," she said again.

He hesitated, then shrugged. "I think it might be good for me," he said lightly. "I have lived at the Eyrie most of my life. They say that change improves everyone. Perhaps it will improve me."

Now she was scowling. "Well, don't let Maga introduce you to any vapid society girls. Rich men's daughters—stay away from them. They have no character and no conversation."

He was laughing. "Yes, angela. Anyone else I should avoid?"

"Angel-seekers," she said promptly. "Maga says they're all over Cedar Hills, new ones arriving every day. She says she's never seen so many, not at Monteverde and not in Velora. You want to watch out for them."

"Thank you so much for the warning," he said sardonically. "For, as you know, those are the sorts of women I'm most inclined to spend my time with."

She came a step nearer, serious now, neither frowning nor pouting. "Yes, but, Obadiah, you really should meet a nice girl, you know. You have too many friends, and not enough—close friends," she ended lamely. "You have such a good heart. You need to find someone to share it with."

"Except someone who is not an angel-seeker, and someone who is not a gently reared Jordana heiress," he said. "Who exactly does that leave for me to bestow my heart upon?"

She gave him a little slap on the arm. "I mean it."

"So do I! Who's left?"

"An Edori girl, maybe. Someone free-spirited and kind."

"Is that how you would describe yourself?" he said in a mocking voice. "For the Edori had the raising of you, and although they did pretty well with the free-spirited part—"

She punched his arm again, a little harder this time. "I'm *serious*. You don't want to fall in love with a—with a—conventional girl. She would be so boring."

"Perhaps I don't want to fall in love at all."

She tilted her head to one side, studying him as if he was a block of marble and she was about to carve out a statue that she particularly liked. "Maybe I'll just have to see to this myself," she said thoughtfully, "since I don't trust Maga's taste, and you clearly are not willing to make the slightest effort. I'll look around and see if I can't find the right woman for you." She straightened and gave him a warning look. "So don't be falling in love while you're gone. I'll take care of everything."

"Angela—"

"Stop calling me that."

"Rachel. I have no intention of falling in love with anyone. Suitable or unsuitable, beautiful or hideous, kind or unkind, Edori or mortal or angel or Jansai. I am content as I am."

She leaned forward and kissed him on the cheek. He stepped back, willing himself not to show his shock and dismay. "No, you're not," she whispered. "But you never know when your life might change."

After that, of course, he couldn't wait to quit the Eyrie at first light the next morning. Stupidly, he replayed the whole conversation a dozen times in his head, that night before he fell asleep and that morning as he flung himself from the high, breezy tip of Mount Velo. He manufactured a hundred different scenarios, recast the entire dialogue, so that she didn't read his mind so well or say such unsettling things. In his mind, he had the gift of handling Rachel. But in reality he had never quite managed it.

It was some comfort to know that no one, not even Gabriel, had ever figured out exactly how to handle Rachel.

The flight was easy enough, for the weather was not bad. The air was a little thick and hot, but Obadiah was cruising at extremely high altitudes, in the zones where the temperature was just right for angels with their superheated blood, but cold enough to freeze mortal bones. Rachel, who did not particularly enjoy flying anyway, hated to be carried at such high levels and would always insist that her escort drop to a lower altitude.

But it did not matter what Rachel did and did not like.

By dint of traveling almost without pause, Obadiah made it to the Galilee River by nightfall, which was starting to come earlier here at the early edge of autumn. The river was dotted with small towns that thrived on trade, and though none of them would be able to boast an inn of true elegance, Obadiah knew that he'd be able to find a reasonable bed almost anywhere. So he began a leisurely descent as soon as he saw the sinuous, glinting shape of the river below him and altered his course only enough to drop into the nearest town in his field of view.

There were two hotels, neither appearing to have an advantage over the other. Obadiah picked one at random and then had to spend twenty minutes in conversation with the proprietor, who was elated to have an angel as his guest for the night. The room to which Obadiah was eventually brought was no doubt the showpiece of the establishment, well-proportioned, overwarm, and featuring its own connected water room.

"Very attractive," Obadiah said, smiling cordially at his host. "I shall be quite comfortable here."

The proprietor hovered a few more minutes, inviting the angel downstairs for dinner or some really most excellent wine, "made locally, angelo, I know you will like it." He stopped short of asking if the angel would be willing to sing for the customers gathered downstairs in the common room, though Obadiah knew such an event would be a great coup for the innkeeper. And any other night, Obadiah would gladly have performed, made his host happy and dazzled the neighborhood merchants, who did not often have angels come their way. But not tonight. Tonight he was tired and lovelorn and not able to summon his usual easy charm.

"Thank you, I believe I will follow you back downstairs and have a quick meal," Obadiah said. "And then I must return to this excellent bedchamber to sleep, for I must make an early start tomorrow."

"This way, then, angelo. Please follow me."

The food was good, the few brief conversations with the merchants who had nerve enough to approach him were painless, and the local wine was, in fact, superb. Obadiah had a second glass and felt his spirits lift a little. It would be good to see Maga and Nathan again, and he had many friends among the other angels transplanted to this new hold. He actually began to look forward to arriving in Cedar Hills.

Magdalena, it was clear, was overjoyed at the news that Obadiah had come to live with them. "Obadiah, *really?* Oh, this will make everything so much better. It's been so hot and dull here, and Nathan is *always* gone, and you would not believe the petitioners who gather here, every day, with question after question after question. I don't know how Ariel has been able to stand it all these years. Though, I swear, it was never this chaotic in Monteverde. There are simply not enough of us to do everything that must be done."

She had flung herself into his arms when he finally tracked her down, hiding away in an acoustically imperfect chamber where she had been practicing a new song. She had refused to leave the room, claiming that someone would then force her to solve a problem or make a decision or fly off to the Caitanas to sing for rain, and so they had simply plopped themselves on the floor and begun to talk. That surprised Obadiah a little, for Maga was not an angel who liked to forgo her comforts. She was dark-haired and dark-eyed, pretty, and amiable, but she had the materialistic soul of a Manadavvi heiress.

Living in Cedar Hills, he saw, had changed her already.

"Poor Maga," he said lightly. "You seem uncharacteristically fretful. I will do what I can to alleviate your various burdens, but I have to tell you that Gabriel specifically wants me to deal with Uriah and the other Jansai. So I don't know how available I will be to head out and do weather intercessions or track down plague flags."

"I don't mean to be fretful," she said quickly. "And I don't mean to complain. It is just that—well, it will be better now that you're here."

"How's Nathan holding up?" he wanted to know. "It is a daunting task to lead a host, I know—and in a place like Cedar Hills, where everything is so new—"

"He is so busy all the time that you would think he would be exhausted, but the work seems to energize him," Maga said. "Or perhaps it is Gabriel's faith in him that gives him so much strength and resilience. Nathan would do anything to please his brother—"

"Gabriel would entrust anything to Nathan," Obadiah said gently.

"Yes, but you don't understand exactly," she said. "Nathan is so grateful for everything Gabriel has given him. Not just the responsibility of Cedar Hills, but—well, *me*. We would never have been allowed to marry if Gabriel hadn't needed us here so desperately. And we both know that. And Nathan is determined to prove to Gabriel that he made the right decision by installing us here—together."

Obadiah watched her closely. "And you don't think it was the right decision?"

"Oh! Of course I do! It is just that—it has been so hard. And the summer has been so hot." She had said that already. "And—and I have so much on my mind. But it will be better now that you're here." She smiled over at him. "We must have a party in your honor right away so that you can meet all our important local merchants— and some of our major landholders. They are all quite angry at having been duped by Raphael, and so they are *very* interested in hearing all our plans and offering their ideas on everything. They can be quite opinionated."

"Have you made allies among them?"

"Oh yes, everyone loves us," she said with the carelessness of the charming girl who, indeed, had always been loved by everyone. "Nathan listens to them all quite attentively, and so they always leave feeling that their every concern has been heard."

"And you flirt with all the men and coo over all the women," he said with a grin.

"Obadiah! I do not! I am just very friendly with everyone."

"I will see for myself at this party you're planning. But I warn you, Rachel has told me not to let you interfere in my life."

"Interfere! What does she mean?"

He held up an admonishing finger. "She doesn't want you to set out finding me a bride. She's reserved that privilege for herself."

Maga smiled again. "Oh, no, she's had her chance this past year, and she hasn't managed to get the job done. It's my turn now. I'll find you a proper young woman—"

"Not too proper," he teased.

"Hush. A nice young girl who will be infatuated with your blond hair and your muscular shoulders. I would think you'd be very easy to marry off, in fact."

"Thank you, angela. You make me feel quite eligible."

They talked and bantered for another half hour, and Obadiah had the satisfaction of seeing some of the worry lift from Magdalena's face. She had always been one of his favorites—she was a favorite with everyone—though she didn't have Rachel's force of will or her sister Ariel's strength of personality. She was merely a kind, gentle soul who had only once, in her entire life, fought for something outside the orderly dictates of a conventional life—and that was her union with Nathan. Angels had been forbidden to intermarry by decree of the god. And yet, it was the god who had given dispensation to these two particular angels a year and a half ago, when the whole world was in chaos. Surely Jovah had had a reason for that.

Obadiah wondered if her pale face and listless manner could be blamed on more than the heavy burdens of leading a hold and rebuilding a province. He would have to watch carefully to see if there were other woes troubling Magdalena. He would not for the world have her grieving and not be willing to turn to him.

Maga escorted him to one of the angel dormitories, a rather utilitarian building a couple of blocks over from the main square of Cedar Hills. His room, on the second floor, was small and unimaginative, its only furnishings a bed and an unadorned armoire. The bed, fortunately, had been made up with fresh linens, but there were no towels in the adjoining water room and nothing at all in the armoire.

Magdalena looked around a bit doubtfully. "It will look better once your own things are here," she said.

Obadiah's gaze followed hers around the room. "I'm thinking perhaps I need to buy a few more things," he said. "Do you have any commerce here in Cedar Hills?"

"Of course we do. Our market is not nearly as grand as Velora, but there are quite a few nice little shops where you can get clothing and furniture and—" She gestured at the bare windows. "Curtains."

Obadiah crossed to the window and gazed out. It was hard to tell where the angels gathered, in this collection of buildings, and where mortals lived and did business. Everything was spread out and pretty much equal. That was the point, he supposed, but he had a feeling he would miss the compact intensity of the Eyrie.

"Where do you eat?" he asked.

"Oh, you can eat with us," she said quickly.

He turned to face her. "You mean, there's not one dining hall where all the angels gather?"

She spread her hands. "Each dormitory has its own kitchen. We do have a big hall in the main complex where we can have banquets that everyone can attend, but we haven't used it very often." She shrugged. "In fact, there aren't even enough angels here to fill the whole hall. But we've been planning at least one meal a month where we all get together. It has become a somewhat festive occasion that we all look forward to."

"So when I'm hungry, I can go downstairs to a little dining room here."

"Or you can come join us," she said again.

"I take it you and Nathan have quarters elsewhere?"

"We have rooms in the central complex, and there's a smaller dining room there. Usually a few of our angels join us every night, and sometimes a couple of the petitioners who are here—landholders, usually—and I'll be very unhappy if you don't come sit with us for meals."

He smiled at her. "Well, I will, tonight at least. I certainly would like a chance to talk to Nathan. But I don't want my dorm mates to think I'm too haughty to dine with them, so I'll take some of my meals here in the future."

Now she looked troubled. "I would have put you in the central complex with us, but there are only a few rooms there, and they're all taken. I could have Daniel moved, though—he wouldn't mind, I'm sure, and you could take his room—"

"Don't you dare! I'm not displacing anyone for my comfort. I think I'd rather be here, anyway, away from your watchful eye. So I can consort with angel-seekers and other low company," he explained.

She smiled. "Well, you'll find plenty of them here. Or they'll find you. But I would hope you would hold to your usual high standards."

He made her a graceful bow. "Angela," he said gravely, "I shall live by your direction."

After Maga left, Obadiah showered and changed into his last remaining set of clean clothes, and wondered how long it would be before his belongings arrived. But he discovered, to his relief, that the dormitory featured a laundry room where he could drop off his soiled clothes to be washed and returned to him. The girl working in the steamy room blushed when his hand accidentally brushed against hers. *Angel-seeker,* he thought immediately, but he smiled at her anyway and thanked her for her help.

Then he strolled through Cedar Hills for about an hour, killing time till he needed to join Maga and the others for dinner. The three or four main streets that intersected at the town center were, he had to admit, lined with a lively variety of shops and restaurants. If he hadn't been promised to Maga, he might have been tempted to step inside one of the little cafes to sample a meat pie or a roasted chicken, and see if the local wine was as good here as it had been in the river town where he stopped the night before. He came across three clothing stores that appeared to cater to a mix of angelic and mortal clientele, for the samples in the window included flying leathers and backless shirts that would accommodate angel wings as well as formal jackets and gowns that humans would be more interested in wearing. On one corner, a cheese shop sat next to a bakery, while across the street were a jeweler and a cobbler. Everything a man might need.

Obadiah was in need of some jewelry himself. He hesitated a

moment before going in, but there was no need to delay due to sentimental attachment to his Bethel roots. He pushed open the door, which chimed merrily with the motion, and greeted the friendly proprietor with his own ready smile.

CHAPTER FOUR

Nathan welcomed him with as much enthusiasm as Magdalena had, though he seemed more relaxed and satisfied than his edgy wife. "Obadiah! Gabriel had mentioned that he might be sending reinforcements, but I hadn't dared to hope for anything so good. How long are you staying? Forever, I hope."

Obadiah smiled and leaned back carefully in his chair. So far, he had only spotted two chairs in this small dining room that were conventionally built, intended to hold mortals. All the rest were constructed like this one, with a thin cutaway back designed to support the spine but not interfere with angel wings. He had often seen mortals, invited to important hold conferences, squirming awkwardly in such seats; and it was true, some were ill-made and uncomfortable even for angels. But not the ones at Cedar Hills. These had been built to the highest standards and the most complete specifications. Maga must have chosen the furniture maker.

"Forever it may very well be," Obadiah agreed. "At any rate, Gabriel seems to want me here for the foreseeable future. Or at least until the crisis with the Jansai is over."

"Which means you'll be here forever," Nathan grumbled. "Has there ever been a time in the history of Samaria when the Jansai weren't causing trouble for someone?"

"Raphael seemed to get along with them well enough," Obadiah pointed out.

"Which is only added proof that he was an evil man."

"But you haven't been spending all your time wrangling with the Jansai," Obadiah said, changing the subject. "Tell me what's been happening in Jordana."

Nathan talked with great animation for the rest of the meal. Obadiah watched his face—so like Gabriel's, though his features were warmer and his eyes were brown—and had to agree with Maga. Nathan had been energized by his daunting commission. He thrived on the long hours, the constant demands, and the unbroken series of challenges.

"And in the Caitanas, as you can imagine, they are all reeling still. For with Windy Point so close at hand, they had supplied much produce—and many young women—to the angels, and considered themselves sort of a de facto support system for the hold. And then to find so much treachery on Raphael's part—and so many of their people dead on Mount Galo or poisoned at Windy Point—well, there are families that might never recover. So I spend much of my energy in negotiations with them, trying to prove that I am an honorable man and that angels are trustworthy creatures. I don't know that I will ever convince them, though."

"What about the weather patterns?" Obadiah asked. They had learned, late in Raphael's tenure, that he had ignored his people's requests for weather intercessions, so that parts of Jordana had been in danger of flooding, and parts of it in danger of drought.

"The Caitanas never suffered quite as much as southern Jordana— because, of course, Raphael was so close to hand. But the harvests are still thin and disappointing in the southern regions, and I have had to send angels out every week to make sure the rains fall just as they should—"

They talked crops and storm systems for a while then, till Maga interrupted and demanded "more *interesting* conversation, for the love of Jovah!" When asked what that might be, she answered, "Gossip," so Obadiah filled them in on all the personal stories he could remember from his last month or two at the Eyrie.

"And Rachel's not pregnant yet?" Maga asked.

"If she is, she hasn't informed me."

"She wants children, I know it," Maga said.

Obadiah had never heard Rachel voice this particular desire, but he said lightly, "All the angel holds are looking to their residents to reproduce, and as speedily as possible."

Nathan shook his head. "It's crass, I know, but there are days I want to call a general convocation here and shout, 'None of you are doing your duty! Go forth and multiply! We need babies—lots and lots of angel babies!' We lost more than fifty angels last year. We will not recover from that in less than a generation."

"It would be such a simple thing if we could be sure all those children would be born angels," Maga said in a tight voice. "But even when the angels do mate—well—we can't know what will result."

Nathan didn't seem to notice anything strange in her voice, but Obadiah found himself wondering. Had Nathan been taking his own advice extremely seriously, and helping to sow the next generation of angels? Hard to credit, considering how devoted he was to Maga, but fidelity had never been the forte of the angels. Indeed, most of them were a promiscuous lot, encouraged by the structure of their society to mate often and diversely.

If trouble lay between Nathan and Magdalena, Obadiah would never trust romance again.

"Well, I stand ready to do my part," Obadiah said cheerfully, hoping to change the mood. "Both Rachel and Maga have promised to find me a nice suitable girl. Perhaps I can install one in each hold and travel between provinces as the mood strikes me, populating both Bethel and Jordana with my offspring. And if Ariel is willing to set me up with a third consort in Monteverde, well, I think I can colonize Gaza as well."

The silliness had its effect. Nathan grinned, and Maga laughed aloud. "Shame on you!" she cried. "And I always held you in such high esteem—"

"Not for nothing do all my friends say I am the most charming man of their acquaintance—"

"I *used* to, but not anymore!"

"Well, we'd better schedule that party, then," Nathan said, "to introduce you to the first of your prospective partners. How quickly can such a thing be planned?"

"I need three weeks, at least," Maga said. "And a little help with the guest list. I know the lowlanders well enough, but I haven't been up around the Caitanas as much as you have."

"We'll work on it tonight," Nathan promised. "It's time Obadiah started doing his duty for his hold and his province."

In the morning, Obadiah flew out with Nathan toward the southern edge of Jordana to perform one of the weather intercessions that was required so frequently. He was giving himself a day or two to orient to the province—and to allow his formal clothes to arrive by wagon—before heading into Breven and setting up a meeting with Uriah. But there was no reason he couldn't make himself useful before he undertook his primary task.

So he joined Nathan on a three-hour flight through the green and gentle countryside of southern Jordana. It was rain that was wanted now, Nathan had informed him, although earlier in the season they had had to offer the prayers that held off precipitation, and later still they would have to fend off winter storms. The angels' prayers forced the cycle of wind and weather into a pattern favorable to certain crops; without divine intervention, this corner of Samaria failed to yield any appreciable harvest at all.

Flying high enough to stay comfortably cool but low enough to watch the terrain, the angels arrived at their destination around noon. Nathan signaled to Obadiah and then angled his body for an upward climb, cutting through the harsher currents here at the higher altitudes to position himself closer to the god. Obadiah followed, feeling the cold air wash over his skin like delicious icy silk. When they were so high that the thin air began to trouble their lungs, Nathan slowed to a hover, and Obadiah circled around to face him. Nathan gave two beats with his right hand, and they begin to sing simultaneously.

They were both tenors, and their ranges were identical, so their harmony was close and inventive. Nathan let Obadiah take the melody and borrowed snatches of harmony from the bass and alto lines. Their voices were both strong, rich from years of practice, angel voices designed to build stairways to the god's house, and Obadiah was pleased with the well-polished seamlessness of their carpentry.

They had not sung more than twenty minutes before the air around them tensed and shifted, growing saturated with moisture that would soon be released. Still they sang another verse or two, just to be sure—and just because they enjoyed the sound of their well-matched voices. But when the air grew suddenly and sharply frigid, and the atmospheric winds brushed them both off course, Nathan abruptly closed his mouth.

"I think we're done here!" Obadiah shouted, and Nathan nodded. Diving to more hospitable levels, they stayed long enough to watch the first raindrops fall, and then set their course back toward Cedar Hills.

Two days later, Obadiah's belongings arrived. Two days after that, dressed in formal black and white and wearing a new gold-and-ruby bracelet on his wrist, he headed out toward Breven.

Of the three provinces, Jordana was the most geographically diverse. The lowlands were farm country, though a few stony peaks broke the skyline and provided some interest to the southern portion of the land. The Caitana foothills nestled against a curving, spiny ridge of mountains that ran north and south through the middle of the province, creating farmland on the west and desert on the east. The long coastline offered a softer climate to farmers who had settled on the northern border, and an abundance of fishing opportunities to villagers on the southern edge, but there was pretty much nothing but desert in the middle region between the Caitanas and the coast. And that strip of sere, barren desert was precisely where the Jansai had chosen to set up their sloppy, half-formed, dirty, unwelcoming city.

Obadiah left early in morning, for it was an all-day flight to Breven, and he wanted to arrive while there was still some daylight left. At first he traveled so high he was above the cloud layer, unable to see the land below except in bits and patches, but after an hour or so, he dropped to a more accessible altitude. He was an angel of Cedar Hills now. It was one of his responsibilities to pay attention to the terrain any time he passed over it, to note floods or droughts or snarling rivers or curious falls of rock. It was his duty to check for plague flags, raised by some desperate traveler or isolated farmer to signal that someone below was in dire need. An angel could pray for the god to send down medicines, if someone was sick; an angel could carry a mortal to safety, if someone was injured. Obadiah should not fly so high that he might miss these pleas for attention.

It was an hour or so before sunset when he arrived in Breven, cruising at an altitude that was lower still. After the prosperity of Velora and the bustling new energy of Cedar Hills, Breven was hard to view with anything but disdain. On the outskirts of the city was a deep ring of tents and wagons—Jansai gypsies encamped for the week or the season. There did not appear to be enough room to accommodate them all or enough sanitation to keep them disease-free. Obadiah always imagined a miasma of foul odors drifting up to him from this section of the town, though he was not really close enough to the ground to catch such a smell—if there was one.

Inside the ring of tents was another roughly circular arrangement of living quarters grouped around the city center, more permanent but nearly as unattractive. The houses of the wealthier Jansai were built of gray stone in unadorned, uninviting blocklike shapes; there appeared to be minimal gardens, very few fountains, almost nothing to soften the sharp edges of life here. Even more disturbing was the fact that every house was constructed so that there were only windows on one half, or one floor. The sections where the men lived. In the portions of the houses were the women dwelled, there were no windows at all. No way to look out upon the world.

For the Jansai kept their women locked away from curious eyes, covered in scarves and veils if they were out in public, and immured behind stone when they were home. Obadiah had seen Jansai women from time to time at the campsite of a traveling caravan, but they had always hidden their faces behind their draped cloaks or ducked inside their tents so that he could not see them.

Strange life. Strange people. And he was here to treat with them.

In the center of the city was where most of the commerce occurred. A colorful, transient market of canvas stalls and striped tents formed the very heart of Breven, and today this appeared to be thronged with people buying and selling goods. Not everyone in the market was Jansai, Obadiah could see from above, for peddlers and traders of all descriptions would come to Breven to seek the finest wares. Most of the buyers and sellers were men. A few heavily cloaked women worked in the fruit stands or the cloth merchants' booths, and a few similarly clad women made their purchases from them. But these were the lower-class Jansai women, Obadiah knew. Anyone whose father or husband or son had any pretensions to wealth would not have the women of his family demeaned in such a public fashion.

Obadiah glided in to land near the market. The closer he dropped to the ground, the hotter and more oppressive the air felt, and by the time his feet touched ground, his face had begun to glisten with a faint sheen of sweat. The very dirt felt hot beneath the soles of his leather boots. Breven was a city that simply exhaled discomfort.

His appearance excited some commotion. Everyone in his immediate vicinity was staring over at him, frozen mid-barter, and a few of the wild young Jansai boys came running over. They were thin and tall, dressed in cool, colorful linen tunics and wearing, even at this young age, a ransom in gold around their throats and wrists.

"Angelo! Angelo! Why are you here?" one of them cried.

He smiled at them, for surely they could not be as duplicitous and scheming as their fathers and uncles. "I've come to make my fortune," he said gaily. "To buy and sell in the market."

"Angels don't buy and sell," another one scoffed.

"He might come for wine," the first boy said.

"Or jewels. He might want to buy jewels," a third one guessed.

"I know who has the best gold in Breven," the first boy said. "I'll take you to his tent right now."

"He's not going to your grandfather's stall! No angel wants to be cheated by that old man!"

"My grandfather is not a cheat! *Your* father is a cheat and a liar—"

They were that quickly squabbling among themselves. So much for their status as uncorrupted youths. "Could you—excuse me a moment—before you get too deeply into a discussion of whose father is more despicable, could you possibly tell me where the merchant Uriah can be found?"

"I'll take you to see him," one boy said promptly. "For a copper."

Obadiah had to laugh. Contentious *and* enterprising; yes, they had been bred up from the cradle to enact all the vices of their heritage. "Done," he said before someone else could make a counteroffer. "Is it far?"

"You'll see," the boy replied, and darted off into the makeshift alleys of the market. Ignoring the hoots and insults of the other boys, Obadiah followed his guide as best he could. It was hard to thread his way through the crowded pathways of the market, but he held his wings tightly behind him and hoped no one stepped clumsily on one of his trailing feathers. He murmured apologies as he brushed past bulky, impassive Jansai who did not bother to give way for him, and he nodded in a friendly way whenever he caught someone's speculative eyes upon his face. Angels did not often come to Breven just to frolic for an afternoon. They all knew he had arrived with some purpose, and they were busy trying to deduce what it might be.

"Angelo! Here we are! Where's my copper?" his thieving little escort announced. "Here" was a fairly impressive booth consisting of a broad table covered by a bright red awning, which was attached to a roomy tent made of a similar red fabric. Three lean, dark, dangerous-looking Jansai men worked behind the table. A crowd of ten or fifteen gathered on the buyer's side, picking through merchandise. Obadiah thought the items for sale looked like Luminaux weavings, but he didn't pause to examine them too closely.

"Thanks," he said, flipping a coin to the boy, who plucked it neatly from the air. Then he turned to one of the young men working. "Is Uriah to be found here? My name is Obadiah, and I've come to speak with him."

The young man looked him over with hostile eyes. He had fair skin burned dark by the sun, muddy blond hair, and the physique of a runner. *Don't be so proud; you'll be fat in another five years*, Obadiah thought uncharitably. But it was true. He had never seen a thin Jansai who was over the age of thirty.

"He's inside," the man said at last. "But I don't know if he's got time to talk to visitors."

Obadiah nodded pleasantly. "That's fine. I can wait."

The young man hesitated a moment. "I'll tell him you're here."

"Thank you. You're so kind."

The man disappeared inside the tent. Obadiah found himself

wondering what he would do if he really had to kill a few hours in this godforsaken town. Find a hotel for the night, he supposed. He would have to stay overnight in any case, since the flight back was too long to accomplish this evening, whether or not Uriah chose to speak to him now.

But the Jansai chieftain was disposed to be gracious. He emerged from the tent with his arms flung wide and a smile spread across his broad, greasy face. Uriah embodied the full flavor and style of the Jansai elder. He was heavy, sly, oily, well-dressed in the Jansai fashion, covered with jewelry, and wholly untrustworthy.

"Obadiah! What a pleasure to see you in Breven, and at my tent of all places! Come in, come in! It is a hot and uncomfortable day, but it is cool inside, and I can give you all manner of refreshments."

"Thank you. I would greatly appreciate your hospitality."

They stepped inside the red tent, and indeed, the temperature was at least ten degrees cooler. The interior was crammed with comforts—overstuffed chairs, piles of pillows, metal candelabra in whimsical shapes—and so many baubles and ornaments that it resembled a market booth itself. Still, it was more appealing than Obadiah's own living quarters at the moment. The angel chose the only appropriate seat in view, a four-legged stool covered in a painted purple leather, and let his wings settle behind him.

"Sit, sit! Will that be comfortable? What would you like to drink? Water? Wine? My wife makes a concoction of mixed fruit juices that is most refreshing on a hot day—"

"Yes, I would like some fruit juice, if some is available."

"Instantly, angelo, instantly."

It was a few more minutes before they were settled in, and one of the sullen sons had brought a tray of refreshments to set on a table by Uriah's hand. The Jansai handed him a glass filled with pulpy red liquid.

"So! Tell me, Obadiah of the Eyrie. What brings you to Breven on such a hot day?"

Obadiah smiled. "I understand that all days are hot in Breven, so if I am to come at all, I must choose to come in the heat."

Uriah laughed more heartily than the joke warranted. This was another feature of Jansai hospitality: a great pretend warmth that could evaporate in seconds. But the Jansai always led with a show of friendliness. It was a strategy Obadiah could appreciate.

"Not all days—come visit us in winter sometime, and you will see how miserable a hot climate can be," Uriah said. "The wind is bitter indeed when there is nothing but sand to shield you from its malice."

"The wind at high altitudes is bitter as well, but I have grown accustomed to it," Obadiah said. "Still, my guess is that I prefer your city in summer or fall, so I am glad this is the time I have chosen to arrive."

"And to what purpose? To examine goods in our market? Just tell me what you're seeking, and I will be happy to advise you on where to spend your money. I would want an angel to be shown only the highest quality merchandise, of course."

"No, I'm not here to buy. Or sell. I'm here—" He lifted his glass and smiled as winningly as he could. "To lend an ear to the Jansai. The Archangel Gabriel has told me that there are troubles among your people, and he knows he has not done what he can to address them. Gabriel is busy—Nathan is busy. I merely sit on the high plateau at the Eyrie and sun myself, so they didn't think I was quite as busy. And they have sent me here to treat with you."

"Ahhhh," Uriah said on a long sigh and sat meditatively sipping from his glass. "Well, that was generous on Gabriel's part," he said at last. "It is good to know he takes me seriously."

"Gabriel takes everyone seriously. Gabriel is a serious man."

"Gabriel is a blind, pigheaded, stubborn fanatic, and no one can deal with him," Uriah said roundly.

Obadiah smiled again. "I assure you, you aren't the only one to hold that opinion. But I have to say I don't share it. I have found him always thoughtful and well-reasoned, though a bit high-handed, I must admit. Gabriel likes things his own way. But I have seen him bend when he has been convinced his way is wrong."

Uriah leaned forward in his chair. "The liberation of the Edori—"

Obadiah shook his head. "It will not be reversed."

Uriah flung his hands out. "But it will bankrupt the city! And if the Jansai fail, let me tell you plainly, your country will crumble within a year."

"The last thing Gabriel wants—the last thing any of us want—is to see the Jansai fail," Obadiah said quietly, with such sincerity that Uriah nodded. "Let us begin with the assumption that we are both working to ensure the success of the Jansai. But let us also work with the assumption that the Edori are to be in no way jeopardized. The Edori are no longer an option for you. Thus, we must look at other options."

"I am not ready to relinquish the Edori," Uriah grumbled.

"Then perhaps we will not get very far in our discussions today," Obadiah said, still pleasantly. "But these are matters that will take some time to sort out, don't you agree? We do not have to solve everything in one evening."

Uriah brooded for a moment, then suddenly his face lit in a smile. "You're right; I am not in favor of negotiations that are finalized in the snap of a finger," he said, striking his fingers together in just such a gesture. "I distrust a man who arrives with his mind all made up, knowing just what he wants of me without seeing what else I have to offer. We will spend a little time together, and we will talk again later in the week—or later in the month—and we will see how we like each other. That is how the strongest deals are made. When you know the best of what your opponent has to offer."

"Or the weakest spot in your opponent's defenses," Obadiah said.

Uriah roared with laughter. "You're a witty one!" he exclaimed. "Did Gabriel send you here because of your quick tongue?"

"He claimed it was my charm of manner," Obadiah said.

Uriah smiled widely, revealing rather large and dirty teeth. "I can be charming myself," the Jansai said. "When it suits me."

"Then I think we shall deal together extremely well."

"Agreed! Are you staying for dinner? You must, of course! Jovah's bones, you will have to spend the night, I suppose, for your puny wings won't carry you all the way back to the Eyrie in a single night."

"My puny wings are more impressive than any wings I have seen you sprout," Obadiah said genially, "and I am not headed back to the Eyrie. I am staying in Cedar Hills for the foreseeable future."

"Still too far to travel by night."

"I agree. I was going to find a hotel."

Uriah nodded. "I can recommend a good one."

That was a relief. For a moment he had been afraid Uriah would insist that the angel stay with him, either in this tent or whatever unfriendly stone house the merchant might own in the central district. But no; the Jansai were not known for accommodating strangers. There had been no real chance that Uriah would take him in. "Thank you. I appreciate your kindness."

The night that followed was only an inch away from debauchery. Obadiah constantly had the sense that, had he appeared the least bit interested, Uriah would have supplied him with fallen women, opiate concoctions, and even stronger liquors than the ones that were served. They took their dinner in another tent, an even more expansive one on the border between the city center and the stone houses of the residential district. The furnishings were opulent, the food magnificent, their companions inebriated and happy. Obadiah was careful to drink enough to appear convivial but not so much that he lost his sense of purpose. He laughed even when he was not amused, complimented his host extravagantly on the food, and listened attentively to every interminable story of hunting and trade offered up by Uriah and his friends. He thought possibly he had never spent a more miserable night in his life.

Well past midnight, Obadiah came to his feet, a little more shakily than he would have liked. "I'm a working man with a report to make in the morning," he told Uriah. "I must be off to bed now if I've any hope of leaving the city before nightfall tomorrow."

"I knew that an angel could not match ale pots with a Jansai," Uriah said in satisfaction. "But you made a brave try! And I like you for it."

"Thank you," Obadiah said. "I was hoping you would like me for something."

"Michael!" Uriah roared, and one of the drunken companions stumbled to his feet. "Escort the angelo back to his hotel. He is staying at the Desert Wind, near the viaduct."

"It is not so far. I am certain I can find it on my own," Obadiah said.

"You can, but if you are on your own, other things may find you first," Uriah said, briefly serious in the middle of this hedonistic evening. "There are people here—other Jansai, I admit it, friends of mine, perhaps—who might not be so happy to see an angel in our midst. I would rather see you under safe escort than open you up to— hostilities—so late at night."

Obadiah could not credit the idea that he could be in any real danger, but he allowed Uriah the chance to prove himself a watchful host. "Thank you, friend," he said soberly. "Your concern for me does me honor."

Michael, when he came weaving up to Obadiah's side, did not look prepared to fend off any Jansai dissidents who might happen upon them during their walk to the hotel. He was short, stout, and almost too drunk to stand. But he tried to arrange his features into some semblance of ferocity. "Are you ready, angelo?" he growled. "Then let us go."

The night air was cool enough to be pleasant, and the streets empty enough to seem devoid of threat. Obadiah breathed deeply, glad to get away from the close confines of the tent and the over-powering scents of incense and alcohol. His companion paced beside him with his eyes trained on the cobblestone street, as if afraid to miss a gold coin left carelessly in the gutter.

"I see no one bent on taking my life," Obadiah said as the Desert Wind came into view around the corner. "You can part with me here."

Michael lifted his eyes to give Obadiah one quick, scorching look, then returned his gaze to the ground. "Every Jansai hates the angels," he said in a gruff voice. "I do. Do not be so sure someone wouldn't hurt you if he could. I would."

Obadiah shrugged, unimpressed. He had come to a halt and now faced his Jansai escort in the dimly lit street. "How do you think you could harm a man who can leap to the sky and fly away the minute you show him menace?"

Moving more swiftly than Obadiah would have thought possible, Michael plunged a hand in his pocket and emerged with a knife, which he laid against Obadiah's heart in one deft stroke. "I could run you through so fast you would not have time to take wing," the Jansai muttered.

Obadiah's hand closed around the other man's wrist with such power that Michael yelped. "Has no one ever told you," Obadiah said coldly, "that angels have the strength of two or three men? I could break your arm with no real effort."

"Do it, then," Michael panted. "You've broken us in every other way."

Obadiah released him and took a step backward. "The angels have done nothing to the Jansai but right a wrong the Jansai perpetrated on others," he said rapidly. "You cannot think you will win our favor through threats of violence. The world has changed in these past two years. You must learn to live in it, or see your people disappear entirely."

"If we disappear, all of Samaria will suffer."

We have suffered enough because of the Jansai; let us see how deep our suffering runs if they are gone, Obadiah thought. He did not voice the words. "The angels would like to see an end to suffering," he said instead. "That is why I am here. You do your cause no good by attacking me. I am here to befriend you."

"No angel was ever friend to Jansai, except the Archangel Raphael," Michael said and turned away. Sheathing his knife somewhere in the folds of his clothing, he stalked off into the night. Obadiah made the rest of the short trip to the hotel unescorted and extremely alert.

Obadiah woke up earlier than he would have liked, and feeling much less clear-headed than he would have preferred. Still, he had been neither knifed nor poisoned the night before; he supposed he must consider that a victory of sorts. He showered and shaved, donned a clean shirt and his flying leathers, and inspected himself in the mirror. His blond hair was still damp from washing but otherwise unaffected by a night of heavy drinking. His face looked a little tired, with faint circles emphasizing the light blue eyes. He appeared to be slouching a little, so he pulled himself upright, straightening his broad shoulders and unfurling his wings to their fullest extent. There, now he looked more like an apparition out of the Librera, the holy book that told of "Jovah's winged creatures, mighty and just and fierce." For the moment, he would simply settle for "winged."

Once he grabbed a quick breakfast, he would go aloft and be on his way.

He was airborne within the hour, but a building headache kept him flying low so that he did not have to contend with the thin air of high altitudes that could make his ears ring even when he didn't have a hangover. He flew on a southwestern course directly back toward Cedar Hills, marveling at how heavy and sticky the air felt when he was forced to fly this near to the ground. Now and then he flew over Jansai caravans, some heading in toward Breven, some traveling away. He was close enough to see the upturned faces of the men watching him pass overhead. He was not close enough to see their expressions of dislike and calculation, but he imagined them in place all the same.

A little past noon, he became aware of a raging thirst that nearly draining his canteen did nothing to alleviate. There was not much water near Breven, but he was close to one of the rare oases that dotted the perimeter of the desert, so he angled downward. He would drink from the small geyser till his thirst was slaked, eat a piece of fruit, refill his canteen, and be on his way again. The farther from Breven by nightfall, the better.

He was only a couple hundred yards above ground when a searing pain ripped through his left wing. He cried out as he began tumbling through the air, madly beating the wind with his good wing but feeling the heavens spin around him. A second streak of fire caught him across his thigh, and he shouted again, drawing his body into a tight ball. He could not hold a course—his injured wing could not lift and beat—the ground rushed up at him from a crazy angle. When he was too close to even attempt to ease his fall, he wrapped his wings protectively around his body, ducked his head, and hit the ground hoping to roll.

Heavy impact on hard, hot sand—a few moments of motion as he skidded across rocks and desert—another few minutes of stunned immobility and deep, desperate breathing. He lay sprawled across the ground, heart hammering, head spinning, half of his body on fire. He could breathe and he could think—barely—so he must be alive. But what had brought him from the sky? And how badly was he hurt now?

Shakily, he forced himself to a sitting position, though the pounding in his head was so severe that for a moment he could not focus. Sweet Jovah singing, there was a bloody gash across his left leg that looked like it had been ripped there by a burning-hot iron. The edges were crisp and black, and the whole of it was so raw and so red that it looked like it should be causing excruciating pain. The fact that he felt only a low throb in his leg made him shift with worry. He must be going into shock; he must be even worse off than he thought.

Slowly—because this limb did shudder with an exquisite agony—he extended his left wing. There, dead center in the lavish overlapping spread of white feathers, was a hole about half the size of his fist. It, too, was black and powdery around the edges, as if a streak of fire had tunneled through his wing and left a singed opening behind.

Someone had deliberately shot at him, and with a fearsome weapon. He was so near Breven that he would have to assume his attacker was Jansai.

He must tell Nathan. He must tell Gabriel. But first, he must drag himself to water and safety.

He lifted his head, squinting against the sharp afternoon sun. He had been close to the oasis when he was brought down; surely he could not be far from it now. Yes—there—a smudge of green against the undulating gold and tan of the desert. It did not appear to offer even the thinnest, sorriest tree to give shelter against the sun, only a patch of forlorn grass against a feeble spout of water. But he needed water now, even more than he had a few moments ago, both to slake his thirst and to clean his wounds.

And then he would need to rig some kind of shelter from the sun, maybe by stretching one of his shirts over a pile of stones. And then he would need to raise a plague flag—again, perhaps, one of his dirty shirts tied to a stick plunged into the ground—if he could find a stick—if he had the strength to paw through his pack and dig out a shirt—

The oasis could not have been more than seventy-five feet away, but Obadiah was not sure he could get that far. He could not fly, that was certain. His wing was quivering in pain, twitching a little; there was no way he could force it to hold his weight. He could not walk the distance either, for his leg felt numb and peculiar.

He would crawl there. It was so far, but he had no choice.

Accordingly he forced himself to his hands and knees and began a slow, dreadful journey forward. The gritty sand was hot and unpleasant against his palms and his knees, and now and then he would put his hand down too hard on a sharp rock or a colorless but prickly plant. He had not gone ten feet when he stopped and, moving clumsily, wrapped a shirt protectively around the open wound on his leg. Sand had already spit up from the ground and come to lodge inside the red heart of the injury. If, as he half-expected, he ended up flat on his belly, pulling himself by sheer will the final yards to his destination, the wound would be even more compromised if he did not bandage it. He refastened his pack and sat there a moment, forcing himself to breathe evenly, shutting his eyes against the glare of the sun. Then he tipped himself back to his hands and knees and resumed his slow crawl toward salvation.

He had to stop three more times to rest, and each time he grew more frightened. His breathing was shallow and his hands felt clammy; if he was cold in this hot environment, he was even worse off than he'd realized. He didn't think he'd lost much blood, but shock was shutting his systems down. His head was swimming from the trauma of the landing, or creeping dehydration, or both. He must reach water soon.

It seemed like hours before his hand crossed the border from hot sand to sleek grass. Now, with a grunt that sounded more like a cry, he did collapse, and he pulled himself forward by grasping fistful after fistful of that tough desert weed. The sharp-leaved plant cut the bare skin of his chest and left his hands even more raw than the sand, but he didn't pause. He dragged himself forward the last few inches and plunged his face into the low, gurgling jet of water. It was warm and tasted of earthen metals, but he didn't care. He drank and drank, sloppily, letting the water spill across his cheeks and down his chin. He would never be able to drink enough.

Finally, too tired to hold up his head any longer, he placed his cheek against the wet soil and let himself rest a moment. He must sit up; he must clean his leg wound and wrap his head and torso in a covering of some sort. Water or no, he would die if he lay too long out in the relentless sun, and infection might destroy him even sooner than exposure.

But he could not move. He could not make the effort. He lay there with his face turned into the gentle stream of falling water and did not stir again.

CHAPTER FIVE

Rebekah had begged to be left behind, to stay at her cousin Martha's, but her mother would not have it. "You spent most of last week with your cousin. It is time you spared a little attention for your own family. You're coming with me and your brothers and your father, and that's the end of it."

"He's not my father," Rebekah muttered.

"What did you say?"

Rebekah lifted her head defiantly. "He's—not—my—father," she said.

Her mother slapped her once across the face, not hard, an action repeated so often between the two of them that they had almost come to expect that every conversation would end in a blow. Rebekah didn't feel like her mother's heart was really in it anymore. It was clear that Jerusha was too tired to deal with her rebellious daughter, too taken up with the demands of a new husband and a new baby to spare any real energy for a girl who could clearly take every ounce of strength she could summon. Besides, it was obvious even to Rebekah that her mother was merely awaiting the day a husband could be found for her—a good strong Jansai man who would know very well how to deal with a willful young wife.

"He's the nearest thing you have to a father, and he's the only man providing for you, so you'd best speak of him with care, *kircha*," Jerusha said. *Kircha* was a not entirely affectionate term for an unbroken filly. "Who would feed you and offer you a tent over your head if not for Hector?"

"My uncle Ezra would," Rebekah said.

Jerusha lifted a hand as if to clout her again, but didn't have the strength to strike. She let her hand fall. "Yes, and you saw how happy he was to have us in his care after your father died," her mother said. "That is exactly how welcome you would be in his household now."

"There were three of us then. There would only be one of me now. He wouldn't mind. I could keep Martha company."

Jerusha gave a little sniff. "You're not going to live with your uncle Ezra. You're not going to stay with him while we travel to Castelana. You're coming with us. And what's more, you're going to help me with the baby, and you're not going to complain. Not one word, for the whole trip."

They both knew this was unlikely.

"When do we leave?" Rebekah asked sulkily.

"Tomorrow. So make sure your things are packed. And talk to your brother. Get his clothes ready, too."

"Let him get his own clothes ready."

Her mother gave her a dark stare, and Rebekah just huffed in irritation and left the room. She would, of course, organize her own traveling case as well as her brother Jordan's. That was what Jansai women did—looked after the men in their family. It was only rebellious teenage girls who ever thought otherwise.

She stormed up the stairs to the hot, still warren of tiny rooms on the second story that she shared with various aunts and cousins and even more distant relatives of her stepfather. Jordan and the baby both had their own rooms on the cooler, more spacious ground level of the house, and naturally her mother shared quite a pleasant suite with Hector, also on the bottom floor. As the woman married to the head of the household, Jerusha had free run of the entire house and was responsible for overseeing the cleaning and upkeep even of the rooms where only men were allowed. Of course, whenever Hector had company—men who were not related to him—Jerusha kept in the women's side of the building, not wanting to show her face where it should not be seen. The rest of the women kept to their own part of the house at all times, except during the common meals that allowed the sexes to mingle when there was only family present. Rebekah had never seen half of the rooms in this house.

Throwing open her bedroom door with a crash, Rebekah flung herself onto the brightly colored mattress on the floor and buried her face in a soft, expensive pillow. Well, she had to admit their lives had improved—materially, at least—since Hector had married her mother. Ezra's house was bigger but filled with many more people, and Jerusha's family had had to be content with the cast-off clothes and furniture the other women of the family no longer wanted. Rebekah had shared a room with Martha and worn many of Martha's clothes, so she had not suffered much, but Jerusha and Jordan had always looked a bit tired and ill-dressed during the three months they had lived with Ezra. But they had had no place else to go after her father had died in Raphael's company when Gabriel brought down Mount Galo.

Rebekah turned over onto her back to contemplate the blank ceiling. Truth to tell, she had not cared much for her father, either, who had been a scheming, tightfisted, somewhat brutish man. Jordan had hated him; but then, Jordan had spent much more time with him than Rebekah had, since Jordan was a son and therefore his father's heir. Jordan had been happy enough in Ezra's crowded household, cast-off clothing or no, but he seemed even more content in Hector's. Hector treated him like he was a man—which, at fourteen, he almost was—and allowed Jordan to join him on business trips and some social outings with the other men. In vain did Rebekah point out that Hector was stupid, mercenary, loud, and coarse. Jordan would shrug.

"He's nice to me," her brother would say, and that was all that seemed to matter to him.

As it happened, Hector wasn't cruel to Rebekah, either. He did, as her mother said, provide her with good clothes and costly jewelry, and he spoke to her civilly if without affection. But she could tell he watched her with a weighing air, as if gauging how much she might be worth when he arranged a marriage for her with some fat Jansai merchant. She had turned twenty last month. If she was not wed within the next year, she would be practically unmarriageable. Which would mean she would be a burden on her stepfather for the rest of her natural life.

Rebekah was very sure Hector would find a husband for her within the next year. It was a prospect that filled her with faint misgiving.

She had just flopped back over on her stomach when there was a knock on the door. "Bekah? Are you in there?" It was Jordan.

She sat up. "Yes. Come on in."

He slipped inside the room and let the door bang shut behind him. "Jovah's bones, it's hot in here," he said, as he always did. His own room had windows that allowed in whatever fresh air the city might muster by day's end.

"We're leaving tomorrow, did you know?" she demanded.

He sat on the floor near her mattress and stretched his legs out before him. He was a tall, lanky boy, exactly her height, and they looked a great deal alike: They both had large, expressive brown eyes, masses of curly brown hair (though his was shorter), and fair skin of a creamy texture. Jordan's skin had been baked brown by exposure to the sun, but Rebekah's, always hidden under a veil when she walked outside, was still a luscious white. She was a little vain of her complexion, she had to admit. Even Martha envied it.

Jordan was nodding. "Yes, Mother told me. You're supposed to help me pack my things."

"I don't understand why a relatively intelligent, though admittedly lazy, young man can't figure out on his own how many tunics and leggings he might require to make a ten-day trek across the desert, which he has crossed at least eight times a year since the day he was born—"

Jordan laughed. "I already threw all my clothes in a bag. I only have about five clean outfits anyway, and two pairs of boots. I'll just bring everything."

She drew her knees up and propped her chin on them. "I don't want to go," she grumbled.

"To Castelana? Oh, it'll be great. Why not?"

"I want to stay here. Martha's having her birthday party, and all her girlfriends are coming, and Uncle Ezra's buying special foods from Luminaux, and I wanted to *go*."

"I'll buy you some fancy foods from the market," he offered.

"It's not the same. I want to visit with all the other girls," she said petulantly. And then, after a pause, "But thank you. You're a good brother."

He grinned. "I just don't want you to be grouchy for the whole trip. That's no fun."

"Who else is going, do you know?" she asked.

"Simon and his wife and his sons. And I think Reuben and his wife, though Reuben might be still deciding."

Rebekah nodded. This was both good news and bad news. Good news, because the other wives would keep her mother company, and they would all share in the cooking, so that Rebekah wouldn't have much to do except watch the baby. Bad news, because there would be no other girls her age along on the trip. Which meant the only people she would have to talk to would be Jordan and the older women. She would not even be allowed to be visible while the other men were around, since no man could see her except the members of her family. She would have to skulk in the hot wagon while the others sat around the campfire to take their meals or talk over the day's travel. She would be so bored she would be practically unable to endure it.

"Don't abandon me," she said. "Don't go off with Simon's boys every day and leave me there by myself."

He grinned again. "Well, maybe not *every* day," he said. "But I like them! They're older than me, but they let me hunt with them. Isaac let me use his bow last time we were out, and I brought down some grouse. I want to do that again."

"What's Isaac like?" she asked.

Jordan shrugged. "He's smart. Asks questions all the time. He can look at a pelt or a weaving and tell you how much it'll go for in the market, and he's always within a few coppers. Hector says he'll be one of the great peddlers because he understands merchandise and he likes to travel. Mother says he'll be rich one day."

"Our mother thinks Hector might want to marry me off to him."

Jordan looked over, an inquiring expression on his face. "Really? That wouldn't be so bad. You might like him."

"You think so?"

"Well, he's not *mean*. You always said you didn't want to marry a mean man."

"He's not mean to *you*. The way men treat their friends and the way they treat their wives are two different things."

They had had this discussion a thousand times. Years of whispered conversations with her cousin Martha and Martha's friends had yielded all the young women of Rebekah's acquaintance with a fairly unnerving picture of married life. Their mothers and their older sisters would appear from time to time with unexplained bruises or reappear after the absence of a few weeks looking frail and starved. Most of the married women made a big show of downplaying the evils of their situations when talking to the younger girls, but every once in a while they slipped; they dropped a few details about a beating or a humiliation. Not every Jansai wife. But enough of them that Martha and Rebekah and their friends looked ahead to married life with a touch of trepidation.

Rebekah turned on Jordan, coming off the bed to kneel before him on the floor. "You have to be kind to your wife," she said fiercely. "You can't ever hit her or scream at her. And you have to be kind to your daughters, too. Marry them off to gentle men. It's really important, Jordan."

"I know," he said, seriously enough for a fourteen-year-old boy who couldn't really envision the day he'd have someone else's well-being entirely in his hands. "I remember. I'll be good."

She sat back on her heels. "You better be. Now tell me more about Isaac. You think he's going to be rich?"

Jordan grinned. "That's what Hector says. Uncle Ezra, too. And you might think he's good-looking. Our mother says he is."

"But then, she married Hector," Rebekah snapped.

Jordan laughed. "Maybe you can get a good look at him on the trip and decide for yourself."

"Maybe." Rebekah sighed. "There won't be much else to do on the road."

Indeed, for the first two days of the journey, Rebekah was just as bored as she'd expected to be. She and Jerusha rode in the tented wagon, its canvas closed against dust, heat, and the eyes of unrelated men, but the dust and heat managed to penetrate, anyway. They jounced on an unsprung carriage through the uneven terrain, till their muscles were sore and their legs were tired from bracing against the wooden floor. Jerusha seemed completely serene and sat cross-legged on a bench, nursing the baby or stitching him a shirt. The baby himself seemed drugged by the heat and the motion, and only gave out faint, intermittent cries when he was hungry. Rebekah worked on the baby's shirt now and then, just for something to do, though it was hard to keep the needle steady against the wagon's constant motion. Eventually, she gave up and stretched out on her own thin mattress, attempting to sleep away the afternoon and the discomfort. She dozed, though she never really slept, but at least lying down required less effort than trying to sit upright in the rock-ing wagon.

When they made camp on that second day, the travelers set up their wagons in a ring around the fire. As soon as the horses had been unhitched and watered, Jordan lifted the back flap.

"We're not hunting tonight," he informed his sister. "Want to go off and run with me?"

Jerusha nodded, so Rebekah leapt to her feet and made sure her soft-soled boots were laced. "Thank you, dear lord Jovah," she mur-mured, and slipped out the back of the tent so none of the other men could see her. "Released from this prison at last."

They headed west onto the glittering gold pathway painted across the sand by the setting sun. There was little to see out here—they were miles from any narrow creek bed or friendly waterhole—but just being free of the confines of the tent put Rebekah in a giddy mood. They chased each other across the gentle dunes, found small rocks and aimed them at boulders in a fairly equal contest of skill, and came across a marrowroot bush where they least expected it.

"Aren't we lucky," Rebekah exclaimed, bounding forward to strip some of the blue green leaves off the low bush. Jordan was right beside her, and each of them stuffed a handful of the waxy leaves into their mouths. The taste was gingery but not so bad once you got used to it, and this was a plant they'd been familiar with since they were toddlers. Hardy and deep-rooted, it grew all over the desert and offered a refreshing mouthful to the thirsty wanderer. There was such a high liquid content in its leaves that it could replace water, at least temporarily, in the diet of a traveler. People had been known to survive a week in the desert with nothing but marrowroot leaves to sustain them.

"We should bring some back for Mother and the others for the cook-fire," Rebekah suggested, so they plucked a dozen more leaves and stowed them in their pockets. They didn't denude the bush; that would cause it to wither and die, and marrowroot was too precious a plant to treat so badly.

Some of their energy spent, they wandered more sedately for another hour or two, idly talking. A small creature hopped across their path, and Jordan threw a rock at it but missed. He spent the rest of their excursion bemoaning the fact that he hadn't brought a bow.

"I'm sure we have plenty to eat, at least these first few days out," Rebekah said.

"Yes, but Isaac would have been so impressed! And Hector would have been proud of me."

"Well, tomorrow, then. Just never leave the tent without your bow in hand."

They had roamed about an hour before it started to get really dark. True children of the desert, they had no fears about finding their way back to the campsite by barely distinguishable landmarks, but they turned homeward anyway. Jerusha would be worried if they were gone for long, and supper would be ready soon. And they were both hungry.

Still, for Rebekah, the evening meal was not very enjoyable. She ate it alone in her tent, while the men gathered around the campfire to eat the food the women had left out for them. After the men had finished their food, they lingered before the flames, talking and smoking a pipe filled with a pungent weed. The three women gathered behind one of the other tents, eating their own meal and gossiping with each other. Rebekah heard the quickly smothered cries of laughter and the occasional exclamation of surprise. They were far enough from the circle of men that she could have slipped out and joined them, but she didn't really want to. She'd had plenty of time with her mother already this day, and she didn't particularly care for Simon's wife or Reuben's. No, once her mother slipped a plate to her through the back flap, Rebekah was content enough to sit there and eat her meal all by herself.

When she was finished, she lay the plate aside and checked to make sure the baby was sleeping. Well, in fact, he wasn't, but he seemed happy to simply look around the interior of the tent and wave his fisted hands at invisible visitors. She patted him on the cheek and rose noiselessly. Moving carefully, so as not to draw any attention to the wagon by making it creak or shudder, she crept to the front opening of the canvas. It was drawn shut fairly tightly, but there was still a roughly circular opening that overlooked the driver's bench—which overlooked the campfire and the men collected before it.

Luck was with her. Ezra, Simon, and Reuben sat together with their backs toward her. Jordan and Simon's sons sat across the fire from them, heads bent over some contraption in Isaac's hands. The bow, no doubt, though from this distance it looked nothing like a bow. It was long and thin and looked more like a slim stick picked up from the side of the road.

Whatever it was, Jordan was fascinated by it and kept asking quick, excited questions. Isaac threw his head back and laughed at something the younger boy said, and Rebekah smiled in sympathy. Jordan was right; Isaac *was* a handsome man. He had straight dark hair that fell to his shoulders in a rather careless way, and his face was narrow and watchful. But not unkind. Thoughtful, rather, Rebekah decided. He was slimly built, but that didn't mean much; good living and a fondness for food caused virtually every Jansai man to grow ponderous as he aged.

Rebekah glanced at Simon. Now, *he* was not as fat as Hector or Ezra or most of the Jansai men she knew. So perhaps Isaac would take after his father and remain a reasonable size as he matured. For a moment she wished Simon would turn away from the fire and look in her direction, so she could see how time had restructured his face and guess from that what Isaac might look like in twenty years. But the older men remained engrossed in their conversation.

She turned her attention back to the young men. Isaac's brother had leapt up and was holding the thin stick up like a club, brandishing it in the air. That got everyone's attention. Simon jumped to his feet and snatched it away from him.

"Give that back to me! Who told you that you could play with weapons as dangerous as this?" the older man demanded, swatting his son with some force.

"I'm the one who got it out," Isaac said swiftly. That was good; he was quick to take responsibility for his own actions. "They wanted to see it."

Simon made a sudden move in Isaac's direction, as if to strike this son, too, but merely growled and stepped back toward his place before the fire. "You boys leave this alone. It's a man's weapon, not to be put in hands like yours."

Reuben and Hector had come to their feet in a more leisurely fashion and stepped forward to look at the stick in Simon's hands. Rebekah inched forward a little to try to see more, but it still just looked like a long, straight staff of wood. Or maybe metal. It was hard to tell.

"What is that?" Reuben asked. "Doesn't look like any weapon I ever saw."

"Firestick," Simon said with some pride. "It can shoot a bolt a couple hundred yards and hit whatever it's aimed at."

Hector grunted and bent over to look at it without getting near enough to touch it. "Where'd you get it?"

Simon stroked the sleek barrel. "Belonged to my brother."

Reuben looked over at him. "The one who died on Mount Galo?"

Simon nodded. "He got this from Raphael." Simon shrugged. "Told me he wasn't supposed to have it, but that the Archangel had a handful of them and wouldn't miss just one. We were going to try to sell it, down in Luminaux maybe. After the Gloria."

There was a moment of silence. At the Gloria, Raphael had challenged the god, and Jovah had brought the mountain down. The mountain and everybody standing on it, which had included Raphael, and some of his angels, and dozens of Jansai and other followers. Simon didn't have to explain that his brother was dead.

He shrugged again. "So after that, I decided to keep it. Use it for myself, if I felt like it. It's not really good for hunting game, though, because it rips too big a hole in a small creature, and it's too bright if you're hunting herd beasts. You might bring down one animal, but the others'll run off as soon as you use it. A bow's still better."

"Why'd you bring it, then?" Hector asked in his usual blunt, nasal voice. Rebekah just hated to hear him talk.

Simon lifted it to his eye as if to sight down the long, smooth stick. "Might find me something else to shoot someday," he said, and his voice was calm and deadly. "Say the Archangel Gabriel flew into town some afternoon. I might try to set his wings on fire."

"Gabriel," Reuben said, and spat to one side of the fire.

"Kill an Archangel, and the god might kill you," Hector suggested, and for once Rebekah had to agree with him.

"I think I'd die happy enough," Simon said. He glanced down at the weapon another moment, then said, "I think this goes back in the wagon." He strode off to his own tent and the others redisposed themselves around the fire.

Rebekah returned her attention to the younger set, but they had their heads bent over a game of chakki. The only expressions she could see on Isaac's face were greed and calculation, and those weren't designed to make him more attractive, she thought. Anyway, just then the baby gave out a hesitant, irritable cry, and she turned around and crept back to his side.

"Yes, aren't you the sweetest thing?" she crooned, holding him up in the dark tent and trying to catch the liquid shine of his eyes by the dim firelight that filtered in. "You're not going to grow up to be a mean, harsh Jansai man, are you? Oh, no, not my little baby brother. I'll see to that. I'll take care of you, and I'll kiss you every day, and I'll love you so much that you'll want to spread love everywhere you go."

She talked nonsense to him until he smiled and chortled at her in return. Truly, he seemed like the sweetest child. Jordan, who had been born when she was six, had been a dreadful baby, screaming at the top of his lungs any time he was hungry, dirty, or bored. Strange that he had become such a good-natured and easygoing boy now. She hoped this did not mean the baby, so happy now, would grow difficult and loutish as he reached his early manhood. She kissed him again on his soft, warm cheek and assured herself that he would never change.

*   *   *

The next day was exactly the same, until shortly after their noon meal. They had not been traveling very long when there was an ominous crack from Simon's wagon, and the whole back end tumbled untidily into the sand. Simon's wife yelped and scrambled out the back, then hastily ran to conceal herself in the tent with Reuben's wife. Simon brought the team of horses to a halt and jumped off the front bench to see what the trouble was. His sons reined in their mounts and circled back.

Jerusha and Rebekah peered out through the front of the tent, gazing out over Hector's shoulders. They were directly behind the fallen wagon, so they had an excellent view.

"Damn axle," Simon called from his hands and knees. "Broke clean in two."

"You got a spare?" Hector said.

Simon backed himself out from under the wagon and stood up, looking disgusted. "No. Didn't bring one. You?"

Hector shook his head. Reuben, who strode over at that point, also replied in the negative. The three men stood together in a tight conclave, discussing options.

"What do you want to do?" Reuben asked. "Go on or go back?"

"I can make it to Catter's Creek in about a day," Simon said, naming the nearest stretch of land that boasted a body of water and a stand of trees. "A day to get back, another half day to plane the wood. You might not want to wait that long. We can fix the wagon and go home. You two head on."

Reuben looked over at Hector. "Hector? You're the one with a delivery. I'm just selling."

Hector lifted his shoulders in a halfhearted shrug. "There was no exact date set. I'm in no particular hurry. We can wait here till the new pole is ready."

Such conversations had happened on virtually every trip that Rebekah ever had been on. Something was always going wrong: A horse went lame, a driver got sick, a wagon fell apart. The Jansai were never in much of a hurry, and it was rare that some members of a caravan would forge ahead, leaving the unfortunate party behind. But the discussion always had to be held anyway.

"I'll leave my boys here to take care of their mother," Simon said. "Make them hunt. Give them any chores you need done. Don't let them sit around being lazy while others are working."

Reuben nodded. "You'll leave now, then?"

"I can make it to Catter's Creek tonight or tomorrow morning. I should be back sometime tomorrow."

It was a quick matter to set him up with some provisions, make sure he had enough water for the journey, and hand over extra waterskins that he may as well fill while he was at the creek bed.

"But there's a waterhole not three miles from here," Reuben said, "if we run low while you're gone."

"I know the one," Simon said. "Only weeds there, though. No wood for the axle."

"You'll find what you need at Catter's Creek."

In another fifteen minutes, he was ready to go. He'd unhitched one of the horses from the wagon and fitted it with a makeshift bridle and saddle pack. Not that he had a saddle, since Jansai rarely bothered with such amenities. Just his food, his water, some bedding, a bow—and his firestick, Rebekah noticed from the back of the wagon as she watched him ride away. He might be planning to bring down game after all.

Once he left, the others got down to the business of making a more permanent camp. They would be here two days at least, so they arranged the more mobile wagons around the one that had broken down, and the boys began to collect tumbleweed and dung for a small campfire. The women gathered in Reuben's tent to look over their food supplies and gauge how much more they might need now that they would be on the road another two or three days. All the males were sent off hunting, the men in one party, the boys in another.

"Rebekah!" Jerusha called once the women were alone in the camp.

She knew what was coming but did not feel like being cooperative. "What? I'm watching the baby," she called back.

"He's sleeping. I just checked him. Come out here."

Mutinously, moving as slowly as possible, Rebekah climbed from the front of the wagon. "What?" she said again, in a most unencouraging tone.

Jerusha handed her a fistful of waterskins, all on long straps that would fit easily over her shoulders. Over a long distance, a woman could carry a dozen skins more comfortably than two buckets, and bring home more water once it was all measured out. "Here. The whole camp needs water. You know where that waterhole is that the men were speaking of?"

"It's too far away," Rebekah complained. "And it's so hot. I'll go when it's cooler."

"You'll go now."

"What, we don't have any water at all? In the whole camp?"

"Listen to me, my girl, we all have to do our share of chores, and your chore is to go fetch the water."

"I'm too *hot*."

Jerusha snapped her hand out and gave Rebekah a little slap across the cheek. "We're all hot. Soon we'll all be thirsty. You go bring us water."

Rebekah cast a sullen look at the other two women, half-expecting one of them to speak up. *No, no, Jerusha, let the poor girl rest in the cool of the tent till the sun has gone down.* But they both just looked at her expressionlessly through the veils they had not taken off even after the men left the camp. None of them would reprimand Jerusha for the light blow or the firm stance. In fact, they would have treated their own daughters the same way.

Rebekah jerked the straps from her mother's hand. "Where is it, then? This stupid waterhole."

Simon's wife pointed. "Straight that way. East about three miles."

"And don't you dawdle on the way back," Jerusha said in a scolding voice. Rebekah had already made up her mind that she would linger at the oasis till the sun went down. She could find her way back blindfolded over three miles of desert; she would have no trouble in full darkness.

"All right," she said vaguely enough and leaned down to check her bootlaces.

"And cover your face," Jerusha added.

Rebekah straightened and gave her mother a look of deep irritation. "All the men are gone. No one will see me."

"You don't know what other travelers might be about, camped

by the waterhole. Jansai or even Edori. You don't know. Wear your veil."

"I'll bring it," Rebekah said. "I won't put it on unless I have to."

Simon's wife came a step closer and ran her fingers lightly down Rebekah's cheek. "Such soft skin," she said in a whispery voice. "You put that veil on, now. You don't want to ruin your complexion in the sun."

"Keep yourself beautiful for your husband," Reuben's wife added.

Rebekah divided a sharp glance between them. Had that been one of their topics of conversation while the women all gathered together after the meal? Who Rebekah's husband might be? She was tempted to shock them all by saying something about Isaac, his face or his body, but she wasn't supposed to even know what he looked like, let alone that he might be under consideration as her groom.

Even more she was tempted to ask his mother, *Is he a kind man? Have you raised him to be gentle? Or is he just another Jansai brute?* But that would shock them all even more.

"I'll get the veil," she said instead, and ducked quickly back inside the wagon. A quick kiss on the baby's forehead, and she was outside again, taking up the packet of food her mother offered. In a very few moments, she was trudging east toward water.

It was not so bad once she was in motion. Hot, yes, almost unbearably so, but that was a fact of life; it was always hot in the desert near Breven. And it felt good to be free of the wagon, free of the camp, of the gossiping women and the overbearing men. Her clothing was loose and comfortable, the outer jeska all white, the inner hallis that peeked through at the hem and throat a cool sage green. She was actually glad she'd brought the veil, for it shaded her eyes from the sun and kept her cheeks cool. But she would be sure to pull it off once she got near the Jansai camp again, just to annoy her mother.

Moving at an easy, steady pace, she took about an hour to cover the three miles. Just as she thought she really might want to sit and rest for a while, she saw the shadow of green on the horizon before her and increased her speed a little. She had brought one full waterskin but had rather squandered it along the way, and now she was getting thirsty. She would take a good long drink before she made herself comfortable in whatever coolness the waterhole offered, lying down in the sand and drowsing away the hours till nightfall.

But when she came a few yards nearer to the oasis, this admirable plan flew out of her head. There was already someone else sprawled before the small fountain of water, looking half-dead and half-drowned.

An angel.

CHAPTER SIX

Obadiah thought he was hallucinating when he opened his eyes to see the ghostly white figure bending over him.

He was in a great deal of pain, and he had drifted in and out of consciousness for the last hour—or some considerable period of time. Maybe a day, or a lifetime. He couldn't tell. It was possible he was now delirious. Or dead.

And yet, he had always believed that Jovah mercifully erased your pain when he gathered you up into his gentle arms. So perhaps he was not yet dead, after all. In which case, this rather shaky apparition might be a living creature come on him by chance at the fountain of water.

"Help me," he whispered.

For a moment, the creature did not stir at all, either to bend closer or to draw away. Then finally it dropped to its knees beside him and spoke in the voice of a woman. "What happened to you?" she asked.

He tried to shake his head, but that did nothing but stir up water and sand. "I don't know. I was flying . . . home. Something burned me."

"*Burned* you?" she repeated, as if she could not believe it.

"I know," he panted. "Crazy. But it was like—fire touched me— twice. My leg—and my wing."

She was silent a moment. "What do you want me to do?" she asked. "I don't know if I can help you."

"I need—I just—I'm so hot—" he said, and then fell silent, too winded to talk.

She sat there a moment, just out of arm's reach, surveying him. Or so he assumed. Her face was completely covered by a mesh scarf—her whole body was draped in flowing robes that concealed her size and her sex. A Jansai woman, he guessed. The last person in the province who would be likely to aid him. He felt the last of his strength ebb away as he realized there was no succor here after all.

"What do you have in your pack?" she asked suddenly.

"A few shirts—all dirty," he answered.

"Any food? Any medicines?"

He tried to smile. "Angels never need medicine."

"But they can carry it for others, can't they? Or beg for it from the god?"

"I don't have—the energy—to sing," he said.

She nodded once. "Very well," she said and rose to her feet. Without another word, she stepped away from him. The sun, which had been blocked from his face by the shape of her body, fell harshly into his eyes. He squeezed them tightly shut and wondered if it was possible he would die here.

Ten minutes later she was back beside him, carrying the skeletons of three or four small, round bushes in her hands. They were gaunt and spindly even in the spring, when they shot up from nothing and flowered in the desolate landscape. She laid these on the sand a little to one side of him and knelt by his head. "Can you move back from the water a little?" she asked. "I don't think it's good for you to keep your wounds wet like that. And give me your pack so I can see what's in it."

He edged himself over a couple of feet, an excruciating process. When he had fallen in front of the water, he had managed to land on his right shoulder, with both his wings stretched out behind him, but they did not easily travel across the sand. He summoned the strength to lift them a few inches as he shoved himself backward, till the ground beneath him shifted from soggy to dry, then he collapsed again. He absolutely could not lever himself up into a sitting position so he could pull the pack off. "I can't," he said. "You'll have to help me."

She regarded him, unmoving. "I can't touch you," she said.

"I can't sit up."

"I shouldn't even be talking to you."

"I know. I can't thank you enough—I can't—there are no words—"

She shook her head, which he took as a signal to fall silent. "Hold very still," she said. Daintily, as if he were a rotting corpse and she a finicky grave robber, she set her fingers on the buckles of his pack and slipped open the leather strap. Gingerly she withdrew every item of clothing stuffed inside—four shirts, two pairs of trousers.

"This ought to be enough," she said. "Are you comfortable there where you are?"

"As comfortable—as I can be," he said with an attempt at humor.

"Then let's make you a little tent."

He had thought the very existence of his wings would make it impossible for anyone to rig a shelter over him, but the Jansai woman had obviously been considering the problem. She placed one spidery bush at the back of his shoulders, right above the join of muscle and wing; another one at his forehead; another one near his navel; and a forth one behind him again, near the bend of his knees. Tying sleeves together and weighting everything with rocks, she made an awning of the shirts and stretched them over the insubstantial framework of shrubbery. Instantly, he felt the assault of the sun get turned aside. The air around his face could not have cooled by a degree, but he felt relieved, refreshed, hopeful.

"That helps a great deal," he murmured. "But now I can—no longer see you."

"You are not supposed to see me," she said, though without much conviction. "Can you stretch out your wounded leg? I'll try to clean it."

He extended it as far as he could outside of his makeshift shelter, and the woman gently peeled back the fifth shirt, the one that had served as a bandage. No way, in this delicate operation, could she entirely avoid contact with him, and he felt her small, quick fingertips brush across the surface of his skin. He shivered, surely the aftereffect of shock.

A small sound of dismay escaped her when the wound was laid bare. "What—is it?" he gasped. "Infected already?"

"No—it looks cauterized. You may not get an infection at all."

"Cauterized? Then—"

"Then it *was* a burn," she said quietly.

There was a small ripping sound as if she tore off one of the sleeves; then he heard her turn away and dip the shirt into the jet of water. "There's some sand in it," she said. "I'll do what I can, but this will be painful."

"I know," he managed. "Thank you."

In fact, it was agonizing, and it was all Obadiah could do not to shriek and jerk his leg away from her hands. She obviously moved as rapidly as she could—or quickly concluded that she might be doing more harm than good—because the ordeal did not last long. "I can't do any more," she said at last. "Except bind it."

Now her hands competently and firmly wrapped a strip around the gash, an action which seemed to hold the torn edges in place and actually reduced the pain.

"What about your wing?" she asked when she was done. "How badly is it injured?"

"The wound—seemed smaller. Maybe cauterized as well. I don't know. I didn't get—a very good look."

She stood up and moved around his body. He felt her shadow bending over his tent, throwing its coolness along the feathers stretched pitifully over the sand. She did not touch his wing, though, merely straightened up and circled around him again. She sat near his face this time, though he could not see much of her through the weave of the bushes except the white folds of her tunic around the triangles of her folded knees.

"Small and also clean," she pronounced. "I don't think there's much I can do for you there. I can't even guess how to bind such a thing."

"No—I don't know that—anyone has attempted to bandage—an angel's wing," Obadiah said, trying to speak lightly again. The effect was rather spoiled by the long breaths he had to take between phrases.

"If I had some manna root salve . . ." she said, and then her voice trailed off.

"It will soothe a burn?"

"Oh yes. There's nothing it won't help to heal."

There was a moment of silence. He wondered what she was thinking. "I know you must want to know," he said at last, "how I got such wounds. In truth—I don't know myself. I thought perhaps—an arrow dipped in fire? But—I didn't see any arrow. It was like fire—thrown by itself through the air."

"It doesn't matter what caused it," she said, her voice a little cold, he thought. "All that matters is that you have been hurt."

"You have been so kind."

"I've done very little. There is very little more I can do."

"I don't think I should—ask you to seek help—from the others in your party."

A small, short laugh. "No indeed. The men I travel with are out-spoken in their dislike of angels."

"So you will not tell them you encountered me—alone and helpless—out in the desert?"

"Believe me, I will never be able to tell anyone of this adventure. I would be locked in Hector's house for the rest of my life."

"Who's—Hector?"

"My mother's husband. Do you have any water?" she asked abruptly.

"There is a geyser right before me," he joked. "All the water—even I could need."

"Closer to hand, I mean. You must have a waterskin with you."

"A canteen. I think I dropped it when I landed—"

She stood, and he saw her feet moving through the sand around the fountain. When she found the dropped metal container, she filled it from the fountain and brought it over to him, sliding it under the fabric of the tent.

"Here. How long will this last you? Maybe I should leave you one of our waterskins as well."

"Not if you will be punished for that."

"No one knows how many skins I brought with me, or how

many are in the camp," she said dismissively. "They will not miss one or two. Do you have any food?"

"No," he said.

She made a small tsking sound of annoyance. "How did you come to be traveling across the desert so ill prepared?" she demanded. "You don't have water, a tent, supplies—"

"I didn't think it would take me—more than a few hours—to cross," he panted. "I did not plan—to linger. Or be shot from the skies—by mysterious weapons."

"I have food," she said, her hands going to a packet at her waist. "I'll leave it with you."

"Not if you'll go hungry," he protested.

She laughed, a surprisingly girlish sound. For the first time he found himself wondering how old she might be. He had taken her for an adult woman, very probably married, but now he doubted it. He had never seen a Jansai wife who looked prepared to disobey the laws of her culture, no matter how far away her husband might be at the moment. If she was a rebel, she was a young woman.

"Oh, I ate well enough this afternoon, and I'll be back in time to eat dinner at the campfire tonight," she said carelessly. "You can have the few scraps I brought with me. It's not very much, but if you haven't eaten all day—"

"Since morning," he agreed.

"And you're weak—well, you'd better have it." She paused. "Unless it might make you sick to your stomach."

"I'll just eat—a little bit," he said.

She unwrapped a small bundle. "Some bread—that should be easy enough to digest. Some cheese. Oh, and some strips of dried meat. That ought to last you a day, at least."

"Thank you so much," he said.

"Are you hungry now?"

"Not really. Just hot. And hurting."

"Would you like to sleep awhile? I'll just sit here and be quiet."

"Don't you have to get back to your camp?"

She made a rude noise. "I don't want to go back. It's too hot to walk three miles across the desert. And there's nothing to do there." A little pause. "But if you want me to go away . . ."

He smiled. "No. I'd like you to stay and keep me company. I don't feel—quite so much pain—while I'm listening to you talk."

She resettled herself on the sand, spreading her clothes around her more comfortably. "But I won't talk if you want to sleep," she said again.

"No. Please. Talk. Tell me—about yourself."

"Tell you what?" she asked doubtfully.

"Your name—to start with."

A small silence. "I'm not supposed to do that."

She wasn't supposed to be talking to him, helping him, allowing him to even be aware of her existence, but he didn't point out any of those facts. "I'm Obadiah," he said.

"I'm Rebekah," she said after a pause.

"Where are you and your family traveling at the moment?"

Another little discontented noise. "To Castelana. I didn't want to go, but my mother said I had to."

"Why not? Castelana is a pretty place. Not nearly as beautiful as Semorrah, but more interesting than Breven, I would think."

Through the scrim of the bushes he could see her fingers pick idly at the threads of her tunic. "Yes, but I wanted to stay in Breven with my cousin. I don't like to travel. It's so hot and it's so boring."

"Boring?" he asked, smiling. "Most people think traveling is an adventure."

She flung her arms out. "Sitting in the wagon all day! Nothing to do but sleep or rock the baby. Sometimes once we've camped I can leave for a couple of hours, but it's not like there's much to do on the road between Breven and the Galilee River. It's just so dreary."

"Who's the baby? Yours?"

"*No!*" she exclaimed, giggling. "He's my brother. My half brother," she amended. "I don't usually like babies, but he's really good. He hardly ever cries. Hard to believe that Hector's his father."

"So your mother remarried after—something happened to your father?"

She was quiet a moment. "He died at Mount Galo."

"Ah. I'm sorry. No wonder you aren't very fond of angels."

He saw her drapes lift and fall as she shrugged. "Hector and my uncle Ezra and all the men—they hate angels. Or, I guess, they hate Gabriel. I don't know much about what happened. I don't know why Raphael hated Gabriel or why Gabriel wanted to bring the mountain down—"

"It wasn't Gabriel," Obadiah said softly. "It was the god."

"See? I don't know much about it. The men don't tell the women very much, and the women don't tell the girls anything."

"Raphael was Archangel before Gabriel—"

"Well, *that* I knew!"

"But he didn't want to give up power," Obadiah said, speaking slowly so that he was not so breathless. "And he claimed that the god did not truly exist. And, he said, if the god didn't exist, then all the people of Samaria did not need to gather on the Plain of Sharon, as it is prescribed in the Librera, and sing the Gloria to honor Jovah. And Raphael convinced a good many people—including your father, apparently—that if they all stood on the Plain of Sharon on the appointed day and failed to sing the Gloria, that nothing would happen. The god would not strike, and the world would go on as before.

"So Raphael and all his followers stood on the Plain—or rather, stood on Mount Galo that overlooked the Plain, and waited for sunset to fall on the day of the Gloria. And when sunset came and the Gloria had not been sung, the god struck the mountain with a thunderbolt, just as the Librera promised he would do. And all those people died. So a day or two later, Gabriel and Rachel sang the Gloria, and there were no more thunderbolts."

"So why isn't everyone angry at Raphael instead of Gabriel?"

"Well, some people are. But Raphael was a friend to the Jansai, and Gabriel is not. So the Jansai don't really like him much."

"Do you know him?"

"Yes, very well."

"Do you like him?"

"I admire him more than anyone I've ever met."

"That's not the same as liking him."

Obadiah smiled. "You're right. Yes, I do like him. He is not an easy man to be around. I would not call him my close friend. But I do like him."

"I've never met an angel before," she said next.

"No, I imagine not. As I understand it, Jansai women don't meet many people—except other Jansai women."

"Well, of course, I know all the men of my family: Hector, and Ezra, and my cousins, and Jordan—"

"Who's Jordan?"

"My brother."

"It sounds like a very strange life," he said cautiously.

"Really? Why strange?"

"Among the angels—and most mortals—women intermingle freely with everyone else. There are no laws that prevent them from talking to anyone or going anywhere—and doing anything—that they please."

"Really?" she said again. "But—don't the men mock them when they appear in public? Or abuse them?"

Obadiah laughed softly. "Most of the women I know would not allow themselves to be abused," he said. "They speak out quite strongly if there is something they do not like. And I know many women who are much wiser than the men of my acquaintance."

"I would be afraid," she said, "to voice my opinion to a man."

"Are you afraid to talk to me?" he asked.

There was a moment's startled silence. "No," she said wonderingly. "But—I just assumed—you are not like other men."

"Well, of course, I *am* very special," he said. "Much wiser, much kinder, and definitely more interesting than most men."

She laughed. "And much more injured."

"True," he agreed. "You can hardly be afraid of a man who cannot even sit up or fend for himself."

"But I don't think I would be afraid of you anyway," she decided. "Not like I am of some of the Jansai men."

That was telling, he thought. "There must be some good men, even among the Jansai," he said. "I'm sure that's the sort of man you'll fall in love with."

She laughed a little. "Fall in love! What are you talking about? Hector will find me a husband, and I'll marry him when Hector says. He may have found one for me already."

"Really? Who?"

"A man called Isaac. He's on this trip with us."

"What do you know about him?"

"Not very much. I've been watching him from the tent. He's kind to Jordan, which is good. And I've never heard him say anything harsh to his mother. But I've only watched him a couple of days." She toyed with a bracelet on her wrist. "He's not bad to look at either," she added. "Though he's not as handsome as you are."

This last statement caught him by surprise. He laughed. "Thank you. Though I would think I do not look particularly handsome in my present miserable state."

He could hear the smile in her voice. "Or maybe it is that I am not used to blond-headed men. Most of the Jansai are darker than you. But your hair is so pretty. And I liked your face."

"Thank you again," he said softly. "I wish I could see your face and compliment you in return."

Another startled silence. "Oh no. I can't remove my veil."

"I know. And, anyway, it wouldn't matter to me if you were the most beautiful woman in Samaria, or the most hideous. You have been so kind to me—you may have saved my life—I would be bound to look at your face and think you the incarnation of enchantment."

"No man has ever seen my face. I mean, except the men of my family."

"I know. And soon Isaac. Or someone like Isaac."

"And I'm very ordinary. You'd be disappointed."

"I don't think so."

"My mother says I'm beautiful," she said wistfully. "But I think mothers always say that to their daughters. Don't you?"

"They should, if they don't."

"But what I mean is, you can't believe your mother when she says something like that."

"There are more important things than beauty, anyway," he said.

"Yes," she said, as if she was not convinced. "But it would be good to be beautiful, too."

"Perhaps Isaac will think you're beautiful," Obadiah suggested. "If you are to marry him, when will he first lay eyes on you?"

"After we're married. After the ceremony, when he takes me home."

"He has his own house?"

"No, he lives with his father and his uncle and the women of their family. But one day when he is wealthy enough, he'll have his own house. With room for his mother, if she's widowed, and his sisters, if they're not wed, and other family members."

"So a Jansai man must always be prepared to take care of the women he is related to."

"Well, of course. Who takes care of your women?"

"We don't think of them as so frail they have to be guarded by someone else. They are free to choose their own lives," he said.

"That would be nice," she said a little enviously.

"What would you do with your life if it was yours to dispose of any way you wanted?" he asked.

"Oh, I don't know—" she said, but it was clear she was considering. "I would—I would marry and have children, I think. What else would I do? But I might marry someone other than Isaac."

"You might not want to marry," he said. "You could go to Luminaux and become a painter, or move to Bethel and buy a farm. Raise wheat and chickens and sell them in the markets."

"Yes, but I'd be more likely to sell them to the Jansai, who would sell them for me in the market," she said. "And then I'd be stuck on the farm all day. That doesn't sound like much fun."

"Move to Semorrah. Marry a rich man and lie about in luxury all day."

"But then I'd still be married," she pointed out. "And a rich Semorran merchant might not be any nicer than a Jansai man."

"Very true. Well, you could open your own stall in the Semorrah market and tell fortunes to the travelers. Or sell gold and other baubles."

"That I bought from the Jansai who came straight from the artisans in Luminaux," she said. "You see? There is no way for me to avoid the Jansai. They touch every part of my life."

"Move to an angel hold," he suggested. "We do not deal overmuch with Jansai at the Eyrie and Cedar Hills."

"I wouldn't think I'd be very welcome at either of those places."

He laughed a bit cynically. "Attractive young women are always welcome at the angel holds."

"No, I think I will stay in Breven with the life I know and the family I love," she said. "But it is interesting to think about the possibilities, even if I know they'll never happen."

He laughed. "Sometimes," he said, "a dream is all the more powerful simply because you know it will never come true."

They talked for another hour or two, Obadiah drawing her out with questions about her cousin, her brother, and the rest of her family. Her life sounded appallingly circumscribed to him, and she seemed moderately discontent with it, but no more so than any young girl resentful of the interference of her parents and the contours of her existence. He supposed she was not much different from a wealthy Manadavvi's daughter, who was also expected to marry a man of her family's choosing and live a life very similar to the one her mother had experienced. The Manadavvi women, of course, appeared to have much greater freedom and a more attractive array of privileges, but all in all, he guessed, their lives conformed to certain strict guidelines. How many pampered young Manadavvi heiresses had he met who had been as rebellious as Rebekah at the age of twenty, and as traditional and serene as their mothers at the age of forty?

She did surprise him once, in the middle of a story about her cousin Martha, who sounded like a rare handful. Obadiah found himself wondering if even the repressive Jansai system would be able to smother a girl so lively, and he said something of the sort to Rebekah.

"Yes, but I'm the only one who knows how wild she really is," the young woman replied. "I'm the only one who went with her to the fair last year—" She stopped abruptly as soon as the words left her mouth.

"Went to the fair?" he repeated, instantly intrigued. "What fair? Are girls allowed to go to fairs?"

"No! We can't even go to the market."

"Then what did you—how did you—"

She leaned forward to whisper. "We dressed as men. Last year at the harvest festival. As boys."

He took a startled breath. "And no one caught you?" he demanded.

"No. It was the most exciting thing! A little scary, though. But I want to go again when they have the festival in a few weeks. I know I shouldn't."

"What would happen if someone discovered you?

She didn't answer directly. "We would just have to be very careful so that no one *did* catch us," she said. "Maybe we won't go. Probably we won't. But if I'm ever to see the festival again, it has to be now, before I'm married. It might be harder to leave Isaac's house than Hector's."

He wanted to discuss this astonishing revelation at greater length, but the sun had gone down and the air had cooled noticeably. Rebekah rose to her feet and shook the sand from her garments. "I suppose I've stayed away as long as I possibly can," she said. "The men must be back from hunting by now, and the women will be making dinner. I'd better return to camp."

"I can't thank you enough," Obadiah said seriously. "If you had not helped me—"

"It will get cold when the sun goes down," she interrupted. "You might want to pull your tent down and cover yourself with your shirts."

"Angels are never cold," he said, amused.

"Angels who have been wounded might be," she retorted. "And the sand will be quite chilly underneath you. If nothing else, you might want to put some of your clothes under your body. I pulled out your trousers when I unpacked your bag. You could make yourself a little mat from them."

"Thank you. I would not have thought of that."

She bent over the geyser, filling one skin after another. "Do you still have enough water? Do you want me to refill your containers?"

"One of them is empty. That would be kind of you."

She took it from him as he extended his hand out from the edge of the tent. "I can't think of anything else I can do for you."

"As I said, you have been very kind."

"You might take a fever in the night," she said. "And there are predators who roam the desert who wouldn't mind a little angel meat for dinner."

"Since I don't have any weapons, I'll just try to stay alert."

"I'll bring you some stones. You can frighten off some of the smaller ones if you hit them with a rock. Or you might bang a rock against the metal of your canteen. Most of them don't like noise."

He had never in his life thought about primitive ways to discourage night hunters from wanting to feast on his flesh. He'd camped out in the open land more times than he could count—though he'd never particularly enjoyed it—but he'd always been facing a fire, and he'd never felt either helpless or in danger.

She stepped away, returning about ten minutes later with a dozen fist-sized rocks. These she piled up neatly within easy reach of his hand. "If you have more night visitors than this, you may just as well lie back and let yourself be eaten," she said with a smile in her voice.

"Good advice," he said. "And someday a Jansai caravan will stop by and find my bones spread out before the fountain and wonder what manner of man was so foolish he died in the presence of water."

"What about your wings?" she asked with interest.

"What about them?"

"Do they rot away like flesh, or hold their shapes like bone?"

This, again, was not something he had ever had occasion to consider, though he had heard historians in Velora talk about old sites they had dug up from the time the settlers first arrived on Samaria. "The wings are mostly tissue and sinew, so they rot away," he said. "But if I die just right, or if I'm buried under a layer of soil and rock, my wings will leave an impression in the dirt, and anyone who finds my body in a hundred years or so will know that I was an angel."

"And if they find your body in a week or so, your wings will probably still be intact," she said. "Because I don't think the mountain cats eat feathers. Or do they?"

"You're a sort of gruesome girl," Obadiah said.

Her laugh pealed out, lilting and happy. "I don't really think you're going to die," she said cheerfully. "But I'll come back tomorrow to check on you."

He was silent a moment. "You will?" he said slowly. "Truly, I would not have asked it of you. You have done so much for me already."

Her garments fluttered with her shrug. "We'll be camped here another day at least. I don't see any reason I can't come back. And I'll bring you more food, because that isn't going to last you long."

"I don't want you to get in trouble."

"Oh, I won't. I won't even have to sneak away. I'm sure my mother will send me back here tomorrow for more water."

"Well, be careful. Don't come here if it will make anyone angry."

That smile in her voice again. "I know how to leave a campsite without being seen. I think I'll be able to come back tomorrow. I just hope you aren't delirious with fever when I get here."

"Or dead," he added.

That laugh. "Or eaten. Then I won't get a chance to see what happens to your body."

Now he laughed. "Good-bye, Rebekah of the Jansai. I hope to see you tomorrow."

"Good-bye, angel Obadiah. You will."

He spent the first hour after she left reviewing their conversation and marveling at the fact that she had appeared at all, in the hour when he was so greatly in need of aid, and then that she had consented to help him. Not one Jansai woman in a hundred would have done such a thing, he believed. Well, maybe her cousin Martha. Wretched as he felt, he could not help a smile from coming to his lips. He had learned enough about Martha to think that Rebekah probably passed for a model of decorum in comparison.

Although, perhaps not. Perhaps even Martha would have fled the scene, leaving the angel there to drown or bake or starve. And how many of those silent, shielded, frightened young Jansai girls he had glimpsed would have stayed beside him a whole afternoon, trading stories and making him laugh? Surely, even among the rebels of her peers, Rebekah was unusual.

She was also adept at predicting the future, for every evil she had warned him against came true in the next few hours. He had been feeling stronger by the time she left, sustained by the food she'd given him, rescued from the wrath of the sun, and buoyed by the conversation. But as the night grew darker, he started to feel worse again. The gash on his leg felt as if someone was holding a brand to the flesh; his wing twitched constantly with the memory of fire. The air cooled alarmingly, and the sand against his skin began to feel like so many grainy pellets of ice. Struggling and swearing with the effort, he managed to worm his two worn pairs of trousers under his body, and that helped a little. But his skin was so cool. The trauma seemed to have leached all the excess heat from his veins, leaving him shivering and pathetic as any mortal.

So he took her next suggestion, which was to tug on the fabric of his tent and bring his shirts tumbling down to cover his body. They were thin and fancy, not designed to act as blankets in a chilly, hostile environment, but he still felt better as he made a nest of his soiled clothing and curled all his limbs together for warmth. The expenditure of energy left him completely drained, so he took one last sip of water and let himself fall asleep.

He woke a couple of hours later, hot and achy and fuzzily aware that some other creature waited nearby. He thrashed about until he achieved a sitting position, though the action caused his wing to crackle and his leg to spasm with agony. Then he saw it: the shadowed but unmistakable shape of a mountain cat maybe ten yards away on the other side of the fountain. Little was visible except the cat's distinctive silhouette and glinting eyes, but that was good enough for Obadiah. Letting out a frightful yell, he grabbed up one of the rocks and hurled it as hard as he could at the night hunter. The cat whipped to its feet, snarled, and bounded away, but did not go far. Obadiah could still see it, a moving patch of sand and shadow against the sand and shadow of the desert. As its lashing tail stilled and its pointed face lowered to the ground, it grew almost invisible. But Obadiah was not likely to forget that it was still there.

Maybe not such a good idea to sleep.

Now that he was awake and in a sitting position, he took inventory. His flesh, so cool just a few hours ago, was now even hotter to the touch than an angel's skin should be, and his head swam a little if he moved it too suddenly. Fever, after all. Damn her for being right.

But he could not damn Rebekah, not after she had saved him. He apologized to the night air and tried to clear his head.

What had she said earlier? About angels begging for medicine from the god? Had he come across any bruised and broken traveler, that was exactly what he would have done: raised a song to the god to pray for drugs. He even knew the exact melodies of the prayers for medicines that would take care of fever; he could hear them running through his head in his own clear tenor. But, merciful Jovah, he did not think he had the strength to sing.

He drew his knees up, moving his left leg carefully, and linked his hands around his ankles. The posture made him feel more secure, as if he would not suddenly lose his balance and fall back to the ground. Then he tilted his head back so he could see the stars, the glittering map of the heavens that seemed, in his delirious state, even closer to his hand than the equally glittering expanse of sand. He opened his mouth and willed himself to sing.

The music came out like a whisper, like a breath, a lullaby so soft he could have sung it at the ear of a sleeping baby. Doggedly, he sang the piece through, panting a little at the first chorus, pausing for breath several times during the second verse, and practically wheezing by the time he arrived at the second chorus. There was no chance this prayer would find its way to Jovah's ear. Obadiah himself could hardly discern the melody. The distracted god would not be able to catch the arrangement of the notes, understand the mumbled words, and toss down lozenges of medicine to ease the angel's hurts.

Obadiah's head fell forward to rest on his knees. He was so tired. He was so drained. He did not care, at that moment, if the fever burned him up or the mountain cat claimed him for dinner. His eyes shut and his mind closed down. Locked in this cramped position, he slept.

CHAPTER SEVEN

When Rebekah returned around noon the next day, Obadiah was in seriously bad shape. He had spent the night dozing in his upright position, then jerking awake every time instinct warned him that danger was approaching. Maybe seven times he spotted the mountain cat only a few feet away, and he drove it off with badly flung rocks and a cacophony of shouts and hammerings. Each time, it slunk away with a little less alacrity; each time, it settled down to wait just a few inches closer.

Every time he woke, defended himself, and then assessed his situation, Obadiah felt worse. His head was beginning to pound, the pain from his wounds was fierce and insistent, and fire ran through his veins. There was nothing much he could do about any of this except drink water, try to rest, and try to stay alive.

When dawn yawned and sat up, he more or less surrendered. He was too tired to maintain his semi-seated position, and he no longer cared if the mountain cat ate him for breakfast. Shuddering, he lowered himself back onto his trousers, untidily bunched into a bed on the sand, and pulled his soiled shirts over his face and torso. He had scarcely adjusted himself twice, seeking a more comfortable position, before he was asleep.

He woke once, so hot and so thirsty that he did not think he would live long enough to fight free of his linen coverlet and find the mostly empty waterskin. A few gulps of water—almost as hot as he was—and then he lay back down, panting. It took a moment for him to realize that he was still alive. So neither infection nor predator had killed him yet. The mountain cat was a nocturnal animal and had probably slipped away with the sunrise; but a fever would hunt any time, night or day, and might easily bring him down before nightfall.

When he woke again, Rebekah was there.

She apparently had been there for some time, because everything was different. It took him a moment to identify why he felt so much better, so he stared at her for a long time, trying to marshal his thoughts. She did not seem to be aware that he was awake. She sat before the fountain, splashing quietly but purposefully in the water, and he could not bring himself to wonder what she was doing. He could only marvel at what she had done.

She had constructed a real tent for him, for one thing. Stretched over his head was an actual length of stitched fabric, and it had been attached to four short poles that were stuck in the ground around him in a rectangular pattern. The pain still throbbed in his leg and his wing, but it was numbed, almost bearable. She must have—while he was still sleeping—spread his hurts with an incredibly efficacious salve. And he was no longer so hot. His skin felt cool, as if someone had wiped it down with water.

But he was still beset by a raging thirst.

"Rebekah," he croaked.

Instantly she turned from her task and came to kneel beside him. Again, she was completely covered in swirling veils, so he could not see her face or her shape; it was like having an attentive ghost perch at his bedside. "So you *are* still alive," she said. "I was not sure, when I arrived this morning, that there was a breathing man beneath those tangled shirts."

"Can I have—something to drink?" he whispered.

She already had a waterskin in her hand. She held it to his lips because his hands were so shaky he could not keep them steady. Expecting another mouthful of hot, tepid water, he was astonished to taste a sweet fruity drink. He gulped it down greedily, spilling some down his chin and onto the sand.

"What is that? Where did—you get it?"

"I brought it from camp. Water and mashed apple and marrow-root. It's good for you."

"It's wonderful. And all this—this tent—"

She laughed. "Yes, I was very pleased with this myself! I brought the broken axle from Simon's wagon and a strip of canvas we carry to repair our own tent. Much better than shirts and shrubs."

"But how did you carry it so far?"

She spread her hands out as if uncertain of how to answer such a ridiculous question. "I made a bundle and slung it on my back. It wasn't difficult. And I brought you some food. And medicine."

"Medicine," he repeated. "I think you must have already given me medicine. You've dressed my wounds again, haven't you?"

She nodded. "Yes. You cried out when I touched you, but you didn't seem to wake. I'm sorry if I hurt you."

"If you did, I don't remember. But the pain is—so much better now."

"Is it? Good!" she exclaimed. "It's manna root salve. Nothing as good as that in any of the three provinces, not for an injury. But that's not what I meant when I said I brought you medicine."

He could only stare at her dumbly.

The smile was back in her voice when she spoke. "Last year, we were traveling in Gaza. There was a farmer there, a poor man, but he desperately wanted to buy something in Hector's wagon. Some farm tool, I don't remember. He didn't have any money, and nothing to barter with except some drugs. Apparently his wife had been sick the summer before, and he'd put out a plague flag, and an angel came down and prayed to Jovah for medicine. I suppose you understand about all that."

"Oh, yes."

"So the god sent these tablets down from the sky like rain, and the man gave them to his wife, and they cured her fever. But he didn't need them all, so he hoarded the rest. And that's what he traded to Hector for this farm tool he wanted."

"And that's what—you've brought to me today?"

"Yes. Jordan was sick last winter, but these pills made him well in two days. They're really quite amazing."

He managed a slight laugh. "Yes. I'm familiar with these particular gifts of the god. Last night, I was wishing I had some, in fact. But I didn't have the strength to summon the god's attention."

"Let me give you one now."

She handed him a small white lozenge, and he put it on his tongue, then he tried again to lift his head to sip from the waterskin. It took him a few sloppy attempts before he was able to swallow the pill. He lay back on the sand, panting and exhausted.

She sat beside him a moment, appearing to assess him. "It's not good that you're so weak," she said at last.

"I agree," he managed.

"I've brought some broth. I think that will make you stronger. Do you think you can sit up and eat some?"

"No."

Another short silence.

"If I held your head up," she said more slowly, "and I fed you, could you swallow some then?"

"I think so," he whispered.

She rose and stepped around the fountain to the place where she had accumulated quite a pile of waterskins, linens, and other objects. He thought she must be one of those naturally efficient people who understood what was necessary and the simplest way to achieve it, and then didn't make any fuss about getting it done. Unless it was something her mother had asked her to do, of course. But that came from youth. His guess was she would be quite a capable woman once she left her mother's care.

When she came back, she settled on the ground even closer to him. "Here," she said, and lifted his head so it could rest on her thigh. "How's that?"

Immeasurably improved, in fact. It was amazing how any perspective higher than a completely prone one gave a person a better sense of control over his world. But that was not the only advantage. Now that he was actually in contact with her, he could smell the scent of her body, a mingling of sage and sun and sweat and sweetness. Through the mesh of her veil he could catch glimpses of smooth cheeks, wide eyes, curls of dark hair.

"It's good," he said.

"We'll try a little at a time."

Slowly, carefully, she fed him spoonful after spoonful of a hearty, meat-based broth. He couldn't believe how hungry he was, how wonderful the salty liquid tasted in his mouth. After every five or six spoonfuls, she gave him another drink of the fruity mixture. He made no attempt to disguise how eager he was for another taste, and another. He felt like some kind of sightless, ravenous baby bird, snatching morsels of food from its patient mother, swallowing as fast as it could, and opening its mouth wide for the next offering.

"I think you shouldn't have any more right now," she said finally, laying down the spoon. "I don't want you to get sick."

"That was—that was so good. Thank you so much."

"It's just soup broth," she said.

"It was wonderful."

A silence fell between them, and he wondered if she would edge away and lay his head back on the sand. But she made no move to do so. He could not be sure through the veil covering her face, but he thought she looked pensively across the sand in the direction from which she'd come.

"This morning, Isaac's mother was crying," she said at last. "She went whispering to my mother, but I couldn't hear what she said."

"Do you think Isaac was unkind to her?"

"I don't know. All the young men were gone to hunt before I came out of the wagon." She hesitated. "She said Isaac's name, though. I heard that much."

"Well, maybe it was just an argument between mother and son. I've argued with my mother often enough."

Now he had caught her attention; he could make out the shapes of her eyes, trained on his face. "Have you? About what?" she asked.

"Not anymore, of course. When I was younger. If she thought I was rude to my father or lax in my lessons or not as tidy as she would like or late or sarcastic, she would sit me down and lecture me. And I would cross my arms on my chest and say, 'Don't tell me what to do,' and then she'd really start scolding. People are always telling me how charming I am—" He paused and smiled and went on. "You might not think it, seeing me in this condition, but I *can* be charming. But I owe all my manners and any gentleness I possess to my mother. A most gracious lady indeed."

"And you are a good son to her still?"

"Well, I try to be," he said with a grin. "Both dutiful and generous. She lives in Velora, though, so I won't see her as often now that I'm living in Cedar Hills."

"Why are you living in Cedar Hills?"

Because Gabriel asked me to befriend the Jansai. This hadn't been exactly what Gabriel had had in mind, though, Obadiah was pretty certain. "We lost a lot of angels in the destruction of Mount Galo," he said instead. "The Jansai weren't the only ones to suffer when the mountain came down. So now the angels from two holds are spread over three, and there is too much work for all of us to do. And more hands—more voices—were needed in Jordana. So I'm here."

"And will you be going to Breven often?" she asked.

It was said innocently, and surely she meant nothing by it, but the question silenced him for a moment. He peered up at her, making no attempt to conceal the fact that he was trying to see beyond her disguise. "I might be," he said slowly. "Cedar Hills has business with Uriah."

"Next time you fly over the desert," she said primly, "you might remember to come a little more prepared."

"I wish you'd take off your veil," he said.

She drew back a little, but did not, as he half-expected, shove his head off her knee and jump to her feet. "I'm not allowed to do that," she said.

"You're not allowed to be here. But you are."

"I can't."

"I'd like to see your face. You've done so much for me, and I don't even know what you look like."

"I'm a dark-haired girl with brown eyes. I'm just ordinary."

"I don't think you'd look ordinary to me."

"Then you'd be disappointed."

"I don't think so."

"My family would abandon me in the desert if I showed my face to you—a man, a stranger, and an angel."

"I would not for the world bring harm to you."

"Then don't ask me for such a thing." She lifted a finger and placed it, gently, on the curve of his cheekbone. "I'm glad I got to see your face, though," she said.

The touch was whisper soft, as vagrant and curious as a spring breeze. As he had last night, he shivered at the faint contact, and this time he was pretty sure it was not shock or trauma. Or, perhaps, both shock and trauma, but not caused by his severe wounding.

"How long will your family be on the road?" he asked, the words sounding tight and constricted. "When will you be back in Breven?"

She shook her head. She had finished tracing the line of his cheek and now she folded her hands back in her lap. "I don't know. How long will it take Simon to find a branch to serve as his axle, how long before the wagon is repaired, how long will we linger in Castelana? Anything could happen on the road. I hate to travel."

"I imagine I will be back in Breven in a week or two," he said.

She laughed. "You will be recovering in a sickroom in Cedar Hills—if you make it that far."

He smiled. "No, no, angels heal very rapidly. You'll see. I'll be well enough to fly back tomorrow or the day after."

"You can't even hold your head up," she said.

"I'd rather rest it against you," he whispered.

She stilled all over, and suddenly the flirting girl was gone and the brisk matron was back. "Well, it's true you should be resting for a while," she said. "I'm going to give you another one of those white pills, and then I want you to sleep."

"I don't want to sleep. I want to talk to you."

"You can talk to me when you wake up."

"I don't think I'll be able to close my eyes. I know I won't fall asleep."

She made a *well, now* gesture with her hands. "But I won't talk with you again until you've napped. You can lie here all afternoon, fighting to stay awake, but I won't say another word to you until you've slept and woken again. So you'd be better off to sleep."

He couldn't help laughing. "Sounds like something you must have said to your brother when he was little."

She didn't reply, but he could see fragments of smile through her veil. She lifted his head and returned it gently to the ground. Instantly he felt a great lassitude steal over him, but he resisted it mightily. "I'm not *tired*," he insisted.

She placed a finger on his lips to silence him, instantly achieving the desired effect. Rising, she stepped over to her pile of belongings, sought through them quickly, and returned with another pill in hand. He didn't argue anymore, just swallowed it down with the water she held to his mouth. He closed his eyes just a minute against the brightness of the day, and the next thing he knew it was a couple of hours later and he was just waking up again.

He lay there quietly a moment, not struggling to sit up, not even trying to look around, wondering what he would see when he did take in his surroundings again. Would Rebekah still be here, or had he slept so long that she had refilled her water vessels and returned to camp? If she had already departed, she would have left him well-provisioned, of that he was certain: There would be waterskins close to hand, and the rest of the soup, and the container of juice. Perhaps a handful of the precious white pills, a small pot of salve, all within easy reach.

But he hoped she had not gone.

Moving slowly to avoid jarring any injured limbs, he stretched his body and craned his neck, looking around the small oasis. Rebekah was nowhere in sight. He felt a profound strike of disappointment, a clutch in the stomach so brutal it felt like nausea, but what had he expected, after all? She had done more for him than any Jansai girl should have—more than most any stranger might have done for a wounded wayfarer encountered by chance. Both his leg and his wing felt markedly improved since the application of the salve, and his fever had responded quickly to the medicine. He would be on his feet tomorrow, in the air and headed toward Cedar Hills by the day after that.

Cautiously he pushed himself up on one elbow, and when that did not cause him to swoon with pain, he fought to a sitting position. His head just fit under the low roof of the tent, and his wings spread out limply behind him, feeling twice their normal weight and completely stripped of glory. Grunting a little, he stretched his hurt leg out straight before him and poked around at the bandage. That woke a few shivers of agony, but the area of injury appeared to have shrunk to a smaller size, so he was clearly healing. Once he could stand and force the leg to take his weight, it would heal more quickly still.

He peered out from under the canvas to try to get a look at the sun and judge what time of day it might be. Late afternoon; no wonder Rebekah had left. He must have been asleep three hours or more. As he had suspected, she had left waterskins piled by his own canteen, all within reach of his hand. Thirst made him reach for the closest one. Water merely, but he drank it down as if it was sweetest wine.

He was just recapping the container when Rebekah strolled into his line of vision, holding a handful of bushy objects before her.

"Good, you're awake," she said. "How are you feeling?"

He was so happy to see her that he smiled like an idiot. "I thought you'd left!"

She made a little sound. "I'm not going back there till the sun goes down."

"You'd better be careful," he said seriously. "There was a mountain cat around here last night. If you go back after dark—"

"It won't come after me," she said serenely. "They only go after small game and helpless big game."

"Well, be careful anyway."

She came close enough to drop beside him and sit cross-legged on the ground. "How are you feeling? You look much better."

"*So* much better. I think the fever's gone. And the pain is almost nothing now. Just an annoyance."

"I'd still be careful for a day or two if I were you. Don't try to fly off to Cedar Hills tonight."

"No. Tomorrow or—more likely—the day after."

She held up a handful of leaves and some long, snaky tubers. "I've been out foraging. I found some marrowroot not far from here and some reskel roots. The reskel roots don't taste like much unless you cook them and season them, but you can eat them raw, and they'll fill you up. So that will get you through tomorrow, I think."

"I'm starting to feel hungry again."

She nodded. "I'll give you the rest of the soup before I go, and I brought some bread. But you're probably going to be really hungry in a day or two, since you've missed so many meals. I can't do much about that. Sorry."

"So I won't see you again tomorrow?" he said, trying to sound careless and wholly failing.

"I don't know. If Simon made it back this afternoon and fixed the axle, we could be on our way at daybreak. If he's still on the road, we might be here another day. Or two. But I would expect him to be back tonight or early tomorrow."

"So when you leave today, that will be it. Last time I see you."

"Yes. It might be."

A silence fell. She sat there, apparently at ease, but Obadiah felt awkward and eager, wanting to say more, knowing he should not. There was no hope of any kind of lasting friendship between a Jansai girl and an angel, even an angel renowned in three provinces for the gift of charm. They were companions of chance, need, and kindness, comrades of the desert, and once he flew away from this precise spot, he would never see her again.

Not by his choice, however.

She spoke suddenly. "I've washed your shirts out."

"What?"

She gestured to an array of white tacked down with small stones on the other side of the fountain. "Your shirts. They were so dirty. I washed them out so you'd have something clean to change into."

He couldn't keep himself from leaning forward as if to stare behind the face scarf and look into her eyes. "You did not have to do any more chores for me. You have done so much already."

She laughed. "All part of caring for an invalid. Making him more comfortable."

"If only there was something I could do for you in return, some way to thank you, or pay you—"

She shook her head. "Nothing. I was glad to do it."

"But your family—you took such a risk."

"Oh, that's one of the reasons I wanted to help you! It would make Hector so mad if he knew! I sat in the wagon last night, and I watched him and Reuben at the fire, and I couldn't stop laughing. If they knew where I had been all day yesterday, where I was today—"

"I don't think that's why you helped me," he said quietly. "I think you did it because you have a kind heart."

She was silent a moment. "A willful heart," she said. "Don't think better of me than I am."

He smiled. "Very well. I will believe that you are willful, and stubborn, and hard to please, and impossible to control. But you are also kind. I have known willful women before, and not all of them would have stopped on the roadside to aid a stranger."

"I'm sure you know a lot of women," she said lightly.

His heart quickened. Was that just the merest hint of jealousy? "Angels and angel-seekers, Manadavvi heiresses and Bethel farm girls, Luminaux artists and the daughters of Semorran merchants," he agreed. "And not one of them is half so amazing as you."

The smile was back in her voice. "I feel certain that you have said something very similar to all those farm girls and heiresses, angelo."

He put a hand to his heart as if it, too, had been wounded by a bolt of fire. "You think I'm a flirt?"

"I think you are—a man who knows how to be delightful to women."

"And you know so much about men! Perhaps they are all like me."

"Silly and funny and kind and complimentary? I don't think so. Not my uncle or my father or my cousins or Hector or the men who are married to the women I know. I can't imagine all angels are just like you, either. No one has ever said very flattering things about the Archangel, for instance."

"No, Gabriel is not silly or funny, I have to admit, although he can be kind and complimentary when he chooses. And Nathan can be quite charming upon occasion. Now, he's an angel you would like, I think."

"Oh, no. I'm not interested in meeting more angels. It's been adventure enough to meet you."

He smiled. "An adventure so shocking you can't even tell Martha about it."

A giggle. "If you knew Martha and the things she's done . . . I can't think of anything I'd do that could shock her."

"It's good to have a friend like that."

She tilted her head as if to consider him. He would swear he could feel her gaze drifting across his face, touching his cheek as lightly and as curiously as her fingertip had touched him before. "I wouldn't think you would need friends who weren't shocked by your behavior," she said slowly. "I wouldn't think you'd done too many shocking things."

"You're right," he admitted. "I've always been—a fairly conformable individual. Not much of a rebel. Easygoing. Dependable."

"So maybe it's been good for you to meet me," she said.

"In so many ways," he answered.

"That's nice to know," she said.

"I wish you'd let me see your face," he said.

He could tell she was smiling even before she spoke. He had gotten that good at reading the small patches of skin he could see through her veil. "I think I need to keep it covered," she said. "So there is still some mystery in your life. Since your life doesn't hold many secrets."

"But this is a secret I don't want to keep."

"You don't want to keep a memory of me?"

"That's not what I meant!"

She laughed and got to her feet. "I was teasing."

He eyed her with a little scowl. "It seems to me," he said, "for a girl who has spent most of her life around women, you have learned very quickly the art of flirting with a man."

"It is because you are so skilled at flirting," she said. "I cannot help but learn from you."

"I'm not flirting now. I'm entirely serious. Let me see your face. Don't go without letting me know what you look like."

"I've already told you. You're not supposed to know what I look like."

"Does it upset you that I want to know?"

"Oh no. I like it that you keep asking. Maybe that's why I don't want to lift my veil. Because the question is so sweet."

"Are you really leaving?"

She nodded and gestured at the horizon. "Almost sundown. My mother will have been watching for me these past two hours."

"But not really expecting you."

Rebekah laughed. "But not really expecting me," she agreed. "But I must get back." She glanced down at him. "If I can, I'll return in the morning. But I can't promise."

"Then, if I don't see you tomorrow—"

She shook her head. "No. Don't even say it."

"I might run into you accidentally in Breven."

"I am never in the public places where you might see me."

"Sometimes you are. At the festivals. You said so."

"Only men are allowed at the festivals."

"Are angels allowed?"

"I don't know. Certainly other travelers come from time to time—merchants and farmers and Luminauzi. So perhaps an angel would be permitted to attend." She glanced down at his outstretched leg. "If an angel wasn't afraid of what might happen to him if he encountered a Jansai with a grudge."

"I'll be in Breven again in a couple of weeks."

"I hope you enjoy your visit," she said.

She would make no other promises or acknowledgments; she would not even promise to return in the morning to secure more water before the caravan got under way again. There seemed to be a certain restlessness in Rebekah that led her, once she had made up her mind to act in a certain way, to be completely intractable, and she had decided to leave without any more coquettish exchanges. So she responded politely when Obadiah spoke, but she went methodically about the business of filling her waterskins, gathering up her bundles, retying her boots, and glancing around the camp for anything she might have left behind.

"Don't forget to eat," she said as she knotted a bundle of tubers and marrowroot leaves around her waist. "And take another one of those pills before you go to sleep tonight."

"I won't sleep," he grumbled. "I'll be thinking about you."

She laughed. "Then I hope you dream about me as well. Good-bye, angelo. Perhaps I will see you in the morning."

"Obadiah," he said.

"What?"

"Say, 'Good-bye, Obadiah.' Perhaps it won't sound so final then."

"Good-bye, Obadiah," she said.

"Better," he said, "but still chilling."

"Sleep well. Heal quickly," she said.

"Walk safely. Watch out for that mountain cat."

"She is more likely to come looking for you again."

"No, no, I have regained so much strength she will not waste her time on me."

"I am glad to hear it. You will be well by morning."

And with those optimistic words, she waved once and set out into the bright haze of the westering sun. Obadiah watched her for as long as she was visible, a sturdy figure against the flat, gold landscape. But it was not long before her shape slimmed and shimmered and disappeared into the indeterminate shadows of oncoming night. In a small fit of temper, then, Obadiah threw himself back on the ground, his wings incautiously brushing against the ceiling of his canvas tent and almost bringing the whole structure down.

He did not know how he would get through the night without the certainty of seeing her again in the morning. And he was far from sure that it was simply the great kindness she had shown him that made him feel so connected to her, so depressed at the thought that she might be gone from his life forever.

Ridiculous. The only angel who had ever married a Jansai woman had been the Archangel Raphael, and that had turned out about as disastrously as a marriage could. Not that Obadiah was thinking about marriage. Not that he was thinking about anything, or capable of thought, or capable of reason or even movement. He slowly eased himself into a more comfortable position, and he slept.

CHAPTER EIGHT

In the morning, he was ravenous. He had woken intermittently to drink water, rearrange his body, and check for night predators, but he hadn't bothered to eat anything. Now he could hardly cram the food in his mouth fast enough to quiet his insistent stomach. The reskel roots Rebekah had left him were scarcely enough to satisfy him, but they did at least stop the gnawing in his belly.

It was only after he'd consumed every last scrap of food in the vicinity that he realized how well he felt.

Testing himself, he stood and fluffed his wings out behind him. Not so good, some weakness still in both the bone and the feather, but dramatically improved over yesterday.

He smelled like a barnyard, though, and his skin had the dull, matted texture of a sick man's. He stripped naked and bathed himself in the warm geyser, splashing water all over his small camp. Sweet Jovah singing, it felt good to be clean again. He didn't have soap or a towel, but the water itself was refreshment enough, and once he was done, he felt closer to human than he had for three days.

He donned a clean shirt, then looked with disfavor at the bunched-up trousers that had served as his bed. And at the pair he had been wearing ever since he was wounded, ruined by a tear and a smear of blood. Not possible to put any of these back on his body. So he rinsed out a pair in the fountain, then spread it to dry in the hot sand, under the hot sun. Hoping Rebekah did not arrive before it was fit to put on again.

Hoping she did arrive, whether or not he was practically naked.

He forced himself to walk a few yards in every direction around the camp, to readjust his muscles to the notion of movement and to test the strength in his leg. His wings felt good, powerful enough to lift him, but he didn't think his leg would hold him when he came in for a landing. One more day of healing, perhaps—more salve, more medicines—and then he would take off in the morning. Surely he could get out of the desert, closer to civilization, even if he couldn't make it all the way to Cedar Hills.

But he was still weaker than he'd thought. Even that brief bit of exercise wore him out, and he returned to camp to rest for a while. His trousers were still damp, but he felt foolish walking around without them, so he slipped them on and did not mind the cool feel of the wet fabric against his skin. He crawled under the shelter of his tent to get out of the sun and fell asleep without intending to.

When he opened his eyes, Rebekah was kneeling by the fountain.

He scrambled out from under the canvas and stood as quickly as he could, still favoring his hurt leg. "I didn't think I'd see you again!" he exclaimed. "Hasn't Simon come back yet?"

She turned her head to look at him and then stilled all over, regarding him through the veil. Something about her pose or her silence made him think she was taken aback.

"What is it?" he said at once. "Are you astonished at how well I'm doing? I told you angels heal fast."

"No. I'm astonished at how—you didn't seem so tall when you were lying helpless in the sand."

He laughed now, pleased, because what man didn't want women to consider him tall and strong? And she had already told him she thought he was attractive. "It's the wings," he said. "They add to the illusion of height and size."

She nodded. "They do. They are most impressive."

He couldn't keep himself from puffing them up, just a little, fanning the feathers out behind him so that they looked even more imposing. His wings were not so white nor so broad as Gabriel's, but they had a particularly graceful shape, perfectly belled, and he had always been just a bit vain of them. "Much more impressive than when they're spilled out helplessly over the desert floor," he agreed.

"How are you feeling?"

"Much better! I—"

But before he finished his sentence he was distracted by a gurgling sound coming from the small bundle of belongings Rebekah had dropped by the fountain. Glancing in that direction, he was astonished to see two small fists waving in the air. The gurgling laugh came again.

"You've brought company," he said.

Rebekah looked over at the pile. "A chaperone," she said with a laugh.

"Your brother?"

She nodded. "My mother said he fussed and cried all day yesterday while I was gone and that I was not to set foot outside the camp today. And then everybody needed water, so she was going to send Jordan, but I said I'd get water and I'd bring the baby with me. That made everybody happy. Even the baby."

Obadiah was not much interested in babies, but he was curious to see this small creature of whom Rebekah had spoken with such affection. He moved forward a few paces so he could look down at the boy's round, smiling face. "Goo-ah," the baby said to him, and waved his fists again.

"He seems very happy," Obadiah remarked.

"He likes movement. He just laughed and talked the whole time I was carrying him here."

"Talked? Not—I mean, he doesn't say real words, does he?"

Her laughter pealed out. "No, you silly man. He won't talk for months and months. Haven't you ever been around a baby?"

"Not really. There are always some at the holds, but—" He shrugged. "None of them ever belonged to people who mattered to me. I just never had occasion to—" He shrugged again.

"Would you like to hold him?"

"Hold him? You mean, in my arms?"

"Yes, of course that's what I mean! Are you afraid to touch him?"

"No, of course not. I just don't want to break him."

"Well, you won't break him if you don't drop him. And even if you drop him, he'll probably be just fine here on this soft sand. You don't have to be nervous at all."

As she spoke, she came to her feet and crossed over to where the baby lay. "Hey, sweet child," she said fondly, bending over to lift the cooing boy in her hands. "Aren't you being good! Are you showing off for the handsome angel? Maybe if you're nice he'll sing you a lullaby. Wouldn't you like that? Angels have beautiful voices, they say. He could sing you straight into Jovah's arms."

She turned and offered him to the angel, and Obadiah took him a bit gingerly. But the bundle was warm and instantly familiar in his arms, as if the accumulated human memories of child-rearing had all crowded into his nerves and muscles at once. He was surprised at how comfortably the small form fit along his forearm, against his chest, as if measurements had been taken and they had both been designed, just so, to come together in this arrangement.

"What's his name?" he said, automatically slipping into a slow, rocking motion, shifting his weight from foot to foot and allowing his shoulders to sway. He felt the trailing edges of his feathers drift first this way and then that against the sand.

"He doesn't have a name yet," Rebekah said.

That caused him to look up sharply from the round, sweet face. "He doesn't have a *name?*"

She shook her head. "Jansai don't name their children till they're seven or eight months old. In case they die young, as so many babies do."

"That's horrible!"

She shrugged. "Not so horrible. Most babies, especially boy babies, bear the names of men in the family who are still living. It is bad luck for a baby to die while that man is alive, and carry both their names with him to Jovah. We don't want to confuse the god."

"I think Jovah is not so easily confounded," Obadiah said, giving his attention back to the child. "I see he has a Kiss, though. He receives that before he has a name?"

"So if he does journey to Jovah while he is still an infant, his soul will find its way easily to the god."

He looked over at her. It had not occurred to him to wonder

about this before, and under her maze of garments he had not been able to see any personal adornments except the occasional flash of gold. "And you, too? You bear a Kiss?"

She nodded. "As do you, as does everybody."

"Except the Edori," he said. "Most of them don't bother to get Kissed. They say Jovah knows their names anyway."

She shrugged. "If Jovah is interested in the Edori."

He did not want to get into a discussion about the Jansai and the Edori and their long history of hatred. Not now, not on the last day he might ever see her. "I'm glad you came today," he said. "How long can you stay?"

She shook her head. "Not long. We're leaving at noon. Simon returned last night, and they worked on the axle till midnight. The wagon should be ready very soon now."

"Then I'll give you your gift now."

She had come a pace closer to smile down into the baby's face, but now she stepped back warily. "You don't owe me a gift. You have nothing to give me, anyway."

He smiled. "I do. I thought of it last night. Hold out your arm."

But she merely looked at him and did nothing.

"Wait, let me put the baby down," he said, and laid him gently on a folded blanket. Straightening up again, he repeated, "Hold out your arm."

"Why?"

Obadiah stripped the two bracelets from his wrist, the silver and sapphire one, the gold and ruby one, then slipped the gold one back over his hand. "Angels wear bracelets that identify them, that tell what hold they live at and what family they're descended from. I used to live at the Eyrie, but I make my home at Cedar Hills now. So the bracelet I wore at the Eyrie is not proper for me anymore. But it's a beautiful piece of jewelry, and I haven't wanted to just lay it aside." He extended his hand with the slim circlet sitting in his palm. "I want you to have it."

She backed up a step. "I can't take that."

"Why not? The Jansai love jewelry, so I've always been told."

"Oh, we do. I do, anyway," she said. "But you don't—I don't—you don't owe me anything. And even if you did, that's much too expensive. I couldn't take it."

"Well, I don't expect you to sell it," he said with a grin. "So it shouldn't matter how expensive it is."

"But I can't take something that matters so much to you."

"You have given me my life, which matters to me even more," he said softly. "I want to give you something precious in return."

Still she hesitated, though he sensed she was torn. "But what will I say if my mother sees it, or Hector?" she said. "They will know that no one in the family gave me such a bracelet."

"Say you found it in the street."

"People don't usually lose something so valuable."

"They lose their hearts all the time. Surely a heart is even more valuable than a bauble like this?"

"I shouldn't take it."

"Hold out your hand," he said.

She hesitated, but then she extended her arm, the folds of her sleeves hanging gracefully from her elbow. She already wore three bracelets on this wrist, one a twisted gold rope, the other two flat circlets etched with patterns. She narrowed her fingers to a point and he slid the bracelet over her knuckles, letting it come to rest on her wrist. It made a small, smug clinking sound as she gently twisted her hand from side to side.

"It's so beautiful," she said. "Thank you."

"It is a small gift to repay a great debt."

She stood there a moment, hands now folded before her and head tipped down, seemingly lost in thought. "I have a gift for you, too," she said, and raised her head.

"You of all people owe me nothing," he said.

The smile was back in her voice. "Oh, but this is something you'll like," she said. And without another word of explanation, she raised her hands and pulled back the scarves from her face.

He stared at her, as much from astonishment as from a greed to take in every detail. Her eyes were dark as rich earth, her hair a glossy brown with a completely untameable curl. There was an exotic tilt to her eyes and her cheekbones; her chin was pointed and determined. He had never seen a complexion so rich and flawless, absolutely untouched by sun. And her full lips held a smile so hopeful and nervous that it almost broke his heart.

"That is the face that will haunt my dreams for days and nights to come," he said slowly. "I could not have fashioned a more perfect set of features if I had sat down with the god to give him my specifications."

Color rose through the creamy cheeks, and she cast her eyes down. "I am nothing out of the ordinary to look at," she said.

He put his hand under her chin and tilted her face back up. "You are extraordinary to look at," he said quietly. "And your gift is even more precious than the one I gave you."

She gazed up at him with those dark eyes, an expression so intense on her face that he felt sure he should be able to read it. They were so close; nothing would be more natural than that he bend down and kiss those generous lips. He wanted to. He thought she might want that kiss as well. But he had transgressed so many boundaries with her already. He did not want to put her Jansai soul in mortal danger.

A moment longer they watched each other, and then she pulled free, stepping away from him and putting her veils back in place. "I have to go," she said. "They're expecting me right away."

"Thank you for coming by," he said quietly.

"I had to get the water."

She knelt by her pile of belongings, organizing things, wrapping the baby closely in some fine white cloth, pulling out a small packet and laying it aside. "That's for you," she said over her shoulder. "Some bread and meat. I thought you would be hungry."

"I am. Thank you."

In a minute she was on her feet, laden down with several bundles and one brother. She looked smaller than usual but just as efficient. "It was an honor, angelo," she said.

"I'll see you in Breven," he replied.

She said nothing in response to that, just settled her burdens more securely over her shoulders and took the first few paces away from the oasis. Obadiah stood there, watching her walk away, waiting for the moment when she would turn back one last time and wave a final farewell. But he stood there till the shimmering heat hid the contours of her body, while the sun made its slow crawl up the bowl of the sky, and she never once turned back to look at him.

In the morning, he took off for Cedar Hills. His initial ascent was a little shaky, as he had not been able to achieve a running start, and both his wings felt cumbersome and ill-trained. Yet, here he was, airborne, and feeling more confident with every downstroke, though he kept low to the ground in case trouble developed. His head was not entirely clear, and he felt a certain shivery weakness along his nerves and muscles—a consequence of too little food or too little exercise, he was not sure. But he could not lie helplessly in the desert one more day, especially when there would be no one arriving to offer him succor. He would rather die in the attempt to get home than die from lack of trying.

The day was fine, although—as long as he flew over sand—hot enough to be uncomfortable, especially at this low altitude. But he thought it might take him only an hour or two to get clear of the desert, and he would be better off then, even if he had to land and make camp for the night. He would be in the soft, green hills of southern Jordana, and any man could survive in that terrain.

The first hour passed slowly, almost tentatively, and Obadiah was conscious of every beat and lift of his wings. The sultry wind in his face made it hard to breathe, and rather soon he began to fear he might not have enough water in his canteen to slake his constant thirst. But the second hour was better. He felt strong enough to cut upward into a cooler layer of air, and his wings had resumed their usual steady, unconscious rhythm. And there, ahead of him, shades of green bordering the endless gold mantle of the sand. He was nearly to safety, nearly home.

Crossing out of the desert made him so happy he felt a burst of energy surge through him, and he increased both his speed and his altitude. The farms and pastures of Jordana spread out below him, cool and inviting and veined with small, silver streams. He was more accustomed to flying over Bethel, but here in the southern territories, the landscape looked much the same. He felt so good that he decided against making a noontime stop, just digging out the last of Rebekah's bread and munching on it as he flew.

But somewhere he had miscalculated. About an hour later, he felt a wave of dizziness cause his wings to falter and his head to swim. He angled downward precipitously, hoping a denser oxygen mix would clear his brain, but the opposite happened; his vision grew more blurred and an intense pressure started building up between his ears. It was all he could do to concentrate enough to keep his wings beating, to guess how rapidly the earth was rising up to meet him, and to slow his descent.

But he had miscalculated again. An errant breeze rushed by him, playfully as a child, and turned him in a half circle from his path. Normally he would have compensated for such a wind without a second thought, but at this moment he was so weak and so faint that he could not correct his course. He felt his wings flutter and his arms flail, and he tumbled the last few yards from the sky onto the ground.

CHAPTER NINE

It was not so easy as Elizabeth had hoped to make friends with an angel.

It wasn't that they were hard to find. They were all over Cedar Hills, cluttering the skies with their great white wings and filling the shops and restaurants with their musical voices and their distinctive shapes. She was reminded of a visit she and her mother had made once to some obscure family connection, an old woman who had had a fondness for cats. The whole house was full of them, and you could not step into a room without your eyes automatically seeking them out: one on the bookshelf, two on the sofa, three in the corners of the room licking their paws or curled up in sleek elegance to sleep away the afternoon. It was like that at Cedar Hills. You could not turn a corner without seeing an angel.

But the angels had even less interest in random humans than the cats had had. They did not step forward to be petted or fed; they did not even seem to notice that they shared their world with another species of life altogether. They just continued on their way, arrogant and beautiful, and filled Elizabeth's whole being with longing and desire.

She wanted to be just that gorgeous, just that careless, just that exquisite and divine. And if she could not be an angel, she wanted to touch one, put her thin arms around a man's chest and feel the silken fabric of his wings as her hands met behind his back.

So far, she had not succeeded in this plan, and she had been at Cedar Hills for nearly a month.

She had fretted over just exactly what she would tell Bennie when she announced that she was not returning with him to James's farm. But it turned out that Bennie was way ahead of her. They had not driven half a mile down the miraculous streets of Cedar Hills before he gestured at a little side street they were on the point of passing.

"There's a woman down there, owns a boardinghouse. She'll take you in if you tell her I sent you," he said.

Elizabeth had looked at him with wide eyes. "She'll—take me in? But I—how did you—"

He had given her that rakish grin, and she reflected, not for the first time, that he was a nicer man than she had given him credit for, back when they both lived on the farm. "No girl runs off with a man she scarcely knows if she's planning to run back home," he said.

"What will you tell Angeletta?"

"Oh, I think she'll have figured it out on her own by now."

She studied him. "I don't want you to get in trouble over this," she said at last. "I don't want you to be fired."

He shrugged and grinned. "Not a job I love so much that I'll mind it if they let me go," he said. "Don't you worry about me. It's you that you should be thinking about. Tola will give you a place to stay for a day or two, but you'll be needing money soon enough."

Elizabeth sat up proudly on her side of the bench. "I can work," she said. "I can cook or clean."

"And you're a beautiful girl who might find a different kind of work in pleasing men," he said, much more seriously than she'd ever heard him speak. "But take my advice, if you'd value something so worthless from such a feckless man. Never be so bent on pleasing a man that you forget you need to please yourself as well."

"I don't know what you're talking about," she said.

He sighed. "Well, you do, but I guess I can't expect you to admit it. Good-bye and good luck, Elizabeth. I enjoyed the trip with you, and that's the truth. I hope you find what you're looking for in Cedar Hills."

"Good-bye," she said, and then hesitated. He had pulled the wagon to the side of the road so she could hop out easily, and she already had one foot perched on the rim of the wagon. But she felt that she owed this man something more for all the kindnesses he had shown her on this weary journey. "I can't repay you for all you've done," she said.

He grinned easily. "Ah, I don't need coins. You'll repay me by finding happiness."

"Thank you," she said, and leaned forward and kissed him on the mouth. She felt the roughness of his whiskers and the firmness of his lips, and for just a moment, his hand lifted and brushed the hair on the back of her head. Then she pulled away and gave him a straight look. He was smiling again.

"There. That's all the payment a man could ask," he said. "Now grab your bags and go. I've got chores of my own to get to today."

That had been more than three weeks ago, and she had not seen Bennie since. She hadn't, truth to tell, thought about him more than once or twice in all that time, either. She was too busy figuring out the demands and duties of her new life.

Tola had proved to be a friend indeed, not only taking Elizabeth in and providing her a place to stay, but helping her find a job within three days of her arrival at Cedar Hills. Tola was a stout, no-nonsense, gray-haired woman in her late fifties, and she ran a boardinghouse that at the moment was home to a dozen other young women, all come to Cedar Hills to make their fortunes. Elizabeth was a little shocked, at first, to hear how openly the other girls talked about their goals and desires—which were, almost universally, to find an angel lover and bear his angel child. They discussed the venues where they were most likely to encounter an angel, the clothing that might be counted upon to catch an angel's eyes, and where a girl and her angel lover might find the necessary privacy.

Because angels were not permitted in Tola's place. "For I don't run a whorehouse, no matter what anyone might say," she commented once. "I provide a place for young girls to live, because some-one's got to offer them a safe bed at night, and it's not up to me to tell them how to run their lives. If they want to chase after anyone with wings, who am I to stop them? But they won't be carrying on inside my house. Angels or no angels."

In fact, Elizabeth learned to her astonishment, Tola had a low opinion of angels in general, and of certain Cedar Hills angels in particular. If she heard one of the girls in her boardinghouse waxing enthusiastic over David's wings or Stephen's eyes, Tola would make a hrummphing sound, and everyone would know that David or Stephen had found a way to earn Tola's contempt. This didn't stop the girls from pursuing David or Stephen, or even from talking about them in Tola's hearing. Nothing, Elizabeth soon realized, could keep these girls from talking madly about the angels.

"He *spoke* to me!" Faith breathed one day as they all sat down to dinner. Faith, who was tall and thin and wore her light brown hair fashionably short, was a lively and well-liked girl who could not have been more than eighteen. "I was in the shop, and Nathan came in and *spoke* to me!"

"Huh. Nathan. He's kind enough to everyone, but he won't look at a girl like you," said Ruth, a plump, dark-haired girl with a wicked tongue. "He won't look at anyone except Magdalena."

"Everyone looks away from his wife from time to time," purred Shiloh. She was statuesque, blonde, and poisonous, and they all hated her. "Even the saintly Nathan."

"No, he won't!" Faith said hotly. She had a grand passion for the leader of the host at Cedar Hills, but it was a pure sort of love. She desperately wanted to believe that he would be true forever to his angelic wife, because that meant, someday, when she found him, a loving angel might be true to her. "He loves Magdalena! He was allowed to marry her by a special dispensation of the god! He would not betray Jovah by betraying his wife."

"Not even Jovah would consider it a betrayal if a little indiscretion on Nathan's part brought another angel child into the world," Shiloh said cynically.

"Yes, but Magdalena would!"

"Then why doesn't she bear him an angel child herself?"

The argument was quickly under way, but Elizabeth ignored it. She had heard it, or variations of it, ever since she had first moved into Tola's house. Faith was in love with Nathan but actively pursuing an angel called Abraham; Ruth spoke rapturously of an angel named Matthew; Shiloh had managed to "enjoy liaisons," as she put it, with two angels, but nothing had come of these trysts. Well, to put it bluntly, she had not gotten pregnant. Which was what all of these girls wanted—to become pregnant with an angel child.

It was what Elizabeth herself wanted, even more fervently now that she was actually here in Cedar Hills. But somehow, now that she was here, the goal seemed both more desirable and less romantic. More like a job—one she could actually get, since she was qualified for it—and less like the misty dreams of her sleepless nights at her cousin's farm.

To bear an angel child! It was an event that would not only reshape her world, but cause the whole of Cedar Hills to dance with celebration. This Elizabeth had learned in her first three days here. Since the founding of the hold, only two angels had been born to the citizens there—only two, and so many angels were so desperately wanted. One of them had been born to a boarder at Tola's house, and Elizabeth had heard that tale over and over in the weeks since she had arrived. Magdalena had been informed of the pregnancy, of course; that, it appeared, was standard procedure any time there was the possibility of an angel birth. When the girl had gone into a harsh and difficult labor, Magdalena had come by the house in a swirl of scented silks and fluttering feathers, to check on her progress.

She had not been there when, screaming and bloody, the girl had delivered herself of an angel child, a boy, half-smothered in his own wings and furious at his violent passage into the world. He had survived; his mother had not. Magdalena had reappeared minutes after the child was born and swept him away with her to be raised by angels, and none of them had ever seen him or had word of him again.

But the death of one of their own—that had shocked the inhabitants of the boardinghouse down to their brightly painted toenails. To come so close to the dream that you died attaining it! It had not occurred to any of them that their own roads could lead to such destruction. It had not occurred to them how high the price might be to finance their dearest desires.

They knew about the other potential costs and factored these into their calculations. They knew that they were five or ten times as likely to bear a human child as to bear an angel child, even if they took no lover but an angel. They knew that there was not much market for such children in Cedar Hills or elsewhere. There were already two orphanages in Cedar Hills, overflowing with children barely a year old, born to the residents of the new hold but missing a crucial feature. Other babies mysteriously vanished, taken home to farm families who were willing to feed an extra mouth, or a sister in one of the river cities whose own child had died just the year before.

Or so the stories went. Sometimes a woman disappeared with her infant one week and reappeared without it the next, and no one could say with certainty where she had deposited the child. No one inquired too closely. No one knew what her own fate might hold, what her own decision might be if such a disastrous event unfolded.

Two such situations had developed at Tola's boardinghouse in just the last year. One of the young women had left the house with her newborn daughter in her arms, never to return to Cedar Hills. The other one, a quiet, intense girl, had gone to visit relatives and reappeared three days later unburdened by a child. Neither Tola nor anyone else had asked about the details.

Elizabeth could not imagine what she would do if such a calamity befell her. But she was sure it would not. She had come to Cedar Hills to make her fortune, and she had to believe she would succeed. She would meet an angel, and he would love her, and he would love her even more when she bore him angelic daughter after angelic son. Her heart was set on it.

Still, she had not made much progress since her arrival.

Tola had found her an empty bed, and Tola had arranged a job for her doing laundry at one of the angel dorms. It was hot, wet, heavy work, and Elizabeth did not care for it much, despite the proximity of angels. She did not appear to her best advantage with her face flushed from heat and the front of her gown smeared with soap. Besides, not all the angels made a point of delivering their dirty clothes personally to the laundry room. Some just left their sheets and shirts piled up in cascades of linen outside the doors to their rooms, and it was one of Elizabeth's duties to walk down the hallways every day and see what kinds of messes had been left behind.

She would much rather have a job like Faith's and work in a bakery, selling bread and waiting on all kinds of customers. But Faith shook her head when Elizabeth said so in a grumbling voice. Faith was her roommate, and the only person in the dorm that Elizabeth truly liked.

"Oh, no! The bakery's a dreary sort of place to work," Faith said. "Well, first, of course, I have to be there *so early* in the morning so we can get the bread started. And then I'm stuck back by the ovens most of the day. It's so hot, you wouldn't believe it. I only get to wait on customers out front if somebody else is gone on an errand, and even then you can imagine how I look, my face red and flour all in my hair. *Not* very attractive."

Elizabeth laughed. "But then, who does have the best job? And how can *we* get it?"

"Yours isn't so bad, you know. You have a chance to—" Faith paused delicately. "To see angels in their most intimate surroundings. You could casually step into someone's room someday, while he was still sleeping, or at least lying in bed. . . ."

Elizabeth laughed again. This had never occurred to her. "And say *what* to him? 'Oh, I accidentally unlocked your door'?"

"Oh, you say you thought he was gone and it was the day to strip his sheets. Make sure you find out ahead of time, of course, who exactly lives in that room! You wouldn't want to walk in on Calah or Lael or one of the other women."

"I'm not sure I can be that forward."

"Well, you have to be a little forward if you want someone to notice you," Faith said sagely. "And you could also—I know! You could launder someone's shirt and then pin a romantic note inside the collar. *That* would get his attention, I promise you."

"What if he just took the note out and threw it away? Once he saw my name and realized who I was?"

Faith shrugged. "Then you're no worse off than you were before."

"It would be so humiliating!"

"Angels expect that kind of attention. They don't think much of it. It's not just girls like us who throw themselves at the angels, it's Manadavvi heiresses and the daughters of rich landowners. Except they expect a promise of marriage, and we'll settle for—well, a little less. But they're all the same. Every girl wants to be next to an angel."

Elizabeth sighed. "It all seems so calculating. I guess I just hoped I could meet an angel who would fall in love with me."

"And so he might. Why shouldn't he? But first he has to meet you. First he has to realize you're interested in him. Now. Who exactly lives at your dorm? Let's see what your potential is."

So Elizabeth outlined for Faith the ten angels who resided in the nondescript three-story building, just mentioning the women but going into some detail about the men. Faith had a comment to offer about each of them: "Yes, he's good-looking but he keeps to himself"—"Oh, he's got a terrible temper, or so I've been told"—"Shiloh spent *three weeks* trying to catch his attention and he never even looked at her. But Shiloh is a nasty girl, and he was probably smart enough to see that, no matter how pretty her face is. He might like you better, because you're so much nicer."

None of this was particularly helpful, as they both realized by the end of the discussion. "Is there someone there you particularly *like*?" Faith asked at last. "Maybe you should concentrate on him first."

"I've only really talked to one or two of them. There was a new man, he arrived a few days ago, called Obadiah."

Faith shook her head. "I don't know him. Where's he from?"

"The Eyrie, someone said. But he's going to be living here from now on. Blond and blue-eyed. Really beautiful. But, I don't know, he didn't seem—"

"Didn't seem—?"

Elizabeth made a gesture with her hands. "Like the kind of man who would consort with an angel-seeker."

"Let me tell you, the best of men will consort with an angel-seeker. Don't have any illusions about that."

"Not Nathan," Elizabeth said.

"Not Nathan." Faith sighed. "But most angels aren't like Nathan."

"And there was another one. David. He's got these beautiful dark eyes and a sort of brooding expression, and his wings—do you know him? His wings are sort of shadowy, like they've been sprayed with bronze paint. He's very striking, I thought."

Faith was nodding. "Yes. I know who you mean. Somebody said that he was seeing one of the girls who lived in the other part of town—I think she was a shopkeeper's daughter—but nothing came of it. Well, she was gone for a couple of months, so maybe something did come of it, but nothing *important*, if you know what I mean."

"So, I kind of like him. I like the way he looks, anyway."

"Good! That's where we'll start then," Faith said briskly. "You'll just have to find a way to put yourself in his path." She thought of something. "And once he's noticed you—once you're alone with him—do you know what to do next? With a man?"

Elizabeth hesitated before answering. Twice in her life, on James's farm, she had found herself in the arms of an attractive man whom she had thought might really come to love her. Both had been the sons of Jordana landowners, young men traveling with their fathers and staying at the farm for a few days. Each time, Elizabeth had been excited and hopeful, sure that now, finally, she had found the route back to happiness and prosperity. Each time, she had been wrong.

"I'm not a virgin," she said at last.

"Good," Faith said again. "Then—let's see—how can we make sure someone in the dorm notices you?"

They sat up late, concocting ridiculous schemes and laughing a little more hilariously as the evening wore on. When the market clock struck midnight, Faith gave a little shriek and dived under the covers.

"Sweet Jovah singing, I have to be at the bakery in four hours! Turn out the light and don't say another word! I'll think about it some more tomorrow and see if I come up with any more good ideas."

In the morning when Elizabeth woke up, Faith was gone. She quickly washed and dressed, and had a light breakfast in the kitchen. Tola provided dinners for all her boarders, but not a morning or noontime meal; anyone who was home at those hours could forage for herself, as long as she made sure the kitchen was tidy again before she left. Tola had kicked out boarders who were too sloppy to clean up after themselves. Not a mistake Elizabeth intended to make. She knew she was lucky to be here, and she planned to stay until she had figured out the best way to achieve her goal.

Life with an angel . . .

The laundry room seemed particularly full of piled sheets and crumpled shirts and soggy towels this morning, and Elizabeth eyed the mounds of work without much enthusiasm. She'd only gotten three steps into the foggy room when Doris met her, a bundle of sheets piled high in her arms. Doris was the scrawny, acerbic, impatient woman who was in charge of the laundry room. She looked ninety but could carry twice the weight that Elizabeth could and moved like a flickering ghost through the heavy atmosphere of the room.

"Here—I've just got a tub started over in the corner," Doris said, transferring her armload to Elizabeth's hands and jerking her head in the appropriate direction. "Dump those in and then start stirring."

"You've already put the soap in?"

"Yes, and set the temperature. Just stir."

The women looked nothing alike, but Doris reminded Elizabeth of Tola: blunt, gruff, competent, and unemotional. But both had been kind to Elizabeth in small ways, and she liked both of them better than she had ever liked her cousin-in-law Angeletta, and so she made some effort to please them.

"All right," she said now. "I can stir the neighbor pot, too, if you like."

"Good. I'll set Helen onto scrubbing the shirts."

So the first hour of the day was consumed with the tedious labor of washing and rinsing and rerinsing the two big cauldrons of bed linens. The second hour, devoted to towels, was not much better. The third hour was at least enlivened by voices at the door—those of a man and two women, or so it sounded to Elizabeth.

"More shirts," Doris commented, carrying the soiled items back to Elizabeth. "Are you about done with those towels?"

"Yes, in a minute. Who dropped off the clothes?"

"Let's see. Calah and Myra. Oh, and David, but he was just with them, I think. Not bringing in anything to be cleaned."

"David?" Elizabeth said, looking up quickly.

Doris's sharp eyes fixed for a moment on Elizabeth's face. "Yes, the good-looking one with the ginger wings. Is he the one you've settled on?"

Elizabeth felt her face burn with embarrassment. At Tola's house, such things were commonly discussed, of course, but she had not realized her thoughts and her motives were so transparent to Doris. She might as well carry a sign around attached to her head, shouting out, Angel-Seeker Here! All Inquiries Welcome.

"I—I've only seen him a few times—he isn't—"

Doris grunted and began picking through the shirts to see which ones might need extra attention. "Oh, don't fuss about it. Pretty girl like you comes to a town like Cedar Hills, there's only one thing to expect. But you work hard, and I like that. And if you want to spend your free time chasing after angels—well, that's your choice. Maybe not such a bad choice if things work out right."

"I've never even talked to him."

"Well, maybe we can do something about that," Doris said, still inspecting the collars and the sleeves. "Damn! Will you look at this? Wine on the cuff. I don't know if we'll ever get this out, and *she's* got a temper when her clothes don't come back just right. You get to the rest of this lot, and I'll see what I can do about Miss Picky's stained shirt."

That was the only conversation they had on the topic that day, but Elizabeth worked with extra energy, trying to prove to Doris that she wasn't just a flighty girl, looking for liaisons. In the evening, she joined four others from the boardinghouse who went on a little shopping spree before the main shops closed for the night. She'd gotten her first salary the week before and had been delighted at how much was left over after she paid Tola her rent. But then, she'd been used to working at least this hard on her cousin's farm and not receiving a copper for her efforts. No wonder she felt glamorously affluent now.

Still, the shops in Cedar Hills sold merchandise at a shockingly dear price. Elizabeth saw maybe a dozen things she would have liked to buy, but each would have consumed the entire portion of her salary that was left or, in some cases, required a loan from the sum she would get next month. She might be a giddy farm girl, excited to be in the angel hold at last, but she was also a product of a hard life, and she was not about to squander everything in her purse on a beaded scarf or a pair of fabulous, fabulous, pink silk shoes.

But her attention was caught by a small dress shop on an unfashionable corner of the city, and Elizabeth headed there when the other girls stopped at a cafe for refreshments. A tired young woman was working behind the counter and gave Elizabeth a halfhearted smile. "We close in about fifteen minutes," she said. "But maybe you'll find something you like before then."

And, indeed, she did—a dark green dress in a sleeveless style, with clingy fabric that made Elizabeth remember she did not always look like a lumpy laundress. The rich color brought out the red highlights in her auburn hair and made her green eyes look deep and compelling.

"I have to have this," Elizabeth said. "I hope I can afford it."

She could, and they completed the transaction with both of them happy. She might never have an occasion or a place to wear this dress, but if circumstances ever conspired to make her need to appear beautiful, she was ready. *That,* she was beginning to learn, was the secret to being an angel-seeker or a sojourner or any kind of adventuress: being prepared for the next eventuality, even if you could not guess what it might be.

The next day did not offer anything so exciting as a chance to dress up for the night, but it did provide an opportunity even more rewarding: her first conversation with the angel David.

It happened midmorning. Doris had been sorting the clean, folded laundry by floor and by room, and she handed Elizabeth a stack of shirts and trousers.

"Third floor," Doris said. "You can come back and get the sheets on your next trip."

It was something of a privilege to be allowed to deliver laundry instead of merely cleaning it, and Elizabeth was smiling to herself as she skipped up the back stairs. She still hadn't had much occasion to go exploring through the dorm. In fact, she had only delivered laundry once, and that was fresh towels to the cedar closet on the second floor, so she wasn't sure which angels were situated where. Although at this time of day, most of them were likely to be gone already.

And indeed, the first three rooms she entered were deserted, though it was clear they were occupied most of the time. Such disarray these angels lived in! Shoes and boots strewn across the room, clothes balled up in corners, beds half-made, water rooms damp and messy. Elizabeth herself couldn't abide disorder, and she had been relieved to discover that Faith was as tidy as she was.

The fourth room Elizabeth walked into was occupied.

The angel David stepped out of the water room, clad only in a towel and his great glimmering wings. "Yes?" he said. "Oh, it's the laundry. I didn't hear you knock."

Elizabeth gaped at him, turning all shades of red, unable to look away. He had a magnificent body, still wet and glistening, and his muscled chest was covered with dark curls. His damp hair was smoothed back from his heavy-boned face; there was a sleepiness to his gray eyes that made her think he had barely climbed out of bed. Out all night on some important mission, no doubt, praying to Jovah for rain or medicine over some desperate hill farm in the northern Caitanas . . .

"I'm—I'm so sorry, angelo, I didn't knock," she stammered. "I did not realize—I just brought in your shirts."

He shrugged and gave her a grin. "Well, you almost got a better look than you bargained for," he said. "Ten minutes earlier—"

She blushed even more deeply. She was willing to be forward, as Faith had told her she must be, but it was still embarrassing to be perceived as being so bold. "No, I didn't realize—everyone else has been—their rooms have been empty—"

He yawned widely and scrubbed a hand over his eyes. "Everyone else no doubt didn't have a headache from drinking too many bottles of wine last night," he said. "If I'd been better behaved, I might have climbed out of bed at a more reasonable hour, too."

"I'm sorry, angelo," she said, finally able to tear her eyes away from him and cast her gaze to the floor. "Next time I will most certainly knock."

He laughed. "Next time? So you're going to become my personal laundress, are you?"

"No, I—I just meant that the next time—if I'm sent to your room with clothes or towels—"

He strode forward a few paces, his bare feet making light slapping noises on the wood floor. She heard the sibilant glide of his wings trailing behind him, an eerie and chilling sound. Her skin prickled into goose bumps. "I was just teasing," he said softly, coming to a halt directly in front of her. "You look so little and scared."

She glanced up quickly, to see him smiling down at her. This close to him, she could see a faint pocking across his cheekbones, a harshness to his skin that she somehow found appealing. Along with his weary eyes and air of exhaustion, the scarred skin made him look weathered but enduring, an indomitable creature who had withstood much and emerged strong. "I'm not scared," she said in a faint voice.

He laughed and continued to smile down at her. "No, don't you just look like the bravest girl! Cowering here in my doorway. What do you expect me to do? Shout at you for bringing me clean clothes? Beat you about the head? It was an honest mistake, that's all. You thought you were stepping into an empty room. And instead you got—me."

"I didn't mean to disturb you, angelo," she said.

"What makes you think I'm disturbed?"

She risked another look up at him and saw him waiting for her reply. She wished briefly for Faith to be standing beside her, whispering encouragement in her ear. All she could think to say was, "I just arrived in Cedar Hills a few weeks ago, angelo. I am not entirely sure what might—disturb—an angel and what might not."

At that, he actually flung his head back and laughed even louder, to the point that Elizabeth hoped no one was in the room next door, hearing the sound and wondering what in Jovah's name might be so amusing at this hour of the day. "No, you certainly haven't learned much in your few weeks here if you haven't figured that part out yet," he said at last. "I could show you a thing or two about disturbing men, but I'll bet you've learned some of those on your own."

"Angelo?" she said, not sure what to reply to that.

He opened his mouth as if to explain, but there was a rough knock on the door. "Hey! David! If you're not still asleep, you lazy dog, get out here and come have breakfast with us. Or lunch, more like it."

"In a minute!" David called back. "I have to dress."

"Quickly, then. We'll be in Lael's room."

Elizabeth proffered the shirts with a formal gesture. "Your clean clothes, angelo," she said.

He lifted them negligently from her arms. "Thanks for your service, kind lady," he said. "Will I see you tomorrow?"

"Will you—well, I'm here most days, down in the laundry—"

He smiled. "Will I see you—somewhere else? Up here, perhaps, delivering more clean clothes?"

"If you have something that needs to be washed, certainly I'll make sure it's returned to you."

"I should be here tomorrow afternoon," he said, turning away and heading back toward the water room. "Bored, no doubt. I'll answer the door myself—" He looked back at her over one bare shoulder and one arched wing. "That is, if you bother to knock."

She made a little bobbing motion with her head, signifying compliance or respect or remorse, even she wasn't sure. "Yes, angelo. Tomorrow, angelo. Just bring your dirty clothes down to the laundry room on your way out today, and they'll be ready for you tomorrow."

He was still laughing when she let herself out of the room and stood there in the hallway a moment, trembling. But, remembering that friends of his were awaiting him down the hall and that he might come bursting out of his own room any moment, she hurried back downstairs as quickly as her dancing feet could take her. She spent the rest of the day dreaming of love and adoration amid the sultry, oppressive fumes of starch and linen.

But David was not in his room the following day.

Elizabeth stood outside his doorway a good ten minutes, knocking at intervals, an armload of towels and trousers held carefully before her. He might be in the water room; he might be (unlikely at this hour) sleeping. She waited another few moments and knocked again.

No answer.

So she unlocked the door and stepped cautiously into the room, to find it completely untenanted and extraordinarily disorganized. Her heart grew both heavy and bulky in her chest, cumbersome with disappointment, and she moved clumsily across the room as if searching for the missing occupant. But he was clearly not here. Had forgotten the assignation, it seemed, or had remembered it but been forced to abandon it—when he was sent out this morning by Nathan, perhaps, to pray for sun over a river city. In any case, he was not here. She smoothed a neat place into the coverlet on his bed and laid the clean clothes there.

Perhaps he had just been teasing again, she thought as she stepped out of the room and locked the door behind her. Laughing to himself.

See that silly girl, angel-seeker, no doubt—let's have some fun with her. Or maybe he simply had not remembered the conversation. Girls must gape at him every day, his handsome scarred face, his sweeping wings with their faint bronze sheen. He flirted with all of them and forgot them. That might be it. She just did not know how the game was played. She had only been in Cedar Hills a few weeks, after all.

Nonetheless, she was devastated, and she moved as slowly as an old woman when she returned to the laundry room to work for the remaining hours of her shift.

She had told no one but Faith of her triumph on the previous day—thank the great good god—so there was no one but Faith to tell of her failure. Not that Faith needed any telling. The truth was plain on Elizabeth's face the instant the friends met in the dining hall at Tola's.

"What happened?" Faith whispered, sliding into the seat next to Elizabeth's.

"He wasn't there."

"Oh, is that all?"

Elizabeth glanced over at her quickly. "I think he forgot me. Or never meant anything by it at all."

Faith shrugged and spooned some potatoes onto her plate. "He was probably called away. Sent to Semorrah or Luminaux. And even if he did forget, which he probably didn't, it just means he hasn't remembered you yet. You haven't made that extraordinary an impression on him. But you will. Wait till he sees you again."

"I don't want him to see me again. I'm so embarrassed."

"This is not the time to be embarrassed," Faith said firmly, ladling potatoes onto Elizabeth's plate, too, and passing the bowl over to Ruth. "This is your future you're protecting. You have to be outrageous. Next time you see him, you must do something or say something that will make him remember you."

They were claimed by the general conversation then, but Elizabeth spent the next few hours, off and on, thinking about what Faith had said. And what she could do to make herself memorable to the angel David. Nothing occurred to her that evening, but she knew the advice was sound. Her future was at stake. She must be bold and notable.

But the following day, it was clear no laundress was going to draw anyone's attention at the dorm. The angel Obadiah had returned after a weeklong absence, wounded, delirious, and escorted by strangers. It was not just the dorm but the whole city that was in an uproar.

CHAPTER TEN

Elizabeth heard the news the minute she got to work, for the angel had arrived not half an hour before. He had been brought in by some Luminauzi merchants who had taken a leisurely route around the Heldoras, peddling their wares at small towns all across Jordana. They realized, as they saw an angel fall from the sky one afternoon, that they had acquired far more valuable cargo than their dyed silks and gem-set baubles, and they had made all haste to the hold.

Elizabeth barely had time to hear the details of how the Luminauzi caravan had pulled into Cedar Hills, and how Magdalena had instantly spotted the broken shape of the angel sprawled in the back of one wagon. Chaos and confusion had ensued, no doubt, but Obadiah had ultimately been carried here, to the room he had called his own for only a few days. And here, said Doris, he would be nursed back to health.

"*Double* the load on us, you'll see, for a sick man uses twice the bedding a well man does, and think of the visitors he'll have," Doris grumbled. Privately, Elizabeth thought she was as excited as everyone else to have such events occurring under this very roof. "People rushing in and out all day—well, *we* won't even have the worst of it; the cooks and the housekeeping staff, now, *they'll* be run ragged, just you wait."

A breathless figure burst through the door, indistinct through the coiling steam. "Please," a girl panted. "We need more cloth for bandages."

Doris whirled to face her, instantly professional. "Plain strips? How wide?"

"I don't—some very narrow, I think, to bind his fingers, and some—wider ones, I suppose, for his leg, but I don't know—"

Doris pointed. "Elizabeth. That cabinet against the wall. Get an assortment and take them up to the angel's room."

All the other women watched with envy as Elizabeth hurried across the room, quickly snatched up a selection of cotton strips, and followed the girl out of the laundry room and up to the second floor.

The sickroom seemed overfull of people, Elizabeth thought, glancing around quickly to see as many details as she could. The blond angel lay, pale and motionless, on the bed in the middle of the room. His wings hung limply over both sides of the bed, looking as rumpled as soiled linens. One dark-haired angel sat beside his bed, mopping his face with a damp cloth, and two other angels milled about the room, whispering to each other and glancing over at the hurt man. A middle-aged mortal woman sat on the other side of the bed. Her efficient air and general confidence led Elizabeth to suspect this was a healer. The angel showing such compassion for the fallen Obadiah was, she was fairly certain, Magdalena herself. The girl whom Elizabeth had followed into the room was nowhere in sight, but splashing from the water room made it clear she had gone back to a task she had merely abandoned for a moment.

No one looked up when Elizabeth walked in, so she spoke in a carrying voice. "I brought the fresh bandages," she said.

The healer looked over and smiled. "Good. Bring them here. Do you know how to set a bone?"

Elizabeth felt her eyes stretch to their widest. "Set a—I can't do it myself, but I've helped hold a man when someone else set it," she said. That was true, too; on the farm, workers were forever being hurt, and Angeletta would no more aid in the doctoring than she would labor in the kitchen. Elizabeth hadn't liked it much either, clinging to a cursing, sweating, smelly man while a splint was put in place, but she had considered it basic human kindness to help ease a man from his misery.

"Oh, thank you," Magdalena said in a soft voice. "I can't do it—
I just can't—"

Elizabeth didn't ask why the other angels or the girl washing out
something in the water room weren't able to aid the healer. She just
placed her pile of bandages within easy reach of the healer's hand
and stepped up to the bedside. "Where's he hurt? What would you
like me to do?" she asked.

"His left arm and three of his fingers are broken," the woman
said. "I want to start with the small bones."

"However did you manage to get so hurt in so many places?"
Magdalena wailed, but in a soft voice, pitched to cause an invalid no
stress. "For your leg is a mess and there's a tear in your wing—"

Elizabeth had thought the angel barely conscious, so she was startled when he answered in a low, breathless voice. "I told you. I fell
from the sky—and I must have landed on my arm. That part is—
rather hazy."

"You did not wound this leg falling from the sky," the healer
observed. "*That's* a burn mark, I'm certain."

"Yes," Obadiah said faintly.

"A burn!" Magdalena exclaimed. "But—Obadiah—how could
you—what did you—"

"I'm not entirely sure. I need to—talk to Nathan."

"What? You'll tell him secrets you won't tell me?"

A smile lit the pale, handsome face. Elizabeth thought him very
attractive, even in his present sorry condition. "I will tell—you, too.
When you are both here—and I don't have to tell the story—twice over."

"You just look so battered," Magdalena said in a worried voice.
"I am so concerned about you."

"He'll be fine," the healer said briskly. "But we've got to get
these bones set. You—are you ready? What's your name, girl?"

"Elizabeth. Yes, I'm quite ready."

It took them the next hour to splint and wrap the broken bones
of the angel's forearm and fingers. By the time they were done, he
was tense with the stress of withstanding agony and covered in a
light film of sweat. While they worked, the splashing girl and one of
the angels left, and two more visitors arrived and departed. The
healer ignored all of them, so Elizabeth did as well.

"I can't say—that your ministrations—have made me feel any better at all," Obadiah panted when they were done.

The healer permitted herself a small smile. "No, I imagine you feel much worse at the moment. But I'll give you something for the pain, and I would think you would feel better by morning. You angels are lucky. You have no idea how long it takes a mortal man to heal."

"I'll stay with you," Magdalena said.

He turned his eyes her way, not moving his head from the pillow. "I'd rather you didn't," he said. "I just want to sleep."

"Then I'll come back later tonight."

"Yes—I'd welcome that."

"I'll bring Nathan, so you can tell us all your secrets at once."

The healer turned her serious gaze on Elizabeth. "You. Elizabeth. You work in this building?"

Elizabeth nodded. "In the laundry room. Yes."

"Can you come back and check on him from time to time? Make sure he doesn't have a fever and that his bandages have not come loose?"

Could she? She would be elated to do so. "Certainly," Elizabeth said coolly. "And if he does have a fever, what should I do?"

The healer was laying an assortment of pills and potions on a bedside table. "One of these for fever, a teaspoon of this for pain. Only two more doses of each by day's end, though. Can you remember that?"

"Yes."

"Can he eat?" Magdalena asked.

"Broth. Soft foods," the healer said. "For a day or two. After that, anything he wants. I imagine he'll be plenty hungry by then."

"I'm hungry now," he said in a whisper.

"No doubt, but right now you're likely to throw up everything we pour down your throat, so we'll just be cautious," she replied. "Is there anything else you need? If not, I'm clearing this lot from the room, and you should sleep as long as you can."

He moved his head weakly on the pillow, an attempt to shake his head no, Elizabeth thought. "I need nothing I can think of. Sleep. I am so happy to be here I cannot tell you—"

The healer rose, and Elizabeth jumped to her feet. Magdalena more reluctantly stood up. "I hate to leave you," the angel said, looking down at the patient.

"Go," he said. "I'll see you later. Thank you. All of you."

Elizabeth gave the healer a little nod and said, "I'll check on him," and the healer nodded in return. Then Elizabeth stepped from the room, trying to move with the measured gait of someone who could be relied on to watch over a sick man, a wounded *angel,* with the closest attention. Once out into the empty hall she paused for a moment and had to squeeze down her squeal of delight. Then she ran back downstairs toward the laundry room to tell everyone there every scrap of information she had obtained in the overheard conference of the angels.

Three times that day Elizabeth returned to the sickroom to check on the angel. He was asleep the first two times she stole in, so she lay her hand tentatively across his forehead to check for fever. The skin of an angel was hotter than the skin of a mortal—she knew that already, mostly because of some very revealing things Shiloh had said—so she was not too concerned when his flesh felt a little warm against her fingers. Still, she wet a cloth and wiped his face with cool water, then checked his bandages to make sure all was well.

The third time she crept inside, he was awake. It was late afternoon, and her shift would soon be over, but she did not want to leave again without a final visit. He resettled himself on the bed as she crossed the room and gave her a faint smile.

"You're back," he said in a thready voice. This afternoon he was lying on his side, and his wings spilled behind him, down the edge of the bed and onto the floor. She could not help thinking of the down stuffing pouring from the hole in a torn mattress.

She gazed at him, convinced that he looked more flushed than he had when he was sleeping, which might not be a good sign. "How are you feeling?" she asked. "I haven't been able to tell if you have a fever."

"I am hot enough to say yes, I think," he said, so she put her palm on his forehead. Yes, even by angelic standards, his body seemed overwarm. "And every separate bone feels broken, and each individual muscle is bruised."

"Well, you haven't had any medicine since this morning, so let me give you some drugs. You'll feel better."

"I'll fall asleep again."

She gave him a small smile. "That might make you feel better, too."

He moved restlessly, though not very energetically, on the bed. "I feel like I have been—sick or sleeping—for days now."

She had picked up a pill and a glass of water, but if he wanted to talk a few moments before she administered the drugs, she was more than happy to oblige. "Why, when did you first get wounded?"

He appeared to think for a moment. "Five days ago? Maybe six? I am tired of lying about helplessly." He smiled up at her again. He seemed like a man whose face was formed for smiles. "Though I have not minded the part about being nursed by pretty girls."

"If by that you mean me and the angela Magdalena, I thank you for the extraordinary compliment," she said.

He gave a weak laugh. "Yes, but—someone else helped me, too. When I was first injured. Or I might not have survived."

Now there was a tale Elizabeth would have liked to hear, but she didn't think the angel would be confiding any secrets to her. "Where did you get injured?"

"In the desert. Outside of Breven." He looked at her, then looked away. "I was very fortunate to find help."

"They say it was Luminauzi who found you and brought you here."

"Luminauzi—yes—who else would help a fallen angel?"

Which was a strange thing to say, so Elizabeth assumed he had acquired delirium along with the fever. "Here, you'd better take this," she said, holding the pill to his mouth and following that with a glass of water. "How about the pain? I've got some kind of powdery mix here I'm supposed to give you if you're hurting."

"Yes—I think a powdery mix is just what I need right now."

She frowned. "Would you like me to bring the healer back again? Do you feel worse?"

"No—no worse—just no better. I *hate* being such a pathetic creature!"

She could not help smiling. "Well, I'm sure you're magnificent when you're feeling whole."

He laughed shakily. "I am—at any rate—not as contemptible as I am now."

"I can't imagine anyone would think you were contemptible ever," Elizabeth said softly. "Here. Drink this, and maybe you'll feel better."

He obediently pushed himself up on one elbow and swallowed the glassful of medicine. When he lay back on the pillow, he gave her a smile of great sweetness. "Thank you, Elizabeth," he said. "Isn't that your name?"

She felt such a flutter in her blood that she almost could not keep her hold on the glass. An angel calling her by name! "Yes, angelo," she said with assumed calm.

He appeared to be straining to keep his eyes open, and then he gave up and let the lids fall. "Come by tomorrow and see me again," he said drowsily. "I will feel better then, I assure you."

"I will," she said, setting down the glass and straightening up. "I hope you feel very much better in the morning."

And as she stepped out into the hall and closed the door behind her, she realized that she had never been so happy. Frail, helpless, and fevered he might be, but the angel Obadiah had thanked her by name. She had been right to come to Cedar Hills after all. This was the place she was meant to be.

Elizabeth was quite a celebrity that night in the dining hall as she recounted her tale of Obadiah's arrival and her role in caring for him. Everyone else had heard of the angel's fall and rescue, of course, for the story had been talked of on every street in Cedar Hills, but no one else had firsthand information about the disasters that had beset him. She was pelted with questions, for Obadiah was a newcomer to Cedar Hills, and not much was known about his looks or his personality.

"He seemed very sweet—he thanked me more than once—and he has the prettiest smile," Elizabeth said. "But I think he was embarrassed to be seen like that. He said he must seem contemptible."

"He's one of Magdalena's favorites," Shiloh said.

"Oh? And just how do you know that?" someone asked skeptically.

Shiloh tossed her long blond hair. "I hear things. They have been close since the days she lived in Monteverde and he resided at the Eyrie. She's the one who wanted him brought to Cedar Hills."

"Well, heavens, I suppose she can have friends if she wants to," Faith said. "And who else are the angels friends with except each other?"

Shiloh shrugged. "But they're *close.*"

Faith rolled her eyes and turned back to Elizabeth. "So what else did he say? Why wouldn't he say how he got injured in the first place?"

They went over the same material three or four times, everyone chiming in with her theory as to what might have brought an angel down from the skies over Breven. Elizabeth was happy to speculate along with the rest of them, but she doubted they would ever find out.

She had not counted on being in the invalid's room the following day, just as Magdalena and Nathan arrived.

She had presented herself to Doris as soon as she arrived in the laundry room, and the old woman had grunted at her, "You're wanted up in the angel's room."

Elizabeth's heart gave a little bounce. David had come looking for her, realizing that he had missed their tryst? Or—"Which angel?" she asked.

Doris glanced over with a look of wry amusement on her face. "That's true, how would you know, in a houseful of angels, once you'd gotten cozy with one or two of them?"

Elizabeth felt her face flame. "I haven't—"

Doris shrugged and waved her toward the door. "I meant the hurt one. Obadiah. The healer's back this morning and stopped by to ask if you could be spared to help her with the rebinding. Well, I knew you had your heart set on soaking the shirts this morning, but I said to myself, just this once, she can tear herself away from her true calling to help out a soul in need."

It was the most humorous speech Elizabeth had ever heard the dry Doris utter, and she couldn't help giggling. "Thank you, ma'am," she said. "I'll be back as soon as they're done with me."

She flew up the stairs and knocked only perfunctorily before entering Obadiah's room. He was sitting up on the bed, his wings spread out behind him like some kind of grand robe of royalty. He looked remarkably improved, even cheerful, though he was wincing away from the healer even as Elizabeth walked in. "Ouch! Do you have any idea how much that hurts?"

"A little," said the woman, who was bent over his wounded leg and slowly peeling back the bandages. "But I've never had the bad fortune of getting caught in the crossfire of some scorching weapon, so I can only speculate."

"It's not like I did it on purpose," he said indignantly. "But if I— Elizabeth! Good morning! Mary says I am much better today."

Mary must be the healer's name. The woman glanced briefly in Elizabeth's direction. "Good. I need to rewrap all the wounds this morning. I was going to leave them for a day or two, but I want to try a new salve."

Elizabeth stepped up to the bed and smiled shyly down at the patient. "You look better," she said. "How's the pain?"

"The pain comes and goes," he said. "But the fever has waned. I told Mary how good you were to me."

Elizabeth shrugged. "I only handed you a pill."

Mary smiled at her. She appeared to be somewhere in her mid-fifties, though thin blond hair and a fair complexion gave her a look of sustained youth. "Sometimes it's just knowing someone is there to hand you that pill that makes all the difference. How long can you be spared from your duties?"

"As long as you need me."

"Good. Let's get started."

But they had barely finished unwrapping the bandage on Obadiah's leg before two more angelic forms came marching in. Elizabeth had only seen Nathan a few times before, and never close up, so she watched him covertly a few moments. He was a well-built, dark-haired, serious-looking angel with quite a magnificent wingspan. Magdalena swept in beside him.

"Oh, so you've finally deigned to come visit me, miserable creature that I am," Obadiah greeted the host of Cedar Hills. "I've only been here—let's see, one whole day—and not a word of comfort or condolence do I hear from you. I think I'll pack my bags and head back to the Eyrie. I'm sure *they* would not leave a wounded angel to rot by himself in agony."

Nathan had reached the side of the bed and was smiling down at Obadiah. Elizabeth could see why Faith was so infatuated with him. His brown eyes added seriousness to a clear-cut and somewhat haughty face, but the shape of his mouth was kind, and there was a general air of pleasantness about him. "I came by last night— twice—but you were sleeping. Probably pretending to sleep," the leader added. "I had been told not to wake you, since sleep would do you more good than a rambling, inconsequential conversation with me. But had I known I would be abused for neglect, I'd have shouted in your ear and shaken you from whatever dreams you were enjoying, just for the pleasure of my company."

"You look better," Magdalena said. "How are you feeling?"

They discussed the state of his health for a few moments, while Mary and Elizabeth continued to work on the wounded leg. Elizabeth had glanced over at the healer, expecting that the two of them would remove themselves while the angels visited, but Mary just kept on working, cleanly and methodically, and Elizabeth said nothing. It wasn't as if she *wanted* to leave.

Nathan glanced around the room, then hauled two narrow-backed chairs to the bedside. "Now. Tell us what happened. Maga says you were secretive last night."

Obadiah shrugged. "With a roomful of gossips, it seemed the best course. But I think this is news Gabriel needs to hear."

Elizabeth concentrated on making herself invisible so she would not be dismissed at this interesting juncture.

Obadiah continued slowly. "I was only a couple of hours outside of Breven when I felt a sudden pain in my wing, and then a second one on my leg."

"You were airborne?" Nathan interrupted.

"Yes. Flying relatively low. I didn't see where the shots came from, but there were definitely weapons of some sort and aimed deliberately at me. And, Nathan, they felt like fire."

"The wounds they've left behind certainly look as if they could have been made by flames," Magdalena said.

"Did you see any projectile—an arrow, a rock wrapped with some kind of flammable material?" Nathan asked.

"No. I saw nothing. I just felt fire. I managed to land and make it to an oasis, where I stayed for a couple of days until I had recovered enough to attempt the trip back."

"Which you were obviously not well enough to make," Magdalena said.

He smiled over at her. "No, but I was fortunate to fall in with friends. Fall in—a joke, you see."

"Not funny," she murmured.

A little silence settled over the room. Nathan appeared to be thinking something over, and the other two angels were lost in their own thoughts. Mary had finished retying the bandage on the wounded leg—much improved, Elizabeth thought—and had now turned her attention to the broken fingers. Elizabeth doubted these really needed to be rewrapped at this point, but she could appreciate Mary's motives; neither of them wanted to leave the room and miss a word of the conversation. The cloth came away oh so slowly from first one finger and then another.

"This weapon," Nathan said at last. "It just shot bolts of fire?"

"So it seemed," Obadiah said apologetically. "I know it sounds impossible."

"There was a weapon like that," Nathan said, "in Raphael's hands. Shortly before the mountain came down."

"I don't remember that," Magdalena said.

"No, I don't either," Obadiah said.

"But there was. Raphael and a few of his followers had these— sticks of fire—and they brought these with them to the Plain of Sharon on the day we were supposed to sing the Gloria. They were fairly powerful weapons. They could be aimed from a hundred yards away or more, and send a tree or a bush up in flames. Everyone was afraid of them."

"Where would they have gotten weapons like that?" Obadiah demanded.

Nathan shrugged. "Left behind when the first settlers came to Samaria five hundred years ago?"

"The settlers brought no weapons with them at all," Magdalena said. "They wanted to leave war and violence behind."

"So we've been taught," Nathan said. "Who knows what one or

two of them may have smuggled to a new land along with their clothes and their copy of the Librera?"

"And you say Raphael had these weapons?" Obadiah said. When Nathan nodded, he continued, "Then perhaps he left some of them behind with his Jansai allies. Malachi, perhaps."

"Malachi perished on the mountain along with Raphael."

"He might have bequeathed his—his firesticks to a nephew or a son."

"So then you think it was Jansai who shot you from the sky?" Nathan asked.

"I was not two hours from Breven. Who else travels that desert and bears a great hatred for angels? But I didn't see them. I can't prove anything."

"Jansai would be my first thought, too," Nathan said.

"But the question would be," Obadiah said softly, "why did they not come after me to make sure I was dead? If I had wounded an enemy, I would follow through on my spite."

"They thought you *were* dead," Magdalena said. "If you fell some distance, hurt and alone in the desert, they would not have expected you to survive. They don't realize how great an angel's regenerative powers are."

"Even so, I should have died," Obadiah said. "It was sheer luck I was close enough to water to drag myself there."

"Gabriel has to know," Nathan said.

"Yes," Obadiah said, "but then what? We are already at odds with the Jansai. Who can we accuse, and what good would it do? I don't believe Uriah set any of his cohorts after me. Though it was clear from my visit there that any number of the Jansai would like to bring the three holds down, not just one random angel."

"So the mood in Breven was unfriendly."

"To put it mildly."

"And Uriah was hostile?"

"No, Uriah was welcoming. I think he liked the idea that I would bargain with him, though I can't say we got very far. The first word out of his mouth was 'Edori,' and that's not negotiable. But we might be able to strike a deal. I don't know. At any rate, he seemed to like the thought that I would return to Breven and discuss alliances. That was the only real outcome of our conversation."

"I can't send you back there in this condition."

Obadiah laughed. "No, but I'll be well in a day or so. A week at the longest."

"But if someone in Breven has a grudge against you—"

"What I think? Some bad-tempered, vengeful Jansai traveler had his hands on an exotic weapon, and he saw the shape of an angel fly-ing overhead. More in a gesture of hatred than in any real attempt to do harm, he lifted the stick and aimed. He was probably as surprised as I was when the bolt struck home."

"Two bolts," Nathan said. "That argues intent to harm."

"I still think it was—fortuitous, if you will. He got lucky. I got unlucky. I don't think he knows my face or was particularly hoping to bring me down."

"But don't you think," Magdalena said in a soft voice, "that he might start to worry once he thinks things over? A dead angel— surely that's something we would notice. Surely that's something we would avenge. He must be starting to dread the consequences, no matter how lucky he felt at the time."

"Maga has a point," Obadiah acknowledged. "And I don't think Gabriel's the only one who needs to know about this. If Uriah really does want an alliance with us, he won't be condoning—what would you call it?—angicide."

Magdalena said, "That's not funny," but Nathan burst out laugh-ing. The leader of the host said, "Good point. Whether or not he's been informed of the incident, he needs to know what we suspect. Though you must tell him of our suspicions very gently."

"I will," Obadiah said.

"So you plan to go back there?" Magdalena asked in some alarm.

"Of course. In a few weeks. There's supposed to be—a festival of some kind? Someone mentioned it, but I didn't catch all the details."

"Yes, it's a harvest fair," Nathan said. "They bring in singers and winemakers and performers and have contests in the streets. A few of the Cedar Hills shopkeepers went last year and said it was some-thing of a brawl, but it appears to be a main event in Breven. It would be good if you were well enough to attend that."

"I'll plan on it, then."

Nathan gestured at Obadiah's hand, which Mary was now, with infinite care and patience, finally finished rewrapping. "How does that feel? It looked like hell when she uncovered it."

"It feels like hell," Obadiah said with a laugh. "But that salve you just put on—whatever it was—that's good. That makes the pain go away."

"Manna root salve, angelo," Mary said. "It's truly an astonishing ointment. I am so glad it's available to us again."

Nathan looked over, clearly attempting to feign an interest he did not feel. "Oh? The manna root stopped growing for a time, did it?"

"All the seeds were gone, gathered up by silly girls to make love potions," Mary said. "So of course we could grow no more plants, and we could make no more salve. It was very distressing to all the healers."

Elizabeth didn't know this story. She'd never heard of manna root before, though she liked the sound of love potions. She didn't want to seem stupid in front of the angels, though, so she didn't ask what miracle had occurred to revive the plants that bore the seeds.

But Nathan, still attempting to be courteous, asked for her. "So how did you bring the plants back?"

Magdalena laughed. "You know that story, Nat. Rachel found an old song of Hagar's and prayed to the god, and all those seeds came raining down, sent by Jovah."

"Yes, and no doubt the lovesick girls gathered up bucketfuls of them, but the healers harvested their share, too," Mary said. "So we've had manna root again ever since Rachel became angelica, and we've all been grateful to her for it."

"That's my Rachel," Obadiah said in an admiring voice, but Elizabeth thought he was laughing a little, too. "Determined to bring love and joy into the world wherever she goes."

Mary patted him lightly on his newly bandaged arm. "We're all done here, angelo. I'll leave drugs for you again, but I don't think you'll need many. You're healing nicely."

"Can I eat?" he demanded.

"Yes. Whatever you like."

"Good. Because I'm starving."

Magdalena rose. "I brought a basket of food and I left it in the hall. Can I stay and eat with you?"

"I'd be happy if you did."

She stepped past them and went out the door. Mary put a hand on Elizabeth's shoulder, and they both stood up. "We'll be going now. I'll check on you in the morning, and I'll make sure this one comes by at least once more today to see if you need anything."

"I'd appreciate that," Obadiah said, giving them each a friendly smile. There was something about him that seemed both warm and genuine, as if he was quite happy to have landed in their circle of friendship and would call them by name if he ever encountered them again, no matter what exalted company he might be in at the time. So it seemed to Elizabeth, anyway. "You can't have too many friends when you're a sick man."

"You," Nathan said in a scoffing voice. "You don't think you can have too many friends when you're well. I never saw a man who collected people the way you do."

"I collect friends so nobody realizes how uninteresting I am on my own," Obadiah said lightly. "Mary. Elizabeth. Thank you so much for your ministrations."

"You're welcome, angelo," Mary said sedately, and Elizabeth repeated her words, though in a rather more breathless voice. Magdalena stepped back into the room, a huge picnic basket in her hands.

"All your favorite foods!" Magdalena exclaimed. "I was in the kitchen all day nagging the cooks—"

The mortals were across the threshold before they could hear the rest of her sentence, and Mary closed the door behind them. Then the healer turned to give Elizabeth one long, serious look.

"Don't think I wasn't as curious as you were," the fair woman said. "But that doesn't mean I'll be repeating a word I heard in there, and you shouldn't either. That story will get around in a day or two—impossible to keep such a tale a secret—but it shouldn't be you or me who repeats it. We hold positions of trust, and we shouldn't abuse that trust by gossiping."

"I won't," said Elizabeth earnestly. "Not a word to anyone."

Mary's face relaxed into a smile. "You're a good girl," she said. "If you ever get tired of working in the laundry, come see me. I could teach you a thing or two about healing and see how you liked it. Might be a better career for you than soaking and scrubbing, who knows?"

"Thank you," Elizabeth said. "But I—right now—I'm promised to Doris at the moment—"

Mary grimaced a little. "You have friends in the angel dorm, I take it. That's all right. I wish you luck. But come see me someday if things don't turn out so well here. I'll find work for a good pair of hands like yours."

And that compliment warmed her almost as much as Obadiah's smile, almost as much as the consciousness of knowing a secret that everyone else would be agog to hear. Elizabeth was humming as she returned to the laundry room, and not even the foulest-smelling detergent or the hottest splash of water could turn her mood from sunny to sour.

CHAPTER ELEVEN

The following day was also alive with angels. Elizabeth was starting to think she'd caught the trick of it, had learned how to draw the great winged creatures into her sphere through the sheer power of her desire. Though that was silly, she knew in her heart. Like Obadiah, flying over the desert, she had been marked by fortune, either good or ill. None of her own actions had had the least bearing on shaping the patterns of her days.

In the morning, after making an appearance in the laundry room, she headed upstairs to do a brief check on Obadiah, as the healer had asked her to do. It was not presumptuous at all. Her tentative knock on the door was followed by a quick, "Please come in," and she entered to find Obadiah standing half-dressed in the middle of the room.

"Oh!" she said involuntarily, because the angel on his feet was quite a different proposition from the helpless creature sprawled in a sickbed. He was taller than she had thought, for one thing, with an air of such negligent grace that he might have been posing for Jovah's concept of an angel the first time the god decided to fashion one from the materials of the universe. And his wings, which had drooped so miserably the past few days, were arranged behind him like a proud retinue, polished, gleaming, and poised for action.

Even the angel's face seemed different, sharper, more handsome, though it retained its general expression of sweetness—and, at the moment, a comical look of dismay. "Elizabeth," he said. "Thank the god you're here."

"What's wrong?" she said, immediately trying to cover up the fact that she was staring at him and attempting to seem professional and helpful instead.

He gestured at his shirt, clumsily settled over his shoulders and completely undone in front. "I can't—my fingers are so clumsy in these splints—I can't get the buttons done. I got my trousers on, but that was a feat, I can tell you."

He sounded so indignant that she couldn't help laughing a little. "Well, I can help you with your shirt."

But he turned his back to her before she could take a step forward. "It's not on right. Can you see? It feels all bunched up over my wings."

It had never occurred to her before that angels must have special seamstresses to design their clothes, but naturally some accommodation must be made for the magnificent appendages springing from their backs. As much out of curiosity as a desire to help, she came close enough to study the construction of the shirt. Yes—that was efficient—there was a central panel of cloth that unrolled down the spine between the two great feathered joints and buttoned underneath the surge of sinew and feather. Not only was the back of Obadiah's shirt not buttoned, that center panel had hooked itself over one of the belled wings and refused to fall properly in place.

"Here, stand still," she said, and carefully tugged all the fabric into alignment. She made some effort to avoid touching his feathers, since she had learned that angels hated to endure casual contact with their wings. Still, it was impossible not to be aware of them, spilling down on either side of her to pool on the wood floor. They emitted a faint odor, and she sniffed cautiously, trying to identify it, but she could not name the scent. Starlight, maybe, or the fragrance carried by the wind shortly before the arrival of rain. Something elemental.

"There," she said. "That's all done. Now turn around."

He made one elegant pirouette, moving with such perfect understanding of spatial relationships that not a single quill edge touched her as he turned. "I cannot tell you how annoying I find it not to be able to care for myself," he told her. His voice was light, but she suspected the emotion was sincere. "I have never been sick a day in my life! *I* am the one who has called down plague medicines for fevered farmers who were convinced they were about to die. *I* am the one who has brought comfort and ease to hurt children and crying mothers. I promise you, I will be much more patient with them in the future."

She smiled and concentrated on the shirt. His chest beneath the fabric looked too lean, the chest of a fit man who could ill afford to go a week or so on a starvation diet. It was a matter of a minute or two to thread all the ornate buttons through their proper slits, and then fasten the cuffs as well. She did not have the nerve to suggest that she tuck the ends of the shirt into his trousers, so she stepped back once her task was completed.

"There you are," she said with a smile. "Fit to go out in public."

"And once more I'm thanking you for your kindness," he said. "Now I know what they mean by the term *godsend.* You have been so good to me these past few days."

She allowed herself to look up into his face. Yes, quite handsome, but more kind than handsome; he had a smile that made you want to confide in him. Not that she would, of course. "I did very little," she said. "Let me know if you need me to do anything else."

"No, I'll be completely well by tomorrow, you'll see. I'll even figure out how to work these stupid fingers so I can dress myself like an adult. But I do thank you for your help."

"You're welcome, angelo."

He stood there for a moment longer, smiling down on her like the first noon of springtime, and then widened his eyes with consternation. "Damn! I'm late. Come check on me again from time to time."

And he leaned in, kissed her quickly on the cheek, and blew out the door like a flock of summer birds. Elizabeth stood there with her hand pressed against her face, feeling like the god himself had laid his palm against her skin with a touch like fire and fate. Oddly, she felt less like an angel-seeker at that moment than she had since the day she had first set foot in Cedar Hills.

Later she was to wonder if that kiss marked her like some kind of brand visible only to other angels. For she had just stepped into the hallway, dazed and unsteady, when Calah poked her head out of her own doorway down the hall.

"Is that—aren't you one of the laundresses?" Calah demanded.

"Yes, angela."

"Step in here a moment, could you? My dress has a tear, and I'm very clumsy with a needle. You can sew, can't you? As well as wash?"

"Yes, angela."

So she slipped inside the young angel's room (as untidy as all their rooms were; who had raised these people?) and set a few stitches in an impossibly delicate silver gauze gown. Just as she was finishing this task, three other young angels—two female and one male—tumbled into the room, talking and laughing together with so much energy that Elizabeth felt her skin prickle with borrowed excitement.

"What—now you've got servants waiting on you? How do you rate so high?"

"No, I just grabbed her as she was walking down the hall. She works in the laundry room."

"Well, I have a stack of clothes that need mending."

"Don't be silly, the poor girl's just trying to do her job. She wasn't sent here to keep your wardrobe in order."

"Well, she's keeping Calah's wardrobe in order!"

Elizabeth glanced up, wondering if she was supposed to be taking part in this conversation, but they were all happily bickering with each other, ignoring her. She carefully folded the gossamer gown and stood up, laying it on her chair.

"All done, angela," she said.

"What? Oh—thanks. You're very good," Calah said distractedly, and put out her hand. She was holding half a dozen coppers—a nice tip for such a small job—and Elizabeth gave a little bob and accepted them. Faith had said that angels could be generous from time to time, and that it was rude to refuse their gifts, or Elizabeth wouldn't have known quite how to behave at this moment. She was still unused to being paid for her services, let alone receiving a thank you that came in spoken or monetary form.

"Thank you, angela," she said, and left the room.

And then, on her way down to the laundry room, she encountered three more angels in the hallways. All of them bid her hello in an absent but courteous fashion, when she didn't remember a single angel ever even noticing her presence before when she passed one in the corridor. Perhaps Obadiah's kiss had held some magic in it, lifting her across an imaginary border from the invisible to the visible world. Perhaps once one angel acknowledged you, they all would.

Or perhaps the magic would only last a day.

At any rate, the spell was still in effect that evening as Elizabeth left the laundry room and stepped outside to go home. She paused a moment to take deep breaths of the clean, cool air, feeling half smothered by a day of inhaling steam and starch. No more pretending that it was still late summer; true autumn was firmly entrenched in southern Jordana. The days could still be delightfully warm, but the nights held a whispered promise of chill to come.

"Well!" came a voice behind her, and she nearly jumped off the stairs. She hadn't heard anyone come out of the door. "If it isn't the elusive little laundry girl."

Elizabeth spun around in astonishment to find herself staring up at the angel David, two steps above her. She had a moment's quick impression of darkness, for he stood in the overhanging shadow of the building, and his hair was dark, and his eyes, and his wings. That notion quickly evaporated in her blinding happiness at seeing him again. "Good evening, angelo," she said a little breathlessly.

He came slowly down the last two steps so he stood very close to her on the edge of the cobblestone street. There it was again, that aroma of starlight or moonlight or distance—the god's own scent, perhaps, divine and mysterious. He was so close she could see the individual scars across his olive skin, each separate lash around his intent eyes. "I have not seen you around these past few days," he drawled. "But I have heard word of you—the laundry girl who joins the healers in saving the lives of angels."

"I—I was asked to help, and I helped," she said, stammering slightly. "I did very little."

"But you have been preoccupied," he said in a low voice. "And nowhere to be found when I looked for you."

She almost could not form the words. "You—looked for me?"

He nodded. A small smile was warming the blackness of his eyes, causing the full mouth to curve. "Of course I did. We had an assignation, you and I."

"You—I could not find you that day," she said.

"Yes, but there have been other days since then," he said. "And you did not find me those days either."

She did not even try to reply to that.

He put a hand up to her cheek—the very cheek that Obadiah had kissed, had marked with an angel's approval—and stared down at her. "I am expected elsewhere just now," he said in a slow voice, "but I will be back before midnight, if you wished to return and wait for me then. Unless there are other duties you have? Other friends you have made while I have been waiting so patiently?"

She could not believe it. He knew she had been called in to aid with Obadiah, and he was—he was not *jealous,* no, that was ridiculous, angels weren't jealous of the attentions of mortals—but he had been reminded of her existence. Just as Faith had promised. She had become memorable.

"No, angelo, my time is completely at your disposal."

He dropped his hand and immediately assumed an air of briskness. "Good! Then I will expect you to be waiting for me when I return. Sometime before midnight."

"And I should be—?"

"In my room, of course. You know where it is." A small grin as he said that.

She blushed. "Yes, angelo."

"You may call me David, you know."

"Yes, David."

"And I should call you—?"

"Elizabeth."

"Elizabeth. Good. A pretty name. I will see you in a few hours, Elizabeth," he said, and took off jauntily down the street.

Elizabeth stared after him, her heart pounding, her face prickling with receding heat. To meet an angel in his room at midnight! What did it mean, what else could it mean than that she was to take her first angel lover? She must go home and bathe and cover herself with scented creams and braid her hair and put on that new green dress.

She must tell Faith, because this was not a secret it would be possible to keep, but she must let no one else know, in case the tryst turned out badly.

But surely it would not. Not this time. Surely David would be there as promised, would take her in his arms and make love to her with his fevered angel body? She shivered as she hurried home, trying to imagine what that act would be like, how much different it would be from love with a mortal man. This would be better; she knew it. This would be a union with an angel.

She tried not to let it bother her that, until five minutes ago, her angel lover had not even known her name.

It was cold in David's room.

After three hours of waiting, cold was all Elizabeth was really experiencing anymore. Excitement had worn off after the first dull hour passed, and eager speculation had carried her only another thirty minutes or so. Boredom had crept up and curled around her toes as she sat, stiff and uncomfortable, in one of those narrow-backed chairs designed to accommodate angel wings. Disappointment had circled the ceiling like a nervous carrion bird till she finally lost the energy to glare it away, and then it had come to perch on her shoulder and squawk hoarsely in her ear. *He lied, he forgot, he does not plan to see you tonight. You were a fool to believe that the angel David would ever take you in his arms.*

But he had to come back sometime, she thought, drunk or sober, alone or in the company of friends. And he had told her to be here. And if she was not here, and he did remember, would he not be angry with her for failing him a second time? Would he not refuse to offer her a third chance, and would he not whisper to his angel friends, "She cannot be relied on. Do not waste your time with her"?

So she waited, and she shivered, because the green dress was thin, and the room temperature was set to suit an angel's blood. And she wished she had brought some sewing with her, or even a book, and certainly a shawl.

And she wondered if she should leave.

And she wondered if David was laughing at her, even now, in a tavern with some friends who all despised angel-seekers and loved to relate tales of the tricks they had played on those unfortunate women.

And she stayed.

It was perhaps two hours after midnight when a curse and fumble at the door jerked Elizabeth from an uneasy sleep. She came to her feet with a gasp, feeling her heart pound and her hands clench into cold fists at her sides. She had no time to do more than take two steps from the chair before the door shuddered open, and David lurched in. The hall lights were on behind him so it was impossible to see his face, just the great, dark shape of his winged body.

She tried to say his name, but a finger of fear pressed against her throat, so all that came out of her mouth was a muffled squeak. His head swung in her direction, clumsy as a bear's, and it was clear his eyes were having trouble penetrating the shadows of the room.

"Who's that? Who's there?" he demanded in an overloud voice.

"It's—Elizabeth, angelo."

"Elizabeth?" he repeated in amazement. She could not tell if he did not recognize her name or was astonished that she was still awaiting him.

"Yes, Elizabeth. The laundress," she added, feeling like a fool. "You told me—when you saw me this evening—you asked me to wait for you in your room."

"Elizabeth!" he exclaimed, his voice suddenly jovial. "Yes! The pretty red-haired girl. You're here tonight? A gift from the god himself."

That reaction sent some of her deepest fears scuttling off into the darkness, but she still felt some misgivings as she saw him stumble across the floor. He did not look very steady on his feet, leading her to guess that he might have been drinking fairly heavily since he had left her earlier this evening. His hands slapped the wall, looking for a light switch, which it seemed he had forgotten how to locate. All the major buildings of Cedar Hills had been fitted for gaslight, Faith had informed Elizabeth; not even Luminaux and Semorrah could claim such a distinction. But it was only on the third or fourth try that David managed to find the knob that brought light springing into the room.

Both of them cowered back a bit, and he immediately dialed down the intensity to a dim but pleasant glow. Then he came a few steps nearer and peered down at her. "Elizabeth," he said again, more slowly, savoring the syllables like a tasty wine. "I remember."

Part of her wanted to run; part of her wanted to take complete advantage of this moment. "You told me to wait," she said again.

In this light, it was hard to see the rough texture of his face, but his general air of mysterious darkness was very pronounced. "And I cannot tell you how glad I am that you did," he said. "You are just the person I most wanted to see tonight."

And taking two more quick strides, he was suddenly right upon her, and without another word, he snatched her into his arms. His kiss was heavy and painful on her mouth, sloppy and redolent of wine. His arms wrapped around her too tightly, and his wings folded over her from both sides. She thought she would not be able to breathe. She struggled in his arms, tried to pull her mouth free, but his grip only tightened. His wings drew down even closer over her head, suffocating her, blocking out all light. Panic ran silver through her veins and gave her a measure of strength. She got her hands up against his ribs and pushed hard, taking them both by surprise with the strength of her resistance. He dropped his arms and folded his wings down, stepping back to stare at her.

"Jovah's hells and fountains, what's wrong with you?" he demanded. "What did you come here for if not for that?"

She stared back at him, panting, poised on the balls of her feet to make a sudden dash for the door. Almost, almost, she ran for it. But ambition held her in place, ambition and desire. This was something she had dreamed of, schemed for, something for which she had been prepared to sacrifice a great deal. She could not dart away now; she could not let fear cost her this great achievement.

"I could not breathe," she said at last. "You held me too close— and your wings—I was smothering."

He bellowed with laughter and lay his arms loosely about her again. "Most women love the feel of angel wings draped around their bodies," he said.

"Yes—I want to feel them—I do," she stammered. "But just—I have to be able to breathe."

Now he looked down at her with a mocking expression on his face. "You're afraid."

"No."

"You're cold. Your skin is like ice."

"This room is chilly for mortal blood."

"I can warm you up," he suggested.

She hesitated just a moment. "Yes," she said.

He laughed, gave her one more quick, hard kiss, and moved back another pace. "Then take off that dress—lovely as it is—and join me in my bed, Elizabeth the laundry girl."

She had not quite imagined how awkward it would be to step out of her shoes and pull off her dress while the angel watched her, unnervingly absorbed. Perhaps she had thought they would progress to this stage after a few minutes of tender kissing, after cuddling on the bed for a while and whispering silly, meaningless endearments in each other's ears. Instead, she stripped naked with a few economical movements, then stood there shivering before him, feeling neither attractive nor eager. He approved of what he saw, though; that was evident in the sudden tautness of his face and the sharp, reckless flickering of his eyes. He came close again, not pulling her into an embrace this time but closing his fingers tightly around her upper arms and drawing her against his chest. She felt the heat of his body flare against her skin the moment before his mouth covered hers again in a rough kiss. The scents of cloud and starlight were over-powered by the odors of wine and lust.

Less than half an hour later, Elizabeth was creeping down the deserted streets of Cedar Hills, making for the boardinghouse. She was trying hard not to think, not to catalog caresses or results, but it was difficult to overlook the various distresses of her body. Sore in a few very private places, bruised in half a dozen more; she felt less like she had been loved than mangled. She had expected more from a union with an angel, she really had.

She had thought she would be dazzled by the heat and poetry of an angel's body, brought to ecstasy by the teasing touch of those deliciously impertinent feathers. Instead, it had been nothing more than a series of drunken lunges and some brutish grunting, body to body, the heavy wings trailing over either shoulder like a winter quilt that hadn't been fully aired out. She had closed her eyes and willed herself to be in delirious awe, an *angel* making love to her, an *angel* with his mouth pressed against hers and his hand groping across her breast. But she had not been able to achieve the trick. She had felt no more delight or radiance than she had felt during those stolen trysts at James's farm. Truth to tell, she had been rather relieved when David had caught his breath and then released it on a long, choked gasp.

"Ah, Elizabeth," he breathed, and collapsed on top of her, pressing all the air from her lungs. "Little laundry girl, I am so very glad you waited."

She waited again, for him to say something else—give her permission to leave, beg her to stay the night, ask her to return tomorrow evening or the day after that—but he said nothing. He did shift a little, collecting his own arms and legs and gathering them to one side of the bed, freeing her from his weight, though one of his wings still lay across her like a spill of down. In a moment or two, she heard his breathing change. He was sleeping.

She slipped out from under the disappointing wing, dressed in her inadequate clothes, and hurried into the clean, disinterested night. She had never walked these streets before at such a late hour, and it occurred to her that she should be afraid, because all classes of people came to Cedar Hills and not all of them were trustworthy, but she couldn't summon the energy. She actually felt she was trudging as she took the final few yards down the alley that led to the boarding-house. No one stirred as she made her way silently through the sleeping building, not even Faith, who had promised to lie awake no matter how late the hour.

Elizabeth undressed and cleaned herself as quietly as she could. A faint moonlight came in through the shuttered window, and by it Elizabeth inspected the souvenirs of her evening. She had thought— she had so desperately hoped—that when she lay with an angel for the first time, the Kiss in her arm would light with gaudy blushes, Jovah's signal that true lovers had met at last. But the Kiss was crystalline and clear, untroubled by iridescence. The only colors on her arm were the dark and scattered bruises left by David's careless hand.

CHAPTER TWELVE

Rebekah paced the garden wall and listened to the words of her betrothed.

"I don't think grain is the commodity to invest in, not if you are making only one investment," Isaac said. He spoke solemnly and with great self-assurance, as though his audience were grander than a fourteen-year-old boy and an old man, strolling beside him on the other side of the wall from where Rebekah walked. "It is the luxuries where you should put your money and your attention. Crops fail, tastes change, the wheat farmer you dealt with last year may decide to sow corn this year, who knows? The market for grain and produce is always unreliable. But rich people will always want their baubles. And the price of gold never goes down."

"Where do you buy your gold?" the old man asked.

Isaac answered, but Rebekah didn't pay as much attention to the words as to the voice of the speaker. He was remarkably easy to hear, even through the thick stone that divided the inner garden from the outer one. Or perhaps he was deliberately pitching his voice to carry through the rock and mortar, knowing someone listened on the other side. He was supposed to pretend he did not know, of course. It was Hector's uncle, the old man who now joined Isaac on his tour of the grounds, who had proposed that the two of them take a walk after the satisfaction of a bountiful meal.

"Let's take Jordan with us, too," the old man had said. "And go by the garden. The evening is fine, and I would like to hear your thoughts about the markets."

So the men had put on their sandals and made their leisurely way to the outer wall, and Rebekah had scrambled into her own shoes and joined them, invisible, on the other side. In such a way affianced brides always grew to learn the tone of their husbands' voices and their public views on the world. The women did not respond with their own thoughts and hopes and aspirations—oh no—the fiction was that the groom was not aware that any hidden observer overheard him. The charade was all to benefit the woman, who might be expected to be nervous and shy at the thought of going to the arms of a total stranger. In this artful way could she become accustomed to the voice of the man who would be her master and learn how wise and thoughtful he could be.

"Luminaux," Isaac was saying now. "Any trader who does not stop there is a fool, for he could make his fortune twice over by buying and selling goods in the Blue City."

"You might buy your bride a wedding gift there," suggested the old man.

"So I might!" Isaac agreed cordially. "Jordan, does your sister like jewels? And if so, what kinds?"

"All kinds," Jordan said. "The brighter the better."

"Then I know just where to shop on my next trip to the city."

Rebekah actually lost a step, pausing on the well-worn path to twist the bracelets on her wrist. She wore up to a dozen on any given day, most of them gifts from her father or her uncle or her brother or Hector. All of them, in fact, except the silver one set with sapphires, and that one the most recently acquired.

She tried not to wear it every day. She tried to leave it in a box at the bottom of her wooden chest, under her outgrown linens and outdated jeskas. But every morning as she prepared to step from the room—on her way to breakfast or to her mother's room to watch the baby or to the fabric room to look over a new roll of cloth Hector had purchased in the market—she paused at the door and looked back. And every day—for two weeks now, she had counted every day—she had turned back into her room and knelt before the chest and pulled out the flat, inlaid box. And slipped that silver bracelet over her wrist.

She could only hope her new husband never had occasion to ask her where such a trinket had come from. But he never would. Every Jansai woman wore so many chains and rings and necklets that not even the most careful one could catalog the history of each piece. Only a few were so special that she wore them every day of her life: her father's parting gift, her husband's wedding remembrance, a piece she took with her from her mother's collection. The rest were so many ounces of gold and amethyst, loved for their beauty and nothing more.

When she was married, Rebekah promised herself, she would take off the silver bracelet and never look at it again. When she was married, she would not be dreaming of other men.

"Well, young Isaac, it's clear you've studied your roads and markets," Hector's uncle was saying in an approving voice. "You will be a fine provider for your lucky bride. And speaking of fine, didn't I see a spice cake waiting on the sideboard? I've walked far enough for an old man. Now I want sweets to finish off my day."

All four of them returned, by two different routes, to the feast halls set up inside the house. Hector had organized a banquet to celebrate the joining of his house with Simon's, and there were close to a hundred people present. The men, of course, were gathered in the great hall with its domed roof and wide windows open to the sun, but the women had been making merry in the closed adjoining room, where the view was not quite so splendid but the food was just as good. All of Isaac's female relatives were there—his mother, his aunts, his grandmother—and Rebekah had sat with them during the meal, trying to pass herself off as a docile, soft-spoken girl who would be welcomed into any household. But after the interlude in the garden, she headed straight toward the table where her own relatives sat.

Martha was already on her feet and crossing the room to intercept her. "Well?" her cousin demanded. "What did he say?"

Rebekah shrugged. "Grain and markets and trading routes—boring stuff. He has a pretty voice, though, deep and slow. I like to hear the words coming from his mouth."

Martha pouted. "He didn't talk about you at all? About how eager he is to get married?"

"No, not that I heard, anyway. He did say he'd buy me a bride-gift in Luminaux. Jordan told him I like jewels. So that ought to be something rich, I think."

Martha tossed her hair back. She had the deep olive skin tone of most full-blooded Jansai, but thick honey-colored hair that made a startling halo of light around her face. She was a striking woman—unforgettable—and the force and energy of her personality made her even more impossible to ignore, no matter what the company.

"I think no jewels will seem as rich and special to you as the one you came home with from Castelana," she said in a low voice.

"Hush. Someone will hear."

"You're wearing it again."

"I know. I couldn't help it."

"It will be hard to take a Jansai husband when you have an angel's face imprinted on your heart."

"I will never see that angel's face again, so a Jansai husband is just what I need, I think."

"When is the wedding going to be?"

"In six months, Hector says. Or maybe nine. My mother is pressing for a spring wedding, but I don't care. I will be ready whenever the date is set."

Isaac's mother approached them then, so they were forced to make polite, pointless conversation, and Rebekah eventually lost track of Martha in the general press of people. She was just as glad when the banquet ended, when the women donned their veils and joined their men at the narrow door at the back of the house, where they could slip out without fear of being seen by chance passersby. She was exhausted by the effort of smiling so much, of making herself seem demure and biddable. She stopped by the baby's room, just to kiss his smooth cheeks, and then headed for her own room to lie on her mat and brood.

Everyone seemed most pleased with the idea of her marriage to Isaac. For quite some time, Hector and Simon had been discussing the idea of formally going into business together, buying up new wagons with their pooled resources, and making semi-regular trips on the great merchant road between Luminaux and Manadavvi country. The wedding would cement those plans, entailing, as it would, settlements to work out, property exchanges to be made between the households, the forging of monetary bonds that were not easily broken. There were dozens of preparations to complete, but many details could be finalized as the wedding drew nearer. The important decision was already made; the union would benefit them all.

Rebekah had not been consulted on the matter, but apparently her mother had, and very proud of that fact she was, too. "Your father asked me what I knew of young Isaac," Jerusha said on the day she informed Rebekah that she was betrothed. "And I told him how well his mother speaks of him, what a good son he has been to her. And I told your father that this was the kind of man I would want for my daughter."

"He's not my father," Rebekah said automatically, but her heart wasn't really in it. She was too busy wondering what it would be like to be married to Isaac. To anyone. To leave this admittedly dull but relatively safe home and seek out the unreliable benevolence of strangers.

"He acts as your father and wants only the best for you," Jerusha said, lifting a hand in warning. *Another word against that good man Hector and I'll strike you!* "You could not have married half so well anywhere inside of Breven."

"I don't care if I'm married or not."

"No? You want to be a burden on Jordan your whole life, a useless, unwanted woman with no man to watch over her?"

"I'll do that. I'll live with Jordan and *his* wife, and I'll help take care of their children. And I won't eat anything, so they'll hardly notice I'm there, and I'll sleep on a mat in the hallway. No one will mind."

"You'll marry Isaac, and you won't give me any more trouble."

In truth, Rebekah was not opposed to marrying Isaac. She knew nothing bad about him; she knew little good about him either, except that his mother called him a kind man. But mothers tended to be blind to the faults of their sons—that Rebekah knew from firsthand observation—so a mother's word was essentially worthless. Still, Rebekah had to admit to a flutter of excitement at the thought of marrying, of giving her body and her care over into the keeping of a handsome young man, of moving into another house in another part of the city. Of becoming, by any measure, a woman. And she would as soon marry Isaac, she supposed, as anyone else.

Since she could not possibly marry an angel.

She twisted the silver bracelet on her wrist again, realizing that she had not taken it off before she lay on her mat, realizing further that she probably would not, not this night and not for many nights to come. She would sleep with that cool metal against her pulse and feel those sweet-cut sapphires resonate inside her heart. She would take it off the day she got married; she would lock it away and give Jordan the key and tell him to never return the key to her no matter how hard she begged. But until that day she would wear it like a shackle, chained to memory as she was.

It was Martha who insisted that they attend the harvest fair, though Rebekah claimed she did not have the nerve. "We were almost caught sneaking out the corridor last time. Your father was so close," Rebekah protested. "If we were seen—"

"We won't be seen! We'll leave from your house this time."

"*My* house!"

"Hector is much more lax than my father. We won't have any trouble."

"But there's still ten streets to cross—"

"Jordan will come with us. And Ephram." Ephram was Martha's brother, thirteen years old and wilder than she was. More than once Ezra had threatened to kick the boy out of the house, let him fend for himself in the streets, but no one, least of all Ephram, feared this fate would befall him. Ezra doted on the high-spirited boy, who got into fights with men twice his age, who pulled tricks on the bazaar merchants and stole coins from the beggars in the square. He reflected the arrogance of youth back onto Ezra, who basked in it.

He would not be much protection for two Jansai girls stepping out into the Breven streets in disguise.

"Truly, Martha, I have a premonition that such an adventure would not turn out well."

"But it *will!* What could go wrong? It's a masked fair, so half the people in the streets will be wearing disguises. And with our brothers with us—"

"But what if Jordan and Ephram don't want to go?"

"They do. I've already asked them. Ephram said they would meet us at the back gate two hours before midnight. And Jordan said you could wear his clothes. You're practically the same size, you know."

"But if we're caught," Rebekah said desperately. "I am a betrothed woman now. I don't just disgrace Hector's house, but Isaac's as well."

Martha stared at her. "Since when did you care about disgracing anyone? You hate Hector! And you scarcely know Isaac."

"I don't want to go," Rebekah said.

The truth was, of course, she did want to go. The angel would be there. He had promised he would be. He had said it often enough that she had been forced to believe him. The angel would be there, and she would see him—because, in the company of Jansai, he would be impossible to miss—and it would take every ounce of strength she possessed for her to stay away from him. There was calamity, there was madness—going to the fall festival disguised as a boy, hoping to catch the attention of the man who would be the most hated individual in the city. No, better by far to stay in her room both nights of the fair, lying on her mat, straining her whole body till she believed she could just catch the faint sounds of revelry. She was an affianced woman. She had to recognize some of the sober realities of her new life.

Martha shrugged. "Fine. Then I'll go by myself."

Rebekah gave her a sharp look. "By yourself with Ephram and Jordan, you mean."

Martha shook her head, sending the heavy honey tresses back over her shoulder. "I was only bringing them along to protect *you*. I'm not afraid of the streets of Breven. I'll go alone."

"You can't do that!" Rebekah exclaimed.

Martha shrugged again. "I can. I don't see why not. It will be better this way, actually, since I won't have someone tugging on my sleeve telling me it's midnight, it's one, I have to come home now. I can stay till the very end and come home at dawn, and then tell my mother I was vomiting all night and can't get out of bed in the morning."

"Please don't," Rebekah said.

"I won't," Martha said. "If you'll come with me."

For a moment they stared at each other, the two cousins who had known each other their whole lives. Almost, Rebekah balked at that moment; almost, she believed it was a bluff, that even Martha could not summon the courage to take so great a risk. But she knew Martha well enough by now. Even if the thought terrified her, even if she feared she would lose her life on the rowdy streets of Breven at the height of a drunken celebration, she would walk out that door unaccompanied, just to prove to Rebekah that she never made an empty promise.

"If I die of this," Rebekah said slowly, "you must tend my grave."

A wide smile lit Martha's dark face, and she threw her hands in the air with a whoop. "I will be buried beside you, so it will be up to our brothers to bring us greenery and desert roses," Martha said.

"They will be too ashamed to honor us. The sand will cover our bones, and everyone will forget our names."

"I don't think so," Martha said. "The scandalous names live longest."

Rebekah was too agitated to sit still another moment. She came to her feet and circled twice around the room. She and Jerusha were visiting Ezra's house the day after the betrothal party, and the two young women had retired to Martha's room to scheme and gossip. Martha's mother didn't have the fanatical standards of cleanliness that Jerusha did, and so there were clothes piled sloppily in corners and shoes scattered everywhere, tripping Rebekah up as she paced.

"He will be there at the fair," she said at last, still walking, not looking at Martha. "The angel. He will be there."

"I know," Martha said in a smug voice. "You told me."

Rebekah glanced over once, quickly. "I thought you might have forgotten."

"Oh, no. I remembered. He will be there, and that is why you must go as well."

Rebekah stopped and stared at her, but Martha rocked back on her mat, laughing. All this on purpose, to snare Rebekah and punish her heart. At that moment, Rebekah didn't know if she hated her cousin with all her might, or loved her more than anyone else in the world.

Two days later, the cousins were together again, this time in Rebekah's room, slipping into their forbidden clothes. They giggled as they helped each other with unfamiliar buttons and strode around the room, enjoying the unaccustomed freedom of silk trousers instead of long, heavy skirts. Even though they were to go masked, they darkened their chins with a charcoal-colored powder and braided their hair tightly to their heads so that it would lie quietly under a boy's loose-wrapped headpiece. Just in case the mask slipped, just in case the torches were too bright, just in case someone looked too closely.

Rebekah was slim and flat-chested, so a billowing man's shirt covered her figure fairly well, but Martha was more amply endowed. They fitted her with a quilted vest and added more padding at the shoulders to make her whole torso look muscular. She stood with arms akimbo, legs planted wide, a snarling look of arrogance on her face, and faced Rebekah.

"Well?" she demanded. "Do I look like a Jansai boy?"

"Like the greatest bully in the market," Rebekah said. "What about me?" And she tried to summon her own expression of careless insolence.

"You look like you're about fourteen," Martha said with a snort. "And are pretending to look twenty."

Rebekah shrugged. "That's not so bad, though. There are probably hundreds of twelve- and fourteen-year-old boys headed out to the fair tonight, trying to pass as their older brothers."

Once they were satisfied with their appearances, they quickly donned their loosest jeskas and veils over their boys' clothing. They were unlikely to encounter Jerusha or any of Hector's aunts in the hallway, but it didn't pay to take chances. If *anyone* saw unfamiliar young men wandering the hallways of the women's quarters, there would be an instant outcry, and the deception would be speedily uncovered. Rebekah did not like to even speculate about what the consequences might be.

But they glided through the empty hallways without incident. They had brought candles with them in case the gaslight failed—as it sometimes did—but even though it had been dialed down to the lowest for the evening, they could still see well enough to navigate without bumping into things. They passed the bedroom doors where Hector's aunts and sisters slept, then the empty guest rooms, and crept down the stairway toward the kitchen. And past the cold iron ovens and the cabinets of spices, out through the women's door and into the garden.

Here, they stripped off their jeskas and hid them behind a stone bench. Now they moved with even greater caution, sticking to the shadows of the tall, spindly corvine plant and threading through the maze of marrowroot and dera shrubs. If Hector was out tonight and coming back home, he would enter through the door at the front of the house, not the gate at the back; but you never knew who might be watching from the windows above. Twenty people all told lived in Hector's house, and Hector could certainly identify all of them by sight. If he saw two unknown young boys sneaking through his back garden, he would have every reason to be suspicious and sound the alarm.

But no one saw them. They made it to the garden gate, and Martha knocked twice on the solid wood. Three knocks sounded on the other side. Martha grinned at Rebekah and lifted the latch.

"There you are. You're late," Ephram said in a low, complaining voice. "We've been waiting here forever."

"Just ten minutes," Jordan said.

Martha spread her arms in silent invitation. "Well? Do we pass? Would you take us for boys?"

"Yes, you're fine, no one's going to look at *you*," Ephram said impatiently, but Jordan paused to make a more critical appraisal.

"You don't exactly look like ordinary boys," he said slowly, "but I don't think anyone would think anything was strange and look at you a second time, trying to figure out what's different about you."

"Well, they'll look even less when you've got masks on," Ephram said, lifting the flap of his own loose vest and pulling out two carefully folded masks. These were flimsy constructions of cloth and string, both of them marked by golden feathers attached at the brow line. Each brother helped his sister secure the mask in place, and then the four of them looked at each other for a moment or two.

"Well, I wouldn't recognize you," Rebekah said to Martha.

"No, and you don't look like anybody to me," Martha said.

"What if we get separated in the crowd? How will we know each other?" Rebekah demanded. "Half the people are going to look like this."

Martha put her hand to her throat and tugged out a silver medallion that she almost always wore. "I'll play with my necklace. Or, if you want to make sure it's me, put your hand to your neck like you're reaching for your own pendant, and then I'll pull mine out."

"That's good."

"How will I recognize *you?*"

"Come *on,*" Ephram insisted.

"This is important," Jordan said.

Rebekah hesitated a moment, then shook her hand out before her. She had stripped off her rings, which looked like they belonged to a woman, and only kept two bracelets on each wrist. All Jansai wore jewelry; it would have seemed stranger to leave the house with no adornments at all. But for her man's role tonight, she had chosen her simpler pieces: a wide gold band, a thin silver chain, a narrow gold rope—and the silver bracelet set with sapphires.

"Oh," said Martha sardonically. "I'll know it's you."

"Are you *done?*" Ephram demanded. "The festival will be over before we get there!"

"The festival will last another whole day," Martha retorted. "But we're ready. Let's go."

They stepped away from the wall and onto the street, heading toward the central bazaar district. Even from a mile or two away, they could see the haze of light that hovered over the fair, yellower than moonlight and half-enchanted against the velvet richness of the night. Skirls of music and faint sounds of laughter and argument drifted back to them, growing stronger as they hurried closer. Now and then they passed other groups of men, old and young, moving in the same direction.

Finally, they turned a corner and it was before them, all the color and motion and excitement of the harvest festival. Rebekah actually gasped and clutched at Martha's arm, forgetting, for a second, that they were insensitive young men who had seen plenty of marvels in their lives. Martha pulled away quickly and took an indifferent stance, but through the slits in her mask she, too, was staring.

The entire market was crammed with people dressed in colorful, flowing robes or the more form-fitting shirts and trousers. They pushed and laughed their way through crowded alleys formed by booths and stalls and pavilions of every imaginable color and size. Breven on an ordinary day offered an impressive array of goods, but here were treasures hard to locate even in the streets of Luminaux: gold statuary, trays of rubies, folds of cloud-white silk piled higher than a man's head. At other stalls, the wares were more practical: barrels of wine from the Manadavvi vineyards, casks of ale from southern Bethel, fermented juices from northern Gaza and Jordana. The smell of spicy food filled their heads like intoxication, carrying the promise of everything from grilled onions to meats so exotic Rebekah could not name them. Everything was lit from overhead by huge, flaring torches and ropes of colored lights strung from stand to stand all the way across the market.

Two men shoved past Rebekah, laughing as they nudged her off her path and into the cloth barrier of a covered pavilion. "Keep your feet, boy!" one of them called out, careless but good-natured, and he waved a bottle of wine at her before taking another swig from it. His companion belched, said something, and laughed again.

"Be careful," Jordan scolded, pulling her back on the path again. "You don't want anyone to get too close to you."

"I was just *standing* here—"

"I'm hungry," Ephram announced. "Let's get something to eat."

"I want to hear the music," Martha said.

"Well, we can hear the music after we've eaten."

They stopped at the closest booth that was selling food, and Jordan bought them each meat pies and mugs of ale. Rebekah was not entirely sure what kind of meat was inside the golden crust, but it was heavily flavored and delicious, and she ate the whole thing in about four bites. She sipped the beverage more cautiously. She did not have a good head for wine, since Jerusha rarely let her sample it, and she was not sure how well she would fare with the bitter, foamy ale. Martha seemed to have no such reservations; she downed half her glass in one swallow, then gave all of them a big smile.

"This is *good,"* she said, and belched like a boy.

Rebekah was a little shocked, but Ephram and Jordan laughed.

They headed in the direction of the music, but there were so many distractions that they didn't make it very far very fast. Here and there were breaks in the long line of stalls, spaces that had been cleared away for games or gambling events. In one small arena, surrounded by hordes of shouting observers, two young men had stripped to the waist and were engaged in a hand-to-hand fight that looked bloody and completely free of rules. In another clearing, cheering boys were kneeling down around a circular area, watching the forward progress of a handful of small, scuttling desert creatures that appeared to be racing. Ephram paused to watch this for a moment, adding his own shouts of encouragement to the ugly, sand-colored creature in the lead, but Jordan jerked on his arm and tugged him forward. They passed clumps of men laying bets on mysterious outcomes, groups of boys holding unprofessional fights, vendors pushing through the crowds bawling out details about their merchandise, and a few enclaves of people who appeared to be playing various games of chance for high-stakes wagers.

"Oh, a chakki game," Ephram exclaimed, coming to a complete standstill. "Look, there's John and Marcus. They'd let me onto their team."

"You can't play chakki," Jordan hissed.

"Why not? I've got money. See, a whole row of coppers—"

Jordan jerked his head at the two women, a step behind the men and trying hard not to stare like farm boys at all the sights around them. They had snuck into this fair a year ago, and it had been exciting, but there were twice as many booths to see this time out.

"We have company," Jordan reminded him in a low, patient voice. "Our *friends* are with us, and we've promised not to abandon them."

Ephram pouted. "I want to play chakki," he said sulkily. "You can stay with the g—with the others."

"Oh, let him play his stupid game," Martha said. "You can stay with him, too. We'll be fine."

Jordan gave her a look of indignation. Neither he nor Ephram had worn masks, so both their faces were open studies of exhilaration—though Jordan, to do him credit, wore a layer of concern over his elation. "I'm not leaving you!" he said in a low whisper. "And Ephram's not either."

"All right, all *right*," Ephram said in a louder voice. "I'll come with you—in twenty minutes. I just want to play one round. I'll win some silver, I know it."

Martha gave her brother a rather ungentle shove on the shoulder. "Twenty minutes," she said. "Come find us over by the music stage."

"I will."

Jordan protested again, but Martha shrugged and strode forward, and he had no choice but to follow. Rebekah fell in step behind him, but she didn't pay much attention to where she placed her feet. She was too busy swinging her head from side to side, taking in the sights: the huge ruffled hawks chained to their perches and crying out unheeded songs of warning; the painted vistas on wide stretched canvases, mountain ranges and riverbeds that she would swear existed nowhere in Samaria; the cool, tall, handsome Manadavvi lords holding a quiet conversation with three fat Jansai merchants, everyone looking pleased and guilty. She could stand here all night, simply staring, and never see enough.

"Come *on,*" Jordan called, now ten paces ahead of her and sounding as impatient as Ephram. She quickened her step and caught up with him, though Martha was still in front of them both.

"This is wonderful," she said in a low voice. "Thank you for bringing us here."

"We can't stay very long," he warned. "It's too dangerous."

"I know," she said. "But as long as we can."

They wove their way past another dozen booths, turned an ill-defined corner into another brightly lit alley, and came upon a small stage that looked like it had been hastily constructed of raw wood and a few metal reinforcing strips. A ragtag group of musicians sat on this rickety platform, apparently oblivious to their surroundings, hunched over their instruments and wearing rapt, hallucinatory expressions. At a guess, they were Luminauzi, trained in the city of artists but earning their incomes by traveling around the three provinces, playing at fairs and farms.

Rebekah could not even name their instruments: two that looked like oversized flutes, three that bore strings of some sort laid across wooden frames, one that appeared to be nothing more than a piece of stretched goatskin upon which the musician played with a stick he might have picked up on the road. Yet they created sheets of melody that fell on the crowd like savage rain, washing all the listeners with divine radiance and making their skin tingle with wonder. That was wind and this was summer—a short, playful little flirt of song was a baby's first smile—one of the flutes burst free of the strings and drum to make a sigh like love and betrayal. Rebekah stood transfixed, her mouth hanging open, not caring that she looked like an ensorceled idiot. Martha looked just as bemused, and so did half of the men standing around them, their jaws slack, their wine bottles forgotten in their hands.

"That was pretty," Jordan commented as the music came to an end and the crowd broke into thunderous applause. "Did you like it?"

The women did not even bother to answer but applauded madly with the rest of the observers. "More!" Martha shouted out, along with half the men in the vicinity. "Another song!"

Jordan rolled his eyes. He was fourteen, and his idea of illicit pleasure was not listening to scruffy musicians playing complex music. "How long do we have to wait here?" he asked Rebekah.

She smiled at him. She was feeling breathless with beauty and possibility, half in love with the whole world just because it existed, and she was certainly pleased with Jordan for helping her come to this fabulous place. "You don't have to wait with us," she said. "Martha and I aren't likely to get into any trouble. Just come back for us here later."

"I can't leave you two," he said, but he sounded less convinced than he had when he had said the same thing to Ephram.

"You can, if you come back," she said. "What did you want to do? Play chakki? Bet on the races? I hope you don't want to fight."

He grinned. "I'm not very good at punching. Ephram is, if we could pull him away from the chakki. I'd lay money on him and win it all back, too."

She gave him a little shove on the arm. "Go. We'll be right here when you get back."

He hesitated. "Twenty minutes?"

She laughed. She had no doubt it would be two hours or more before they saw Ephram again. "An hour," she said. "Does that give you enough time?"

"Are you sure you'll be all right?"

"No one's paying any attention to us at all. We'll be fine."

He protested another minute or two, but it was clear his attention had already wandered back to one of the booths they had passed on their way in. "An hour, then," he said at last. "You wait right here."

He left, and Rebekah looked around to explain to Martha that their escort had dwindled down to nothing.

But Martha, it turned out, had already acquired another defender.

It took Rebekah a moment to locate her cousin, since the honey-blonde hair and the distinctive face were both hidden behind disguises, and half the crowd was dressed exactly like she was. And Rebekah was looking for a solitary figure, standing a little apart from the mob, circumspect, even, trying to avoid drawing any attention.

What she didn't expect to see was Martha, a dozen yards away, in close conversation with a barefaced young man a little older than Isaac, dressed like a Manadavvi and gazing down at Martha as if he could see beneath the cloth and feathers of her mask.

Jovah's old decrepit bones.

Oblivious to the crowd, Rebekah stepped a few paces closer, staring at the couple so completely absorbed in each other that they might not have realized a fair was unfolding around them. They had not just met a few moments ago, that much was certain; and that the Manadavvi lordling knew he was speaking to a young woman was evident in every strained line of his body. How had Martha met him? Where? Under what circumstances? True, Manadavvi traders came into Breven every day, selling some goods and buying others, but all of the transactions took place at the open market, where the only women present were the poorest of the Jansai or were not Jansai at all.

Had Martha been sneaking into the market for days or weeks now, dressed as a servant or boldly pretending to be a farm wife from the Jordana hills? Only her male relatives or her wide circle of female friends would recognize her once the veils were put away. No other Jansai would have any reason to know her face. She was smart enough to go to market only on days her menfolk were unlikely to be bartering—and brave enough to hope that none of the women of her circle would betray her if they saw her. Even so, such a deception, if discovered, carried such a high price that Rebekah could not imagine carrying it out except to satisfy the most extreme desire.

This man. This Manadavvi. Did Martha imagine she loved him?

Had Martha squealed and sighed over every detail of Rebekah's rendezvous with the Cedar Hills angel, all the while keeping a much more incendiary secret to herself?

Had this been the reason she had insisted on coming to the fair and had threatened to come alone if Rebekah had refused to accompany her? Had she headed straight for the music stage to keep an assignation, not caring if her brother or her cousins saw her in conversation with the most dangerous of companions? Rebekah felt shock and dread alternately heat and freeze her heart. The questions tumbled from her brain into her chest, bouncing between her ribs like rocks set loose by a mountain catastrophe. This could not be occurring. Martha could not be so wanton with her life. This was a crime she could die for.

Rebekah took another step closer, though her feet felt so stiff and heavy they almost refused to move. As if sensing her approach, Martha jerked her head around, and her eyes fixed on Rebekah's through the swaying, surging crowd. Impossible to read her expression at this distance, in these circumstances, but Rebekah caught the message as clearly as though Martha had shouted it in her ear: *Come no closer. I am no responsibility of yours.* Rebekah halted where she stood, moving only when buffeted by the restless revelers. Martha returned her attention to her companion, who smiled at her with an unfeigned delight. Martha, or so Rebekah imagined, smiled back.

As if it was possible for the evening to get worse, that was when Rebekah saw the angel.

CHAPTER THIRTEEN

Music flowered from the stage the instant that she saw him, a hallelujah of brass from some itinerant band that had just now set up its chairs and scores. He was walking through the crowd, approaching the clearing around the stage from the opposite direction of the route that Rebekah's group had taken. He was accompanied by a handful of Jansai merchants, all dressed in bright, flowing robes and pushing each other aside to get a chance to argue with him. He was laughing. Torchlight spangled his yellow hair and threw glitter across his white wings, held narrowly behind his body as if he wanted to keep them from being soiled or stepped on. He looked regal and beautiful and fashioned of pure divine light.

Obadiah.

It was not the night, Rebekah felt certain, for her to have been left unattended by her brother and her cousins in a sea of indifferent and drunken strangers.

But she would not talk to him. She would not follow Martha's reckless example, oh no. She was an engaged woman, a dutiful daughter, a fool who might carry the image of an angel in her heart but who knew better than to reach her hand to that image and see if she could startle it into existence.

Besides, he was surrounded by powerful Jansai men who had no interest in indulging the whims of gawking young boys who wanted to step close enough to see the angel, marvel at his wings, wonder aloud why he had wandered into Breven, where angels were far from welcome. Those Jansai men would be even less tolerant of a Jansai girl in disguise, come creeping into the city by night to sample the delights of the harvest fair.

The brass band played ecstatically on, pumping a rhythmic surge of adrenaline through her veins. She would swear by her love of the god that she had not expected to lay eyes on him again. She had come to the fair knowing he might be here, *would* be here, he had sworn he would attend and begged her to do the same, but she had not really thought she would see him. Had not thought she would be standing this close to him, had not realized that her mutinous feet would carry her, unordered, through the maze of the crowd so that she stood only a few yards from him. Close enough to see his face. Close enough to see the sweetness of the smile he turned on the fat, greasy Jansai leader whom she suspected was the merchant Uriah. Close enough to hear the timbre of his voice when he exclaimed, "I can't imagine I'd be very welcome! But you flatter me."

If he looked over her way, if his eyes had the power of stripping away disguises, he would be able to count the cadence of her fluttering pulse by the way the color came and went across her cheeks. He was that close. She took a step nearer.

The brass band came to an exultant conclusion, and the crowd broke into enthusiastic applause yet again. "More! More! Another song!" the listeners cried out. But this was a night, apparently, that musicians took the stage for only a single number, then yielded their places to the next performers. The players gathered their horns and trumpets, bowed to the horde, and made a rather untidy exit. Rebekah dragged her eyes from Obadiah's face long enough to see who might be ascending the stage now, but it remained empty while the concert masters debated who should take the next turn. The crowd, trading insults and tossing back drinks, waited happily enough.

Rebekah looked back at Obadiah. He was laughing again, hands flung up, palms out, as if to offer a physical protest. Uriah scowled, then laughed, then stomped away from the angel and up the open, rickety steps that led to the stage.

"So!" the Jansai bawled out to the crowd. "We've got an angel here, and he thinks he's too good to sing in our competition."

"That's not what I said!" Obadiah called, but his contradiction was drowned out in the roar of the mob's disapproval.

Uriah held his hand up for silence, and the crowd subsided a little, still muttering. "I told him, we've no love for angels, but we appreciate when a man does us honor. Is that right?"

Every voice in the crowd shouted back a confirmation of that fact.

"And we're Jansai! We can gauge the worth of every item bought and sold across the three provinces! We know what an angel's voice is worth, do we not?"

"We know!" the men cried out.

"So we know the value of an angel's voice, lifted in celebration at our humble fair, do we not?"

"We know!"

"And we've got an angel here! And we want to hear him sing! Do we not?"

"We do!"

Now Uriah pumped both fists in the air. "So let's have him sing! Angelo, take the stage!"

The throng responded with a stamping, shouting, surging howl of anticipation. Rebekah felt herself carried forward a few feet by the motion of the revelers around her, and in a moment's panic, she was afraid she would be crushed by their enthusiasm. Or hatred; it was hard to tell. Emotions were certainly running high, and the crowd was as liable to stone the singer as to cheer him. Breathless and a little frightened, she fought free of the press of people and moved a little away from the main area in front of the platform.

She could still see the stage, though. She could see Obadiah calmly mounting the steps and crossing the dais with the white, orderly grace of a god. Away from his Jansai companions, alone on the stage, he took on even more poise and incandescence. His wings, spread out fully behind him, created an aureole of brightness that wrapped his entire body in luminescence. He stepped to the edge of the stage and looked down at his audience. Incredibly, he was smiling, a winning and infectious smile that invited all listeners to like him. He must know that they all hated him, that they only shouted him onstage so they could humiliate him. He must know that he had never in his life sung for a less appreciative audience.

"Thank you for your kind invitation," he said in a clear, carrying voice. He sounded utterly relaxed and at ease. "It will be a pleasure for me to sing for you tonight. I will not trouble you with formal masses and prayers to the god. Instead, since it is a night of moonlight and magic, I will sing to you of love."

Oh, loving god of the skies and waters, it could not be worse.

Rebekah looked around wildly for the only person she knew, hoping Martha would realize that now, of all times, she must come to her cousin's side and provide strength and support. Martha would instantly know that *this* angel was Rebekah's angel, and that Rebekah would be cowering in the shadows, torn between bliss and agony. Martha would come to her side, grab her hand, give her a squeeze of sympathy.

But Martha and her Manadavvi friend were nowhere in sight.

A different kind of panic drove Rebekah's heartbeat for a moment as she considered where Martha might have disappeared. Well, the Manadavvi might have traveled to Breven with a contingent of Gaza merchants, and he might have his own sheltered pavilion set up on the far side of the fair. Chances were he had a brother or a father or a cousin working the booth with him, but perhaps there was a wagon out back, a covered cart holding the unsold merchandise, and two determined people might be willing to call that privacy. Rebekah's face went hot and her hands went cold at the thought.

She wished she had never come to this thrice-damned fair. Everything was poised to go awry, balanced on the crystal edge of disaster. What would she say when Jordan returned, and Ephram? Martha, no doubt, was counting on both boys being absent for much longer than the promised period, but what if she guessed wrong? What if they reappeared in ten minutes, or twenty, with Martha missing and the whole fair to search? Rebekah felt her stomach knot and her hands clench as she turned this way and that, searching the crowd with her eyes, still hoping to catch a glimpse of the gold-feathered mask and the rich, intent features of the Manadavvi lordling.

And then the angel began singing, and Rebekah forgot everybody in the world but him.

He first sounded a single pure, sustained, wordless note, a feather-light gong of music that brought the entire audience to still attention. Longer than it was possible, so long it was clear he could not have the usual human requirements to breathe, he held the note, seeming to draw it out of the stage and the soil beneath him. When, abruptly, he shut it off, the silence he left behind was so surprised the night itself seemed to shake itself and look around in bemusement. Everybody in the crowd merely stared at him, openmouthed and stupid.

And then the true song began, riffs and trills of melody so light and sweet that it seemed either dawn or spring had arrived early. His voice laughed and beckoned, pausing so briefly on each note that it seemed to spring up behind him like a blade of grass released by a running foot. Rebekah had no way of judging if the song was sophisticated or simple, difficult or easy, but that he was an absolute master of his material there could be no doubt. The music swirled around her like a light breeze, lifting her heart like a pile of fallen petals and spinning it into the infinite heavens.

She was not even listening to the words.

He had called it a love song, so she tried to concentrate, to make out the story line or the text of the refrain. It was not that he did not enunciate, for every syllable was clear as a spoken word; it was that the music itself haunted her so completely that she could not pause to analyze its components. But the words must match the melody, frivolous and fun, for everyone around her was smiling, and these were not men who were easily moved to delight.

A quick-rising series of notes, two sharply dropped ones, a sudden nod of his head, and the song was done. Once again, the silence caught everyone totally unprepared, so that there was a moment's stunned and empty stillness. Then the mob broke into such a wild, sustained ovation that the stage trembled with it. Rebekah saw the angel put out his hand as if to rest it on a support, but there was nothing but bare wood beneath him and it was looking none too steady. He spread his feet to improve his balance and laced his hands behind his back. As the cheering went on and on, he bowed his head again, this time more deeply, and then took a pace back as if to exit the stage.

Uriah was right back up there with him, putting his hand on Obadiah's shoulder as if to hold him in place. It was Rebekah's imagination, maybe, but she didn't think the angel cared for the Jansai's touch. Uriah shouted something at him, and Obadiah shook his head. Uriah shouted something else, and Obadiah reluctantly nodded.

"Quiet!" bellowed the Jansai, and the crowd simmered down, though there was still a murmur of excitement bubbling under the surface. "The angel has agreed to sing a second song!"

At that, the response threatened to bring the platform down again, and Obadiah looked as if he was seriously considering waiting out the uproar on solid ground. But he stood before them all, white and gold and magnificent, showing a courtly patience.

When the noise died down sufficiently for him to be heard, he took one step forward and began to sing. This was a completely different song in a wholly different style, slow, looping, and beautiful. It was not sad so much as wistful, a meditation on a lost love or a vanished home or a dream abandoned long ago. Obadiah's voice easily made the long, elegant sweep from the low notes of the melody to the high, pensive elegy of the chorus. Each time one verse ended and the refrain began, Rebekah felt her heart make that leap with his voice. His music molded her body, sculpted her into so much tense, mute longing. She stood absolutely motionless on the edge of the crowd, but every nerve, every sense, was agitated and primed, pointed straight toward him. If she had been an arrow nocked on the bow, her release would have driven her directly into his heart.

This song did not end as abruptly as the last; rather, its last clear, mournful phrases faded and repeated, faded and repeated, till the very last note merely melted away. Again, the crowd greeted the performance with first silence and then clamorous approbation. The angel bowed again, so low that his blond hair swept the raw lumber of the stage, and then he straightened with an air of great determination. He was down the stairs and onto the ground while the throng was still cheering and chanting.

If Rebekah had had attention to spare for anyone else, she would have felt a wave of pity for the next performers. But she didn't care about those luckless unfortunates, and she didn't give Martha more than one quick thought as she took another cursory look around the crowd. All her energy was concentrated on the angel, visible in patches of glowing white through the unstable construction of the stage, surrounded by the dull, heavy, mundane bodies of Jansai.

She had to get next to him.

She had forgotten all her vows, her responsibilities, the risks she ran of angering Hector or disgracing Isaac. She had to move closer to Obadiah, had to be able to truly look at him, to see the strength and kindness of his face. She would not talk to him—no, she was not that foolish—and, anyway, how could she, surrounded as she was by a sea of pushing, shoving Jansai men? They would have no chance to talk, Rebekah and Obadiah, Jansai girl and Cedar Hills angel, but she did not need to say a word. She merely wanted to see his face, remind her heart of its lines and contours. She asked Jovah for no more than that.

Accordingly, she drifted through the crowd, willing herself to be invisible. There was no shortage of men pressing in the same direction, determined to shake the angel's hand—or, who knew, to tell him all his fancy love songs would never change their opinion of angel laws and angel ways. But fewer than she had thought. She would have expected the whole world to run in his direction, breathless with wonder, and for all men to throw themselves at his feet in adoration.

In truth, there was just a handful of Jansai pooled around the angel as he stood behind the stage. Only a few sputtering torches lit the trampled area behind the platform, so it was hard to make out all the bodies congregated there, but Obadiah was easy to see. His wings clung to him like his own shadow, but constructed of light, moving when he moved, trembling when he gestured. What glow the torches could generate was all concentrated on his face. He was laughing.

"Not at all—thank you, indeed—ah, I am glad to hear that I gauged my audience correctly," he said, handing back graceful replies to the compliments that Rebekah could not catch. In fact, the only sound she could hear in the world was his voice. She knew that fresh musicians had taken the stage, and she believed that they had started playing, but their music did not register with her. Only Obadiah's voice.

"Tomorrow night? The fair goes on another day? Yes, so you did. Listen, that's nice. A Semorran harper, I have met him before. No, but I do not want to monopolize the stage. . . ."

She supposed that the Jansai were asking him to perform again tomorrow, and she found herself wondering if she could make it here again, slip from the house a second night without being caught. Surely Martha would come with her, or Jordan—or did it matter? She could come alone—anything to hear the angel singing one more time.

She had continued to move forward with a ghostlike stealth till she was as close to the angel as she could manage without coming into the flickering light. The group around him had thinned out now, so that only three or four men remained by him, and these seemed to be arguing among themselves. One was Uriah, but his attention had been claimed by a young man who looked enough like him to be his son, and both of them looked furious. The other two men appeared surly and distant, no friends to Obadiah, but waiting on his pleasure now because they were allies of Uriah's and this was what Uriah had required them to do. None of them were paying any attention to the shapes in the shadows, though Rebekah felt she must be hard to overlook. There must be a glow to her, emanating from her hair and her skin and her fingertips; she would not be surprised to learn that she flared and fluttered like one of those backstage flambeaux.

None of the Jansai looked her way. But the angel did.

She didn't know if it was a gesture or a noise that caught his attention, but his eyes turned indifferently her way—and then caught, and held, as he considered the indistinct form crouched beside the support beams of the dais. The faintest smile crossed his face and he looked away, and she was able to breathe again. She guessed that he had seen her and drawn his own conclusions, imagining her to be an awestruck boy too shy to approach the star of the evening's entertainment.

She should leave now, before he looked again, but she could not. She could not walk away from him, deliberately put more distance between his smile and her ability to see it. She would wait here, trying to transform herself into shadow, until he and the Jansai left together. And then she would shake herself back into reality, knead some feeling into her numb cheeks and fingers, and return to the crowd in front of the stage to search for the familiar pieces of her life.

"Jovah's blood and balls!" Uriah growled, slapping his son with a sudden fierceness. "Do you mean to tell me—Joshua! Abe! We've got to get back now. Angelo, my apologies. I have urgent business."

"No apology necessary. I can find my way back to my hotel on my own."

"In the morning, though—"

"In the morning," the angel agreed with a friendly nod. "I shall come see you again. We have much to talk about."

"Damn you, boy," Uriah muttered, cuffing his son again, and then gave the angel another quick look. "I want to hear all the details."

And with a swirl of his colorful cloak, Uriah spun on his heel and strode away. His son and his companions followed in silence.

Rebekah and the angel were left completely alone in the deserted, half-lit clearing behind the stage.

"You can come out and talk to me now, if you like," Obadiah said to her in the low, gentle voice a man might use to soothe a wild pony or reassure a hurt dog. "There's no one to see you disgrace yourself by talking to an angel."

Rebekah could not move or speak.

"Of course, if you've brought a few rocks to stone me with, I'd just as soon you stay where you are and give me a few minutes to fly someplace safer," he said in a whimsical voice. "I know that Jansai don't like angels much. I'm perfectly willing to leave, if you want me gone."

"Nnn—" she choked out, but she could not form the words. Didn't want to form the words. Didn't want to be here, alone with the angel, telling him how much she had thought about him these past few weeks. She put a hand to her mouth as though to keep the words inside through brute regulatory action.

"Did you like the singing? Did you want to ask me about Cedar Hills? Or is there someone in your family who's sick, who needs plague medicines? I'm perfectly willing to help or talk. But you have to step out here where I can see you."

This time she merely shook her head, not even chancing articulation.

"Well, then. I'll go if you want me to. My name's Obadiah, by the way. They didn't bother to introduce me properly when they sent me up to the stage."

She nodded. She knew his name.

His smile grew a little wider. Even by broken torchlight, his face looked both handsome and compassionate. "And your name? Can young Jansai men share that information?"

She shook her head again, more violently, her hand still pressed against her mouth. The bracelets clinked on her wrist as her sleeve fell back from the contagious motion. She could feel the feathers of her mask against her fingers, and she could feel the tingling of her fingers as they itched to rip off the mask.

But she would not have to. She would not have to throw off her disguises in order to engineer her own betrayal. The angel's eyes had been drawn to the musical tinkling of her jewelry, and now his gaze lingered on the circlets around her wrist. She did not even have to look down to know what the fickle torchlight showed him: sapphire and silver, arranged in his own design.

When he lifted his eyes to her face again, he was no longer smiling.

CHAPTER FOURTEEN

Obadiah felt that he had flown to Breven on a breeze of half-truths and outright lies, and he was perfectly comfortable with that.

He had returned to Breven sooner than almost anyone wanted, from Nathan to Magdalena to the brisk healer called Mary. "Yes, yes, angels heal more quickly than children, but you were weaker than you realized, and I would hate to see your fever come back," she said to him sternly.

He had laughed at her. He liked her, and he rather liked being fussed over, though Maga's overdramatic protectiveness was beginning to wear on him. "I haven't had a fever in ten days. I don't expect to have a fever again for ten years. But I thank you for your concern."

She had been easy enough to fob off, but Maga was a different story altogether. He had gone to visit her the day before he planned to leave for the desert city, and had found her alone in the handsome suite she shared with Nathan, sulking. There was no other word for it.

"Why, lovely, you look so sad," he greeted her, dropping an affectionate kiss on her dark hair. In fact, she looked surly, but he opted for the gentler word. "Do you want to share your troubles?"

She gestured at the open window, which revealed a perfect day of windless sunshine. By this time, at the Eyrie, winter would have been well and truly entrenched, and a slow dreary rain would have settled in to sour all their moods. "It's just—look at it," she said crossly. "Nothing but sunshine. Perfect weather all the time."

He settled down in the chair across from her and smiled. "Yes, I can see why you'd find that discouraging."

"No, but why must Nathan be *gone,* then? No one's come asking for a weather intercession for three days! Yet there are some farmers up by the Caitanas who need his help, and he flew off this morning and won't be back for two or three days, and I can't *stand* it. He's always gone."

"So is Gabriel. So is Ariel. You know that, lovely. The leaders of every hold are in high demand."

"Yes, but I need him," she said, and burst into tears.

Obadiah promptly crossed to her side, knelt beside her, and enwrapped her in both flesh and feathers. "Now then," he murmured into her ear, "this isn't like you. You have something on your mind besides Nathan and his absences."

"Oh, I feel so stupid," she sobbed, turning in his arms and clinging to him. He felt her tears wet the front of his linen shirt, freshly washed by the pretty little laundress. "I've just—it's been—never mind me, Obadiah. Just go away."

He laughed at that and gave her a little hug. "No, I won't go away, but I'd like you to tell me what's the matter. You can trust me, you know. Whatever it is."

"I can trust you. I can trust everybody," she answered somewhat wildly. "Everyone will know soon enough."

"Well, then—please. Just tell me now."

She sniffed and wiped her face with a very expensive sleeve, and straightened in his arms. He sat back on his heels, his wings spread on the carpet behind him. "I'm pregnant," she said.

He threw his hands in the air, then leaned forward to kiss her cheek. "But this is delightful news!" he exclaimed. "Cause for celebration, not despair! Though I know women in your condition are prey to all sorts of emotional excesses—"

She stared at him, her face so bleak he stopped speaking. "I'm so afraid," she whispered.

He was at a loss. Yes, there were inherent dangers in childbirth, and to bear an angelic child was risky in the extreme, but he was convinced every healer in the city would attend her delivery, if she wanted. "I know there is some reason to be frightened, but—"

She clutched his arm. "There has never—every time an angel has mated with an angel—there have never been anything but monster children born as a result," she said in a low, urgent voice. "Obadiah! What if the child I am carrying is a horror of some kind—a lucifer? I do not want to bring such a child into the world, then watch it scream and die."

Now he understood. He leaned forward and wrapped his arm protectively around her again. "Yes, that is true, but Jovah has made allowances this time," he said. "He brought you and Nathan together, don't you know? He made your Kisses light when you were in the room together. He must have meant for you to wed and bear children."

"I'm not sure Jovah had all that much to do with it." She sighed. "Nathan and I are together because Gabriel no longer had the energy to try to keep us apart."

"Gabriel always has the energy to continue to do what he thinks is right," Obadiah said with a touch of humor. "If you cannot trust your Kiss, you can trust the Archangel."

"He doesn't know," she said, still in that low, despondent voice. "No one knows. Until this child is born—"

"Well, and until then, there is nothing you can do, and fretting will not make things any easier," Obadiah said practically. "You must wait and see what the god sends you."

She looked up at him with some desperation in her eyes. "And if he sends me something—too awful to contemplate?"

"Then Nathan and I and all your friends will be right beside you. But I do not think Jovah will be so cruel."

"Jovah is as stern as Gabriel when he wants to be," she said, making her own attempt to joke.

Obadiah smiled and sat back on his heels again. "So! When is the event to occur? And why hasn't Nathan told me the great news?"

"I haven't told Nathan," she said.

"You haven't—Maga!" he protested.

"I've been so afraid! And I knew he would be worried, too, and he has so much already to worry about, without me clinging to him every day. It's just that I—I'm so afraid and so lonely. I try to keep busy, and I see all the petitioners who come to Cedar Hills, but they're beginning to think I'm lunatic, because I start crying as soon as they tell me the story of the slightest privation—"

He could not help laughing at that. "You must tell Nathan, though," he said. "And a midwife. You must have someone to watch over you. Aren't there special foods you should be eating now? More sleep you should be getting? I don't know much about these things—"

"Yes, I suppose," she said listlessly. "Someone to calm me when I get irrational—" She smiled over at him with an effort. "I'm glad you're around," she added.

"I leave for Breven tomorrow," he said before he could stop himself.

"Obadiah! No!"

"I must! Truly! Gabriel sent me here to spy on the Jansai, and spy on the Jansai I will."

"But you're not even healed yet! I can still see the marks on your body."

"Show me," he said, extending his wing. She scowled and bent closer, but there was no scar to be found. He knew, because he had searched for it himself the day before and could not locate, by sight or tenderness, where the wound had been. "See?" he said, when she straightened up, still frowning. "Not even a memory of an injury."

"I don't want you to go," she said. "And after what I just told you—"

"I have to go," he said gently. "Perhaps you can find another companion who is more reliable than I am."

"Who?" she demanded.

A month ago, he would not have believed the words would come out of his mouth. "Why don't you send for Rachel?"

So, even though he should have felt guilty about it, he left Cedar Hills with a sense of relief. And excitement. He had learned his lesson about flying in the vicinity of Breven, oh yes; he brought a leather satchel strapped over one shoulder, and inside was an assortment of dried food and potent medicines. He could not really expect to be shot down twice, he thought, but he now knew to respect the treachery of the desert.

He arrived in Breven a day before the harvest fair was scheduled to begin, and found the whole city bustling with activity and anticipation. The only hotel rooms available were the most expensive, but he did not think either Nathan or Gabriel would begrudge him the expense. The Verde Hotel was run by enterprising Manadavvi who wanted to offer the highest-quality accommodations to other Manadavvi coming to the city to trade. Every room was sumptuously decorated with gorgeous furnishings and plush mattresses, and each chamber boasted its own water room, a luxury itself in this desert city. The young man who handed the angel his key had the patrician features and haughty bearing of every Manadavvi Obadiah had ever met.

"It's a dreadful city," he told Obadiah in an up-country drawl. "Barbaric and violent. You can't trust the Jansai to tell you the same story two days running. But you can make a fortune here, if you can stand the company."

"Shall I show you to your room, angelo?" asked a pretty voice behind him.

Obadiah turned quickly, trying to cover his surprise. He found himself facing a slim woman who looked to be in her early twenties, dressed in clothes of simple and expensive elegance. "I thought—I have never seen an unveiled woman in Breven," he excused himself when he had stared for a moment or two.

"My sister," said the man who had taken his registration. "She doesn't leave the hotel unless I go with her, or my father does. But she refuses to cover her face, even in the market."

"That sounds a little dangerous," Obadiah commented.

"They despise me, but they'll take my money if I'm buying," she said, a hint of iron in that soft, gentle voice. "The Jansai are primitive and judgmental, but you can always count on their greed."

"Anyway, they don't care about our women," her brother said. "It's only their own poor, miserable creatures that they want to keep locked away from the eyes of men like you and me. Never saw any people treated so badly in my life."

"The Edori," she said.

Her brother snorted. "Oh, yes, the Edori! Another tale of Jansai greed and cruelty. What I want to know is why Jovah has not struck them all dead any time these past five hundred years."

Obadiah had to admit that he felt some sympathy for this point of view, but it seemed impolitic to say so aloud. "Jovah loves all his people," the angel reminded them, speaking in platitudes. "On the morning of the Gloria, he requires the presence of all of us on the Plain of Sharon. Perhaps they have been brought to this world simply to teach us the principles of harmony, because they create so much dissonance. Jovah has his reasons for all things."

The young man looked skeptical but not prepared to argue theology with an angel. "In any case, we're here in Breven, and we have learned how to deal with them," he said. "I suppose that's why you're here, too."

Obadiah smiled. "Yes," he said. "I am here to get closer to an understanding of the Jansai."

He had gone to his room, changed clothes, stepped back onto the streets of Breven, and wandered through the markets for twenty minutes before he fully realized the futility of his mission. He would not be able to find Rebekah here. The fact that she was physically within reach made no difference. She was as far away from him now as she would be if he were in Gaza and she across the ocean in Ysral.

He had strolled through the Breven markets before, but never with such a sense of strangeness. He had realized—of course he had realized—that virtually every face on both sides of every stall was male. To walk the streets of Breven was to believe that Jansai women did not exist, that the men reproduced themselves and raised themselves and existed entirely without the touch and attention of women. And indeed, some of their coarseness and roughness, Obadiah thought, might be attributed to the fact that all their transactions were male-on-male, that they had no broad understanding of the whims and softnesses and unbelievable strengths that a woman could possess.

To be sure, here and there was some degraded creature, wrapped in five layers of tattered cloth, buying bread or fruit at a market booth and treated by the merchant as if she were a walking pillar of filth. And every once in a while Obadiah spotted a barefaced woman, clearly a landowner of some kind, or a Luminaux craftswoman, or the wife or daughter of a trader from one of the three provinces. But these women were never alone, and none of them looked entirely easy, even when they appeared defiant. He didn't blame them. He felt none too safe himself in the Breven market.

Yet many of the people on the streets—a good number of the buyers and sellers themselves—were not Jansai. Breven was such a rich trading center that anyone with goods to barter would eventually make his way here, think what he may of the city's politics. Obadiah spotted Semorran merchants and Bethel farmers, as well as the ubiquitous Manadavvi. What was strange was to see no Edori, for Edori were as itinerant as the Jansai and could be found in every other city, big or small, across the three provinces. But the Jansai had terrorized the Edori for years, allowed to do their worst under the negligent reign of the Archangel Raphael. Today there was not a single Edori who would willingly set foot inside Breven.

Angels were almost as scarce. In fact, Obadiah was the only one. Another strange facet of a strange city.

But the strangest was: He was here, no more than a mile or two from the woman he was determined to see again, and he had not the faintest idea how he could go about contacting her. She might as well be dead and curled sleeping in Jovah's arms for all the good it would do him to be here and trying to find a way to see her.

Uriah affected to be suitably shocked at the news that Obadiah had suffered harm the last time he had left Breven. "And *what* was this weapon that brought you down?" he asked for the second time. "A— a missile of fire? That's extraordinary."

"Extraordinarily painful, too," Obadiah said serenely. They were drinking a very good wine in Uriah's pavilion, and all of the Jansai's disciples and sycophants had been ordered from the tent. Obadiah wouldn't have minded speaking in front of a handful of listeners, but he thought Uriah liked the cachet of special knowledge and extra privileges. "I have never felt anything quite like it."

"What could such a weapon be made of?" Uriah asked in a marveling voice. "And who might have such a thing?"

"Both excellent questions," Obadiah said. "Although there was talk, a year or two ago, that Raphael and some of his allies possessed sticks that could throw fire."

"Aaahhhh," Uriah said. "So at one time such a weapon was in the hands of the angels! How curious."

"In the hands of the angels," Obadiah agreed, "and in the hands of the Jansai. For Malachi of Breven was seen with such a firestick in his possession."

"Have you any enemies among the angels?" Uriah asked innocently.

"None," said Obadiah. "I am universally beloved in the three holds."

"Then you think perhaps it was a Jansai who shot you down?" Uriah asked with great astonishment. All feigned, of course, but Obadiah gave him credit. He did not show the slightest inclination to laugh.

"I think that must be considered as a real possibility," Obadiah said gravely.

"A shocking turn of events, if it proved to be so," Uriah said.

"Yes, I have to think whoever took aim at me did not think very far ahead," Obadiah said. He leaned back on his chair (specially made for him since his last visit, for which he gave Uriah great credit), and sipped at his wine. "For, just think if I had died. There are not so many angels in the world that my disappearance would have gone unnoticed. And once my mutilated body had been found—"

Uriah made a slight, fatalistic moue with his hands. "Yes, but, how to reconstruct the event? If no one saw an enemy lift this weapon up and sight it upon you, how could anyone be sure who exactly had brought you down?"

Obadiah smiled at him. "An angel felled over the desert not fifty miles from Breven?" he asked gently. "Who else might be blamed for such an act?"

"So you think Gabriel would have pointed to the Jansai, whether or not we were guilty?" Uriah asked.

"Whether or not you were guilty," Obadiah repeated. "Yes, I very much fear so. Which is why I am telling you now. I certainly do not expect you to make yourself responsible for my safety, but I would like you to realize that the Jansai will come under suspicion if anything happens to me while I'm anywhere near your city. It's regrettable, but there it is."

"And yet if a reasonable man could prove the Jansai had nothing to do with something so calamitous—"

"I think you overestimate Gabriel's ability to be reasonable on a subject about which he feels passionately," said Obadiah, even more gently. "I love Gabriel like a brother, but I would not want to cross him on a matter of such magnitude. If something were to happen to me—or any angel—anywhere near the city limits of Breven, I fear that Breven itself would not long survive the event."

Uriah stared at Obadiah from dark, narrowed eyes, trying to weigh the sincerity of the threat as well as the likelihood that it could actually be carried out. Neither man spoke for a moment. "But angelo—" Uriah said at last.

"Furthermore," Obadiah interrupted in an urbane voice, "Gabriel believes that a Jansai who once would use such a weapon to attack an angel might be incautious enough to use it a second time. Against an angel. The Archangel made it very clear to me that he would not be happy until such a weapon was in trusted hands."

"His own, you mean?" Uriah said sharply.

"Or yours," Obadiah said, nodding his head graciously. "He is quite sure you would not do anything so reckless as offer harm to an angel. He said he would be quite satisfied to know that you had located the man who might possess this device—asking no questions about how he may have used it!—and confiscated the weapon for your own."

"And if I cannot find him? Or cannot persuade him to give it up?"

"Then I am not sure how much longer Gabriel will be willing to hazard my person in the pursuit of an alliance between us."

"You would leave Breven."

"I would have to."

"With all our claims left unsettled."

Obadiah shrugged, feeling his wing tips lift and settle over the braided silk rugs that covered the canvas floor. "But I would happily return once you took charge of this firestick," Obadiah said. "I believe that you, at least, intend no harm to me."

Uriah gave a sudden, cracking laugh and slapped a hand along the arm of his chair. "No, for I like you. You've a scoundrel's heart behind that face of a pious saint," he exclaimed.

"Have I been complimented or insulted?" Obadiah wondered.

"Complimented—the Jansai love a scoundrel," Uriah retorted. "But enough of this dancing about! Talking is hungry work, don't you find? Come join me for dinner, and meet my ruffian of a son."

"I am happy to accept your hospitality," Obadiah said. "But we have talked very little business, and we have, as you know, much business to discuss."

Uriah waved a hand and heaved himself from his chair. "There is time," he said. "But for now, I want food, not negotiation."

This second meal in the company of the Jansai chieftain was a little more restrained than the first one Obadiah had sat down to more than three weeks ago. Perhaps that was because it was a little more formal, though still held in some business-district tent and not in Uriah's home. Obadiah was beginning to suspect that until he was actually invited into the man's house he would not be considered trustworthy, and until he was considered trustworthy, no progress would be made on their negotiations.

It seemed like he was about to become a fixture on the Breven social scene.

There were maybe twenty-five men in the big tent this night, most of whom Obadiah did not remember from that last dinner. The brooding, unfriendly Michael was not here, which first pleased Obadiah and then made him nervous. Because if the Jansai wasn't under Uriah's watchful eye, he could be skulking around somewhere in Breven, just waiting to haul out any variety of weapons to bring the angel down.

Though Obadiah was pretty sure his threats would keep him safe, for a while yet. Everyone knew Gabriel was capable of calling down thunderbolts in a moment of extreme displeasure. No one really wanted to find out what events might provoke him.

Uriah was introducing the angel, in a haphazard way, to the other men at the table. "And that's Mark, my son—looks like me, doesn't he? He's a rascal. Over there, Zebedee. Oh, and Simon. You must congratulate him."

"On what?"

"His son has just gotten betrothed to the daughter of a wealthy man. Watch my words, they're going to open up the route to Luminaux like you've never seen. You want luxuries in Velora? They'll get them to you, Simon and his partner."

"I want luxuries in Cedar Hills," Obadiah said.

Uriah gave his sharp bark of laughter. "Well, and you'll have them there, too! They'll make a good team."

"I thought it was the daughter and son who were making the alliance?"

Uriah waved a dismissive hand. "Same thing. They are all extensions of their fathers. Until the boys learn to be their own men and the women bear the next generation of sons."

The food was heavily spiced, the wine was strong, and the conversation covered virtually no topic but trading. Obadiah kept the smile on his face and tried to conceal his thoughts. He did nod and comment when someone asked his opinion on a trade route or a weather pattern, but he only made one unsolicited contribution to the general discussion.

"So I understand there's to be a grand fair here tomorrow evening," he said. "Is anyone allowed to attend?"

"Yes! The harvest festival!" Uriah exclaimed. "I didn't know you planned to stay for it, angelo! You must come as my guest. The crowds can be a little rowdy from time to time—hard to imagine, I know—and I would not want some unwary Jansai treading on your wing feathers."

This was something of a setback. Impossible though it was, Obadiah had been hoping fervently that Rebekah would sneak from her house and make her way to the fair in some kind of disguise. He would not be able to spot her, of course, but she would have no trouble identifying him, and he had thought if he made himself visible enough, wandered through the booths restlessly enough, she might see him, and she might take her courage in hand and approach him. . . .

Not a chance of that if he had Uriah and his minions by his side.

"I appreciate your concern," Obadiah said. "But I would not wish to intrude on your own revels. The presence of an angel might—inhibit—some of the activities of you and your friends."

Uriah roared with laughter and slapped Obadiah on the arm, a gesture the angel endured with only the slightest grimace of distaste. He did not care much for casual contact, certainly not from half-drunk

Jansai, and Uriah's hand had come perilously close to brushing against Obadiah's wing. Such a mishap and Obadiah would not have been able to refrain from jerking his feathers back, reacting as violently as if he had been stabbed or, again, rent with fire.

"There'll be no inhibitions among us, I promise you!" Uriah roared. "Come with us to the fair tomorrow, angelo. You shall enjoy yourself, never fear."

And, in fact, Obadiah had rather enjoyed the evening, though he deeply regretted losing the chance to walk the overrun streets and hold himself up as a beacon to catch a girl's attention. However, a mere half hour among Uriah and his friends in the crowded bazaar led him to believe that Rebekah's chances of being at this event were very close to zero. For one thing, it was a rough and boisterous throng, and individuals faced every chance of being shoved or harassed. For another, he was getting a pretty fair measure of the outlook of the typical Jansai male, and he couldn't believe anyone as dependent as a Jansai daughter would risk the anger of her husband or her father by slipping out into such a melee.

For another, he didn't see anyone, masked or unmasked, who looked like a woman in disguise. Everywhere, in every booth and alley and gaming pit, boys and men as far as his gaze could wander.

There were plenty of other distractions, but Obadiah's presence itself was drawing no little attention, mostly from those boys. The fat, satisfied, older merchants paid him no heed at all, unless they bothered to throw him a look of appraisal or dislike. The restless young men watched him from edgy groups badly lit by torchlight, sneers on their mouths and hatred in their eyes. Those were the times Obadiah was glad for Uriah's escort, though even alone he would not have been afraid, exactly. It was just that he knew the firestick was still at large, and he was not entirely sure all the Jansai had yet gotten the message that the angel was to be left unharmed while he roamed their city, or dire consequences would fall to all.

The young Jansai boys, however, didn't seem to have realized that they were supposed to despise him, and they came tripping up to Obadiah all night. They bombarded him with questions—"How high can you fly?" "Do your fingers and toes ever freeze?" "Can you fly at night?" "Have you ever gotten lost?"—and came so close it was clear they were dying to touch his interlaced feathers. But Obadiah was nimble enough to elude most of those cautiously extended fingers while smilingly answering even the silliest of questions. Uriah alternated between showing great irritation at the constant interruptions and a certain amount of pride in indomitable young Jansai manhood that had no fear of angelic messengers.

"They swarm around like rats in a sewage hole, but how can you tie them to their mothers' jeskas once they've reached such an age?" Uriah shrugged, minutes after chasing off two impudent boys who asked how much an angel's wing feathers might sell for in the open market.

"I don't mind them," Obadiah said. "They're friendlier than their fathers, at any rate."

Uriah laughed. "Give them time, angelo," he joked.

The crowds and the ale and the merchandise and the gaming Obadiah had expected from the harvest fair. What he had not expected was the music stage set up on the far edge of the gathering, and it had not even occurred to him that Uriah would ask him to sing. Or rather, bully him into it, despite Obadiah's protests.

"I can't think your average Jansai merchant will be much impressed with my voice," he said seriously. "They're more likely to stone me than applaud me."

But Uriah was determined, and Obadiah thought he knew why: It gave the Jansai leader a certain amount of prestige to be seen in the company of an angel, especially if that angel appeared to be doing his bidding. But Obadiah did not really mind being constrained to perform, even in front of such a hostile audience. If, by some remote chance, Rebekah *were* in this crowd tonight and had failed to mark him as he made his slow progress across the fair, she would be almost certain to see him when he stepped onto the stage. See him or hear him. He had that much faith in the power of his voice.

Accordingly, he took the stage and smiled at the crowd, and gave them two songs that could offend nobody. He was rather proud of both his rendition and his reception, since it was obvious the audience had not expected to be moved by his performance. He wondered how many of them had heard an angel sing before—had made the pilgrimage to the Plain of Sharon to observe the Gloria, or visited Raphael's debauched hold back when the Jansai and the Archangel were close allies. Some significant percentage of them, surely. And yet all of them appeared to be more moved than they had expected.

He bowed and exited the stage, trying not to give in to an irrational disappointment. Well, admit it, then, he had hoped for some divine reaction, a mark of the god's favor. He had not been able to erase from his mind the tales of how Gabriel's singing had always woken the colors in Rachel's Kiss. He had hoped for some sort of similar miracle, fashioned just for him: a flare in the crystalline heart of his own Kiss, proof that Rebekah was near and had overheard him. And that the god approved.

Ridiculous. How could he have been so foolish? Even if the god had made some effort to bring together Rachel and Gabriel, Nathan and Maga, it was hard to believe Jovah could have such interest in the doomed romance of a minor angel and an unimportant Jansai girl.

He joined the conference held behind the stage and graciously accepted the compliments of the men who pushed back here just to give him their praise. Slowly that crowd dispersed, leaving only Uriah and his attendants, and Uriah's energy was mostly directed to an argument with his son. A little bored by now, Obadiah glanced around the underlit clearing and was amused to see yet another Jansai boy hiding under the overhang of the platform, mesmerized by angel wings but too shy to come out of the shadows. He scarcely heard Uriah's curses and apologies, but willingly agreed to meet the Jansai again in the morning. He was just as happy when everyone left, and he could turn his attention to the lurking admirer.

"You can come out and talk to me if you like," he invited, but he had to continue to cajole for another five minutes. It was quiet and strangely restful back here behind the stage, a welcome break from all the hell-bent Jansai machismo he'd been bombarded with for the past few hours. The Semorran harpist played a pensive melody, neither happy nor mournful, and the sputtering torchlight lent the whole scene flickering unreality.

"My name's Obadiah," he said, thinking to coax the boy's name out of him in return. But no, that just sent his small hand up to cover his mouth, scarcely to be seen anyway under the feathered mask of black and gold. The gesture sent the bracelets jangling on the boy's wrist, and Obadiah's eyes dropped automatically to the sound of gold against silver.

It was the silver that he recognized first. When he lifted his gaze to meet her own, it was the eyes he recognized next.

CHAPTER FIFTEEN

"I can't believe you're here," the angel said.

Rebekah had taken three steps away from the overhang of the stage because, after all, what good did it do her to hide in shadows now that she had been discovered? But she was still having a hard time speaking.

"I looked for you, but then I thought—it would be too dangerous for you to try to come to this event, even in disguise, and so I gave up. But then I thought—if I sang—and you heard my voice—"

Incredible. He sounded as nervous as she felt, his words disjointed and his beautiful voice strained. He kept peering down at her, as if he was still not entirely positive she was the person he hoped to see. He was so tall. Behind him, the white wings lay like untouched snow, drifted into miraculously exquisite patterns.

"But I didn't *really* think you'd be here."

"Obadiah," she said.

He stood utterly mute.

"Obadiah," she said again, just to feel her lips shaping the syllables again. "I wasn't going to come tonight. I was afraid to see you."

"Afraid—of *me?*"

She shook her head. "Of—seeing you. Of learning I had remembered you wrong." She smiled a little, behind the mask. "Or that I had remembered you right. Just as bad, you see."

"Yes," he said with such passion that she was sure he understood her entirely cryptic remark. "But which is it?"

That made her laugh. "I remembered right," she said.

"I can't stand being in this city and having no way to see you," he said. "I've been to Breven a hundred times, and never felt so—how can people live like this? How can you be so close to me and yet completely out of reach?"

"That's just how it has always been," she said. "That's just my life."

"I have to be able to see you," he said.

She shifted on her feet and changed the subject. "How are your wounds?" she asked. "I don't see any scarring on your wing."

He brought his left wing forward with a slow, sweeping motion. It draped from his shoulder to the ground like a carelessly thrown shawl. "Not a mark on me," he said. "I'm completely whole. My leg, too."

"So you made it back to Cedar Hills without incident?"

He gave a rather hollow laugh. "Not exactly. I was sick for a few days. But I mended. How was the trip to Castelana?"

She grimaced. "Boring. No more angels to take care of. And very little to do on the whole trip except argue with my mother and take care of the baby."

"You're wearing my bracelet," he said.

So he could change the subject just as quickly as she could. "Sometimes I do."

"So you can be reminded of me?"

"I like it. It's pretty. I don't have much silver."

"Point out the booth. I'll buy you whatever silver trinkets you like."

"I don't need any more of your gifts, thank you."

"Do you want me to go away?" he asked. "Do you want to forget me?"

She stared up at him. The feathers of the mask imperfectly rimmed the eyeholes, throwing little wavering fronds before her vision, making the edges blurry. Or maybe she was just having a hard time seeing clearly, thinking clearly. "I won't be able to forget you, even if you go away," she said.

"I want to see you," he said.

"You're seeing me."

"Not like this."

"Then what do you want?"

There was a sudden roar from the crowd as the harpist finished his song and then clattered down the steps, making more noise than it seemed one man should. Rebekah drew back into the shadows, saying nothing until the next group of performers tramped up the stairs and began to array themselves on the stage.

"Not like this," Obadiah said again. "Where I'm afraid any minute that someone will see us together and question who you are. I want to be able to *talk* to you. I want to be able to see your face."

"I'm betrothed to marry Isaac," she said baldly.

He was silent so long that the musicians on the platform above them had time to warm up their instruments and dive into the first measures of their music. A reel of some sort, lively and inappropriate.

"When will you be married?" he asked at last.

She shook her head. "Sometime next spring. They have not finished all the arrangements yet."

"Do you want to marry him?"

She shrugged and found herself on the move, unable to stand there so quietly discussing this. She paced away from the shadows and in a tight circle around the angel. He pivoted slowly, following her. "I don't know what I want! Marriage to somebody like Isaac is what my life has always held. Why should I not want to marry him? Because I have met you?" She stopped and stared at him. "I don't even know you," she said.

"I hate to think of you living here," he said, speaking very rapidly. "Trapped in some house, forced to wed at your stepfather's whim, forced to live as your husband says—with no voice, and no choice, in your own life."

"That is the life of every Jansai woman. What else should I expect?"

"You could come back with me to Cedar Hills," he said. She had the impression that the words surprised him just as much as they surprised her, but he pressed on after only a second's hesitation. "I realize—you don't know me—I understand that. But there is a great deal of work to be done in Cedar Hills. There is an entire hold to be built, and there is work for all hands. You could sew or teach or watch the children. You could see me only when you wanted to. A woman can live on her own in Cedar Hills, can make her own way. And I would be a friend to you forever."

"I can't leave Breven."

"You say that because you have never been on your own," he replied. "You're afraid. But it would not be frightening for long. Not as terrifying as living here, compelled to do as someone else decided—"

"But here at least I understand my place and my purpose," she interrupted. "To go to Cedar Hills—to leave here and go anywhere—that is like asking me to jump in the ocean and live under the sea. That is like asking me to do something that is—that's not possible. That's crazy."

"You don't have to decide tonight," he said. "But think about it. Promise me that. You'll think about it."

"Every time I see you I start thinking about things, whether or not I want to think about them," she said crossly.

He grinned. "Well, then, I must hope that you see me quite often! I like to have you thinking about me and things I've said."

"I am not always sure it was such a good thing that I found you by the water and saved your life," she said with a little scowl.

"Well, it was a good thing for *me*, so I'm very happy you found me that day! I'm very happy I found you *this* day. And I want to see you again. How can I see you again?"

"There is no way," she said.

"There has to be."

She looked up at him, shaking her head in the negative, but her mind had not accepted that impossibility. She considered and discarded ideas even while she told him no.

"I will be here tomorrow night as well," he said. "At the fair, I mean. I can stay another full day and another full night. If you will tell me someplace I can meet you."

"There is no place," she said, still trying to manufacture a different alternative.

"Can you get to my hotel?" he said. "I think we might be safe there."

"At a Breven inn?" she said, her voice derisive.

"It's a Manadavvi establishment. The Hotel Verde."

Her racing mind stopped dead on that thought. "The Hotel Verde," she repeated. "Do they have any Jansai servants working there?"

He shook his head eagerly. "No! Only Manadavvi. And there's a woman who works there, the daughter of the owner, she goes about with her face uncovered. All the time. Even in the market."

"Her complexion must be as rough as a man's," Rebekah said without thinking.

Obadiah smiled. "That wasn't my point."

"Yes. I know. Your point was that, if I could make it to your hotel, I would be safe there from prying eyes. But that would mean leaving my house and traveling through the city, and being stopped by no one, and not being missed while I was gone—"

"No," he said, suddenly, and his voice was bleak. "No. I can't ask you to try that. I'm sorry, I—no. I don't realize how much actual danger you face. All I realize is that I—I'm sorry. I don't want to put you at risk."

On the instant, she decided she would do it. "I can't promise anything," she said. "It depends on if I can get out of the house. Nighttime is more likely. But I can't promise."

He came a step nearer, so there were really only a few inches between them. "Rebekah," he said, and his voice was urgent. "I don't want you to risk your life for me. I don't want you to risk your life for anything. I want to see you—more than anything I can think of at this precise moment, I want a chance to be alone with you—but my blood chills in my veins at the thought of you putting yourself in danger. For me. Because if something happened to you—"

"Before midnight," she said, as if he hadn't spoken. "If I'm not there by then, I won't be coming."

He grabbed her arms with a clasp so strong it swayed her almost against his chest. "Promise me you won't even try to come if someone will discover you," he said. "If you'll be in danger, promise me you won't come."

"I'm in danger now," she said calmly. "But here I am."

Silence fell like a warning the instant the words left her mouth. The performers hit their last chords, and the crowd took a moment to react. Still in the angel's grip, Rebekah lifted one hand to tug her mask from her head. They stared at each other like penitents gazing into the face of Jovah.

"Angelo?" said a voice behind them, and then the thunderous applause of the crowd drowned all other noise.

A shove, a swirl of feathers, and Rebekah found herself pushed behind the angel, his wings half folded around her as if to shield her from all hazards. Her heart was pounding and her blood clamored with terror. She had dropped her mask, and she could not see it anywhere on the ground. Who was there, who had seen her, how could even the angel explain away such an intimate conference with a young Jansai boy? Unless, with her mask gone, she had not appeared to be a boy.

"What is it, young man? Who are you?" Obadiah asked sharply. She had not thought his pleasant voice could sound so imperious.

"Angelo, I was looking for someone. I thought he might be back here, with you."

It was hard to make out the voice over the noises of the night, but Rebekah thought there was the slightest chance it could be familiar. She tried to peer around Obadiah's wing, but it was too high, too broad.

"There is no one here but me," Obadiah declared.

"I'm sorry, angelo. There was a boy here a moment ago. I saw him—"

"That boy is no concern of yours."

Rebekah dropped to her knees and stared out through the froth of feathers at the base of Obadiah's wing. It was still hard to see, but she could make out a figure standing beside the platform, casually dressed in trousers and a vest. The new arrival was wearing a mask of black and gold feathers and toying with a pendant hung around his throat.

"But I'm looking for my cousin," the boy said.

Rebekah scrambled to her feet and pushed past the startled Obadiah. "Martha! Where have you been? You disappeared!"

Martha gave her one quick, indignant look, easy to read even through the mask. "*I* disappeared! *You've* been gone forever! And where do I find you? In a dark field somewhere, exchanging kisses with an angel!"

Rebekah didn't know if she was more embarrassed at the accusation or the fact that Obadiah could overhear it. "I was not kissing him," she hissed. "*You're* the one who—"

"I take it everything is all right, then?" Obadiah interrupted.

Rebekah turned to face him. "This is my cousin Martha. I came here with her. But then *she* went off somewhere—yes, you did, don't pretend you didn't, I *saw* you with him—"

"Saw me with who?"

"Some Manadavvi," Rebekah said and had the satisfaction of seeing Martha's defiance melt away. She returned her attention to the angel. "Anyway. I came with her. She won't betray me."

"Then you're safe," he said.

"We have to go," Martha broke in. "Ephram and Jordan are both back looking for us. I thought I saw angel wings behind the platform, which is why I came back here—"

"Ah, so you know all your cousin's secrets," Obadiah murmured.

Rebekah felt her cheeks redden. "Hush," she said before Martha could say anything, and then, to the angel, "I have to go. Remember what I said."

"You remember what *I* said," he answered.

"Where's your mask?" Martha asked.

"I dropped it."

"Here," Obadiah said, bending over to retrieve it from the ground. "I'm afraid I stepped on it."

Rebekah hesitated just a moment too long, so Martha strode forward and snatched it from his hand. "Thank you, angelo," she said somewhat tartly, and returned to Rebekah's side. "Turn around, let me tie this on."

In a moment, Rebekah was back in disguise, and Martha was pushing her toward the main clearing in front of the stage. It had ended too strangely and abruptly, this fortuitous meeting with the angel, and she did not want to leave like this, so many words unsaid. But Martha's hand was firm on her back, and Rebekah could only look over her shoulder at the still, winged shape.

"Good-bye," she called. "Remember."

"I could not possibly forget," he said.

A few moments later they were back in the throng, getting buffeted from their true course by the constant motion of the crowd. "I want to know *every*—" Martha was saying, just as Rebekah demanded, "What *exactly* do you think you're—" and neither of them had time to complete a sentence or answer a question.

"There they are! Eph, here they are!" Jordan's voice, sounding young and relieved, called out right at her elbow. "It's late. We've got to get you back. I'm sorry I was gone so long."

Ephram joined them, smelling like wine and not looking sorry. "Where were you?" he demanded. "We searched all over for you."

Rebekah's mind was blank, but Martha spoke with lofty coolness. "She had to relieve herself and was looking for some privacy. Now, do you mind? We're both tired. I don't know where *you* two have been all evening, but Rebekah and I need to get home."

"Was it fun, though?" Jordan asked a little anxiously. "Did you have a good time?"

"Oh, yes," Martha said, once more answering for both of them. "It was the most wonderful thing ever."

They didn't have a chance to really talk until they were back in Rebekah's room. The return trip through the Breven streets had seemed longer and even chancier than the trip out, as they encountered groups of drunken men and whooping boys intent on squeezing a last few minutes of riotous pleasure out of the evening. And then there was the slow, creeping journey through the sleeping house, through the kitchen, up the servants' stairwell, down the hallway where the big-eared aunts lay on their mats, never as deeply slumbering as a girl might wish. But they encountered no true checks or dangers, and they slipped into Rebekah's room with a series of muffled giggles, shoving the door shut behind them. Then they collapsed on the mats by the wall, still giggling.

"Sshh—shh—you'll wake somebody up."

"Jovah's wicked bones, what a *night*! I love the harvest fair, I *love* it, I shall go every year for the rest of my life—"

"Shh," Rebekah whispered again. "Be quiet."

Martha had been rolling from side to side on the mat, clutching her arms around her chest in remembered ecstasy, but now suddenly she pushed herself to a seated position and pointed at her cousin. "You! You found your angel! Tell me every word he said."

Rebekah sat up, too, and leaned her back against the wall, sticking her feet out straight before her. There were no windows in the room, so it would have been completely dark except for the low flicker of gaslight on the wall by the door. "Oh no," she said. "This is a night for you to be telling tales first."

Martha looked innocent, a hard trick to pull off with the remnants of a charcoal beard rimming her mouth. "I have no tales to tell."

Rebekah crossed her arms on her chest. "Disappearing with a Manadavvi lordling into the night. I think you have plenty to report."

"Oh, very well, but first you—"

"Not a word from me," Rebekah said. "Until you tell me everything."

It was clear Martha was bursting with news, so she didn't need any more encouragement. "Jovah take my bones and bury them in the desert, but I think I'm in love with him, Bekah," she said. "I never thought I could—I mean, our mothers and our aunts don't talk about love—and anyway, who could truly love a Jansai man? So I never thought I'd feel this way. But Chesed—I do love him, I believe. It's so strange."

"Where did you meet him? How long have you known him?"

Martha drew her knees up and rested her darkened chin on top of them. "In the market. I was there one day—"

"How did you get to market?"

Martha hunched a shoulder impatiently. "I go sometimes when no one's paying attention. When my father and Ephram are traveling and the rest of the house is sleeping. It's not hard."

"Do you dress as a man?"

"Oh, no. I put on a stained old jeska over my most threadbare hallis, and I look like one of the campers from the city rim. A poor woman, who has to come to market on her own. Everyone despises me."

"You never told me any of this."

"I knew you would worry."

"Well, I'll worry even more now!"

"I tell you, no one pays attention to me in that house. My mother never asks me where I've been. Or maybe she knows and is afraid to ask. Maybe she crept out of the house herself when she was young—or out of the tent. I don't think my grandfather owned a thing but that tent in his whole life—"

Rebekah shook her head impatiently. "Back to the story. So you've been slipping out to market, and you met this Manadavvi, this Chesed—"

"Oh, Bekah, he is the most wonderful man. His father owns land in Gaza—so much land—and they grow the most amazing fruits there, sweeter than plums, but so fragile they cannot be shipped south of the Verde Divide. He has met the Archangel, only think of it! And dined with Ariel and Nathan. And he has traveled to every hill and corner of the three provinces—"

"So have you," Rebekah interjected.

"Oh, certainly! I've viewed every acre of land from the back of a tented wagon! But he has *seen* Semorrah and Luminaux and Velora. He has walked the streets. He has dined with miners and ship-builders and artists and angels, and he tells me about all of it, and I want to *go*."

"Go? Go where? Go with *him?*"

"Yes," Martha said dreamily. She laid her cheek on her knees and rocked herself gently. "I want to see every mile of Samaria from the back of a Manadavvi caravan, and then I want to go live in Gaza and eat fruit so delicate it scarcely survives the motion of being picked from the tree."

"You can't go with him," Rebekah said blankly.

"I don't see why not. I don't want to stay in Breven."

"What do you mean you don't want to stay in Breven? You belong in Breven! This is your home! You would be so lost and alone out among all those strange people—no one knowing your customs, no one knowing your name, no aunts to care for you when you fell sick, no brothers to watch after you—"

"I am sick to death of aunts and brothers and fathers and *cousins* telling me what I can do! Watching my every move and reporting my every action! Other women are free, Chesed told me so. I want to be free, too."

"So you will ride away to freedom with this Manadavvi man? Will he marry you? Will *that* be your freedom? Or will he merely take you away from Breven to some city where you don't know a soul, so he can abandon you there when he's tired of you? Will *that* be your freedom?"

"You don't understand!" Martha cried.

Before Rebekah could retort that she understood very well, there was a sharp knock on the door. "Girls!" came a low, edged reprimand. "Do you want to wake up the entire hallway?"

It was Hepzibah, Hector's oldest sister, who had the room directly adjacent to Rebekah's. Rebekah gave her cousin a warning look and jumped up to run across the floor. She opened the door just a crack.

"I'm sorry, *awrie,*" she said, using the respectful term that meant "beloved aunt." Though cantankerous old Hepzibah was anything but beloved. "Martha and I sometimes forget what time it is."

"Well past midnight! You should be sleeping!"

"How long have you been awake, listening to us argue? We didn't mean to wake you up," she asked in a contrite voice. She was really trying to determine if Hepzibah had heard them sneaking through the house or caught any of the words of their heated conversation.

"Oh, you didn't wake me up. I didn't hear you till I was on my way back from the water room. But Gabbatha, she sleeps light, she may have heard you arguing all night for all I know."

"We'll be quiet, I promise."

"You'll go to *sleep,* is what you'll do," Hepzibah replied. "Foolish girls. Don't think I'll be telling Jerusha to let you sleep in tomorrow, not if you don't have enough sense to take to your beds at a reasonable hour."

"I'm sorry," Rebekah said again. "We'll be quiet."

She apologized one more time, watched Hepzibah navigate the last few yards down the hall to her own room, and then shut the door. Flying across the room, she landed on the mat beside Martha, who had covered her mouth with her hands to press back the laughter.

"*Quiet!* She'll be awake all night now, straining to hear every word we say," Rebekah hissed.

"Spiteful old cat," Martha whispered. "*She* doesn't know what it feels like to slip out of the house at night and lie in the arms of a lover—"

"*Martha!*"

Martha rolled her eyes. "Well, what do you think? I've known him almost three months! Every time he goes away, I'm afraid I'm never going to see him again. I just want to hold him as close as I can."

"But, Martha—"

"Oh, like you never had such thoughts about your precious angel! Who, I notice, you did manage to find in the crowd tonight, even though *he* couldn't recognize *you*, so *you* had to be the one to walk up and introduce yourself to *him*—"

"Ssh! Be quiet! You still haven't told me—"

"Oh, we're done talking about me now. I want to hear about you and the angel O-ba-di-ah."

A rush of excitement and terror left Rebekah speechless for a moment, just at the sound of his name, and she realized all her preaching at Martha was hollow and hypocritical. Martha had known her illicit lover longer than Rebekah had known hers, but Martha had done nothing that Rebekah did not long to do—might someday do, if the opportunity arose and the temptation was great enough.

Well, the temptation was already great enough. What Rebekah was counting on was keeping the opportunities to a minimum.

"I—he is—he came there looking for me," Rebekah said. "He wants me to meet him again, but I—it is so frightening, because I *want* to, but I know I can't—I mean, I shouldn't, even if I could—"

Martha rolled to her stomach and propped herself up on her elbows. "You can," she said. "If you want to."

Rebekah stared at her. "How? And I don't want to—"

"You *do* want to! Don't lie to me, even if you've been lying to this poor angel. 'Oh, Obadiah, you beautiful angelo, I'm a good Jansai girl, and I don't sneak out of the house without my brother's escort.'"

Rebekah's face was burning. "Well, I don't! Certainly not to meet men! Martha, if your father knew—"

"My father doesn't know anything," Martha said shortly. "And your father is dead. You can do what you like."

"You know that's not true."

"Very well, but you *can* sneak out of this house and meet your angel friend. I can help you."

"You just want to disgrace yourself with this—Chesed boy!"

"If you keep scolding me," Martha said calmly, "I won't help you keep an assignation with your angel."

Rebekah opened her mouth to reply hotly that she did not *want* to keep an assignation with Obadiah, but she could not make the words come. Dear Jovah, blessed god, she was as bad as Martha— worse than Martha, because she at least seemed to have some notion of what was at risk, and she wanted to do it anyway.

"What must I do?" Rebekah asked humbly. "I want to see him again."

Martha returned to her father's house in the morning when Ephram came by to collect her, but her good-byes to Jerusha and Hepzibah and the other women were brief and sunny. "Oh, I'm coming back to spend the night," she said carelessly. "They're recaulking the garden wall at my father's house, and the smell drifts up to my room at night. I can't sleep at all, thinking I'm going to be poisoned."

"You know you're always welcome here," Jerusha said with a smile. "You keep Rebekah out of trouble."

"Yes, *awrie*, that's what I try to do," Martha said.

"Will you be here for dinner?" Jerusha asked.

"I don't think so. Ephram can't be spared till later, so it will be well after sundown, I think."

"Well, we won't look for you till you arrive."

Rebekah spent the day alternating between exhausted lethargy and sweet hysteria, imagining what the night might bring. She was willing enough to watch the baby when her mother impatiently asked her if there was *anything* productive she might be able to summon the energy for, and she spent a few pleasant hours entertaining him while he was awake and dozing beside him while he slept. He had just set- tled into another nap when her mother found her midway through the afternoon.

"Wondrous. You're actually still helping," Jerusha said dryly. "Asa's here and she wants to measure you."

Rebekah sat up drowsily. "What? Measure me?"

"For your bridal dress. Come on, the baby's fine. She's waiting in the fabric room."

Rebekah followed her mother through the shadowy halls of the upper level to the wide, cluttered chamber they called the fabric room. Here, stacked against every wall, were bolts of fabric of all descriptions: cotton for making everyday jeskas, silks for fashioning formal clothes, heavy canvas sheeting for repairing the tents on the traveling wagons, fine linens for bedding. Every woman of the household knew how to sew ordinary clothes or hem a curtain, but Asa was called in when special styling was required. She was a short, heavy woman with dull gray hair and thick features set in a complexion that, to this day, was flawless. She lived with her son's family in a grand house near the market, and every wealthy Jansai woman of the past two generations had hired her to design her wedding dress.

"Oh. You," Asa said when Rebekah followed her mother into the room and Asa got a look at her. Rebekah could only suppose Asa had been to so many houses and met so many young girls that she hadn't been able to remember what this particular bride looked like.

"Good afternoon, *awrie,*" Rebekah said more respectfully than she felt. There were half a dozen women scattered throughout the room engaged in their own projects, and Rebekah was sure they were all watching this exchange with interest.

"Don't just stand there, girl, come here where I can see you," Asa said sharply, motioning her over. Rebekah reluctantly crossed the floor to stand in the center of the room, directly under the skylight. It was the only place in all of the women's quarters that admitted natural sunlight, a decided advantage when a seamstress was picking out colors and textures. On dreary winter days when she'd been confined to the house too long, Rebekah had sometimes come to this room just to be cheered by the cold infusion of white sun.

"Huh. Now lift your arms. Now turn." Rebekah complied. "Where's my measuring string? Hold out your arms again." Rebekah waited patiently while Asa calculated the reach of her hands and the height of her shoulders from the floor. "Very well. Now strip down."

Rebekah dropped her arms and stared at the seamstress. "What?"

"You heard her. Come on, come on, give me your jeska," Jerusha said impatiently.

Rebekah was sure she heard a titter from someone in the room, probably Hector's sister's daughter, a snide and spiteful girl. "I am *not* getting naked here in front of—in front of all of you!" Rebekah said, crossing her arms against her chest.

"Jovah love me, I've seen your body so many times I could draw it from memory," Jerusha said.

"Not since I was about six years old!" Rebekah exclaimed.

"And when you've been bathing in the water room and when I was nursing you through some sickness and—oh, you ridiculous girl, just take everything off and don't be silly."

"I don't—"

"Stop arguing! For once! We will promise not to look at your delicate flesh any more than we can help."

Now there was no chance that anyone in the room was failing to eavesdrop on the conversation. Rebekah was completely mortified, convinced she was blushing on every square inch of her so-far-covered skin. "What does she have to measure my body for? I've never needed to be measured for any of my jeskas, except when I was growing taller."

"Wedding dress is different from a jeska," Asa said. "It shows your new husband how beautiful you are. What a prize you are. What a handful he'll take hold of when he whisks you into the bedroom."

Rebekah choked back a gasp and heard Hector's niece snicker again. "Mother," she whined.

Jerusha appeared to be about fed up. "Come on, now. Off with that jeska. We do not have all day to stand here and indulge your modesty."

Slowly, furiously, Rebekah untied the sashes of her jeska and let it fall to the floor at her feet. Under that was the hallis, made of straight panels of cloth that hung down her front and back, designed to cover her body should the folds of the jeska spread too wide or dance aside in the wind. Once she had slipped the hallis over her head, she was left standing only in a sheer, transparent covering of silk, designed to wick away heat in the summer and coddle the skin with warmth in winter. She stood there adamant, refusing to strip this final shield away.

"Fine, fine, it doesn't matter," Asa grumbled, holding up her measuring string again. "Lift your arms now. *Higher,* do you think I can duck under your elbow like that?"

This was even more intensely embarrassing, as Asa wrapped the string around Rebekah's chest, laying it right across her small breasts and snugging it tight. "She's thin enough to please him, but there's enough here to *really* please him," Asa said with a cackle, and Rebekah prayed that the floor would open along its seams and allow her to melt through. "That's a treat for any man on his wedding day."

"Built like my mother," Jerusha observed. "Of course, she died a fat old lady with a stomach that stuck out farther than her bosom, so this little girl better watch her appetite as she gets older."

"Good hips, though," Asa said, dropping the string to circle Rebekah's waist and cinching it in. "Nice and narrow."

Jerusha groaned. "Too narrow, if you ask me. Makes for a lot of screaming when the babies come."

"And a nice midsection. You want to watch the sweets, or your stomach will swell up big like your grandmother's, but right now you're as scrawny as a young boy," Asa said approvingly. "I had a figure like this one day. Wouldn't know it now."

"We all had figures like this one day," Jerusha said with a sigh. "But three children and a hard life and—" She shrugged. "That's the way of it, though. You're young and beautiful for five minutes, it seems."

"Then you've got a husband who can't be satisfied and babies who won't stop wailing, and you're camped out somewhere south of the Heldoras in a rainstorm," Asa agreed. "And you say, 'Send me back now! To my father's house! Everybody loved me, and I didn't have to lift a finger. I didn't have to wonder what this brute was going to say or do next—' "

"Asa," Jerusha reprimanded her, giving her daughter a quick

ANGEL-SEEKER 213

look. Rebekah was pulling her hallis over her head and trying to pretend she wasn't in the room. "We have a bride here."

"Misty-eyed now, red-eyed in the morning," Asa said incorrigibly. "That's what my mother told me the day before I got married. I was happy when that horse's ass died and I could go to my son's house to live in peace. Happier than I had been on any day since the day before my wedding."

"Asa," Jerusha said again.

"You've been fortunate in your marriages. Everyone says so."

"And Rebekah will be fortunate, too. Isaac is a wonderful boy."

Asa looked skeptical. "Not if he's anything like his father. Though Simon's not as bad as some, I'll give him that. Lucky for her she's not marrying Michael's boy. I told my son to keep his daughter out of that household, no matter how rich Michael is."

"Well, money can sweeten the bitterest poison, and Hector says Michael is not so bad," Jerusha claimed. "But it's Simon who's the far-thinker, Hector says. It's Simon who understands trading. We're better off with Simon. Rebekah will deal much better with Isaac."

"So!" Asa said, putting her hands on her broad hips and looking up at Rebekah. "What colors would you like to wear on this most happy occasion?"

It was another hour of torture before Rebekah could finally slip away from the fabric room and go bury herself in blushes in her own room. She had not, by the time Asa posed the question, been able to think of a single hue or fabric that would seem suitable for her wedding, but under the prodding of Asa and her mother, she had made some random selections. If she remembered correctly now, she would be attired in a collection of silky greens, some the palest sage, some striped with ochre and saffron. The dress would be molded to her shoulders, cling to her upper body, and be gathered tightly at the waist, in a display of immodesty that still left Rebekah speechless.

Everyone would see her in this garb—not only the women, gathered in the garlanded dining hall that would be decorated for the event, but the men as well, attending in the great open dining chamber that adjoined the women's room. It would not just be her male relatives and Isaac's family present to gawk at her in the thin, revealing

dress, but all of Hector's and Simon's business associates and the other
wealthy Jansai men of Breven. It had not occurred to her that she
would have to present herself to them in a state so close to nakedness
it almost made no difference. Her face would be veiled, but her body
would be on display, and everyone in the room would have his chance
to assess what Isaac would be taking to bed with him that night. The
thought was humiliating. She could stroll boldly down the streets of
Breven, dressed like a boy and showing off her bare face, and not feel
nearly the degree of shame she would suffer on her wedding day.

How could women stand to be married? And how could they
stand all the tribulations that came after?

Rebekah shivered on her mattress and concealed her face with her
pillow. She wanted to crawl under the mattress and hide her whole
body.

She was only partially recovered, and therefore fairly subdued,
when she joined the other women for dinner. Hector's niece made a
point of sitting beside her and talking very loudly about her own
prospects for getting married in the next year or so. *Are you insane?*
Rebekah wanted to scream at her. *Didn't you hear anything they were
saying?* But the girl talked on blithely of rich merchants and their
enterprising sons. Rebekah toyed with her food and thought she
might throw up.

Her spirits revived a little as the night wore on, however, and she
thought about what the evening might hold. She dropped by the
baby's room shortly after dinner to find her mother there, nursing
him.

"When did Martha say she would be back?" Jerusha asked.

"Sometime after dinner. I thought I'd go down to the garden and
wait for her."

"Hepzibah said you girls were up all night talking. No wonder
you were so irritable today."

"I wasn't irritable! Nobody wants to be told to go naked in front
of everybody in the household—"

"Well, you just make sure you girls go to sleep at a reasonable
hour tonight. I don't want you dragging around all day tomorrow,
cross-eyed and crabby."

Rebekah shrugged and headed for the door without even giving the baby his customary kiss. "We'll try," she said shortly. "Good night."

An hour later, she was down in the garden, sitting on a narrow ornamental bench and feeling the air cool down around her. It was full dark already, though the generous three-quarter moon cast down enough light to see by. Rebekah had Jordan's clothes on underneath her own, but didn't want to take her jeska off just yet in case Hepzibah or Gabbatha or somebody else came out for a late-night stroll. She could hear voices on the street, boys whooping out their high spirits as they headed toward the fair, men more soberly discussing market values and probable bargains to be had from certain sellers. Now and then she caught the echo of footsteps as a solitary reveler made his way toward the festival lights. Then, for a few minutes, silence.

A few moments later, voices again. "When will you be ready in the morning?" Ephram asked.

"I'm at your convenience," Martha said. "I wouldn't think you'd want to come too early."

"Father's meeting with Uriah at the city rim at noon," Ephram said. "He wants me with him. I'll come for you about an hour before."

"That sounds good. Thank you."

A quick knock on the gate, and Rebekah slid back the locks and opened it. "Going back to the fair tonight?" she asked Ephram.

He shook his head and looked glum. "Merchants at the house that Father's entertaining," he said. "I have to be there. Sometimes I think—" He shook his head as if to shake away the unworthy thoughts, and then burst out, "I don't know that I want to be a man any time soon! It's all talk and barter, barter and talk. Father hasn't been to the fair once this year. He never has any fun."

"Father thinks it's fun to make money," Martha said. "I wouldn't feel too much pity for him."

Rebekah felt a twinge of sympathy, something she rarely felt for the cocky Ephram. She wasn't so sure she wanted to grow into adulthood either.

"See you tomorrow, then," Martha said, and came inside the garden, shutting the gate behind her.

They waited in tense silence until they heard his footsteps die away. Then Martha pulled off her veil and jeska, revealing the boy's clothes underneath. "Charcoal?" she whispered.

"Here," Rebekah whispered back, pulling it out of one of Jordan's pockets. She slipped off her own jeska and folded it carefully, hiding it in the shadow thrown by the bench. Then she quickly wrapped her hair in the loose headpiece the young boys favored. It felt strange to have her face so exposed that she didn't even have locks of hair to cover her cheeks. "Can you see well enough to fix my face?"

"Yes," Martha said. "Hold still."

Ten minutes after Ephram had left her behind, Martha stepped back through the garden gate, Rebekah right behind her. It was exhilaratingly terrifying to saunter down that street with no companion except another woman, totally at the mercy of the god and the inattention of the other fair-goers. Even once she had tied her feather mask in place, Rebekah felt vulnerable and on display. Her first few steps were so shaky that Martha hissed at her to hurry up, hold her head high, walk like a *man* if she was going to walk down the street at all.

Rebekah took a deep breath, envisioning Ephram's customary swagger, and caught up with her cousin.

This night they did not aim for the crowded makeshift boulevards of the festival but skirted the most populated part of the city and headed for the hotel district instead. "I'll come back for you two hours after midnight," Martha said. "*Don't* be late! Be waiting for me outside in the shadows or just inside the door."

"Wait—if you're leaving me at the hotel—you can't walk through Breven by *yourself!*" Rebekah exclaimed.

"Oh, I'll be fine."

"But you—where are you going? How far?"

"Not far. And I'll make sure Chesed comes back with me to the hotel."

"Why can't he meet you at the hotel?"

"Because I didn't know until last night that a hotel was involved," Martha said reasonably. "So I couldn't tell him where to meet me."

"So you—if I hadn't come with you—you were going to go out by yourself? At *night?*"

Martha rolled her eyes behind her mask and quickened her pace. "I'm going to stop telling you things if you act so shocked every time I open my mouth."

"No—but—by *yourself*—it's so dangerous—"

"And I don't think you have any right to scold me, seeing as you're scampering off to meet an *angel,* who is even worse than a Manadavvi, if you were to ask our fathers—"

"Yes, but I—that's not it—walking around alone—"

Martha gave a little snort that fit very well with her costume. "I don't think the world is nearly as dangerous as we have been led to believe," she said scornfully. "We hide in our houses all day—all our lives—and what is there to fear outside their walls? Only the brothers and fathers and sons of our friends! Will they harm us? I—"

"Yes," Rebekah interjected. "You heard that story. Two years ago. About the girl who was caught on the streets of Breven without an escort. She was stoned to death by the men who saw her, and her family never asked for reparation. They would have stoned her themselves, if they'd known where she was."

"Well, that's not going to happen to us."

Rebekah wanted to ask her how she was so sure, but she knew the answer: Martha was sure because that was the way Martha wanted it to be. Rebekah was conscious with every step of the perils around them, but she continued on, determined as her cousin, because that was how she wanted it to be, too.

No, she certainly had no right to scold Martha.

The Hotel Verde finally materialized on a poorly lit street several blocks away from the fair. They could hear faint strains of music and catch the arching halo of torchlight over the market district, but this particular street was both quiet and dark. The hotel itself looked solemn and judgmental, built of thick white stone that was designed to turn away summer heat. Three steps led up to a banded wooden door. There were no hedges or ornamental buttresses behind which a runaway might hide.

Rebekah had never been inside a hotel before. She found it hard to guess what it must be like, though she imagined it to be a very big house with nothing but sleeping chambers. She hoped she did not walk through this door and into someone's bedroom.

"Two hours after midnight," she said, her voice wavering a bit. "I'll be here."

Unexpectedly, Martha leaned over to kiss her on the cheek. Rebekah drew back sharply, hoping no one was near enough to see. Jansai boys did not kiss each other under any circumstances. "Good luck," Martha said, smiling behind her mask. "Enjoy yourself."

Rebekah nodded and climbed the steps. The door resisted a moment before giving way to the pressure of her hand, and she stepped inside.

She was in a huge atrium, tiled in a creamy tan ceramic and filled with plants and vines. She could hear the sound of running water—there was an extravagance in a desert town!—though she couldn't locate its source. Discreet gaslight rimmed the room to create a soft glow, easy to see by though far from harsh. A young woman was seated at a desk in the center of the atrium, looking over some papers.

She looked up when the door shut behind Rebekah and seemed to wait for the visitor to step forward. When Rebekah stayed frozen by the door, the young woman stood and walked over, a pleasant smile on her face.

"Yes, *m'kash?*" she asked in a quiet voice. *M'kash,* Rebekah thought. *She thinks I'm a boy.* Of course, Rebekah had gone to a great deal of trouble to make everyone think she was a boy, but she hadn't been sure the ruse would work. "May I help you?"

"I'm looking—I'm looking for one of your guests," Rebekah said, trying to pitch her own voice in its lowest natural register. "I have a message for him."

"Would you like paper and ink? I can deliver a note."

Rebekah shook her head. "No, I have to see him."

"Is he here? Is he expecting you?"

"He is—he is possibly expecting me. I thought I might await him in his room if he is not here."

The Manadavvi woman looked skeptical. She had huge eyes and perfectly slanted cheekbones, and she was scented with floral creams.

Rebekah wondered why Obadiah would even be interested in seeing a plain Jansai woman again when he could gaze every day at the face of a Manadavvi heiress.

"If he has told me he is expecting visitors," the woman said, "I can allow you to wait in his room. But if not—you understand—our guests value their privacy, and I cannot be certain you truly have business with him—"

"It's urgent," Rebekah burst out.

The woman nodded gravely. "And who is it you're looking for?"

Rebekah took a deep breath. "The angel. Obadiah."

Now the woman gave her a sharp look as if suddenly trying to see behind the mask of black and gold feathers. Rebekah wondered if something had given her away—a change in her voice, the sudden desperation that no Jansai boy would show—but the woman merely nodded. "I believe he is in his room, in fact," she said quietly. "He returned shortly after dinnertime and has not left again. He must surely be awaiting your visit."

"Can you take me to him?"

"Follow me."

They crossed the atrium, passing by a low fountain of rocks and ferns that was the source of the gurgling noise. Hallways opened off the atrium in five spokes, and the Manadavvi led Rebekah down the one guarded by a blue marble statue of an eagle in flight. *Luminauzi work,* thought Rebekah automatically, since that type of stone was quarried only near the Blue City. Not that she cared where it came from or whether or not the artist had been any good. She noted it only so she would know her passage out—or her return course, should she ever be back here.

They passed five doors on the right and six on the left—Rebekah counting to mark her way—before the woman stopped at a door on her right. And knocked. And waited less than thirty seconds before the door was flung open, and Obadiah stood there, feathers making an aureole around his body, his face as eager and boyish as Jordan's on a day he expected a rare treat.

"I brought you a visitor, angelo," the woman said, but she might have been made of porcelain and fabric for all the attention the angel paid her. He was staring straight at Rebekah, and he looked as nervous as she felt.

"You came," he said. "Jovah and all the angels rejoice."

CHAPTER SIXTEEN

At first it was awkward. They stood in the middle of a gracious room crammed with riches, and just looked at each other.

"Do you—are you hungry?" Obadiah asked suddenly. "I have food and—oh, or if you're thirsty! Wine and juice and water. I didn't know what you might like."

"I'm not allowed to drink much wine," she said, and then wished she hadn't said it, because it made her sound like a stupid little girl. "But I like it," she added quickly.

"Maybe one glass," he said. "I could use it myself but—but maybe I shouldn't be getting you drunk! I'm committing all sorts of crimes here. I suppose I shouldn't add that one, too."

She smiled behind her mask. "One glass, then. One small one."

"That's good," he said and hurried across the room to a table where he had set out all sorts of delicacies. White cheese and fresh bread and small purple fruits that she did not recognize. Maybe they were cousin to those delicate crops that Martha's Manadavvi friend harvested on his father's land. He was beside her again in a few moments, two fragile wineglasses in his hands. He extended one to her, and then drew it back.

"I think—if you would—I mean, I don't see how you can drink through the mask," he said.

"Oh." Of course it was silly to think she would leave this

ridiculous mask on the whole time she was with the angel. She had done so many other more unpardonable acts that allowing him to look on her face would be the least of her sins. Still, she felt dreadfully self-conscious as she put her hands up to untie the strings. She slipped the mask into her pocket and then gave Obadiah a tilted, defiant look.

"Oh—" he said and started laughing, though he tried to stop himself. "You are—I remember the face and the eyes very well but—"

She was both humiliated and furious. "But what? But I am not so beautiful as you thought I was?" She clawed for the mask again, but he had set down both glasses and caught her wrists in his hands before she could even lift it toward her face.

"No, your face is perfect and I am *so* happy to be given the privilege of seeing it again. But you—there is—I don't remember this sort of black dust being on your chin before."

"*Oh!*" Now she remembered the charcoal and felt her skin flame under the flimsy disguise. She had had charcoal on her chin last night, too, but he had seen her face so briefly by such unreliable light that he might not have noticed. Now Rebekah turned her head from side to side, trying to conceal her features. "Oh, I forgot. This is awful—"

"It's a different look, but not unattractive."

She pulled away from him and he let his hands fall. "It's supposed to look like a beard. If someone sees behind the mask. So no one suspects who I am."

"Very effective," he said solemnly. "Though I have to confess I am not quite fooled."

"But you *would* be at night on the street," she said. "Is there— do you have some cloth I can dampen so I can wipe this away?"

"Yes, but if you're going back out later tonight, maybe you should leave it in place?"

She gave him one quick look of exasperation. "I am not going to sit here and try to talk to you knowing I have charcoal all over my face. It is too embarrassing!"

"Then let me get a wet cloth. I'll be back in a moment."

He slipped through a doorway, and she heard a series of small splashes. Surely that could not be a water room, his very own, attached to the bedroom? She could not imagine such luxury. He returned quickly with a damp towel in his hands. She reached for it but he pulled it back.

"Let me," he said. "I am not yet accustomed to the thrill of stripping away your disguises."

That made her blush again, but she squared her shoulders and turned her face up to him. "You don't have to rub very hard," she said. "But it will ruin your towel."

"Not my towel," he murmured. He had one hand under her chin, and with the other he slowly and pleasurably ran the thick cloth over her skin. She imagined the charcoal smearing, then wiping away on his second and third pass. His face was so close that she could see the whorls and texture of his skin, not as fine as hers and stubbled very lightly with a true beard. He smelled like soap and feathers, as if he had bathed recently, in anticipation of her arrival.

"There," he said, backing away and dropping his hand. His eyes, blue as summer, scanned her face. He smiled. "All clean."

"Thank you. Now I do need that wine."

He handed her a glass, and she sipped from it as she walked slowly about the room. Her practiced eye priced the wall hangings, the furnishings, and the flooring. "I've never been in a hotel room before," she remarked. "Are they all like this?"

He laughed. "Hardly. Most places I've stayed have been dank little taverns in some town so small it doesn't have a name. Taproom on the ground floor, three musty rooms upstairs, and you're pretty sure the bedding hasn't been changed since the last guest stayed overnight." He made a sweeping gesture with one hand, and his wing rose and fell with the motion. "But this is a Manadavvi establishment, so you can be assured of every comfort."

"I think I'd like to be a Manadavvi," she said, pausing in her perambulations and turning to face him. Six feet of hand-woven rug lay on the floor between them.

He laughed again. "Well, they're greedy, arrogant, and impossible to trust, but they are sophisticated," he said. "I wouldn't like to be one, and I'm not always at ease when I'm with them, but I certainly enjoy their hospitality."

"But you're only here for another day, aren't you?" she asked, sipping from her wineglass.

He was watching her. "But I'll be coming back quite often."

She gave him a half-smile. "It was so easy to slip out of the house tonight," she said. "I always thought more people would be watching. My mother or my aunts. But no one paid any attention at all. And we walked down the streets and no one even looked at us."

"We?"

"My cousin and I. Martha."

"Oh yes. I met her last night. The wild one."

Rebekah nodded emphatically. "Wilder than I even thought."

"I take it she was not shocked when she learned of your destination?"

"*My* destination! Her own is even more appalling. And the things she has been telling me—sometimes I wonder if I have ever known her as well as I thought."

"People will surprise you every day," he said. "You've surprised me tonight."

She gave another little smile. "You didn't think I'd come?"

"I didn't think you'd even want to come."

She started her measured pacing again. He pivoted slowly to keep his eyes on her, his wing feathers dipping and trailing over the sculptured pattern of the rug. "It's confusing," she admitted. "Part of me is shocked at my own behavior. I don't even know you. What am I doing here? Why do I care if I ever see you again? And part of me—" She shook her head and continued pacing, keeping her gaze trained on the carpet. "Part of me is so happy and so excited that I can't even think. That I can't even weigh the risks and stop to examine my own behavior. It's like I have two people inside of me, and one of them is someone I never met before." She glanced over at him, then back at the rug. "But she seems more real to me than Martha, or my brother, or myself—the self I always thought I was."

She fell silent then, not sure if she'd said too much, not sure if she'd said anything that made any sense. He waited a moment, seeming to consider his own thoughts, and then spoke in a similarly flat and quiet voice. "I am having some of those same battles," he said. "You saved my life, and so I owe you something, but that doesn't explain this great—this incredible need I feel to see you again. It's like how you wake up in the morning and all you can think of is food, and until you eat you can't think of anything else. Except it's not just in the morning, and it's not a craving I can explain. You are—what do I know about you? You're a stranger. I thought you could only miss the people you already consider your friends."

She gave him a swift look for that. "Exactly!"

He shrugged. "But that's how it feels. Like I miss you. Like you are a part of my life that's missing. I don't know why that should be so."

"I don't know anything about love," she said hesitantly. "Maybe that's what it always feels like."

He grinned a little. "I have played at love from time to time," he said, "and sometimes I wasn't playing. But this feels different to me."

She stopped pacing and faced him. "I'm glad it's different," she said. "With me."

"I imagine everything would be different with you."

"But I don't know what happens next," she said.

He took a step nearer, and she did not back away. "Why did you come here tonight?" he asked.

"They fitted me for my wedding dress today."

He smiled faintly. "That might be a reason not to come."

"And the things they said—" She gave her head a series of little shakes. "I'm not so sure I will enjoy being married."

He seemed to be choosing his words with care. "I don't know what marriage to a Jansai man is like. Some people—people who are not Jansai—find marriage quite pleasant."

"My mother seems happy enough."

"Do you want to marry him? Isaac?"

She was surprised he had remembered the name of her betrothed—but then, not surprised. She thought she would remember the name of any woman Obadiah might casually mention. "It doesn't have anything to do with wanting or not wanting. It's what my life holds."

He came another step closer. They were only a few feet apart now. "But if you could choose?" he said. "Would you marry him?"

She gazed up at him, aware that her confusion and longing must be showing on her face, not having any idea how to conceal them. "Not just yet," she replied in a low voice.

He put his hands on her shoulders, and she could feel their heat and weight. It was like he was made of heat, fashioned of fever wrapped around solid bones. "If I kissed you," he said, "would it frighten you?"

"No," she said. "It would make me happy."

His hands slid from her shoulders and around her back as he drew her closer in. It was like being embraced by fire, exhilarating and delicious. His wings drifted around her like white flickers of harmless flame. His mouth on hers was heavy, sweet, and slow, and the kiss itself was alchemy; it changed her. She did not know what knowledge her features would show or what shape her body would hold once that kiss was ended.

He lifted his mouth, but the magic was not broken; she was still in the process of transformation. "I don't know," he said, in a slow, drugged voice, "how much of love you want to learn this night."

"I have to leave again two hours after midnight," she said. "How much can I learn by then?"

He gave a soft laugh. "It could take a lifetime to learn the whole library," he said, "but a few hours can give you the basic text."

She could not help giggling. She lifted her hands shyly to put them on either side of his face, marveling at the rough textures, the unfamiliar scents. So strange to have somebody else's body this close, to be aware of every breath and heartbeat of a separate human being. So strange, and so intoxicating. "I think I've learned some of the alphabet already," she said. "I want to see what's in the book."

He laughed aloud. "Well, then," he said, dropping his head to kiss her again. "Chapter one . . ."

Several hours later, lying on her own mat in her own room, with Martha peacefully slumbering beside her, Rebekah just accustomed herself to the idea that she would never sleep again. She had almost convinced Martha that she would never speak again, since she had refused to say much during that long, terrifying walk home, when the streets appeared to be full of drunken rowdies who could not bear the idea that the harvest fair had come to its wild conclusion.

Twice they'd been engulfed by large groups of young men who wanted to assimilate them into their parties. "Come with us! Back to my father's tent!" had been the basic cry, and it had taken Martha's angry rant against "my stupid father who never allows me to have any fun" before they were allowed to go on their way home to beat their professed curfews. Each time, though, they had been forced to drink a few swallows of high-proof liquor from a dirty goatskin bag as a mark of fellowship before they were permitted to pass. Rebekah had never been so relieved to see the back gate of Hector's house, or felt so safe and happy as she stepped inside the garden.

"Sweet Jovah singing, what a night," Martha said, briefly leaning against the gate, removing her mask, and letting her anxiety melt away. Then her face lit up with an impish expression. "And in so many ways, what a *night!*" she exclaimed. "But you! You haven't told me anything!"

"There isn't much to tell."

"You were with the man for three or four hours. I think there is something to tell."

"We talked."

"You *talked!* I didn't spirit you through the streets of Breven so you could *talk* to the angel. Did he kiss you?"

"Yes."

"And?"

"And I am tired and I have to go to sleep," Rebekah said. Without another word, she turned and threaded her way through the garden and into the silent house. Martha followed, perforce silent herself, as they crept up the stairwells and down the hallways. They passed Rebekah's door and went all the way to the end of the hall to clean themselves up in the water room. Under cover of the gurgling pipe, Martha began her interrogation again, but Rebekah would not answer.

"Was it *bad?* Why aren't you telling me anything?" Martha finally demanded.

"Oh no. It wasn't bad."

"Then—?"

Rebekah gave her one last, desperate look. "Because I cannot *talk* about it," she said in a low urgent whisper. "I have to *think* about it first."

And that answer, strangely enough, seemed to satisfy her cousin. They finished their quick baths, put on clean sleeping clothes, bundled up their dirty boys' clothes, and returned to Rebekah's room. Martha was asleep in five minutes.

Rebekah, of course, would never sleep again.

She had thought kissing brought a body close to a body, but the act of love made kissing seem a light thing, a casual touch that was suitable for the public viewing of the marketplace. She had not realized that the angel would touch every inch of her skin, would seem awed by every curve and hollow and hidden architecture of bone. Nor had she thought to wonder how a man's body might differ from her own—not just in his private parts, but in the layering of his muscles and the tailoring of his hips. They had stood side by side and naked before the mirror just so she could absorb the differences.

"And all men look like this?" she had asked.

He had laughed. "Allowing for differences of weight and height and athletic condition, more or less."

"How strange," she had said, and he had laughed again.

They had laughed a lot. He had seemed delighted by everything she asked, every observation she made, and it had not occurred to her that she shouldn't say or ask anything. There was a great deal, she had discovered, that she did not know. Jerusha had fairly briefly outlined to her what she might expect in the marriage bed, and overheard conversations from other married women had allowed her to imagine some variations, but it still had never been clear to her exactly how everything came together.

Obadiah had explained everything, and then he had demonstrated.

Once the initial pain was past, she found the entire experience much more enjoyable than she had been led to expect. She had not known that a breast or a lip or a patch of skin on the inside of her forearm could react with such feeling. It would not have occurred to her that fingertips playing down the length of her spine could cause her to gasp or tremble. It had simply not crossed her mind that her body was an instrument to be played for pleasure. The Jansai women talked of marital duties and the hope of bearing children. They never described experiences like this.

"And this is what it's *always* like?" Rebekah had asked the angel as they lay wrapped together on the bed. Her hand was spread across his chest just so she could feel the fine pale curls under her fingertips; her head was resting on his shoulder. His wing was laid across her from chin to toe, so that she could not even see her own amazing body.

"Actually . . . no," he said. "This was better than most."

"But why?"

"Why was it better?"

"Why isn't it always like this?"

He laughed. "Because sometimes you're in a hurry, and sometimes your partner is not interested in all the—all the exploring, and sometimes you're just interested in quick gratification, and sometimes you're tired and your body doesn't respond as you'd like, and sometimes the person you're with doesn't care if you feel good or not—and, I don't know, there are a lot of different factors."

"And why was this better than most?"

He kissed her quickly on the mouth. "Because it was with you."

"That made it better?"

"It's always better if it's someone you love."

She was silent a long moment. "But you don't love me."

"Actually," he said, "I think I do."

"But how do you know?"

He sighed a little, and his arm drew her nearer. Under the thin silk of hair, the warm layer of skin, and the hard cage of bone, she could feel the beating of his heart. "Because I have truly never felt like this before," he said.

"But you've loved a lot of women," she said. Her voice made it a question.

"Some. Not a lot. Not as many as some angels."

"And I'm different?"

"Oh, you're so different."

"But how? In what way?"

He laughed again, a small, helpless sound that gave her the answer before his words. "I don't know. I don't know. But you are— by every measure I have—absolutely unique."

"Will you be here tomorrow night?" she asked.

He had lifted his head to look down at her. "You think you can come back tomorrow night? I hadn't even dared to ask you."

"I don't know. I've been trying to work it out. I think I can. I can try."

"I'm so worried about you. I'm so afraid something will happen to you—and because of me."

She shrugged a little, feeling the caress of feathers across her skin as her shoulders moved. "I'll try. If I can't leave the house, I won't come here. But if you think you'll be here—"

"Oh, if you think you might be able to sneak out, I'll be here. I'll sit in this hotel room all day, and I won't even go out for food."

"You can leave during the day. I won't be able to come till the night. I think. Unless . . ." Her voice stopped as she considered possibilities. "No. Not during the day. Tomorrow night."

"Around the same time?"

"I would think so. But I might not be able to make it."

"I won't count on it. Except I'm counting on it already."

"I know. So am I."

They talked like that, circuitously and sleepily, for another twenty minutes. And then it was time to dress and say good-bye, and head to the lobby to meet Martha. Obadiah had wanted to come downstairs and wait outside with her, but Rebekah had refused. "You are too noticeable," she said. "If you were just some Manadavvi lordling or a peasant farmer—but you cannot hide those wings. Everybody knows who you are."

"But I'm worried about you. I wish I could escort you safely home."

"You certainly can't do that!"

"What if something happens to you on the street? You don't show up tomorrow night, and I think it's because you can't slip out of the house, and it's really because you were killed walking home?"

She laid her hands flat against his chest, a gesture that had new sense and meaning now that she had touched his bare skin. "I'll be fine," she said. "Don't worry about me."

He gave her a small, unhappy smile. "I'm afraid that's what my life holds from now on," he said. "Worry about you."

"Good night," she said, lifting her head for a kiss, which he dropped willingly upon her mouth. "Tomorrow, if I can."

And she had let herself from the room, and swiftly had gone past the eleven doors and the blue statue and the lobby fountain. A young man was now sitting at the desk in the middle of the atrium, but he merely nodded and said, "Good night, *m'kash*," as she walked by. She pushed open the heavy door, and there was Martha, just now stepping up to the hotel, toying with her silver necklace just in case Rebekah couldn't tell who she was.

"Excellent timing!" Martha greeted her gaily. Her voice was pitched low, but it still carried an exultant note. Rebekah didn't need to ask how well her cousin's evening had gone. "Or have you been peering out here every five minutes for the past hour?"

"No, I just got here."

"And how did your evening go? My own was wonderful."

"It was very good," Rebekah said. "Come on, we have to get moving."

And so they had begun that perilous journey home, but Rebekah had never felt truly in danger. For she was aware, by some greatly heightened lover's instinct, of the instant they were joined by a ghostly but inexorable companion, flying above them too high and silently to draw attention. He escorted them all the way from the market to Hector's garden, hovering overhead when they were approached by strangers—perfectly willing, she was sure, to swoop down and snatch her off to safety should the need arise. She felt the shadow of angel wings pass over her face as she locked the garden gate behind them. She knew then that he had made one great circle in the night sky and was heading back to the Hotel Verde now that she was safe.

She didn't tell Martha this. She didn't tell Martha any of it. She didn't know how you could ever talk about things that mattered so much.

CHAPTER SEVENTEEN

Elizabeth was more disappointed than she had thought possible when her monthly bleeding arrived, right on schedule.

She had made her way to David's bed three more times in the intervening weeks, always after some not-so-chance meeting in the hallways in which she contrived to remind him of her existence. Each time he had given her first a blank look, then a slight frown of concentration, before his face broke into that roguish smile and he pronounced her name with real pleasure. "Elizabeth!" he said each time, and sashayed down the hall to place his hands on her shoulders or drop a kiss on her cheek. "My little laundress! Still working hard for your living, I see."

Each time, she had returned some answer but combined it with a flirtatious smile, and he had asked what she was doing that night or the following night. And she had been available, and he had always arrived more or less on time, and they had, as Faith put it, "given in to their emotions." David had never been entirely sober at any of these rendezvouses, and none of them were any more romantic than the first one, but at least Elizabeth knew what to expect now, and she didn't really mind.

It bothered her that she didn't feel any deep emotion for the dark angel. She had thought surely some kind of passion would develop between them, or at least a certain affection, but to date she hadn't been able to muster up more than a fierce sense of triumph each time he asked her back to his bed. *Yes. A victory.* This was what she had come to Cedar Hills for; she was on the way to achieving her destiny.

So it was with great bitterness that she discovered her blood-stained undergarments that morning and knew that her destiny was still at least a few assignations away.

Faith tried to cheer her up as they sat together in the kitchen, scrounging up an early morning meal before heading off to their work-stations. "It's very difficult for an angel to sire a child," Faith said in a sympathetic voice. "And just as hard for an angel to bear one! That's why there are so few angels in the world and so many more mortals. Don't be discouraged! You just have to try again. And maybe again."

Elizabeth sighed. "Well, I don't even think David likes me that much. I don't know how many more chances I'm going to have."

"With David! But there are other angels in Cedar Hills!"

"None that I've had any luck with."

"You can't give up, though. You just got here, after all. Some girls have been here *years* and never had an angel baby."

"That doesn't make me feel any better!"

Faith giggled. "Come out with me tonight," she said. "They're having a concert in the square. There will be plenty of angels singing there, and who knows? Maybe one of them will stop to talk to you."

So Elizabeth had put on her green dress and accompanied Faith to the concert, and stood there the whole night shivering, because it was really too cool to be standing around outside, even with a coat on. The only angels she saw were traveling in pairs and bunches, great disdainful flocks of otherworldly creatures who didn't even notice the frail human forms flitting around them. David was among them, his wings glittering in the light thrown by the ornamental lamps, his mouth curved into a perpetual halfwit's grin. She stayed long enough to hear him sing a quick, rather risqué folk song, and had to confess she didn't much care for his voice.

It was going to be hard to make herself keep trying to love him, but she was determined to do it.

The following day she was yawning over one of the soapy cauldrons when Doris hunted her up. "You've got a visitor," the older woman said.

Elizabeth looked up hopefully, but Doris shook her head. "Not one of *them*," she said. Not an angel. Nonetheless, Elizabeth dried off her clothes and batted her way through the steam to the front of the room, to find the healer Mary waiting for her.

"I'd bet half the girls who work here go home with lung troubles," Mary said, glancing around and deliberately inhaling the heavily starched air. Her thin blond hair was already frosted with moisture. "How can you breathe in here? Must kill everybody off in a few years."

"Doris has worked in laundry rooms her whole life, and she seems pretty healthy," Elizabeth said. She was smiling, though; she was pleased to see the healer. "And so far, I seem to be fine."

Mary appraised her. "Yes, you're the type. You look languorous and fragile, but you're strong as a Bethel farm girl. Probably never been sick a day in your life."

Elizabeth smiled again, a little more ruefully. "Only when I was a little girl and there was someone to take care of me. Since I've been caring for myself, there hasn't been time."

"Listen, my assistant just took off for northern Gaza with her young man, says she'll be back in two weeks, but I need some extra hands while she's gone. I'll pay you what you're making here if you'd like to come work with me. The job might be permanent, you never know. She says she's coming back, but she's got the smell about her, and I wouldn't be surprised if she's carrying when she gets back."

"The smell?" Elizabeth repeated. "Carrying what?"

Mary sniffed. "That baby smell. She'll be carrying a child when she returns."

Elizabeth paused for a moment to reflect what a useful skill that would be to have—the ability to know just by scent if someone was pregnant—and then she focused on what Mary had said to her. The healer had made the offer once before, but Elizabeth had never seriously considered it. "You want me to come work for you?" she said slowly.

Mary nodded. "For a couple of weeks first, to see if you like it, and then longer if everything works out. But I don't want you to lose this job if it's one you particularly like."

Well, it was hard to develop any true love for doing laundry, but the job did put her in a position to see angels on a somewhat regular basis, and she had been able to parlay that to her advantage a few times. Though it hadn't worked out all that well so far, she had to admit. And it would be nice to spend a couple of weeks away from the damp heat and the constant chemical smell of soaking clothes.

"Can I talk to Doris?" she asked. "And see what she thinks?"

"By all means."

Doris, perennially philosophical, shrugged and nodded. "We always need extra hands here, so if you don't like nursing, come on back," the small woman said. "It might do you good to get a change of scenery."

"If anybody comes looking for me—" Elizabeth began, and then blushed and fell silent.

Doris gave her that small smile. "I know where Mary can be found. I'll send anyone who inquires after you down to her address."

So Elizabeth took off her limp apron and gathered up her posessions and followed Mary out into the bright day.

"I have rooms in the main hall, there," Mary said, pointing to the central building of the Cedar Hills complex, where Nathan and Magdalena lived. She didn't pause, though, and Elizabeth walked on beside her. "People come looking for me there, but most of the day I'm out checking on patients. I try to leave behind a list of where I might be found in case an emergency comes up."

"Are you the only healer in Cedar Hills?"

"Feels like it sometimes. But no. There are two others, both good. But the city grows a little every day. We could use five healers, or eight." Mary glanced over at her. "Maybe if you're any good at it, you could become a healer someday. You've got a cool head and a sharp eye."

No one had ever given Elizabeth such a compliment before, and she contemplated it as they kept on walking. She herself rarely strayed past the main four blocks that made up the heart of Cedar Hills: the dorms and halls and shops whose construction had been completed before Elizabeth ever arrived in the city. Now they were traveling down streets that were mostly mud and debris, past framed-in structures that were starting to resemble houses, cafes, and stables. Wagonloads of brick and hay were everywhere; the sounds of hammering and sawing and shouting added weight and color to the breeze.

A cool head and a sharp eye. It was true that she didn't panic at the first sign of trouble, but that was usually because she was so frustrated at the thought of the extra work that was going to be caused by this fresh problem that she didn't have time to have hysterics. She tended to act fast if a crisis erupted, since that generally meant she'd have less to do later to fix things up. Like the time there'd been the fire in James's kitchen. She hadn't particularly wanted to be rushing for the cistern while she called for help, but she had figured the sooner she doused the flames, the less soot she'd have to clean from the kitchen walls the next day.

"I'm practical, I guess," Elizabeth said at last. "Not by nature, though. By necessity."

Mary snorted. "No, by nature all of us are lazy little brats who whine for attention and cry when we don't get what we want," she said. "It's the ones who stop whining and start working that appeal to me."

"I don't know anything about medicine," Elizabeth said.

"No. But I'll bet you learn fast."

In a few minutes they arrived at a massive construction site on the very edge of town. Dirt was piled all around a deep hole in the ground, and loads of lumber and brick had been dumped randomly on either side of the excavation. Part of the structure was already standing, though it looked like the central portion had collapsed. Half a dozen men stood in a cluster, arguing over a long scroll of paper, and a few others stood in isolated groups, watching or taking a pull on a waterskin. Another small group knelt around a tarp spread on the ground, and one of the men in this group waved them over.

"What happened?" Elizabeth asked, more curious than apprehensive.

"Beam fell on his head and could have killed him. There's probably not a lot I can do for him if he's alive, and nothing if he's dead, but if he's awake, I can give him something for the pain."

The group stepped back to allow them access, and both women knelt on the edges of the tarp. The man was indeed alive, grunting from pain, and twitching aside when Mary put her hand to his skull.

"Hold still if you can," she said. "I need to see how deep this goes."

Elizabeth was a little shocked at how much blood was smeared all over the man's face and shirt, and how much blood had soaked through the tarp near the back of his head. Good thing she wouldn't be doing this man's laundry. She listened as Mary asked him a litany of questions about whether he'd lost consciousness and whether he'd thrown up, and she opened Mary's satchel when the healer told her to.

"Get out that big needle—see it?—that's it. And the black thread. We're going to have to sew this man up."

"Sew up my *head?*" he exclaimed, writhing on his blanket. "Jovah's bones, Jovah's balls—"

"Jovah will thank you to speak of him with a little more courtesy," Mary said crisply. "Elizabeth, first we'll need to clean the wound. And then numb it, before we try to sew it. I'm afraid he's not going to lie still, though, so I may need you to hold him down. Though you might not be big enough—"

"I'll hold him down," said one of the men who had stood guard over the injured fellow.

Elizabeth glanced up at him—and then held the glance a moment when he smiled down at her. He was fairly tall, rangy, and spare, a man who looked like he'd been built to be bigger but had suffered too many years of privation. His brown eyes were huge, and his broad facial bones seemed set over hollow cheeks, but his smile was still easy and friendly. It took her a moment to absorb the significance of his mahogany-colored skin and silky black hair, cut somewhat carelessly around his face. He was an Edori.

"I'm pretty strong," the Edori added. "He won't be able to shake me off."

"Good. I'm sure we'll need you. But first can you bring me some water? This looks nasty."

"Sure."

The Edori departed, and Mary motioned Elizabeth to come closer. "Can you put his head on your lap? I need a better angle. Can somebody get me a towel to put over her dress? You're going to be covered in blood."

Normally she was covered in grease and soap and starch. It

wasn't like she wore her best clothes to work. "I don't mind," Elizabeth said with a shrug.

But someone brought her a scrap of canvas, none too clean itself, and she laid that across her knees before she lifted the hurt man's head. In a few moments, the Edori returned with a bucket of water, and they went to work on their patient. Elizabeth watched in detached fascination as Mary carefully picked out splinters and bits of dirt from the deep cut that drew a bloody line diagonally through the man's matted hair. He continued to grunt and jerk as Mary's hands touched tender areas, but the healer worked on without paying him much attention.

"Now, can you mix a little of this water with the fluid in that bottle—yes—just stir them together with your finger in that little bowl. All right. I'm going to hold his head pretty tight and you just pour that over the wound. He's not going to like it—"

Indeed, the hurt man yowled and tried to twist away from his torturers, but by then, the liquid was splashed all over his open cut and working its painful magic. After a moment, he lay still, panting and scowling.

"Now. We'll put some manna root on it—but first, I think, some numbing salve. You see that blue jar? Yes. That's dera leaf. It doesn't have any restorative powers, but it shuts pain down for a little while. Always use that if someone has a burn or a deep wound—or a cut like this, that you're going to suture, or any time you're about to do something else that might cause additional pain."

"Jovah and all the angels bless me," the man muttered.

Mary patted him rather absently on the shoulder. "You'll be just fine. You don't have any alarming symptoms, and you haven't lost nearly enough blood to put you in danger."

"It looks like a lot of blood to me," Elizabeth said doubtfully.

"Head wounds are always gushers. That's usually not your biggest concern in a case like this. It's concussion."

So Mary explained the symptoms of a concussion while she gently layered a sticky gray ointment over the cut. The injured man seemed pleased with her ministrations for the first time, giving a loud sigh of contentment and slightly unclenching his body. They spread manna root cream over the gray ointment and let it soak in a moment before Mary began to thread the needle.

"I need you to push together the edges of the wound for me so it's easier to sew—yes, like that—you're very good at this," Mary praised.

"What are you doing?" the man asked apprehensively, lunging away from the healer's hands.

"We're attempting to repair your scalp," Mary said. "Lie still."

The Edori man dropped to a crouch beside them. "Would you like me to hold him now?"

"Yes," said Mary. "I think he's going to be troublesome."

The Edori straddled the patient, using his knees to clamp the man's arms to his sides. The hurt man yodeled with indignation, but all three of them ignored him.

"And his head?" the Edori asked.

"Yes," said Mary. "If you can keep it still."

So the Edori placed his broad hands on either side of the patient's head and essentially rendered it immobile.

"Very good," Mary said with satisfaction, and began to sew. Elizabeth kept her hands just ahead of the healer's, closing the open gash with her fingers until the needle could do its work. Even so, the wound still looked pretty raw once the black thread was crisscrossed over it to hold it shut, and Elizabeth was predicting their patient would have the god's own headache by the time the numbing ointment wore off. The same thought had occurred to Mary, because she was rifling through her satchel to put together a little medical kit to send home with the hurt man: a small vial of the salve and a handful of white lozenges.

"What are those?" Elizabeth asked.

"Drugs. Sent by the god. They'll ward off infection."

"I've never seen anything like that," Elizabeth said, and Mary handed her one of the small, perfectly shaped pellets. It appeared to be constructed of a white powder that had been mixed with some kind of adhesive and set in an exceptionally fine mold, for it had no rough edges or irregularities. Elizabeth marveled at the god's workmanship.

"Where did you get it?" she asked.

Mary gave her a quick look. "The angels pray for medicines when there's a need. They have different prayers that result in different pills of all sorts of colors. They bring me the extras, because the god always sends more than the job requires—and now and then, if I'm running low, I ask Nathan or Calah to make a special request. It's very handy."

Elizabeth handed back the pellet. "I'd like to know those prayers."

"Oh, only the angels can make such requests. Jovah can't hear anyone else's voice."

The Edori stood up, but looked down at Mary with a smile. He was still poised with one foot on either side of the patient's chest, as if ready to drop down again at any moment and subdue him. "That's not true," he said.

Mary glanced up at him. "What's not true?"

"That the god can only hear angels' voices. Yovah hears the voices of all of his people."

"Yovah?" Elizabeth repeated.

Mary shrugged impatiently and began repacking her satchel. "The Edori have their special name for the god."

"But he is the same god, and he is the same to all people."

"Yes, well, we can discuss religion some other time," Mary said, and then turned her attention to the patient. "Listen. You. Can you sit up? Good. How do you feel? Now, I'm going to tell you what you must do for the next few days. . . ."

As soon as the man's head was lifted cautiously from her lap, Elizabeth came to her feet and shook out the folds of her dress. Between the dirt, the starch, the soap, and the blood, this poor garment had suffered a rather grueling day. Elizabeth had a feeling the rest of her days as Mary's assistant might be just as messy.

"Let me see your hands," she said to the Edori.

He gave her an easy smile that was impossible to resist. "Nothing wrong with my hands," he said.

She held her own out imperatively. "Let me see."

He acquiesced, extending them palm down, so she took hold of them and flipped them over. Scraped raw and filled with splinters. She thought she had glimpsed those abused palms as he lay them against the hurt man's face. "What exactly did you do?" she asked.

He shrugged. "Pulled the beam off him. Didn't take the time to put my gloves on."

Mary was still giving instructions to the man with the head wound. "Mary," Elizabeth said. "I need the needle to get these slivers out, and then I need to spread his hands with something. What should I use?"

"Get a fresh needle, for one thing, and then—oh, the manna root's as good as anything. And two of the white pills. Five, if any of the splinters go too deep."

"Well, let's go someplace where we can be comfortable," the Edori said, and led her to an empty wagon that still smelled of pine and cedar. They seated themselves, and then Elizabeth grasped the man's right hand. "I can't believe this doesn't hurt," she said, examining the dozens of chips of all sizes that had embedded themselves in his skin.

"It does," he said, smiling again. "But not so much as a log falling on my head."

"I'll try to be careful."

Indeed, she was fairly good at this particular chore, since field hands at James's farm had always come home with splinters when they had spent the day repairing the fences. The Edori never flinched or protested, though she knew that more than once the point of the needle probed painfully deep.

"What's your name?" he asked after she had been working on him for about five minutes.

"Elizabeth."

He waited a beat, then supplied his own. "I'm Rufus."

"Hello, Rufus," she said, not even lifting her head.

A moment of silence, and then he tried again. "So how long have you been living in Cedar Hills?"

She answered as briefly as she could. "About two months."

"And you like it?"

"Sometimes."

"Where did you live before?"

"On my cousin's farm."

"Why did you leave?"

"I wanted to learn how to sew up the heads of careless men."

He laughed. "Why don't you want to talk to me?" he asked next.

That was so unexpected that she actually looked up at him. "What?"

His eyes were so dark that she thought he must be able to see even in pitch black. "Why don't you want to talk to me?" he repeated gently.

She flushed and returned her attention to his hand. "I'm trying to concentrate."

"You don't like Edori," he hypothesized.

"I don't even know any Edori."

"You don't like men?"

She dropped his right hand and picked up the left one. "I don't like some of them," she said dryly.

"Well, there's no reason not to like me," he said cheerfully. "Could we have dinner tonight? Or some night?"

This caught her completely by surprise, and she transferred her gaze to his face. She couldn't remember the last time her social interaction with a man had been preceded by something so innocent and friendly as a dinner conversation. "I don't know," she said.

"Won't Mary allow you any free evenings?" he said, giving her that easy smile again. This was ridiculous; she was not the kind of woman who melted at a friendly grin. "Maybe if I talk to her."

"No, that's not it—it's just that I—why do you want to have dinner with me?" she floundered.

"Because I got paid yesterday, and I haven't had dinner with a pretty girl since I left Semorrah, and I thought it might be nice," he said. "And look! Yovah sent me you."

"Why do you do that?" she said, her voice almost petulant. "Call the god by a different name?"

He laughed. "Oh, there are many things the Edori do that are different from your ways. We don't live in houses, we don't rely on the angels to care for us, we don't ask the priests to set Kisses in our arms—"

She almost stared at that. "You don't have a Kiss? But how can you—how does the god know who you are and where you are?"

Rufus shrugged. "He knows. He watches over all of us."

"But how do you—how can you tell when you're in love?"

Now he looked amused. "And the Kiss can tell you this?"

She was furious with herself for betraying such girlishness. "They say," she said stiffly. "The legends. That when you meet your true love, your Kiss will glow with fire. But if you have no Kiss—"

He was laughing. "I think I will be able to tell, all on my own, when I've fallen in love. I won't need the god's guidance for that."

She shook her head and went back to work on the maltreated hand. "Well. Whatever you say."

"No, whatever *you* say," he said gaily. "Will you have dinner with me? If not tonight or tomorrow, sometime next week? I can wait till you're free."

She shrugged. "Actually—tonight or tomorrow—either would be fine. You might just want to stay home and wrap your hands tonight, though."

"Oh, no," he said. "I never choose solitude and brooding when there's any other option."

She shrugged again, but she felt a tiny, almost unnoticeable curl of pleasure unroll beneath her ribs. He wasn't an angel, of course, and he didn't even have the social status of one of James's field hands, so naturally she intended nothing more than some light conversation and, she hoped, a meal better than the one she might expect at Tola's. But it was still no bad thing to have a man call you pretty and to ask to spend time in your company. "Where would you like me to meet you?" she asked.

"In the square? Does that suit you? When are you done working?"

"I don't know. I'll ask Mary."

He seemed jubilant at the thought of the outing. She thought he might be the kind of man whose standards were not particularly high, who was pleased by everything, so it meant very little that he was pleased by her. "I know just where we can go," he said. "I'll walk back with you and point it out. I can't remember the name."

She teased out the last sliver of wood and then set the needle into the fabric of her skirt so she wouldn't lose it. "Salve now," she said, "and I think we're done."

That night as she got ready for bed, Elizabeth reflected that only the first few hours of the day had gone as she'd expected. Once she left the dorm to accompany Mary to the construction site, she was deep in unfamiliar territory, and the rest of the day held nothing but surprises.

They had returned to the center of town, where Rufus had pointed out a sidewalk cafe and Mary had looked amused. Then the healer had towed her new pupil off to a series of appointments, to check up on a pregnant woman, to visit a sick child, and to doctor an angel with a sore throat. "Angels are never sick, so I'm sure she doesn't have an infection, but they're all just singing themselves hoarse," Mary observed as they left the unfamiliar dorm. "A little honey and a little tea—you'll find that's almost as good as the god's drugs, sometimes, when it's nothing serious."

They also paused briefly in the suite that Mary occupied in the central building. The front room was almost an apothecary's shop, lined with shelves of drying herbs and colored jars and smelling of sage and lemon. The back room, Elizabeth supposed, held a bedroom and perhaps a water room.

"Why don't you just come here in the morning?" Mary said. "We've got a handful of patients to check on tomorrow, but I'd like to show you a few things here. We might have time to mix up a bit more manna root. I noticed I was running low. Oh, there's lots to do here if there was only a free minute!"

"What time do you want me?"

"How early do you rise?"

Elizabeth shrugged. On the farm, she'd been up before dawn. At Tola's, she'd gotten accustomed to sleeping in, but it still felt like a sinful luxury. "As early as you want."

Mary nodded approvingly. "I knew I liked you. Let's say two hours past sunrise. I'll have breakfast ready. We can get a lot done before the first emergency comes calling."

"I'll be here."

And she was looking forward to it, too, oddly enough—and, even more strange, looking forward to the evening with Rufus. The occasion didn't seem grand enough to call for her green gown again—and anyway, it was really getting too cold for such flimsy material—but she had a nice burgundy dress she used to wear when she was serving fancy meals at James's, and she could accessorize it with a black shawl and a braided black belt. Faith cooed over her appearance when she pirouetted before the closet door. There was only a small mirror tacked high on one wall, so she couldn't really judge how she looked.

"That's a nice color for you. You look so pretty! So what's this Rufus like, anyway?"

Elizabeth shrugged and checked her hair in the mirror. She hadn't had time to wash it again, and after the day's travails, it was both limp and a little dirty, so she'd pulled it back into a smooth auburn bun. She always thought the style made her look elegant, though she didn't think Rufus particularly cared if his companion was elegant or not.

"He's an Edori," she said. "He seemed very friendly. It's just dinner. There's nothing more to it than that."

"I've met some Edori men," Faith said in a dreamy voice. "Very nice, all of them."

"I'm sure," Elizabeth said, a little sarcastically.

"I'll wait up for you," Faith said, as she always said, as she never did. "I want to hear all the details."

Rufus was waiting for her on the green, sitting on the ground with his back against a tree, his whole attitude one of loose relaxation. Elizabeth frowned a little. He didn't seem to have much energy—much gumption, as Angeletta would say. She didn't like to be quoting Angeletta, but she had to admit she preferred a man with a certain amount of drive.

He saw her from some distance off, though, and was on his feet and smiling by the time she drew near. He smelled of soap and clean linen, so he had obviously had time to freshen up since they parted.

"Don't you look nice," he said in an admiring voice.

She smiled. "It's just an old dress."

"It's not the dress that looks so good. It's you."

She shook her head, but she was still smiling. "You shouldn't give me such compliments. It'll make me conceited."

"One or two kind words? I doubt it. I bet it would take years of compliments to make you vain."

"My roommate said this was the nicest cafe in Cedar Hills," Elizabeth said. "Is it very expensive?"

He laughed. "I don't know. I haven't been there yet. But I've been working for three months straight, and I've spent hardly a copper, so I can afford our meals, no matter how much they cost."

She was a little embarrassed. "I'm sorry. I didn't mean to imply—"

He gave her a shrewd look. "When you start worrying about money, it becomes a habit," he said. "It's what you start to think of first. Before happiness, before home."

She made a little gesture with her hands. "If you don't have money, sometimes you can't have happiness or a home," she said.

He shrugged. "It's not the Edori way to think too much about possessions. What to wear or where to sleep. We've usually thought the god would provide—and generally he does."

"And yet you've been taking a salary for three months," she said, not entirely kindly.

He grinned. "That's laziness," he said. "I haven't been sure what else to do."

"You work because you're lazy?" she demanded.

He took her elbow with an unself-conscious gesture and turned her in the direction of the restaurant. "Well, now, if we're going to get to the story of my life, we'd best be comfortable and eating," he said. "Let's go find a table."

But what with crossing the road, picking out a table, looking over the menu, placing their orders, and trying their first glasses of wine, it was some time before they got back to the subject of Rufus's life. Which was fine with Elizabeth. She was not all that interested in the story of a rambling Edori's undirected wanderings.

She did like the restaurant, though. It *looked* expensive, built of a fine-quality brick and hung with thick-woven curtains. The tables were highly polished wood inlaid with an inch of darker material at the rim, and the wine was better than anything she'd stolen from Angeletta's cellars. And there were angels here, two she recognized from the dorm, and two she hadn't seen before. Visiting, perhaps. Her eyes kept going to their exquisite, graceful forms as Rufus studied the menu and theorized about what he might want to eat.

"How about you?" he asked, though she had scarcely glanced at the selections. "What are you hungry for?"

"Oh, I haven't decided."

So she had to take a moment to peruse the offerings, consider whether Rufus really had as much money as he claimed, and decide on a moderately priced item just in case. Their server was a sleek young man with a haughty, beautiful face. Elizabeth, inexplicably, was seized by the notion that he was an angel-seeker's mortal son, left to fend for himself when he proved to be a disappointment to his mother. She brushed the thought aside.

"More wine?" the server asked.

"Of course," Rufus replied. The Edori smiled at Elizabeth as their server glided away. "I haven't had wine in a year," he said. "Maybe more. Good thing I don't have far to walk home."

Elizabeth took a sip from her own glass and held it on her tongue a moment before swallowing. "I love it," she said. "But I've never had more than a glass or two at a time."

"It gives you a headache?"

"It—it never came my way that often, or in much quantity."

He nodded. "Right. On your cousin's farm."

She had forgotten she had mentioned that to him earlier. "Exactly."

"So why did you leave the farm for Cedar Hills?"

She glanced around expressively. "Why not? Who'd pick a farm over this?"

"And your cousin doesn't worry about a young woman being all alone here in the city?"

"I'm not so young."

"But you're all alone."

"I have friends."

He tilted his head to one side. "Maybe. It's not the same as family, though."

She gave a short laugh. "Better than my family."

"So that's all you have? Your cousin?"

"And his wife. Neither of them—well, I don't think they've missed me or worried about me much since I've been gone."

"So you're an orphan."

She nodded. She wasn't particularly interested in his life, but she certainly didn't feel like talking about her own. So she turned the subject. "What about you?" she asked. "What's your family like?"

He gave her that effortless smile again. "Ah, you know what my people say. All Edori are family."

Which was an evasive answer, she thought. He might not want to talk about his past much more than she did. Perversely, that made her more interested. "And why did you come to Cedar Hills?"

"I heard they were building, and I had some skill with my hands. And I was tired of Semorrah."

"I don't think I'd ever get tired of Semorrah," she said frankly.

He laughed. "It's a beautiful city," he said. "And absolutely soulless. I was happy to go."

"How long did you live there?"

"Seven years."

She arched her eyebrows. "So long in a place you hated?"

"And five years in Castelana before that. A city I also did not love so much."

"So why stay?"

The waiter arrived just then with their food, which smelled divine. "I'm starving," she said as soon as the young man had left the table.

"So am I," he said, and picked up his fork.

She had eaten three mouthfuls and given herself up to the sheer rapture of taste before she realized he hadn't answered her last question. "I thought Edori didn't like cities," she said.

"They don't."

"Then why did you spend so long in Castelana and Semorrah?"

He gave her another smile, this one laced with hurt. "Why did any Edori of the last twenty years live in places with people they despised?"

She lifted her fork again, then set it down without tasting the food. "You were a slave," she breathed.

He nodded. He did not look eager to talk about it, but he did not look entirely unwilling, either. "Almost half my life," he said.

"But you—but they—but how did that happen?"

"As it happened with so many Edori. The Jansai came upon us by night and raided our camp. Most of the grown men were killed. The women and the boys my age were kept. Taken to the city and sold."

"But how did they—you can't just kill people!" she exclaimed. "Even Jansai. Jovah doesn't allow it!"

"Yovah allowed it for nearly twenty years," he said with a certain grimness. "Or, rather, Raphael. It was a great day for the Edori when Yovah chose an Edori girl for the Archangel Gabriel's bride. Although from everything I know of Gabriel, he would have freed the Edori even without Rachel's intercession."

"Rachel isn't really an Edori."

"Raised by them. She understands the people."

"So when Gabriel became Archangel—"

Rufus gestured with both hands, shaping the world. "All the Edori were released, most often reluctantly, from their merchant and Jansai masters. Hundreds of us. Thousands. Many, many, *many* had died in captivity, because Edori require freedom the way you require food. But some of us—the younger ones, the ones who didn't know any better—we survived all those years. Till we were set free."

She was fascinated now. "And then what?"

His expression was ironic. "Yes, and then what? That's been the question for a lot of us. We don't belong anywhere. We hate the cities where we've lived so long, but we've forgotten how to live as true Edori, wandering the world and living in harmony with the earth. I know a few who have tried to be farmers, but they're not used to coaxing a living from the land. Most of us have ended up back in cities of one sort or another, doing the kind of work we did before. Getting paid for it, this time, but not loving it any more."

"Have you tried to go back?" she asked. "Back to your people?"

"My whole tribe is dead."

"But you said all Edori are family."

A slight smile for that. "True. And any branch of that family would welcome me. Or so I tell myself. Maybe I don't want to find out if that's really true. Maybe I want to believe the Edori are exactly as a thirteen-year-old remembers them, loving and kind and welcoming. Maybe it is easier to hold on to that belief while living in Cedar Hills."

She took a mouthful of her food and chewed and swallowed while she thought that over. "I think you should find out," she said.

"Oh, I've gotten used to the comforts of the city by now," he said. "I'm used to a roof over my head when it rains, and food available when I want it. I'm used to buying my clothes instead of making them, and used to sleeping by myself in a big room instead of sharing my small tent with ten others. I don't see myself traveling with a clan from storm to drought, from summer to winter, and smiling through it all like it's Yovah's great adventure."

"I'd go back," she said. "If I could return to my childhood? I'd do it. Without a second thought."

"Oh? And this was a childhood before you moved to the farm?"

"Yes. We were rich. Or it seemed rich to me then. I had beautiful clothes and everything I wanted, and my mother loved me more than she loved anything else in the world. I'll never feel that safe and happy again. Never."

"You may find someone else who loves you more than the world itself. Then you won't miss the riches."

She thought about her joyless trysts with David, the stolen embraces with rich lordlings at James's farm. "I think money lasts longer than love," she said.

"And that's what you came to Cedar Hills for?" he asked. "Money? I wouldn't think you'd get rich apprenticing with a healer."

She just stared at him and did not try to answer. She didn't have to. It would never have occurred to her that she could be so deep in conversation with a mortal that she would fail to notice the approach of an angel, but that was exactly what happened. A laugh, a footfall, the coolness of a shadow falling over her, and she looked up to find David standing beside their table. He was dressed in formal black and white, and his dark hair fell picturesquely over his eyebrows. He did not look like he had had his full quota of liquor yet this night, for his eyes were alert and his pocked skin not yet flushed from wine.

"My little laundress," he said in that low, delighted voice. "How electrifying to see you in another setting! I didn't know you ever left the confines of the dormitory."

"David," she said, her voice betraying both her pleasure at seeing him and her embarrassment at being placed in just this position. She did not expect him to linger long to chat, however; two of his dorm mates stood a few feet away, looking bored and impatient. "Hello."

"Out for an evening of fun? You certainly deserve it," he said. "But it seems so long since I've had a chance to visit with you."

"Well, I'm—I'd like to see you again sometime—when you've

got an evening free," she said, stammering. She couldn't look over in Rufus's direction.

"Tomorrow, then," he said gaily. "I'll look forward to it."

And with no more discussion than that, he spun around, his dark wings adding more shadows to the room, and strode off with his friends. Elizabeth dropped her gaze to her plate and thought how unappetizing the expensive meal suddenly looked.

"Ah," said Rufus. "That's why you came to Cedar Hills."

CHAPTER EIGHTEEN

*O*badiah spent the entire week he was in Cedar Hills wishing he was in Breven.

It wasn't that there was nothing to do in Cedar Hills. He was busier there than he had been during his whole three days in the desert city, when all he did was wait on Uriah's convenience and think about Rebekah. It was just that his heart wasn't in any of his activities. His heart was in the hands of a Jansai girl whom he might never see again.

Impossible to believe that.

She had managed to win her way free that second night and spend a few hours with him, though she brushed off his attempts to seriously examine what risks she was running. "But if you get caught," he said more than once. "If your father finds out—"

"He's not my father."

"The man who acts as your father. Or your betrothed. If they discover you have been roaming the city on your own—let alone if they discover what you have been doing—what happens to you?"

"Nothing very good, I imagine," she answered, shrugging. She wouldn't outline possible punishments for him, and her lack of concern made him think, perhaps, it would not be so very awful if she was found out. A brutal beating, perhaps, confinement to her room forever—he wasn't able to make his mind come up with worse penalties.

And yet he knew, they all knew, how harsh and unforgiving the Jansai could be. Rachel, who was pretty good at hating, reserved her fiercest animosity for the Jansai, and Gabriel admitted that he disliked them too much to deal with them. But they could not be so awful as that, not if they had produced a creature like Rebekah and she was content to live among them.

"I wish you would return to Cedar Hills with me," he said to her again that second night, and again she told him no.

"This is my life."

"You are toying with your life by seeing me."

"Well, perhaps I won't toy with you very much longer." Said with a kiss and a smile. She had learned lovers' ways so quickly.

"I would make sure you were taken care of," he said. "Even if—I know you think perhaps this emotion between us won't last—and even if it doesn't, I would take care of you. I would not abandon you."

"I know that," she said. "I don't want to come to Cedar Hills."

And that was that, this time, anyway. He had followed her home that second night, as he had on the first, having already memorized the overhead view of that square, dour house and its brief desert gardens. He would be able to find it by night or day now, for the rest of his life. Even if he never saw Rebekah again, he would know where she lived; he would be able to throw the shadow of his wings over the roof that sheltered her body.

Until she married, and moved to another man's house, slept under another man's roof.

He could not bear to think about that.

But there had been very little he could bear since he had left Breven a week ago. He had found Magdalena's moods and despondencies even harder to deal with, though he was always kind to her the many times he saw her. She sent for him every day—sometimes twice a day if Nathan was gone—and her attempts to be cheerful in the face of her great fear touched his heart, even while her moping drove him mad.

She had told Nathan her secret while Obadiah was gone, and Nathan had responded with predictable delight. "Did you hear? Did you *hear!*" Nathan had demanded the minute Obadiah returned from Breven. "We're expecting a child! In a few months—I can't wait—everyone says the time will fly past, but to me it seems like every day is a thousand years long."

"Maga seems concerned that the child might be—deformed," Obadiah said cautiously.

Nathan nodded, his brown eyes serious. "Yes, and I can't convince her otherwise. But I just don't think—" He shrugged. "I don't think the god would have brought us together like this to create monster children. So I cannot help rejoicing, no matter how much apprehension Maga feels."

But Maga's condition put an extra strain on the hold, already suffering from too few angels and too many demands. It was rare enough for a mortal woman to bear an angel child; it was even rarer for an angel to carry one, and no one wanted to chance a miscarriage. So Nathan and Magdalena agreed that she should fly on no more patrols or weather intercessions, and that she should even limit the work she did, greeting petitioners at the hold.

Which meant that Obadiah was pressed into service fulfilling the daily responsibilities of the hold and could not even plan for his next trip to Breven.

After one whole week performing mostly local intercessions, one of his commissions took him north. An early winter had already settled in on the valley between the Plain of Sharon and the northernmost tip of the Caitanas. Two heavy snowfalls were followed by an actual blizzard, and the farmers were begging the angels for a respite. So Obadiah went north on the cold aerial road, spending two days on the journey and another two days at his destination. The people of the northern plains had not been willing to have him leave.

The big, homely man who seemed to be unofficial mayor of this frozen community had asked most humbly for Obadiah's continued presence. "If you could stay another day—two days, maybe," the man had said, ducking his head and looking the very picture of pleading. "It's just that—the snow's stopped, but the skies are still overcast, and we've seen what clouds like that can hold."

How could he say no? "I'll go aloft again this afternoon, and then tomorrow two or three times. Jovah will surely hear my prayers then," Obadiah said graciously.

The ugly man gave him a wide smile, all sincere gratitude. "You'll stay with me, of course. I've got the biggest house in these parts. The food's plain, but there's plenty of it. We got the harvest in before the first snowfall—but, sweet Jovah singing! We never expected the bad weather so soon."

"No," Obadiah said. "Storms never come when you expect them."

So he flung himself aloft that afternoon, into the crystal air that even he found almost unendurably cold. He had spent too many days in desert luxury, that was it; his blood had grown thin and lazy. When he was as high as he could stand, he dropped into a hover speed and sang again all the prayers he had offered to the god this morning. He could feel the words leave his mouth and careen upward, dodging through the weighted clouds and their unshed bounty, not stopping till they were clamoring at Jovah's ear. He sang for an hour, supplicant and celebrant, remembering how much he loved this chilled, solitary communion with the god. The clouds bunched around him, drawn by the cadence of his voice, unaware that he was the siren who would lure them to their doom. Mesmerized by that soothing, beseeching tenor, they shivered around him and gave themselves up to dreaming. Once they slept, the god brushed them away with a sweep of his windy hand.

It was in bright sunlight that Obadiah descended, to find his host and half a dozen of his friends gathered around to await his return. They were all smiling broadly, anxious to thank him personally for his aid, to show him the fruits of their summer labors. There was no hope for it; this would be a feast night.

And so it was, thirty or forty people crammed into one sturdy farmhouse, the children spilling out into the barn and the dairy house, and coming in covered with the very snow Obadiah had been praying away. The food was, in fact, plain but hearty, stews and breads and casseroles and a home-brewed ale that was more potent than anything he'd had in the streets of Velora. Obadiah actually enjoyed himself, eating far more than he should have and allowing his host's eight-year-old daughter to sit on his lap for the whole meal and tell him about the neighbor boys that she did and didn't like. No one dared to ask him for another song, a more social one this time, so he brought it up himself.

"Does anyone play a harp or flute? I'd be happy to sing and have you all join in."

It was a suggestion that met with universal approbation and resulted, as he knew it would, in various teenage girls and lanky, unformed boys being brought forward to parade their own voices in solos and duets. Music was the coin of their realm; it represented not only a hard-won harmony between individuals but the grace of their god. And so nearly everyone could sing, or play, or try to; and those who had no musical inclinations at all had trained themselves to listen. Obadiah sang, then listened, then joined in when the music became general, and all in all it was not a bad way to pass an evening.

His allotted bedroom, of course, was inappropriate for an angel in every way: It was too hot, the bed was too narrow to accommodate his wings, and there was not a single chair in the room that he could sit in. But these were common conditions in any small farm town. You didn't accept an overnight invitation with the expectation of staying in comfort. You stayed because the people needed you.

In the morning, he was served a breakfast that was nearly as hearty as the dinner the night before, and returned to the heavens to sing away the hours. Yesterday he had halted the snow and banished the clouds; today he would wish away winter, begging Jovah to send warmer breezes from the edges of southern Bethel. He could imagine the currents of air making their slow, playful spiral from the coastline off of the Corinnis, across the banks of the Galilee River, and threading through the pointed peaks of the Caitanas. Well, the year was almost over; he would not be able to keep the season at bay for long. But he could hold it back a week or two. That much strength and skill he had.

This second evening was not quite as festive as the first one, though a good ten neighbors came calling before dinner was over, eager to thank the angel in person for his excellent work. Obadiah tumbled into his inadequate bed that second night feeling pleased with himself, happy with his role in the world.

He woke with an overwhelming desire to swoop by Breven on his way back to Cedar Hills.

Ridiculous, he knew. Such a detour would take him way off course, probably delay his arrival into Cedar Hills by another full day. He argued with himself while he dressed, while he said good-bye to his hosts, while he catapulted himself once more to the skies overhead to sing a final prayer for sunshine. He told himself he was needed in Cedar Hills or elsewhere in Jordana, that he could not afford such foolish, romantic gestures. He did not even know how to get in touch with Rebekah, should he be so idiotic as to fly into the city with the hope of seeing her. He had asked her that. *How do I get word to you when I return?* and she had said, *You can't. But everyone knows everything that happens in Breven. If you are here to meet with Uriah, Hector will know, and then Jordan will know, and thus I will know.*

But if he came to Breven with no plan of meeting Uriah?

It was pointless. They had invented no system of communication. She was immured in a walled, windowless cell, and he had no way to reach her. There was no reason to fly to Breven to spend a single night, and fly away again, frustrated and disappointed.

But he flew to Breven anyway.

He justified it to himself by flying low, following the coastline south and staying on the lookout for plague flags or other signs of trouble. He was actually relieved when he saw a tattered red banner flying over an isolated farmstead on the second morning of his flight. Illness in the house, most likely. He dipped his left wing and coasted down.

"Angelo! Thank the god!" cried a frantic woman who ran from the house to greet him. "My husband—his leg is broken—and I set it, but then an infection set in. It's been two days; he's delirious—"

"Let me look at him," Obadiah said, holding his wings together tightly behind him so he could make it through the cramped doorway. Nonetheless, he felt a feather catch on the doorjamb and he had to jerk his wing forward to free it.

The hurt man lay panting on a narrow cot, two small children standing beside him looking numb and nervous. The room was dark and cold, even though winter had not fully settled in at this latitude. Obadiah suspected this was not a prosperous home. The man's disability could bring them perilously close to starvation.

Obadiah was not a healer, but, like all angels, he could recognize the symptoms of the most common diseases and pray for the god to deliver the proper cures. This man, fortunately, looked to be suffering nothing more than infection—serious, yes, but not untreatable—and he hadn't developed any illness on top of it.

"I'll pray for him," Obadiah said. "We'll have medicines in an hour or two."

And indeed, the god pelted them with dozens of white tablets not thirty minutes after Obadiah returned to the sky to enter his plea. He wanted to be on his way right then, but common kindness kept him in place another two hours, hauling up buckets of water from the nearest stream, chopping two days' worth of wood, and forking down hay for the animals. None of these chores were made any easier by the presence of his wings, clearly not designed for a man doing manual labor.

One of the little girls who had been standing by her father's bed approached him as he put aside the pitchfork and devoutly hoped he had done his duty. She looked like she would be a solemn child on the best of days, which this clearly was not, but she also did not appear to be afraid of the extraordinary apparition come to spend a few hours on her homestead.

"You dropped this, angelo," she said. She was offering him one of his own wing feathers, torn from his skin by the splintered doorframe, perhaps, or combed out by the spindly branches that had overhung the path from the creek to the house. It was a pristine white and long as his forearm, one of the bigger feathers to be found toward the very back of his wings. "Do you need it?"

He was about to say no when an idea occurred to him. "Yes," he said, reaching for it. "Thank you."

"There's another one, back by the creek," she said, jerking her thumb in that direction. "Shall I get that one, too?"

He had tucked the feather into an inside pocket of his leather vest, where it barely fit. He would have to move carefully to avoid snapping it. "No, I just need this one," he said. "You can keep the other if you like."

Her sober face broke into a delighted smile. "That's luck for me, isn't it?" she asked. "An angel's feather."

He came close enough to pat her on the tangled curls at the top of her head. "I hope so," he said. "And my prayers for you. That'll bring you luck, too."

"Mama says Daddy's better already, since he took those funny white pills."

"He'll be well in a day or two. Trust me."

"I'm glad you came, angelo."

And that, thought Obadiah as he took wing again a few minutes later, was all the justification he needed for this small detour, this illicit but surely harmless jaunt back into Breven. He had brought a little girl luck and quite possibly saved her father's life. That would satisfy Nathan, if he even asked what had kept Obadiah on the road so long. That would satisfy the god himself, if Jovah were keeping accounts.

Shortly before nightfall, he was in Breven and hovering over Hector's house. In Velora and major cities of Samaria, citizens had trained themselves to glance skyward now and then, desirous of seeing an angel, but in Breven, he thought, such traditions were not common. For one thing, angels were rare in this part of the world. For another, the Jansai did not think it such a grand sight to view an angel on the wing.

Still, it would not do for some bored and restless member of Hector's household to look up and begin pointing, and bring the whole attention of the neighborhood to the occupied skies overhead. So Obadiah circled quite high, flicking in and out of thin streamers of cloud, hoping to blend with the haze of afternoon. He could see very little from this vantage point, of course, mostly small sticklike figures that floated down the boulevards around this house, indistinguishable from each other. Now and then shadowy shapes moved in and out of the back gardens of Hector's house, but Obadiah had no way of knowing if one of them was Rebekah. Those who left the gardens for the street he presumed to be men; those who stayed within its walls he guessed to be women.

He thought that at one point he saw someone bend over and pick up an object from the ground, and study it, and slip it inside a pocket; but he could not be sure. If so, he hoped that that person had been Rebekah, and that she had found the wing feather he had tied to a stone and dropped in her stepfather's garden. And that, if it had been Rebekah, she knew how to interpret the treasure she had found.

He stayed above the house till well after dark, not sure what he expected to observe, just loath to tear himself away. In case she had not found his clue, in case she could not get free, in case this was the closest he would be able to get to her this night. But she would never be able to find him if he remained airborne, endlessly wheeling overhead, so he eventually forced himself to cross the city and drop to land on the street before the Hotel Verde.

The young woman he had seen before was sitting at her desk in the center of the atrium, and she smiled as he approached.

"Good evening, angelo," she said. "Would you like a room?"

"Yes, please. And I'd like to have food sent to me as soon as possible."

"Certainly."

"Also, I may be expecting company tonight. I'm not sure. It might be quite late. But if someone could make sure this visitor is admitted to my room—"

"I shall be at this station until midnight," she said gravely. "I can escort your visitor to you."

"Thank you so much."

"Is it the same young woman who's visited before?"

His mouth had already shaped the word *yes* before he took in the enormity of what she'd said. Then all he could do was stare at her, shock making him stupid and voiceless.

She smiled. "I'm sorry. The *m'kash* who's been here."

"How did you know?" he asked quietly.

"The disguise is not that good, angelo. Anyone paying much attention would also know."

"But she—no one has guessed but you."

"I hope for her sake that is true."

He still watched her. She was a quiet, well-mannered, beautiful girl whose patrician face spoke of centuries of wealth and breeding. Not someone he would expect to be entirely in sympathy with a runaway Jansai rebel. "Have you told anyone?" he asked.

"No, angelo. I would not do that. My family maintains the discretion of all the guests at its establishment."

"Does your brother know?"

"I have not discussed it with him."

The next words to come from his mouth surprised him. "It is possible she could stand to have a friend in this city."

"If I ever have a chance to be her friend, I will be."

He watched her a moment longer. His instinct was to trust her—indeed, at this point he had almost no choice but to trust her—and yet, Rebekah's safety was at stake, and that was a gift almost too great to lay in the hands of any stranger. "What's your name?" he asked.

"Zoe."

"Not a name from the Librera," he commented.

She smiled. "Not a name found there, perhaps, but a word in the great book. It means abundance and grace. My mother named me."

"I hope your mother would approve of this secret you are willing to keep for me."

"My mother was a woman of many secrets herself. I think she would agree that this one was worth keeping."

"Let me tell her—my friend—when she arrives," Obadiah said. "It might alarm her to learn the news from you."

"As you wish, angelo. I will see that food is brought to you immediately."

So Obadiah was left to pace in his room for who knew how many hours, beset by a fresh set of worries. He had had his share of dealings with the Manadavvi over the years, and he had always found them tricky and impossible to read. The men were clever, ambitious, greedy, and worldly, but often so charming that you could not hold their vices against them. The women were invariably beautiful and mysterious—all of them, like Zoe's mother, full of secrets. He knew an angel who swore he would never take any woman but a Manadavvi for a lover. "Because you can't tell if she loves you or hates you, you can't tell if you've bored her or roused her to rapture, but she'll smile at you every minute that she's with you, and you'll sleep on silk sheets when you're in her bed." Those had not been good enough inducements for Obadiah—silk sheets and discretion—but he was willing to bargain for just one of those virtues now.

Food arrived almost at once, but he was too tense to eat. He was tired from the earlier effort spent at the troubled homestead, not to mention the long flight and the hours spent circling over Rebekah's house, but he could not throw himself on the bed and attempt to rest. He could merely pace, and stop to try a bite of cheese, and stand at the window and stare out, wondering if anyone he loved walked these streets this night.

When the knock came shortly before midnight, he flung himself from the window and tore open the door. The image of Rebekah was so strong in his head that for a moment he did not recognize the slim boyish figure standing there, face bare, chin raised, shapeless clothes adding to the androgynous look. Then he felt his own face remolded by happiness, joy springing from him like a source of light.

"Rebekah!" he exclaimed, catching her arms and pulling her into the room. "You're here!"

She had so much to tell him, in her serious, unself-conscious way, and they lay in bed talking for at least an hour after lovemaking. There had been a fever sickness in the house, but everyone was better now; the date for the wedding had been set, exactly five months from now; her cousin Martha had grown quite reckless of late and had begun to leave the house in broad daylight to make assignations with her lover.

"How does she manage that?" he asked, having more than a little interest in this trick if it was one that another young woman could replicate.

"She just goes down to the garden in her jeska and veil, and when no one is watching, she steps out of the gate! And then she puts on a *different* veil, the most disreputable thing, something no woman of respect or status would wear, and she walks to the market like a beggar woman. No one troubles her, no one speaks to her, of course, all of them assuming she is the most desperate of women, whose husband and sons must be sick. So she goes where she wants."

"How does she get back home?"

"That's the real danger, of course. She creeps back and stands outside the gate, and listens to hear if anyone else is in the garden. And if she hears no voices, she slips back inside. But anyone could be standing there—anyone! Her mother or her aunts or even Uncle Ezra—anyone could see her stealing back inside!"

"And what will she say then?"

"Oh, she has it all worked out. She is so devious you cannot believe it. She has a little handkerchief that I embroidered for her years ago and she carries it with her everywhere. Everyone knows she has it, just as everyone knows I carry a scarf she embroidered for me. She says that if anyone sees her coming back in, she will just claim that the handkerchief got blown over the wall and she went scrambling after it. She will get in trouble, but it won't be so bad. That will be seen as a little transgression."

"But what if someone has been sitting in the garden for an hour or two, and that someone knows very well that Martha did not just dash out of the gate a moment ago?"

"I know! Or what if her father or her brother come upon her from behind while she is lurking outside the gate, listening for voices on the inside? Then her little excuse will fool nobody, and she will be in very big trouble indeed."

"I don't think you should try to leave the garden during the day," he said reluctantly.

"No," she said. "I've thought it through, and I can't see how it would work."

"But you were very clever to know to come here tonight."

She smiled at him. She was curled next to his body, sheltered under his wing, and she looked utterly content. "I almost didn't get your message! Jordan found it this afternoon and brought it to me. 'Look what I found out in the garden. Isn't this the most curious thing? What kind of bird could this have fallen from?' Well, first, don't be silly, that feather's much too long to have fallen from a *bird,* and what bird ties rocks to its feathers when they fall? I didn't say that, of course! I just told him he should put it in his box of treasures, or save it to give Jonah on his naming day—"

"Jonah?"

"Yes," she said happily. "The baby's finally got a name. We're going to have quite a celebration next week on his naming day."

"I don't suppose you'd want to miss that," he said ruefully.

"Miss it? Why would I?"

He kissed her quickly on the mouth. "If you came back with me to Cedar Hills. Tomorrow morning—or even now. We could leave this instant."

She looked as grave and unprepared as if he had never made the proposal before. "But I can't leave Breven," she said.

"I wish you would think about it. You always say no, but you never stop to even consider it."

"Because I—it's just that—you're right. I don't even consider it. I can't leave Breven."

He sat up, so she sat up, too, drawing the covers around her for warmth when his wing fell away. "You don't think you can leave this life behind, but don't you see?" he said gently. "You've already left part of this life behind, just by knowing me. You're no longer the girl you were when I met you in the desert six weeks ago."

"No," she said, her face troubled. "But I have not changed so much that I have considered leaving my home."

"You think you can marry Isaac and live in his father's house and raise his children—and not wonder? All your life? Where I am, what happened to me, who I might be loving? You think you can love somebody and then walk away into another man's arms? Or do you think—do you honestly think—you can continue to see me after you are wed? Or have you even considered that at all?"

"I have," she said in a small voice. "At least, I've tried to. I can't imagine what it will be like—to be married. What that will feel like. But I can't imagine what it will feel like to know I'll never see you again. And if you say, 'Once you are married, I am done with you,' then I'll understand that, I am even expecting that, but—"

He looked over at her, knowing his helplessness was evident on his face. "The god save me, I will want to see you even when you are another man's wife," he said in a low voice. "I would want to see you if the god himself forbade it. I see you now, even though I know how much it puts you at risk, because I cannot help myself. Because I want you so much that I can't give you up. But I am not so sure you will be able to carry such a thing off—meeting a lover while you act out the duties of a wife."

"I am already two people," she said, her voice just as quiet as his. "I am the person who goes around every day, living in her stepfather's house, eating with her mother, caring for her brothers, laughing with her aunts. I am the person everybody sees. And I am, at the same time, the woman who is here with you. She is inside me every day. She watches that other me, and sometimes she laughs, and sometimes she's sad, and sometimes she marvels at how innocently I can talk or move or behave. But she never goes away. She sleeps beside me on my mat at night, and she puts her jeska on right over mine. Don't think I don't know how to live with deception. She is my closest friend."

He put his arms around her then, drawing her tightly to his chest. His wing wrapped all the way around her body and brushed against his opposite shoulder. "I am so worried about you," he whispered into her dark hair. "You are not safe. I am destroying your world—I am destroying you. And yet I cannot bring myself to say good-bye to you, as I should—as someday, I know, I will have to."

She turned in his arms and kissed him deliberately on the mouth. "But not now," she said. "Not tonight."

"No," he said, drawing her even tighter. "Not tonight."

"And will you be here tomorrow as well?"

He shook his head. "I must go back in the morning. I have delayed so long already—well, I should not even be here at all tonight."

She giggled and came to her knees within the circle of his arms so that she could kiss him with a little more intention. "No," she whispered against his mouth, "neither should I."

Back in Cedar Hills the next evening, Obadiah found himself, like Rebekah, split in two. Or perhaps not even split—perhaps multiplied. He was his ordinary self, joking pleasantly with the angels in his dorm or friends he encountered on the green, promising Nathan he'd come by for dinner the next night and give him a full accounting of his travels. And he was his secret self, his obsessed self, the one who could not move or observe or think without considering how Rebekah might react. Would she approve of the shirt Obadiah changed into? Would she think Nathan was amusing? Would she find Cedar Hills attractive, with its scattering of pretty buildings and its well-planned streets? Would she be happy if she chose to live there?

Would she ever choose to live there?

He spent that first night back dining out with friends, carrying on conversations that seemed friendly but unimportant. He slept well, though, exhausted from the long trip and the lack of sleep the night before. The following day he checked in with Magdalena, who was acting as chief interviewer for the day, and she sent him off to do a quick weather intercession over a farm village not two hours' flight away. This time the plea was for rain, not sunshine. Every once in a while Obadiah found himself wondering if Jovah ever got the mix right all on his own.

That night, he joined about a dozen other of Magdalena's favorites in a boisterous and happy meal held in the private dining room adjoining Nathan's suite. Most of those present were angels, but there were three mortal women in the room as well, friends of Maga's from Monteverde and the nominal reason for the celebration. Obadiah had been seated between two of them. Not so far gone with her own megrims and malaise that she had failed to keep her promises. Maga was out to find him a suitable mate.

"Obadiah! So good to see you again!" the woman on his left greeted him, giving him a casual kiss on the cheek. She had straight black hair and delicate skin, and the classical features of a Manadavvi heiress. Her name was Deborah, and she had lived in Monteverde half her life. "I've been here two days and not laid eyes on you."

"I've been traveling. There's much to do at the angel holds these days, as you know."

She grimaced, but even that expression was pretty on her pretty face. "I know. Ariel is always gone, and so are the rest of them." She laughed. "I keep thinking this must be a lean period for angel-seekers."

"Oh, and we've got scores of them here in Cedar Hills," said the angel on Deborah's other side. "An angel wouldn't have to spend a single night alone, and if he was the kind of man to value variety, he could spend each of those nights with a different woman."

"But of course your scruples prevent you from indulging in such behavior," Deborah said.

He laughed. "Not my scruples, my stamina."

She turned her shoulder to him and smiled more widely at Obadiah. "So tell me about these travels. Whom did you rescue and what kind of prayers did you offer the god?"

Light, meaningless conversation; he'd spoken versions of the same dialogue hundreds of times over the past ten years. Flirtation

and response, jest and rebuttal, and all of it overlaid with the unspoken questions: *Do I please you? Are you the one for me?* Deborah
was classy about it, though; she wouldn't ask outright. So he
wouldn't have to refuse her outright.

Nobody pleased him except the one woman he could not have.

The evening was tedious and interminable, though Obadiah was
pretty sure he was the only one not having a grand time. Deborah
gave up on him after a while and managed to charm more intelligent
conversation from the angel on her left. Obadiah and his other
dinner partner, a quiet blond mortal born of an angel mother, made
stilted but well-meaning conversation the rest of the night, discussing
the probable severity of winter, the new fashions out of Luminaux,
and the new bridge just completed between Jordana and the river
city of Semorrah.

Once the meal was over, Nathan shepherded everyone toward
the spacious front room of the suite. "Entertainment now! Angels
together, must be singing!" the host declared. He paused to clap Obadiah on the shoulder, leaning in to whisper in his ear.

"I don't think you're being social enough. Maga expects you to
form at least one alliance after tonight's little party."

Obadiah grinned and fell back, letting the rest of the group pre-
cede them into the front room. "Maga can just stop trying to orches-
trate my life."

Nathan grinned back. "Still, you have a duty to your Archangel
and your nation. The holds must be repopulated. You shouldn't let
matters of personal taste stand in the way of your responsibilities."

"Maybe I'm holding out for a wife like yours—an angel. Until
Jovah gives me special dispensation, too, I don't want to marry."

Nathan looked suddenly and unexpectedly serious. They were
briefly alone, as the dining hall emptied and the other members of the
party disposed themselves around the sitting room. "Whatever you
do, you shouldn't hold out for a wife like Gabriel's," he said quietly.

"What?" Obadiah exclaimed.

Nathan shrugged, lifting and dropping his great white wings.
"I'm hoping it will do you some good to be away from the Eyrie for
a while. Remind you how many other difficult, fascinating, and
beautiful women there are in the world."

"Oh, please don't tell me this is about Rachel. Don't tell me that I was brought here just to remove me from her dangerous influence."

"Gabriel sent you here to deal with the Jansai. But it didn't hurt you to get away from Rachel."

Obadiah shook his head and strode away. "I can think of a lot of other ways to ruin my life than to mope over the angelica for the rest of my days," he shot over his shoulder.

Nathan hurried to catch up, not at all discomposed by Obadiah's obvious irritation. "That's all we ask—a little creativity in your path to self-destruction," he said cheerfully.

Obadiah was annoyed enough to seriously consider walking out right then and there, but Deborah motioned him over to a seat she'd saved for him, and it was clear that nobody else was ready to call it a night. So he throttled his displeasure and smiled at her, sweeping his wings back to take his seat.

"How could it be otherwise?" he said. "First food, now singing."

"It is how the angels spend their days," she said, smiling back.

At first he was in no mood to sit there and be entertained by voices, but gradually, as always, the music insinuated itself into his heart and put him at peace. Three of the Cedar Hills angels stood together and sang a rapturously beautiful rendition of the Lochevsky *Requiem,* all minor triads and woeful harmonies until the granting of absolution offered in a major chord at the end. Deborah and Magdalena sang a sweet country ballad that Obadiah would have sworn was not in Maga's repertoire, since she generally stuck with the sacred music, and then Maga performed a solo that left them all dumb and breathless. She had always had a vibrant mezzo soprano, darker and richer than her sister Ariel's high voice, but on this piece she sang with such depth and range that one or two people in the audience actually appeared to be crying. It was one of the prayers of thanksgiving, usually performed after great trials or particularly expressive displays of the god's affection. Obadiah could not help wondering: Was this her way of thanking Jovah for the gift of the child that she was still terrified to be carrying?

Yes, he was to conclude in the very next moment, as Nathan came to his feet to address the group. He looked flushed and happy; Maga, standing beside him, looked equally flushed and a little nervous.

"Friends," Nathan said, taking his wife's hand and holding it possessively, "we didn't just gather you all here to have a pleasant meal with us. We have news—the best news, the most exciting news—and we wanted to share it with our closest friends and staunchest supporters."

"Jovah rejoicing, you're going to have a baby!" the blond mortal girl shrieked, and the room was suddenly alive with cries of wonder and congratulations. Everyone swarmed around the mother-to-be and her beaming husband, offering hearty hugs and best wishes. Nathan laughed and shook hands all around and let the girls kiss him. Magdalena accepted all the cautious embraces and stroked her stomach and tried not to look frightened. Obadiah blew her a kiss from across the room, and she smiled at him, too deep in well-wishers to even try to get closer.

"Now," Nathan said in a loud voice to wrest attention back from his wife, "we want to celebrate this great news as angels celebrate everything—with a song. Deborah? Matthew? Lael? If you'll come stand here with me . . ."

Magdalena looked as surprised as everybody else did, so Obadiah guessed this particular number had been written and rehearsed in secret. Nathan was a composer of moderate renown; he had scored pieces that had been performed at the Gloria and his own wedding, among other notable occasions. Obadiah wondered what kind of music he would have considered appropriate to commemorate such a momentous occasion in his life.

It was, as it turned out, a plaintive melody that traded a cascading series of notes with the restless alto line. Its question-and-response format required there to be two sets of singers, each singing in harmony, so Deborah and Lael posed the questions while Nathan and Matthew responded. Obadiah listened with real appreciation as the simple, haunting song unfolded.

> *Who will you love who comes as a stranger,*
> *Love long before that first knock on the door?*
> *I will love no one who's wrapped in a mystery.*
> *Yes, this is one you'll completely adore.*
>
> *Am I expecting a man or a woman?*
> *It could be either or it could be both.*

Might I mistake him for some stray wayfarer?
This is a face you will instantly know.

Then tell me this: Are his eyes blue or hazel?
Will he be dark or will he be fair?
Is he of sullen or sweet disposition?
You will not know till he's standing right there.

Who will I love who comes as a stranger,
Face unfamiliar and features unformed?
This one you'll love above any other,
The child of your heart—the baby unborn.

The room exploded with wild applause when the song was done, and Magdalena flung herself into Nathan's arms, covering his face with kisses. Obadiah thought it was the happiest he had seen her in weeks, but then again, he thought the song was the best present Nathan could have given her.

The next few weeks passed in a sort of agony for Obadiah. The early days of winter always featured turbulent weather, particularly in this quadrant of the country, and there was no way for Obadiah to shirk his responsibilities to the hold. So he spent his days traveling south to the lower coastline, west toward the Galilee River, north again, almost to the burned crater that marked the place where Mount Galo had stood until a year and a half ago. Singing, always singing, praying for rain, praying for sunshine, praying for the harsh winds to unsnarl and lay quiet. Every morning, he woke with the resolution of returning to Breven, and every day passed without offering him a chance to follow his heart. He could not even expostulate with Nathan, could not even pretend that negotiating with the Jansai could take precedence over these desperate journeys to placate the god and keep Jordana habitable. He merely flew, and sang, and tried to set aside his longing.

It was a complete month after his last rendezvous with Rebekah that Nathan—as exhausted and sleepless as the rest of the Cedar Hills angels—finally decreed that Obadiah could go back to work on his foremost mission. "For winter is here, and we've done what we can to ease its passage into our lives," Nathan said. "I don't care if it snows from now until the Gloria next spring. The farmers can do without our interference for a few days."

"Then I'll be off to Breven in the morning," Obadiah said, trying to sound nonchalant.

"And maybe you'll have better luck with Uriah this time. Somehow convince him that we're not such a bad lot."

"And if not Uriah," Obadiah said with a smile, "maybe I'll find someone else who's disposed to look favorably on the angels."

He set out at first light so that he would make it before the early dark of the season, and he headed straight for the house in the wealthy district of the city. The tricky part, of course, was getting close enough to that house to leave a memento in the garden without being seen. This time he and Rebekah had planned ahead. She had given him her embroidered scarf, the one that had been a gift from her cousin; anyone who found it lying about would know it was hers and make sure it was returned to her instantly. He would not need to worry about whether or not she would receive his message. No, he would only have to worry about whether or not she would be able to slip from the house, and whether or not she would be able to navigate the streets in safety.

There—the garden was empty. He made one quick pass overhead and let the flimsy scarf fall from his hand, unwrapping from around a quartz stone as it dropped. Then he canted seaward, toward the city center, and headed directly for the Hotel Verde.

"Good evening, Zoe," he greeted the Manadavvi woman at her desk. "I'll be staying here for two nights at least. And I believe I'm expecting company quite late."

CHAPTER NINETEEN

It was the longest month of Rebekah's life. The angel had warned her, though, that he might not be back for weeks, and it never even occurred to her that she might never see him again. Not until Martha mentioned it.

The conversation about failed love had started off as a conversation about failed contraception. One of Martha's cousins, who lived with her husband in Ezra's house, had become pregnant for the third time in three years. "And I heard my mother scolding her. 'Don't you know about kalaleaf? Don't you understand how the medicine works?'"

Rebekah looked up. "What's kalaleaf?"

Martha looked around as if to make sure no one was listening. But they were alone in the fabric room of Hector's house, hemming sheets. It was a tedious task, but if they agreed to do it, Jerusha left them alone for the day, and sometimes it was worth it to have the chance to talk in privacy. "See?" Martha said. "They don't tell girls about things like that until they're married. But it's a medicine that prevents you from conceiving."

"Well, if no one told you about it—" Rebekah began.

Martha looked smug. "I know about it. I know about a lot of things that haven't been told to me." Her voice dropped. "I've been using it."

"Martha!" Rebekah exclaimed, and then almost immediately

had a change of heart. *"Martha,"* she said, almost breathing the name this time. "Do I—should I—"

Martha flicked her hair back. "Oh no. You can't have a baby with an angel."

Rebekah felt doubtful. "You can't? But then where do all the angels come from?"

"They're all born at the angel holds, and girls drink special potions that help them conceive. And still it almost never happens. It's almost impossible to have an angel baby. Don't you worry."

Rebekah sighed. "Well, I won't have to worry, if I never see him again. It's been so long."

Martha sewed a few moments in silence. "Do you ever think he was lying to you?" she said at last.

"Do I ever think *what?*"

"That he was lying to you. Your angel. When he said he loved you."

Rebekah took a few more stitches. "No."

"Men always say they love you. It means nothing."

At that, Rebekah looked up. Perhaps they weren't talking about Obadiah at all. "Do you mean—your Manadavvi friend—"

Martha shrugged with elaborate carelessness. "Oh, he was in town last week. I know because Ephram was in the market and bought goods from Chesed's caravan, but I didn't see him. He had told me they wouldn't return for another two weeks. I guess their plans changed."

"But why do you think—"

"I don't think anything!"

"Martha," Rebekah said patiently. "Has something gone wrong between you and Chesed?"

"I don't know," Martha said, keeping her head down over her hem and taking very large stitches. Hepzibah, who inspected the linens, would not be pleased. "He has been so affectionate! Has told me—oh, a hundred times—that he loved me. A thousand times. But then the last few days we were together, he has seemed—not as pleased with me. He did not tell me I was beautiful, did not beg me to run away with him. I said something—something like, 'Someday I'll see those orchards in Gaza,' and he just shrugged and said,

'Maybe.' Like he didn't care. And then now, he comes to town, but he doesn't tell me he's going to be here and I think—" She paused and took a deep breath. "I think he doesn't really love me after all."

Rebekah was at a loss. Jansai women didn't often deal in love and betrayal. Dissatisfaction, resentment, and fear, yes; those were often the lot of a Jansai wife, but none of them married for love, so they had no experience in handling it. "I don't—surely he did love you," she said, stumbling over the bleak comfort. "Surely he wouldn't have said something if he didn't mean it."

"All men lie," Martha said with a little sniff. "That's what my aunt says."

"And what does she know about men? She was married once to a husband who died three years later, and she has spent the rest of her life in her brother's house."

"I don't know how she knows. It's what she says. She says a man is no more faithful than a desert cat, even to his wife."

"And how does she know *that?*"

"I believe her, though. Men lie about everything else. They lie when they barter with merchants in Luminaux. They lie when they meet other travelers on the road. They lie about money. They lie about the weather! Why wouldn't they lie about love?"

"Jansai men, maybe. Not all men."

"All men," Martha said firmly. "Even your angel."

"Obadiah doesn't lie."

"Oh, so he's gone back to his hold and told all his friends, all those other angels, how he's taken up with a Jansai girl?"

"No. He said he's told no one."

"So he's lied to the people he's known all his life. Why wouldn't he lie to a girl he just met a couple of months ago?"

Rebekah sewed faster, her stitches hardly any neater than Martha's. "Why would he?"

Martha leaned closer. "Maybe to trick you into loving him."

"He didn't trick me into anything. Everything I did, I did because I wanted to."

"Everything you did, you did because an angel said he loved you. And now he's gone, and you don't know when you'll see him again, and I'm wondering if you haven't just been made a fool of."

Rebekah abruptly laid down her cloth and stood up. Not saying another word, she left the room and went down to the lower level to see if her mother needed help with the baby.

"Here—he's yours if you want him," Jerusha said, handing over the squirming, scowling bundle of irritation. "He's been fussing all day, and I'm about to set him out on the street for the baby-stealers to take."

Rebekah held Jonah up so her eyes peered right into his and her nose brushed against his tiny round one. "No, she wouldn't do that, would she, your mama?" she crooned into his little face. His frown turned into a laugh. "Mama wouldn't give you to the baby-stealers, not my sweet Jonah."

"Keep him the rest of the day, if you would," Jerusha said. "I'm going to sleep for a bit."

So Rebekah took him out to the garden, where it was really too cold to be outside for very long, and sat beside him on the rocky sand. He was just beginning to crawl with any real purpose, and he made his way with great determination from the corvine plant to the dera shrubs. "Gooha!" he exclaimed at her, a word with absolutely no meaning that she could discern, but she scooped him up and kissed him anyway.

"Gooha yourself!" she whispered into his ear. "Aren't you the most precious thing in the world."

And even though she stayed out in the garden until the baby's nose started running and her own fingers grew numb with chill, there was no shadow of angel wings overhead. No mysterious feather came drifting down, full of portent and promises; her missing scarf did not miraculously reappear. The angel was not in town—or, if he was, he had not bothered to contact her.

She avoided Martha the rest of the day and wouldn't talk to her that night when they were alone in Rebekah's bedroom. She was awake, dressed, and out the door before Martha woke the next morning, and she was seated by Hepzibah in the dining hall when Martha came down for breakfast. Martha watched her with the mournful expression that meant she was truly sorry, but Rebekah gave her no chance to apologize. Shortly thereafter, Ephram arrived to take his sister home, and Martha left without Rebekah allowing her a chance to speak.

There was always the possibility that Martha was right. That would make it even more impossible to forgive her.

Two days later, Jordan came down with a stomach disorder that made him weak for three days. He was really too old to be nursed by his sister, but Hector was gone, and Jerusha was busy with the baby, who had also begun to vomit and cough. So Rebekah moved Jordan into her room and cared for him all three days, bringing him soup broth from the kitchen and reading him stories when he was able to concentrate. On the third day, he was feeling well enough to play board games and tease his sister, and on the fourth day he was out of her room.

On the fifth day, *she* got sick.

No one was really available to nurse her, though, so she just suffered through more or less alone. One night she just dragged herself to the water room and lay on the cold tile all night, lifting her head enough to throw up every few hours. She slept for the entire following day. Hepzibah brought her soup that afternoon, and Jerusha checked on her in the evening, but she didn't wish for any more attention than that; she didn't care much for hovering solicitousness when she was feeling bad.

She was sick the next morning, and the next—and even when, by every reasonable standard, the sickness should have been gone, she felt nauseated and a little weepy every morning for the next week or so. She didn't share this news with her mother, who truly couldn't abide illness and considered it a mark of laziness. Since she felt more or less normal by the time lunch arrived each day, she figured she wasn't actually dying, and she just got used to the morning queasiness.

Two weeks after she had made unpardonable comments, Martha was back for the day, deposited at Hector's gate by her brother. The dark blonde didn't look any too sure of her welcome, though Jerusha greeted her with a kiss and Hepzibah observed dryly that she must have remembered where her *true* home lay, since they hadn't had the privilege of her company for so many days.

It was well past dinner—and an informal social hour sparked when the women of the house across the street were escorted over by their men—before the two girls had a chance to talk. They were heading up the stairway, on their way to bed, and Hepzibah and Gabbatha were close behind them.

"Rebekah," Martha said in a low, urgent voice. "I wish you wouldn't—I'm so sorry for what I said—"

"I know," Rebekah said in a flat voice.

"Please don't be mad at me anymore."

"I'm not," she said in the same tone.

"You girls go straight on to bed!" Hepzibah called up in her cranky voice. "Don't be staying up talking all night."

"We won't, *awrie*," Rebekah said over her shoulder.

"Bekah—"

But Rebekah didn't say anything till they were safely in her room, the door shut, the low gaslight on. Martha stood by the door, as if, once she determined for certain that she was not welcome, she intended to slip down to the kitchen and sleep on the hearth all night. Rebekah stood facing the opposite wall, hung with a brightly patterned tapestry that her father's mother had given her on her sixteenth birthday.

"I haven't heard from him," Rebekah said, speaking directly to the wall hanging.

"Oh, sweetie, I'm so sorry."

"I think I will. He said it might be a long time before he could come back. He said it might be weeks, and I shouldn't worry."

"Yes. He might just be really busy," Martha said encouragingly.

"But I do worry, a little," Rebekah said, her voice faltering. "I thought—I didn't think it would be so long—"

"Bekah, I'm sorry, I'm sorry—"

Rebekah whirled to face her. "Don't you say that," she said fiercely. "Don't you ever say anything about him that's—that's mean or distrustful or uncertain. Don't ever tell me he might not love me. Don't ever say that. Even if it's true."

Martha shook her head. She had taken one step away from the door, and her eyes were wide as winter moons. "I won't," she said. "I'm sure he loves you."

"Yes," said Rebekah.

And then they both moved forward at once, falling into each other's arms and sobbing. Despite Hepzibah's warning, they did stay up most of the night, talking.

*   *   *

It turned out that Martha's Manadavvi lover had reappeared, claiming he had never slighted her. Yes, his family had been in Breven a few weeks ago, but he had not been with them, having been left behind to make deals in Luminaux. Successful deals, it turned out, because, look, here was a silver hair clip banded with straps of bronze, a delicate piece that looked demure and expensive when set in Martha's deep blond hair.

"At first I wasn't sure I believed him, but he spoke so prettily that I had to pretend to," Martha prattled on. "He even gave me their schedule for the next two months, but *I* know how travel goes. Anything can delay you on the road, so I can't count on him arriving exactly when he says he will. But he promised to get in touch with me next time they arrive."

"Get in—how will he do that?"

"I told him about you and Obadiah—"

"You *told* him? No, sweet Jovah, no, please swear to me that you didn't tell this Manadavvi boy about me and the angel."

"Oh, hush. I just said that one of my cousins had taken a lover. I didn't say which cousin and I certainly didn't describe her lover! But I told him about the signal you use, a special item dropped into the courtyard. We picked five pieces of cloth from his father's stores— different colors, because wouldn't it be odd if every few weeks another pink scarf blew into your garden?—and he'll drop them in on the night before the day that he wants to see me. It is such a clever system! I'm amazed that you and Obadiah thought of it. You aren't as easy with deception as I am."

"Oh," Rebekah said on a sigh, "it's a skill I'm learning very well."

Late that night, Hector returned from a long trip north to Gaza, the wagons loaded down with merchandise and the man himself delighted at some of his deals. The girls heard all the news through Jerusha, who joined them the next day at the breakfast table, wearing three new gold necklaces and a soft shawl of the most exquisite design. She also looked dreamy and smug, smiling like a little boy who'd left frogs on his sister's pillow. Rebekah knew what that look meant. She'd worn it herself recently, on mornings after a tryst with

Obadiah. Hector had been gone nearly three weeks; no doubt he had missed his wife.

Rebekah found she didn't really want to think about her mother and Hector enjoying the act of love.

She spent the day instead helping the cooks prepare an evening feast, because Hector had invited his new business partner's family over to celebrate the successes of their trading venture. Martha had petitioned to stay for the event, and permission had been granted, so once all the food was ready, the girls retired to Rebekah's room to put on their finest clothes. Simon's sister was spiteful; she loved nothing better than to appear dressed in the most gorgeous fabrics and then make purring little comments about the other women's clothes.

"We'll show her. I sent Ephram back to pick up my green silk jeska. You know it always brings out the color of my skin," Martha said. "And you in that deep red—stunning. She hasn't seen that jeska yet. She'll be jealous and hateful all night."

Rebekah was tugging the close-fitting hallis in place, and frowning in front of the mirror. "No, but it's not laying right. It's making me feel all squishy."

Martha came over to inspect the problem. "What? Here across your bosom? It's all bunched up in back, wait a minute—"

But even with Martha's adjustments, the hallis felt too tight for comfort. "I don't understand it," Rebekah said. "Hepzibah just made this for me a month or so ago."

"Have you gained weight?"

"A little, I think, but not there!"

They both giggled. "It doesn't matter," Martha said, whipping the looser-fitting jeska over her cousin's head. "No one will be able to tell once you're fully dressed."

And, indeed, the two of them were quite pleased with themselves as they stood side by side, examining their images in the glass. Rebekah was all dark hair and brilliant color; Martha was a desert blossom, green stalk and golden tassel of hair.

"So jealous," Martha said again. "I can't wait."

The dinner was sumptuous: rich courses of meats and gravies, flavored with exotic spices and set off by a variety of wines. Hector often reserved the best dishes for the men's table, but because

Simon's wife and sisters were dining with them that night, the fare in the women's hall was just as grand as food in the main dining room. Rebekah and Martha gorged themselves, and everyone around them did the same.

After the meal, Jerusha shooed Rebekah out into the garden. "It's too *cold*," Rebekah whined, but Jerusha merely told her to get a heavy cloak and stroll around the perimeter. Martha giggled and fetched wraps for both of them, and they paced around the garden for twenty minutes, shivering, before Isaac and Hector's uncle made an appearance.

"So I've heard my nephew's account of the trip to Gaza," the old man said. "What were your thoughts?"

"I was impressed by the great wealth of the Manadavvi people, but I found their customs distasteful," Isaac said in a serious voice. Martha elbowed Rebekah in the ribs and made a mocking face.

"How so?"

"They display their riches in pointless ways. I understand the value of a grand house, and I even understand investing in beautiful furnishings, but they overspend. The houses are too grand. There are so many empty rooms just piled on for show. There are too many useless treasures hanging on the walls or standing about in the statuary. I saw door handles made of gold and walkways lined with chips of diamond. A Manadavvi flaunts his wealth, whereas a Jansai merely enjoys it."

"They are ostentatious," the uncle said gravely.

"Yes. And arrogant. They were willing to make deals with us, but their disdain was evident. More than once I wanted to say, 'My opinion of you is even lower than yours of me.' But I did not."

"No, for a good trader pretends every man is his friend, even a man with no goods or money at hand. For who knows when such a man may acquire wealth or merchandise?"

"And their women," Isaac continued.

Now Rebekah and Martha exchanged quick looks, mirthful but curious.

"They treat their women badly," Isaac said.

"Now, that is something I hadn't noticed," Hector's uncle said.

Isaac made a little grunt of disgust. "They parade them around the room like the gaudiest of possessions! They show them off like their women were prizes they had wrested from the marketplace. A woman should be guarded so carefully that no other man knows what treasure you possess. A woman is too precious to be gazed upon by strangers."

Martha made a little bobbing motion with her head, as if she liked the way he phrased his answer, even if she didn't agree with his philosophy.

"Unfortunately, none of the other peoples of Samaria share our views on this matter," the old man said. "They consider women ordinary and commonplace."

"Well, the Manadavvi at least have no understanding of what gives a woman value," Isaac said, a note of contempt creeping into his voice. "And the women themselves behaved with a shocking lack of virtue. We were forced to dine with them, you know—men and women mixed all together at a single table in one room."

"Yes, I have dined with the Manadavvi before."

"And the women spoke shamelessly with the men seated around them, not at all embarrassed to be out in public and on display in such a fashion. And some of the women—young women! unmarried women!—were deep in conversation with men, completely unsupervised by any father or brother that I could see. I swear I saw one girl slip away from the room in company with a Luminaux merchant in our train, and they did not return. I can only guess, with horror, what might have passed between them when they were out of sight."

Now the looks Martha and Rebekah exchanged were half rueful and half apprehensive.

"Shocking, indeed," the old man said. "But again, their customs are not our customs, their ways not ours."

"Some truths are universal," Isaac said firmly. "A young woman is a piece of glass, fragile and beautiful. It takes only a single careless motion to brush that glass to the floor, to see it shatter and break. A young woman who has been compromised is useless—she is valueless. *Kirosa*," he added, using the Jansai word that meant *broken*. "She must be swept aside and forgotten, and a new glass found to fill her place. The Manadavvi cover their broken pieces of glass with bright shawls and expensive jewelry, but I see the shards beneath the finery. I would cast such a woman into the desert. She would have no worth to me."

The men kept on walking, but Rebekah and Martha were standing stock-still, staring at each other with their eyes wide and their mouths parted in horror. All Jansai men felt this way; what he said was no surprise. But it was one thing to know something, to acknowledge it while pretending it had no significance to you. It was another to hear your affianced husband say out loud the words that could seal your death warrant if he ever learned the truth.

Two days later, Jordan brought Rebekah her embroidered scarf. "This is yours, isn't it?" he asked. "I found it in the garden yesterday."

"*Yesterday?*" she exclaimed, snatching it from his fingers. Her imagination, no doubt, but it smelled of snow and starlight. "You've had it all this time?"

He looked surprised. "Yes. I'm sorry. Were you looking for it?"

She tried to choke back her hysteria. "It's just that—I'd lost it, and Martha was upset with me. She made it, you know, and she says I'm so careless with all the gifts she's given me—which isn't *true*—"

Jordan shrugged. "Martha's a little unsteady these days."

She was wholly focused on the significance of the scarf, on the fact that Obadiah was in town—or had been in town a day ago—but something in the tone of his voice caused Rebekah's gaze to lock onto Jordan's face. "What do you mean?"

He shrugged again. "Eph says she's always fighting with her mother and her aunts, sleeping till all hours of the day, hiding in some corner of the house where they can't find her whenever there's work to be done. He says if he didn't know better, he'd think she'd gotten into their father's liquor store, but all the wine is kept in the men's kitchen, and he knows she wouldn't cross the dividing wall."

Rebekah was fairly sure there was no part of Ezra's house that Martha hadn't crept into at some point. She knew for a fact that, whenever the men were gone on an extended journey, Martha would get up in the night and glide through the men's quarters, exploring, while the servants and the young boys were asleep. The wine cellar would be Martha's playground. She no doubt had a bottle or two stashed in her own room at this very moment.

But such transgressions, of course, were the least of Martha's crimes.

"Martha's just—Martha," Rebekah said lamely. "She's always been a little wild."

"Well, she'll need to calm down soon if Uncle Ezra's going to find her a husband."

"Is he trying to make a match for her? She hasn't said anything."

"Maybe she doesn't know," Jordan said a little smugly. "Eph says their father has been talking to Michael and Elam. They both have good trading routes, though Eph says Elam is shrewder and more likely to turn a profit."

"I didn't know Elam had any sons," Rebekah said.

"He doesn't. But his wife died three years ago."

"He's fifty years old!"

"A steady man for an unsteady girl," Jordan replied. "That's what Eph says."

"I think maybe you've been spending too much time with cousin Ephram," Rebekah said sharply.

Jordan looked surprised. "Why shouldn't I?"

She shook her head and was unable to explain. "Because he's—because he—oh, Ephram is always such a braggart, always showing off how much he knows or how much smarter he is than everyone else. He doesn't need to be monitoring his sister's behavior and plotting with his father to see her married off."

"Of course he does. If she doesn't marry, Martha will be his responsibility. Just as you would be mine, if you didn't marry Isaac."

It was too ludicrous. Rebekah had been helping care for Jordan since the day he was born; she'd rocked Ephram in his cradle while Martha tickled his tiny feet. Impossible to think that these little boys would suddenly become judgmental men who saw their sisters as burdens, as objects to be sheltered or bartered. But Jordan was perfectly serious, and Ephram, she knew, had always wanted to race headlong into the duties and delights of manhood.

Something to consider another day. Her hands were nervous on the scarf, winding and unwinding it around her fingers. What had Obadiah thought last night, when she did not appear in response to his signal? No doubt he had waited for her in his hotel room for

hours last night, his hopes gradually fading, his eager face falling
into lines of disappointment or worry. Jovah's bones, he would be
frantic with anxiety, convinced that her failure to appear meant that
some disaster had befallen her on the streets. She must go to him
now, right away, soothe away his fears and remind him that she
loved him—

Not now. Tonight.

She did not think she could endure the intervening hours.

"I wouldn't mind, though," Jordan was saying.

She had no idea what they were talking about. "Wouldn't mind
what?"

"If you never married. Or if you came back to my house after
you were widowed. You've always been the best sister to me, and I
would do everything to care for you, if that task came to me."

She kissed him impulsively on the forehead, though he tried to
duck, and thought how much he looked like Jonah. Sweet Jovah
singing, might it be *Jonah* who someday entertained the same grave
thoughts about how to best care for his aging sister? Oh, very easily.
Hector was twenty years younger than Hepzibah, after all, and she'd
lived in his house for at least a decade.

"I appreciate it," she said, forcing herself to sound serious. "I've
always known I could count on you."

The day took forever to dodder past, creaky and as full of irritations
as an old woman with an achy back. Rebekah had a quick, snappish
fight with her mother over something stupid—the color of her jeska,
perhaps, or the way she'd styled her hair—and Hepzibah lectured
her for ten minutes about her table manners when she failed to
answer a question addressed to her at dinner. Everyone was in line to
use the water room right when Rebekah wanted to take a quick
bath, to freshen herself up for her evening assignation.

And no one, it seemed, wanted to sleep at all that night. Rebekah
stood for half an hour in the hallway outside her door, hand on the
knob so she could pretend she was just stepping back inside if someone spotted her, and listened to all the movement going on up and
down the corridor. Was everyone lying awake, finishing up an embroi-
dery project, or holding a last conversation before bedtime? Was no

one ready to turn off her gaslight and tumble onto her mattress, bid good night to Jovah, and drift off to sleep?

At last she could stand it no longer. She vowed to tell anyone she met that she was hungry (she was, actually), and that she was just stepping into the kitchen for a late snack. She glided silently down the halls, encountering no one, and felt her way cautiously past the stoves and tables in the kitchen. Once in the garden, which seemed quite bright by moonlight after the utter darkness indoors, she stayed in the shadows as she circled around to the gate. She paused a moment to listen to the sounds from all directions—the house and the street—then lifted the latch and stepped out.

Obadiah almost wept when he saw her. She felt the shivers shake his body as he swept her against him, holding her wordlessly for the longest time. She lay against his chest with her eyes closed, reveling in sensation: the heat of his body, the strength of his arms, the sweetness of his scent. His feathers tumbled across her hair, down her back, textured as velvet. She did not know how she would be able to leave him when the evening came to an end.

"I have spent the last day praying for the god to strike me dead," he whispered against her cheek. "I was sure you were already in Jovah's arms, and I wanted to join you there."

"No, nothing has happened. I didn't even get the scarf until today. I didn't know you were here."

"And it's been so *long!* Weeks! And I couldn't get back, I couldn't leave the hold, there was so much to do, and I thought, she will not believe in me, she will think that I have forsaken her."

"No," she lied. "Not for a minute."

"By the god's own heart and heartstrings, I have missed you, Rebekah." He groaned, holding her even tighter, pressing her bones into his bones. "I did not imagine I would ever have to go so long without seeing you again."

"And I have missed you." She gasped, since she couldn't get enough air to speak in a normal voice. "Obadiah, I must breathe—"

"I will give you my own breath," he said, and covered her mouth with his. And it was true, he breathed for both of them, or else she ceased to need oxygen at all. For it seemed she did not once inhale on her own again for the rest of the night, but drew all her sustenance, all her cues, even the pace of her heart, from Obadiah's body; and that was enough to satisfy her.

After they made love, they were both starving, so instead of lying in bed and murmuring endearments, they sat at the fancy table and had a hearty meal. Obadiah told Rebekah of all the farms and provinces he'd visited in the past four weeks, praying for a change in weather or a gift from the god. She was fascinated by the variety of tales, the glimpses into so many different lives, amazed that none of them were like her own.

"And what was *she* wearing?" she asked, every time his tale included mention of a woman. "What did her husband say to her? How did her son treat her?"

Or: "But how did she break her wrist? Working in the *field?* You mean, in the direct sunlight? With—no, you mean those other men were not her brothers?"

Or: "What do you mean, she's a teacher? She teaches the little children? The *adults?* The men, too? Does she—and she doesn't wear a veil? Don't they stare at her?"

She had always known, in a vague way, that women outside of Breven lived somewhat different lives. But she had just assumed they were very much like her own life, except in small, unimportant details—that the foods they preferred featured different spices, that they only covered their faces in daylight, that they walked unescorted in the world, but only to certain destinations. She could not imagine living in a world so free of boundaries, so filled with frightening, constant choices. *What should I wear today? What shall I eat? Whom might I encounter on the street?* How did such a woman know what expressions to hold upon her face, when anyone might see it at any point and guess what thoughts were circling in her head? How could she calculate the cost of food, how could she judge when to plant and when to reap, how could she barter products in the marketplace? How could she lie down at the end of the day, carefree enough to sleep, knowing that she relied completely on her own skill and wit?

Earlier this very day, Rebekah had laughed at the notion that

Jordan would care for her, but she had never considered the implications of having to care entirely for herself. She did not think she could do it. She did not know how.

"I wouldn't want to be that woman," she said quietly, when Obadiah described an isolated farm wife whose husband and son lay sick with fever.

"No, I pitied her sincerely," Obadiah said. "She must have been so lonely out there! But the food was in for the winter, and her older boy looked like he'd be a help around the farm, so I imagine she'll pull through well enough."

She looked at him helplessly. She wouldn't have wanted to be any of those women. But she didn't think she could explain.

"So how have you passed your time?" he asked. "More eavesdropping on Isaac's conversations?"

She laughed. "Yes, just the other day he was telling us—telling Hector's *uncle*—about a trip to Manadavvi country, and Martha and I got to listen. He didn't seem to like the Manadavvi much."

"Well, see? Your betrothed and I have one thing in common."

"He thinks they treat their women poorly."

Obadiah laughed. "The only women treated *less* poorly than Manadavvi women are those who happen to be angels. Spoiled and beautiful, those Manadavvi girls. And powerful and clever and full of secrets. I don't think he needs to feel sorry for them."

She didn't bother to explain. "Full of secrets? How would you know that?"

He grinned. "I've talked to a few of them from time to time. I always came away convinced they were concealing something vital. And now that I've talked to Zoe so often—"

She could not identify the peculiar tingle of heat that prickled across her face and hands. "Zoe? Who's that?"

"The woman here. The one you usually see downstairs when you arrive at night."

"Oh. Oh, that one. I didn't know she had a name."

"Yes, and it's pretty, isn't it? Zoe."

"I've never heard of anyone having a name like that," she said coldly.

"She's lived here almost a year. Can you imagine that? So far from her friends and her familiar places and her customs. The only people she can really speak to are the travelers who stay here, since the merchants and the Jansai men treat her like sin incarnate, and naturally she hasn't been allowed to meet any Jansai women. I imagine she must feel like a prisoner here sometimes, but she's always polite and helpful. Always friendly. You'd never know it if she was unhappy. That's one of the reasons I think Manadavvi women keep secrets."

"All women keep secrets," Rebekah said shortly. "I'm sure this Zoe is not so special."

Obadiah laughed out loud. "What, you can't be jealous!"

Was that the name of this feeling? This sense of cold rage mixed with a hot urge toward murder? "It is just that if I had known you preferred Manadavvi women—"

He leaned forward and kissed her quickly on the mouth. "I have only one preference," he said. "I prefer you."

It mollified her, but only a little. "Still, if you talk to this Zoe person every time you are here—"

"You might consider talking to her sometime as well," he interrupted. "Next time you arrive."

Rebekah arched her eyebrows in disbelief. "And what would I say to her?"

"She is—she might—she could be a friend to you sometime, perhaps," he said, uncharacteristically awkward. And then, all in a rush, "Rebekah, she knows you are a girl."

She jerked back so hard that the fine ribs of the chair bruised her back. "She *what?* How does she—did you *tell* her?"

"No, no, I would never do that. One night I told her I was expecting company, and she said, 'The same young lady who has been here before?' and so I realized that she knew. I thought that—"

Rebekah covered her face with her hands (too late to be hiding her face *now,* she thought savagely), and felt more unnerved than she had since beginning this charade. "Jovah's bleeding bones," she said through her fingers. "Then if *she* knows—if *she* could guess—anyone could tell. Anyone might know me."

He was reaching for her, pulling her tense body over onto his lap and cradling her against him. "No, no, she saw you under strong light, and she is trained to assess whoever steps through that door," he soothed her. "No one else has noticed, no one else has known. You know that women are much more clever than men. They see things that men do not."

She laughed through her panic. "That's certainly true!"

"And she swore to tell no one. I believe her. Manadavvi women and their secrets, remember? But I thought—I asked her—"

She lifted her head then to glare at him. "You asked her what?"

He offered a tentative smile. "If she would stand friend to you if you were ever in need."

Her scowl grew even fiercer. "And what might I ever need from a Manadavvi stranger that I could not get from my own friends and family?"

"I don't know. A safe place to stay for the night?"

"In a Manadavvi tavern!"

"It's a hotel, and a very luxurious one."

"I would never run from my family's house to this place."

"You never know when you might need succor."

"I never know when an angel might say crazy things."

He shrugged and kissed her on the cheek. "So. Anyway. She knows, and now you know she knows, and if you ever have a need that she can fill, you can go to her."

"Nobody does favors for free," Rebekah said suspiciously.

"News to you, but outside the Jansai world of barter and payment, many people *do* perform favors for no cost," he retorted. "But if a fee is involved, I will pay it. So you may ask her with a light heart."

"I don't think my heart can ever be light now that strangers know my identity," she grumbled. It was bad enough that someone had unmasked her; worse still that it was the beautiful Zoe whom Obadiah already admired so much. She did not actually feel that threatened by the exposure. She just was not happy with how the entire conversation had gone. Manadavvi women and their secrets, indeed.

He tightened his arms around her and brushed his lips along her cheekbone and around the curve of her eye. "What can I do to lighten your heart?" he whispered. "I am prepared to make any sacrifice."

She couldn't help herself; she laughed. She slipped her arms around his back, marveling as always at the silky heat of his skin and the cool dazzle of his feathers. "Well, I am very sad," she said in a mournful voice, hard to manage through her smile. "I think you will have to work very hard to make me cheerful again."

He rose to his feet, holding her in his arms. His wings flowed behind him like a robe thrown open. "I shall not rest," he declared, "until you are radiant again with gladness."

The radiant gladness was relatively quickly achieved, and then they both found themselves almost too drowsy to talk. Obadiah actually fell asleep with his head pillowed on Rebekah's shoulder. She toyed with the edges of his wing feathers, brushing her fingers back and forth against the wispy edges, and listened to the slow, steady rhythm of his breathing.

It was a sound that woke her up—which made her realize that she, too, had fallen asleep.

The sound came again—a knock on the door. "Angelo?" A woman's voice. "Angelo? It is quite late—it is almost early—"

Rebekah scrambled from the bed, fired by a choking sense of panic. "Dear Jovah, sweet Jovah, what time is it? My lord, my god, sweet Jovah—"

She was throwing on her clothes and bending to tie her sandals before Obadiah had even shaken the sleep from his eyes. "What's wrong? Who's knocking?"

"Angelo?" came the woman's voice again.

And then he realized. "Zoe! Yes! Thank you! We were just leaving!" he called, jumping up and hopping into his own clothes. "Merciful god, how long were we sleeping? Rebekah, I'm so sorry—"

She was tying the sash around her boy's tunic, adjusting the cap upon her head. It was still full dark outside the windows, but she could hear the slap and rattle of carts going down the roads. In maybe an hour, Hector's household would be awake. She had so little time, almost no time, to make her way across town and sneak inside the garden.

Obadiah's shirt was misbuttoned and his blond hair stood up all over his head, but he looked ready to go. "I'll take you back," he said. "It'll be much faster."

She merely brushed by him and stepped into the hall. "No. Someone will see you."

"I'll put you down a block away. You can go the rest of the way on foot."

She hurried down the corridor, out into the atrium, the angel at her heels. "I can make it. I have just enough time."

"Rebekah, it will be light in less than an hour!"

"It doesn't take me an hour to get from my house to here."

"I want to take you."

"I don't want you to."

"Rebekah—"

"Stop arguing with me, you'll only make me late."

The Manadavvi woman sat at the desk with her head down, pretending not to hear them. Obadiah nodded at her, mouthing a quick thank-you, but Rebekah just hurried on by, furious. At Obadiah, at herself, at everybody. Furious and terrified. The cooks usually weren't up before dawn, but Jerusha might be awake already, roused by a crying baby. Hepzibah was often up at three or four in the morning to use the water room, and sometimes she never fell back asleep. One of the curses of old age, she would say.

Anyone could be awake. Anyone at all.

Her feet hit the street and she almost fell into a run. Obadiah was beside her for a few steps, pulling at her arm, attempting to reason with her, but she ignored him and kept on trotting forward. Soon enough he must have realized that he put her in even more danger by racing along beside her, an angel opportuning a Jansai boy, so he halted and fell behind as she kept striding on. And then—she was waiting for the sounds—a rush and a ruffle and the sensation of a private wind swirling about her, and she knew he was aloft, following her from overhead.

She didn't look up. She didn't slow down. She just hurried forward, head drawn in a little, eyes on her feet, heart pounding, breath trading painfully in and out of her lungs. A cart passed her, the horse's hooves making a steady clopping on the cobblestone road. Strangers walked by on the other side of the street, quarreling in low voices. The darkness felt thin, insubstantial, ready to rip and give way. Two more carts passed, heading toward the market.

She rounded a corner, crossed another street, and was almost in the residential district. Another block, another street crossed, no more carts or pedestrians. These were the neighborhoods where the wealthy Jansai lived, in big multistory houses behind high walls and sere gardens. She could catch the minty scent of the dera leaves, green all winter. She was fifty yards from her own gate.

So close to her goal, she quickened her pace so that she was actually running by the time she reached her destination. She put one hand on her heart to slow its beating and the other one to the gate latch, to pull it open.

But it would not budge. She jerked again, harder, but it would not respond. The gate was locked.

CHAPTER TWENTY

Rebekah stood there a moment, so stunned she couldn't think. Locked out? Who would have been up, roaming the house and gardens, after she had left? Certainly Hector and the other men were often gone from home till quite late, but they entered through the front door or the gate of the outer garden. Which of the women had been abroad later than Rebekah herself?

And how would she get back inside? Back to safety, back to secrecy, back to her own secure room? She tugged on the handle more frantically, causing the wood to rattle against the iron, but the lock didn't give. Sweet Jovah singing, she couldn't climb the wall—it was nearly twelve feet high, and made of smoothly planed wood—and there was no other way in.

But she couldn't stand here all night, waiting for the cooks to stir and the house door to open, waiting to call someone over. *It's Rebekah, I've been out all night, let me in.* She had to get inside. She would have to try the wall.

She had taken a step back to gaze up and gauge her chances when she felt the soft stir and swirl of wind around her. Turning quickly, she found Obadiah had landed noiselessly on the street behind her.

"What is it? What's wrong?" he demanded, coming close enough to whisper.

She gestured helplessly. "The gate, it's locked."

"You don't have a key?"

She shook her head. "From the inside."

"I'll lift you over," he said.

She stared at him a moment, not comprehending.

"I'll carry you over," he repeated. "Set you down in the garden and then take off again."

"Someone will see you," she said.

"Well, someone will certainly see *you* if you're out here much longer."

"And the garden—it's not very big—I don't know if you'll be able to take off again from inside—"

The sky was lightening just enough for her to see the faint smile on his face. "Well, then, I'll unlock the gate and walk out."

"Oh—yes! But I still think you—"

A noise on the other side of the gate caused them both to freeze, then move deeper in the shadow of the wall.

"What was that?" Obadiah breathed.

"One of the cooks, I think. Usually they're not up this early. But she might be going out to pick marrowroot or spices. You can't carry me over."

He stepped back into the street and gazed up, scanning the flat, bare surfaces of the house. "What about the roof?" he said. "Can you get in from there?"

She looked from his face to the house and back again. "The roof? I don't—well—yes. Maybe. There's the winter stairwell."

"The what?"

She shook her head. "In the winter. When it rains. We put pans and buckets on the roof to catch the rainwater. Everybody does, all the houses on the street—"

He nodded impatiently. "And can you get to this winter stair?"

"I don't know. I mean, I don't know if it's locked. I haven't been up on the roof since I was a child. I think Jordan and Ephram still go up there sometimes."

"I'll take you to the roof," he said. "And I'll wait to see if that door, too, is locked."

She was seized with terror. "And if it is?"

"And if it is . . . then you'll have to come back with me."

"I can't do that!"

"Or you'll have to wait outside until someone lets you in, and only you can tell me what kind of story might keep you out of trouble."

She shook her head. "No story. I can't think of anything. I—I have to get in. That's all. I have to."

He stepped closer. "Put your arms around my neck."

Unthinking, she did. She was not quite prepared for what happened next. She felt his whole body collect itself, then explode in one clean burst of energy. A little cry escaped her; she clung to him, her face against his chest. The world swung madly around her for maybe a minute, though she couldn't see any of it; she had her eyes shut tight. Then a little *bump* and a couple of quick steps, and all motion stopped. Cautiously, she opened her eyes.

"We're on the roof!" she exclaimed in a low voice.

He kissed the top of her head and set her on her feet. "Where's this stairwell?"

She took a moment to gaze around her at the unfamiliar perspective on a familiar world. From here she could see down into the gardens of the houses on either side. One of them was crammed with a variety of skinny shrubs, naked and shivering in the winter cold but no doubt quite green and inviting in the summer. The other garden showed very little plant life, but it had been set with stone benches and an ornamental screen that probably shielded the worst of the sun in the hottest months. She had not been inside either of these gardens, because Hector was not friendly with the men who owned the houses. She had often been in the garden of the house across the street, but she could not see into it from this vantage point.

"Rebekah?" Obadiah murmured. "I think we'd best hurry."

She nodded and shook herself from her reverie. The trapdoor to the winter stair was on the women's side of the house, toward the back. "See that? That's the skylight to the fabric room," Rebekah said. "We work in there all winter, just to see the sunlight."

"I'll fly above it from time to time and look down on you. Maybe you'll glance up just as I'm going over, and you'll see me and wave."

"And have Hepzibah and Gabbatha and everyone wonder if I'm crazy enough to be waving at birds. Here it is," she said, falling abruptly to her knees. Obadiah crouched down beside her.

"I hope it doesn't creak when it's pulled open," he said.

"No one should be awake on this level. Not now, anyway. The bedrooms are all on the second floor."

He put his hand out to the carved wooden knob and pulled hard. Protesting only a little, the door swung back on its hinges to reveal absolute blackness inside.

"Can you find your way from here?" Obadiah asked, peering in. His voice sounded worried.

Rebekah had already dangled her feet over the open edge and felt for the first stair with her toes. "Yes. I know exactly where the stairwell comes out. Now the only danger will be running into anyone in the hallway—dressed as I am."

"I wish I knew that you would be all right," Obadiah said.

She kissed him swiftly. "I will be. I am. Thank you for rescuing me."

"I won't look for you tonight," he said. "But I'll be back in a week or two."

"You'll be here again tonight?"

He put his hands on either side of her face. "Please don't come," he said, his voice very low. "I am so afraid for you."

"We'll see," she said, and kissed him again. Then she let her feet take the full weight of her body and stood on the stairwell, only her head and shoulders above the roofline. "I'll be fine," she added and began her descent.

Another ten steps down into total blackness and her feet found solid floor. Above her, she heard Obadiah fit the door back in place. She listened till she caught the sound of three running footfalls on the roof above, then the quick *swoosh* of wingbeats. Her imagination, surely. She stood for a moment at the door leading into the hallway, listening. But there seemed to be no one astir. She pulled the door open and stepped into the empty corridor.

It was a matter of three minutes to glide through the hall, creep down the next stairwell, and hurry the last hundred yards to her own room. Once inside, she stood there a few moments, panting, her back against the door. The sweet god of heaven must love her above all creatures. She could not believe she had successfully negotiated the hazards of this night.

Exhausted and weak with nerves, she wanted nothing but to fall onto her mattress and sleep for a hundred hours. But she had learned already the dangers of unguarded sleep. First she quickly changed into bed clothes, then hid her boy's attire in the bottom of her dresser. She wet an old cloth with water from her nightstand pitcher and scrubbed off any faint traces of charcoal that might remain on her face. Only then did she allow herself to lie on her bed and give herself up to dreaming.

Her eyes opened only a few hours later. She would have liked to sleep till noon, but there were consequences for such foolish behavior. They would think she was sick, and dose her, or think she was lazy, and assign her all the least pleasant tasks of the day. So she forced herself up, promising herself a nap later, and dragged herself down to the water room to wash and dress. She could hear voices the length of the hall as the other women headed downstairs for breakfast. Everything was silent by the time she emerged newly clean, dressed in a fresh jeska, and absolutely starving.

She hurried down the stairs, following the scent of food and the sound of light laughter. It would be dangerous, of course, but if the angel was going to be here another night—he might not return for weeks, she could not wait so long to see him again—and now that she had a second way into the house, a secret way—

At the door to the dining hall, Jerusha met her with a cry of rage and a slap upon the face.

Rebekah froze where she stood, shock making every detail vivid. The room contained about eleven women, all of them staring. Someone dropped a pan, and it clattered on the floor. The smell of burning bread pushed an acrid thread of scent through the hearty aromas of cooking meat and frying eggs.

"You lying little *tramp!*" Jerusha screamed, grabbing Rebekah by the arm and slapping her a second time across the cheek. "The minute your father returns this evening, I will tell him what you've done, and he will throw you from the house."

A murmur of surprise and speculation from the women in the room. Rebekah could not look at them. She stared up instead at her mother's stormy, furious face.

"What—what have I—"

Jerusha slapped her a third time, though Rebekah tried unsuccessfully to flinch away. "Midnight—one o'clock—I come to your room. The baby is screaming, and I need your help. I need to sleep. But you're not there. You're not in the water room or the kitchen. You're nowhere in the house. Where can you be, a young girl in the middle of the night?"

Now the response from the crowd was full of dismay and condemnation. Whispers and words flew around the room.

"But I—" Rebekah stammered.

Jerusha shook her so hard her vision blurred. "Were you out in the garden? No, for I looked! A cold night, but you might have come down with a fever and searched for a cool place to calm your blood. No one was in the garden, but the gate was unlocked. Someone had unlatched it sometime in the night."

Gasps and a rising buzz of speculation from the listening women.

"I don't know who—who opened the gate," Rebekah said. "I was—I didn't leave this house! I was—"

Jerusha hit her again, even harder. Rebekah felt her cheeks spangle with bruises. Her heart had compacted itself to such a small, desperate ball that her chest was tight with pain.

"You liar! You awful, wicked, lying, dreadful girl! Where have you been all night? Who have you been with? What terrible things have you done?"

Rebekah could not answer. Her mind would not frame the lie; her lips could not shape the words. *I am dead,* she thought, and prepared for the next swift blow.

"Jerusha, you foolish, hysterical woman," came a dry voice from the hall behind Rebekah. "What crazy ideas have you got into your empty head now?"

Jerusha jerked Rebekah away from the doorway, and Hepzibah stepped through. The old woman looked frail and exhausted, as if she had had no more sleep than Rebekah had, and needed it more.

"No crazy ideas, *awrie,*" Jerusha said in a low voice, her fingers tightening spasmodically on Rebekah's arm. "Just a wretched truth. My daughter so far forgot all her training, all her dignity, all her worth, to sneak from this house last night. She was gone for hours, and I do not know how she managed to return, because I locked the gate behind her and expected to never see her again."

Before Rebekah had had time to digest that terrible piece of news, Hepzibah laughed. Actually laughed. "Oh, to be young and full of fantasies again," she said in her gravelly voice. "You stupid woman, don't you know where your daughter was last night? She was with me."

Jerusha was so astounded, she dropped Rebekah's arm. Both of them stared at the old woman. Hepzibah patted Rebekah on the shoulder.

"I know I told you I didn't want anyone to know about my back," she rasped out. "But, Jovah's bones, child! I didn't expect you to take a beating on my behalf."

"I—I didn't know what to say," Rebekah choked out.

Hepzibah nodded. Her sharp little eyes were fixed on Jerusha's face. "I can't sleep. Night after night, I can't sleep," the old woman said. "Your daughter—who is a *good* girl, and you're too dull to see it—your daughter has come over many a midnight to rub oil on my back. Last night wasn't the first time she fell asleep on my mattress, and I felt too guilty to wake her and send her back to her own room. Let her sleep, poor thing. An old woman can't grant a young girl too many favors."

"But she never said—and the *gate!*" Jerusha exclaimed.

Hepzibah shrugged. "Maybe it was never locked. Everyone forgets a chore now and then. And as for Rebekah never saying a word, well, I asked her not to. I am old and despised enough already. I don't want pity on top of it."

"No one—no one despises you, *awrie,*" Jerusha said. "You are my husband's beloved sister."

"And you are an empty-headed, hot-hearted, foolish woman," Hepzibah declared. "Are you done mistreating your daughter? I would ask her to bring me a plate of food to the table. I find I am not feeling so strong this morning, and I need to sit down."

"Yes—I—Rebekah, go get food for your aunt," Jerusha said.

No apology first. No apology expected. A woman could abuse her children, just as a husband could abuse his wife, and no one questioned her behavior. Still, Rebekah felt her face must be bright red as a dera berry, half of the color brought by violence and half by mortification.

"Sit. I will bring you whatever you like," Rebekah said to Hepzibah in a voice that was almost a whisper.

"A little of everything," Hepzibah said. "I'm hungry."

There was almost complete silence as Rebekah moved across the room to where the cooks had laid out a buffet. Hector's other two sisters were standing nearby, and Gabbatha reached out and brushed Rebekah's arm as she passed by. A gesture of sympathy. The other one gave her a tremulous old woman's smile. Out of the corner of her eye, Rebekah saw her mother slowly leave her stance by the door and sit down at a table by Hector's cousin and her daughter. Instantly the three women were in a low-voiced discussion, the other two women no doubt reassuring Jerusha that she had done the right thing. *A girl gets wild impulses. Even if she did nothing wrong this time, who knows when such an idea might sprout in her head? Better to warn her now. Better to frighten her so deeply that she never forgets it. Better now, before she does something terrible and it's too late for her.*

It was not the first public fight this room had witnessed between Jerusha and Rebekah, between other women and their daughters. But it was the first time Hepzibah had spoken up to champion anyone. Rebekah moved down the buffet table, filling two plates with food, and could not imagine why Hector's sister had come forward to save her with a lie.

Hepzibah was already seated with her two elderly sisters, all of them deep in gossip about one of the girls in a neighbor's house. "Thank you," Hepzibah said when Rebekah brought over her plate, but in such an absentminded way that it was clear she did not expect Rebekah to sit with them. Rebekah carried her plate to another table, where Hector's niece Hali was sitting with two other girls.

"I hate my mother," Hali said, and they all laughed. That was all that was said on the topic for the whole meal.

The rest of the day passed in an odd, unreal way, Rebekah moving through each sluggish moment as though her whole body was weighted. She went to her mother's room to take charge of Jonah, but then her mother complained that she was so tired, she had to have some rest. So Rebekah brought him with her to the fabric room, letting him crawl through the bolts of cloth and knock over trays of needles. When he turned crabby and fretful, she brought him to her own room and laid him down for a nap, lying beside him on the mattress. Both of them slept for two hours, and Rebekah could have slept even longer if he hadn't woken up and begun to poke at her eyes with his small, curious fingers.

"Frubo," he said in delight when she sat up.

"Frubo indeed," she said, running her hands through her hair and yawning widely. "I wish I knew exactly what you were trying to say."

It was an hour or more before dinner, a time of day when many of the women of the house retreated to their rooms to nap or read. Rebekah scooped the squirming baby into her arms and went down the hall to knock on Hepzibah's door.

"I'm here, come in, don't let an old woman sleep," came the grumble from the other side. Rebekah pushed open the door and went in.

In fact, Hepzibah was sitting at her desk, writing a letter. She had a sister who had married an unusual man; they had moved away from Breven and gone to live in Semorrah twenty years ago. Hector had had nothing to do with her ever since, because she lived like any Semorran woman, barefaced and brazen, but Hepzibah had kept in touch with her all this time. Rebekah could not think of anyone else the old lady would be writing.

"Oh. It's you," Hepzibah said, and folded over her paper.

"I just came—I wanted to thank you."

Hepzibah gestured to an overstuffed red velvet chair, covered with a brightly patterned shawl, and Rebekah sat. Jonah wriggled from her arms and scurried across the room on his hands and knees.

"Let him go," Hepzibah said. "You sit and talk to me."

"I wanted to thank you," Rebekah said. "For helping me this morning."

"For lying for you, you mean."

Rebekah nodded. "Yes. I don't know why you did it."

Hepzibah snorted. "Because your mother is a stupid woman who does not understand that she lives in a prison and that any sane woman would want to break free of it."

Rebekah merely stared at her. Hepzibah gave a parched laugh. "Oh, the prison works for me well enough now. I'm an old woman, and I like to live in a house that someone else provides, eating food that I don't have to cook. I can sit in the garden on a sunny day, and sit under a roof when it rains. I have an easy life. But I'm old. The life wasn't so easy when I was young."

"Did you—when you were younger—"

"Not going to tell you of any of my rebellious actions! You're as foolish as your mother, and just as little to be trusted. But I wasn't a happy girl. I wasn't a happy wife. I don't imagine you're very happy either."

"I was," Rebekah said, "until recently."

Hepzibah nodded her head. "Well, don't tell me anything you've been doing. I don't want to know it. I don't want to stop you, but I can't protect you. I just want you to know that. There will be nothing I will be able to do for you if you are found out."

"You have done so much for me already—today—"

"And I am willing to play that game again. But if you are caught outside these walls, nothing I say will save you."

"I'm going again tonight," Rebekah said.

Hepzibah nodded. "I was sure you would. Be careful."

"I will be."

"Do you need money?" the old woman asked.

Rebekah just looked at her for a moment. Jansai women never had cash, since they were never out in public places where they might spend it. All the household expenses were discharged by the men. "I don't think so," she said. "But why do—how do—"

Hepzibah brushed her hand through the air. "My sister sends me some from time to time. It is a good thing for a woman to have her own coins, in case—well, just in case."

"I won't be leaving Breven," Rebekah said.

"No? And you'll marry this Isaac in—what is it now, a little more than three months' time?"

"Yes."

Hepzibah leaned forward. "Think long and hard before you do that, *kircha*," she said, using the term more fondly than her mother ever had. "A Jansai marriage is not so wonderful a thing. For a girl who is not so docile."

"Hector has decided," Rebekah said. "I have no choice."

"Do you not?" the old lady said. "Don't throw away the choices you do have. And you know better than I do what they might be."

Across the room there was the sound of objects falling and then Jonah's long, accusing wail. Rebekah leapt to her feet. "Oh no, I'm so sorry, he's pulled down your tapestry—"

"Just what I'd expect from a son of my brother's," Hepzibah said with a sniff. "Destruction and turmoil."

Rebekah crossed the room to extricate him from the folds of fabric and upended hanging rods. "Let me give him to my mother, and then I'll come back and fix this. I'm so sorry—"

Hepzibah laughed, her dark little eyes alight with amusement. "You can fix it tonight," she said, "when you come in to rub ointment on my back."

Rebekah was caught so much off guard that she actually opened her mouth to explain where she would really be this night. And then she realized it was a joke. Amazingly, she started laughing, too.

It never would have occurred to her that she would be sharing any jest with Aunt Hepzibah. Particularly one like this, not actually funny.

"If you ever *do* need oil rubbed into your back—" she began, but Hepzibah snapped, "My back's just fine," and they both kept on laughing. Rebekah was still smiling as she delivered the baby back into her mother's arms.

"Thank you," Jerusha said, and that was their only conversation for the day. If you overlooked the conversation at the door of the dining hall that morning.

Dinner was quiet, and Rebekah left early to go lie down. She was always tired these days, it seemed. No wonder, of course, when she spent half the night awake and out of the house, leading a secret, second life. But Obadiah would leave in a day or two, perhaps even as early as tomorrow morning, and she could sleep away every one of the weeks he was gone from her.

She rose from her mattress a couple of hours before midnight and bundled up her boy's clothes under her arms. As before, she stood outside her own door a long time, listening to the noises down the hall. As before, she moved absolutely silently through the sleeping corridor. But this time, on a hunch, she did not take the stairway down toward the kitchen, but up, toward the third story. And from there, she took the winter stairwell up again, pushing open its flat doorway and climbing onto the roof.

The angel was there, waiting for her. She threw herself into his arms and covered his pale face with kisses.

CHAPTER TWENTY-ONE

By now, Elizabeth and David had settled into a routine that seemed to suit them both. He was not a man who seemed to require, as Faith put it delicately, that his physical needs be met with a great deal of frequency. Nor, as Elizabeth put it more bluntly, did he satisfy those physical needs with a great deal of finesse. But he seemed to like the idea of regular sex, without having to go to much trouble to achieve it, and it was Elizabeth's goal to make his life as trouble-free as possible.

So she began to organize their relationship. Each time she saw him—which was always late at night in his own room, no romantic dinners or flowery speeches required beforehand—she inquired into his schedule for the next week or so, and they would agree on the time she should return to his room. Sometimes he forgot, but she never raged or reprimanded him. She simply left him a note: "I see you've been detained. I'll come back tomorrow night." And he was always happy to see her that following night, no matter how inebriated he might be.

His skills as a lover never improved much, but since her expectations had gone down to zero, neither of them was ever disappointed.

And the life suited Elizabeth well enough. She felt she was finally in control of her destiny, working toward all the things she had ever wanted to achieve. She possessed an angel lover—who, truth to tell, took very little of her time and even less of her heart—and the remainder of her life was filled with relationships and activities that she found most agreeable. She and Faith had become truly close friends, confiding all the rather grim details of their previous lives and sharing all their observations about their current existence. They both hated Shiloh, they both adored Tola, they loved the same foods, they had the same goals. They were soul mates.

Faith's own fortunes had turned brighter, as she had begun a romance with a rather callow young angel named Jason. Unlike Elizabeth, Faith seemed to feel some real affection for her angelic suitor, though she was under no illusions about the permanency of the relationship.

"But he's very sweet," she told Elizabeth over dinner one night. They were both earning enough that they could afford a night out once a week, and they looked forward to this evening above all other events in their lives. "He told me yesterday that his mother would like me. And of course you know she wouldn't. But I think if we were up Gaza way where she lives, he might actually take me to meet her!"

"She'll like you well enough if you have his baby."

Faith sighed. "And I thought this month—I really thought—well, you know, I was three days late. But then—" She shrugged. "No baby."

"Listen," Elizabeth said. "They're a little expensive. But Mary's sold me these herbs that are supposed to enhance fertility. You can only take them on certain days, and you can only take them three times a month. I tried them, and they gave me a headache for a week. But if they help—" She shrugged. "You could try some."

"Oh, yes! I'd love to! But why can you only take them three times a month?"

"Because they'll kill you if you take them too often."

Faith's eyes grew big. "Then I guess I'd better be careful."

So Elizabeth asked Mary for a set of the herbs to sell to her friend, and the healer only reluctantly agreed. "You're not lying to me, are you?" the small woman demanded. "You're not pretending these are for somebody else, and then planning to take them all yourself?"

That hadn't even occurred to Elizabeth. "No, of course not! It's just that Faith's seeing this angel, and he's very good to her, but who knows how long it will last? So she wants to improve her chances while she can."

"Well, you be sure to tell her all the warnings," Mary said, shaking some of the dark crushed leaves into a little vial. "This is a very dangerous drug."

"I've already told her," Elizabeth said. "We'll both be careful."

The other reason Elizabeth was enjoying life so much these days was that she loved working with Mary. The initial two-week apprenticeship had become full-time employment since, as Mary had predicted, her original helper never did come back. That was perfectly fine with Elizabeth. Every day she worked with Mary she learned something new, and every day the healer spoke to her with approval. She couldn't remember the last time anyone in her life had appreciated her on a consistent basis. Oh, her mother had loved her, had complimented her often on her beauty and her sense of fashion, but the things her mother had valued had been useless, really, when their old life had fallen apart. These days, she was being commended on her quick wit, her ability to learn, her steady hands, and her cool nerve. Qualities she had not even known she possessed, but qualities that seemed to benefit her more than a heart-shaped face or ropes of auburn hair.

At Mary's side, she had treated broken bones, massive hemorrhages, gangrenous toes, dehydration, rashes, fevers, and hysteria. She'd seen three women give birth, and one almost die from the experience. No little angels had come into the world under Elizabeth's watch, but Mary said she had delivered about a dozen in her time.

"They're rare," she said. "And difficult."

"Difficult how?"

Mary shook her head. "In many ways. So often an angel child is a stillbirth, or a child that dies only a few hours after it's taken from the womb. It's as if whatever there is in angel blood isn't meant to mix with mortal blood—as if there's an alien compound in there somewhere. And the angel children that do survive often kill their mothers on their way to being born. They're too big. You wouldn't think their wings would bulk them up so much, but they make the passage hard. More than once, if I've thought the chance was good that it was an angel child inside, I've knifed open the mother's belly and cut the baby out. Saved more than one life, I promise you."

Elizabeth listened to this recitation with some dismay. "But then—if I become pregnant—or Faith—"

"I know it's what you're both wishing for. But the minute you're carrying an angel child, you're putting your life at risk. Think of that next time you meet that dark boy at night."

Elizabeth shook her head. "If I ever find I'm carrying David's child, I'll move in with you. I'll follow you everywhere. I'll never be more than three feet behind you till the day I deliver."

Mary smiled. "Well, that'll improve your chances, that's for certain. That's the best I can promise."

But nothing—not the frequency of their meetings, not the dried herbs, not the simply wishing for it so much—did anything to improve Elizabeth's ability to conceive. Again, she was intensely disappointed when her monthly bleeding stained her morning clothing. She had had an angel lover for more than two months; she had desperately hoped for better results than this.

But someone in Tola's house, it appeared, was actually able to celebrate. A week later, Shiloh came down to the dinner table, all smug and blushing. "I have news," she informed the rest of the residents, pretending modesty but clearly gloating. "I am carrying the child of the angel Stephen."

Of course, they all had to act as if they were happy for her, and lavish her with attention, and offer to fetch things for her if she grew tired or sick. But Faith and Elizabeth exchanged private glances and shared their true opinions later that night in their room.

"Of all the lucky cows!" Faith spat out. "And I don't know how she can be sure it's *the angel Stephen's* child she's carrying, when she's been in the beds of half a dozen other men. That I know of!"

"How did she get him to notice her? He never speaks to anyone except the other angels."

Faith made an unattractive sound. "All the men notice Shiloh. I think she uses potions."

"Potions," Elizabeth repeated, intrigued by the idea. "I hadn't thought of that."

Faith laughed. "Oh, you know of some?"

"Mary was telling me. Something about a love potion made from manna seeds. Does that really work? Or is it just a fable?"

Faith laughed again. "I've never actually tried any, but the *story* is that if you grind them up and put them in the food of the man you're interested in, he'll fall in love with you."

"Huh," Elizabeth said. "Mary and I use the salve all the time."

"Does she have seeds, too?" Faith asked.

"I'll ask her tomorrow. I'm seeing David again in a couple of days. Now would be the time to mix up a potion."

"Could you—if there was enough—"

"I'll get some for you, too," Elizabeth said with a grin. "Those boys will fall in love with us yet."

Mary was less than impressed by Elizabeth's reasoning when Elizabeth made the request the following morning. "Oh, sweet god of the skies and waters," she exclaimed. "Don't you girls ever think about anything except snaring the attention of an angel?"

"Not very often," Elizabeth replied.

Mary hunted through the sealed jars on one of her tall bookshelves. She did own about thirty books, all tattered and much-read medical texts, but most of the shelves contained other items: boxes, vials, dried roots, a bone or two that Elizabeth had never had the nerve to examine too closely. "Don't you have more pride than to try to make a man love you against his will? Wouldn't you rather have him court you because of your pretty laugh or your kind heart than because you'd poured an elixir into his wine?"

Elizabeth shrugged. "I don't care why he loves me, just as long as he does. Anyway, I don't even care if David loves me. I just want—" She searched for the right words. "A little more of his time."

Mary turned away from the shelves, a tall jar in her hand. It was filled to the brim with tiny white seeds no bigger than grains of rice. "I don't even know if this tale is true," she said.

"How much should I use?"

Mary shook her head. "I don't know that either."

Elizabeth was alarmed. "Well, I don't want to kill him!"

Mary laughed. "It's manna. It's a gift from the god. I don't think it'll kill anybody, no matter how much you dose him with." She opened the jar and shook about a half a cup of seeds into a small bowl. "That being said, I'd use some caution if I were you. No more than ten grains in whatever you serve your angel lover. Grind them up finely and put them in something with a strong flavor of its own."

"Will he be able to taste it?"

"Who knows? I've never been so foolish as to try such a thing! But most ingredients you add to a recipe have some kind of tang. Cover it up as best you can."

"Thank you. Thank you so much," Elizabeth said, pouring the seeds into a blue handkerchief and knotting it up securely. "I'll pay you, of course. What do they cost?"

Mary just watched her with a peculiar smile on her face, shaking her head. "They're a gift from the god," she said again. "And all such gifts are free."

Faith and Elizabeth spent a good couple of hours that night grinding the hard white seeds into powder, a task complicated by the fact that they didn't have the right tools. They'd borrowed a cutting board and some heavy glassware from the kitchen, and these had to serve for mortar and pestle, but they were left with a lot of hulls and over-size chunks that they feared might be visible in water or wine.

"But ale," Faith said. "That's got a strong taste, and you'd be likely to overlook something like this floating around in the foam."

"David doesn't drink ale," Elizabeth said glumly. "Only wine."

"Well, try to crush it down again."

In the end, they came up with a few teaspoonfuls of a respectable enough powder, which they divided equally.

"Will David wonder why you've brought him wine, since you've never come to his room with liquor before?" Faith asked.

"I don't think so. He'll just be happy it's there."

"Will he wonder why you don't drink any?"

Elizabeth laughed. "I don't think so," she said again. "Anyway, I might have a taste or two. Why not? Mary said that, according to the legend, the manna seed is only supposed to have an effect on men."

"And even if the potion worked on you—" Faith began.

Elizabeth shrugged. "Is that so bad? To fall in love with him?"

Faith sighed. "I'm already in love with Jason."

"Then I hope this potion works on him."

*   *   *

They both had assignations planned with their lovers the following night, Faith meeting Jason at a concert in the main hall, Elizabeth, as always, awaiting David in his room. He was just unreliable enough that she did not want to uncork the wine and pour in the powder before he arrived, because what if he never showed up at all? There was a good bottle of wine, and a few hours' worth of work, wasted. But she did not want him to see her sifting substances into his drink. So she carried in the unopened bottle and two white ceramic mugs, and poured the powder into one. He would laugh at the container, but she didn't think he would disdain the offering.

And, in fact, he seemed both touched and greedy when he entered the room a couple of hours later, none too steady on his feet. "Aha! I thought I remembered!" he exclaimed when he saw her. "This was to be our night! I couldn't remember absolutely positively, but I hoped! Yes, I did, I hoped you'd be here. I even left my party early."

She smiled at him and gave him a cursory kiss. "Well, since you've had to pass on a few rounds with your friends, maybe I can make it up to you," she said. "I brought a bottle of wine for us to share. I hope it's a kind you like? It's from a Manadavvi vineyard."

Tola, who knew most everything, had recommended both the brand and the seller, so Elizabeth was not entirely surprised when David let out an exclamation of satisfaction. "Give me anything from a Manadavvi field, and I'll drink it from now till sunrise," he said, snatching up the bottle to examine it. "Well done, my surprising little laundress. Well done."

He pried out the cork and she made sure he drank from the proper container. As she'd foreseen, he laughed at her choice of glassware, but he approved of the gesture so much that the mockery didn't last for long. If the manna root had any bitter aftertaste, it wasn't evident by the satisfaction with which David downed his second and third mugs of the wine. Elizabeth contented herself with one serving, impressed by the wine's smooth taste and heady effects. No wonder everyone raved about the Manadavvi vineyards.

Whether the secret powder had any instant impact on David she couldn't judge. He certainly turned quickly from imbibing to embracing, but the quality of the lovemaking was no different, as far as she could tell. But she thought the potion might be like disease or fever, slow to take hold but impossible to shake, and so she wasn't too worried when the night did not end with any passionate declarations of love.

"Next week, then?" she asked as she was pulling her clothes back on. "Our usual schedule?"

"That sounds good," David said drowsily, watching her body disappear beneath the folds of fabric. "It's always good to see my little laundress."

She kissed him again and let herself out.

Faith had had significantly better luck with her portion, raving so much about Jason's tenderness and stamina that Elizabeth started to feel a little jealous. She didn't get to hear the story till the following day, because Faith spent the night in her angel's arms, listening to him tell her that he loved her.

"I am delirious with happiness," Faith claimed, spinning around the room with her hands clasped beneath her chin and her eyes raised heavenward toward the god. "A gift from Jovah indeed! Thank you, great god, thank you!"

"When do you see him again?" Elizabeth said, throttling down her uncharitable emotions.

"Tonight! And tomorrow night! And maybe every night after that! Elizabeth, I think he may be truly in love with me!"

"I am happy for you," Elizabeth forced herself to say. And it was true, except she would have been happier had she had a similar story to report.

"Maybe he will love me forever, even if I never bear his child. Maybe he will—maybe he will make me his wife. Angels marry, don't they? Some of them."

"The leaders of the hosts at the three holds," Elizabeth said. "I don't know about the other angels."

"But there's no reason they *can't* marry."

"None that I know of."

Faith started spinning again. "I shall be an angel's wife, and live in the hold, and Rachel and Gabriel shall invite me to their dinners, and I shall stand beside the angels on the Plain of Sharon every year when it is time to sing the Gloria—"

Elizabeth smiled, because it was really hard to believe any of this would come true. "Unless you get so dizzy that you fall and hit your head and forget your own name, let alone your lover's," she said.

Faith came to a shaky halt and stood there looking wobbly for a moment. "And I shall invite you to all my angel parties, and you shall meet someone who is much kinder and more attentive than David, and you shall bear twenty angel children, and we shall be happy the rest of our lives."

"Twenty?" Elizabeth repeated. "I think I'd be happy with one."

"Then you shall just bear one," Faith said. "But we shall still be very happy. And always the best of friends."

"Yes," said Elizabeth, who had never had a friend before and was surprised to find out that she really did expect to know Faith the rest of her life. "We'll always be the best of friends."

Elizabeth brought more of her ground-up powder to her next two trysts with David, and he happily drank down the spiked wine, but it still seemed to have no effect on him. Or no greater effect.

"Maybe I'm just not very lovable," Elizabeth said to Mary a couple of weeks later, when the healer asked how the bewitching was proceeding. "David certainly shows me no more affection than he ever has."

"Maybe even before you gave him the potion, he already loved you as much as he's capable of loving anyone," Mary observed. "Did you consider that?"

Elizabeth thought that over for a moment. "That's a little sad."

Mary smiled faintly. "Maybe you'd better look around for someone who's got a greater capacity for love."

The angel Jason certainly seemed to have that capacity, for he had become simply enamored of Faith. He even came to Tola's house once or twice to fetch her, causing all the girls to sigh and coo over his long, silky blond hair and his boyish smile. Only Shiloh affected disinterest in him, smoothing her hands over her stomach when he was introduced to her, as if to communicate without words that Faith might have won a prize, but Shiloh had earned the ultimate trophy.

But even in Faith's sunny life, storm clouds were forming. "He has to go back to Gaza," she told Elizabeth one night through a frenzy of tears. "To Monteverde. And he's leaving in three days!"

"For how long?" Elizabeth asked.

"I don't know! Forever! Ariel is sending some other angel down here, and Jason is going back to Monteverde. I shall never see him again!"

"Yes you will, of course you will. He has said he loves you, and I'm sure he means it. He will send for you, or you can follow him—"

"I can't move to Monteverde uninvited!"

"No, but there is a city nearby. You could live there. You could find work there as easily as you have here, and you could be near him—"

"What if he doesn't want me to come?"

"What if he does?"

Faith paced around the room. It was late at night, and she had been crying since about noon, when she received the news. She looked awful. Her dark, curly hair was tangled and knotted; her face was blotched with red, and her nose looked sore and puffy. The wild expression on her face didn't help, either.

"I think the potion is wearing off," Faith admitted. "I think— these last few days—he still seems fond of me, but he doesn't seem so infatuated. He didn't seem at all upset by the thought of leaving me behind! I think he's tired of me."

"We'll grind up more of the grains," Elizabeth said. "He'll be sure to take you to Monteverde then."

Faith shook her head. "No, I—if he doesn't want me—well, I'll do just fine. I will. I just—I was hoping—*this* time I would have an angel baby, *this* time it would be all right."

A few more incoherent exchanges like this, and Elizabeth had heard enough. "That's it. You're going to bed."

"I can't. I won't sleep. I'll just lie there—"

Elizabeth was already rummaging through a little satchel she'd bought, much like Mary's, only not nearly so full of interesting con-coctions. "You'll take one of these tablets, and you'll sleep well enough," Elizabeth said firmly. "You'll feel better in the morning."

Indeed, Faith slept through the night and seemed much calmer the next day, though pale and apathetic. "You come home early to-night and you go straight to bed," Elizabeth told her.

"I can't," Faith said with a sigh. "I'm meeting Jason for dinner."

"Well, then, you come home and take a good long nap. And when you get up, you put on your best dress and braid your hair back in a fancy style. Make yourself so beautiful that he won't be able to leave you behind."

"Three more days," Faith said in a whisper. "He's leaving in three more days."

"Three days left to love him, then," Elizabeth said.

As for herself, she had no interesting appointments to keep that night, so she agreed to go out with a group of the other women from the house. They went to a new restaurant, one that had just opened on the west edge of town and was designed to accommodate large parties that didn't have a lot of money. Elizabeth looked around the big, open room, all whitewashed walls and dark supporting timbers, and thought she might have seen this place when it was still a pile of lumber and nails. She and Mary had been in this very neighborhood on the first morning that Elizabeth had worked for the healer, when they had been summoned to sew shut a man's bleeding head.

The day she had met Rufus. Elizabeth had never seen him since, though she and Mary had been called down to more than one construction site in the past ten weeks. She wondered if he had moved on, back to Semorrah, or gone off to seek his lost Edori relatives. She wondered if he'd found another pretty girl to spend his salary on. She didn't think about him often, of course, just now and then, when she was in this area or she passed a man who looked Edori. She really scarcely knew him at all.

"I'm *famished*," declared Ruth, who could be counted on to say those exact words at every single meal. "And it smells wonderful here!"

"I'm going to have the fish," Marah decided.

"The beef for me."

"Anything with sauce. The richer the better."

Shiloh put a hand down on her stomach. "I have to be careful what I eat," she said. "Angel babies are very delicate, you know."

"Oh really?" Ruth said brightly. "I never knew an angel yet who didn't eat everything he wanted, down to the bones and gizzard."

"A full-grown angel, perhaps," Shiloh snapped right back. "But when they're this small—in the womb—"

"Yes, I'm sure you're doing everything you can to protect your little one," Marah said soothingly. She was always the peacemaker of the group. "So what can you eat? Do you see anything you'd like?"

Soon enough they had all ordered, and they sat around the table chattering with easy enthusiasm about clothes, men, upcoming social events, and the prospect of a new angel flying in from Gaza. "He's older than Nathan, but not really *old*," Ruth said. "And not as handsome as Jason, but fair, like Jason."

"Have you ever met him?"

"Not to talk to. He was in Castelana a lot one summer when I was working there. They were having trouble with too much rain, and he was the one who always came to town to pray. He stayed at our inn a few times. I thought he seemed very nice."

Shiloh refused all wine, because of the baby. She couldn't choke down any of her meat, because of the baby. She couldn't have dessert, because too much sugar would alarm the baby.

Elizabeth thought she might have to kill her.

Still, it was clear that Shiloh was annoying everyone else as much as she was annoying Elizabeth, and that made the theatrics a little easier to bear. Ruth ordered a huge piece of creamy white cake, decorated with frosting in swirls and loops, and crammed the first bite in her mouth.

"Thank you, Jovah, for making sure I wasn't pregnant tonight," Ruth said, piously turning her eyes toward the heavens. "Because this certainly is the best cake I ever had in my life."

Shiloh turned her head aside and had to brush away a tear of hurt or anger.

Elizabeth caught Ruth's eye, grinned, and had to turn her own head away to try to hide her laughter. The motion brought a few nearby tables into her view, and she idly looked over the occupants. Most of the other diners were mortal, since this was a place that featured hearty food without a lot of fancy touches, but there were two angels that she hadn't noticed when she first came in. One was Lael, who lived at the dorm where Elizabeth used to work.

One was David. And he was with a mortal girl.

Elizabeth felt herself turn motionless and cold as she watched the two of them across the room. The woman was small-boned and dainty, with finely cut features and dark ringlets of silken hair. She was dressed in some kind of floating, diaphanous material of dark red, and she gestured as often as possible to cause the fabric to fold and glitter around her arms. Her face was animated, and she seemed fascinated by whatever it was that David was saying.

Elizabeth transferred her gaze to the angel. He was talking rapidly and with great exuberance, now and then throwing his head back to laugh. But then he would quickly focus his eyes back on the woman's face, as if unwilling to miss out on a smile or overlook a single expression. He looked attentive; no, that was not strong enough. *Captivated,* Elizabeth thought. As if this slip of a girl had captured his heart.

She hadn't thought David had a heart.

Or perhaps he did, and the manna root had worked its magic well enough after all. It had just delayed the release of its enzymes until Elizabeth was out of the room, until his eyes had fallen on this wispy beauty instead, the next morning or sometime later in the day. And he had capitulated instantly to infatuation as he usually succumbed to alcohol. Look, he wasn't even touching his wine. He was subject to a completely different sort of intoxication tonight.

Elizabeth forced her eyes away and snatched up her own glass of wine, downing the contents in a swallow. So much for potions. So much for love. So much for angels, or men, or friends, or *anything.*

"Can somebody pass me the wine?" she said, and Marah obligingly handed the bottle down. She didn't care if she had the worst headache of her life in the morning. Tonight she was going to drink so much that she wouldn't even be able to feel her feet as she made the long, dreary walk back home.

Still, impossible as it seemed, the rest of the evening was convivial enough, and Elizabeth found herself laughing more than once at the outrageous things Ruth said. She only looked twice more in David's direction; the second time, he was gone. That was worth another glass of wine, or at least half of one. She was actually not nearly so drunk as she'd planned to be by the time they paid their bill and headed back home. The air was sharp with a winter bite, and Marah squealed with cold when they first stepped outside.

"I wish I'd worn a warmer coat," Shiloh complained. "I don't want the baby to take a chill."

Elizabeth, walking directly behind the new mother, eyed Shiloh's back consideringly. It would be easy to give her a little shove, knock her into a puddle, perhaps. The air was not so cold that the muddy wheel ruts along the construction sites had entirely frozen over.

Beside her, Ruth gave a muffled laugh. "Don't do it," the other girl warned. "She's vengeful, and she's vicious. If something causes her to lose this baby—"

"Better that than all of us losing our minds," Elizabeth grumbled. But she kept her hands down loosely at her sides.

"I'm glad you came out with us," Ruth said. "You and Faith are such good friends that the rest of us don't see you much."

"I'm glad you invited me," Elizabeth said.

"So why didn't Faith come? Seeing Jason?"

Elizabeth nodded. "So I expect it'll be one of two things by the time I get back to my room. She'll be home already, sobbing because he'll be gone in two days, or she'll still be out with him, spending the night at his place."

"Because he'll be gone in two days," Ruth repeated.

Elizabeth nodded. "And for her sake, I hope she's still out."

Faith was home, though, as Elizabeth saw the instant she stepped through her own door. Home and lying quietly on her bed as if too exhausted even to lift her head when Elizabeth arrived. She was still dressed in her long black gown, which she thought was elegant and which Elizabeth thought made her look sickly, and she didn't say a word in response to Elizabeth's hello. But her eyes were open, and she blinked when Elizabeth crossed the room to stand beside her.

"So? I guess it didn't go so well if you're back this early," Elizabeth said in a gentle voice. "You look like you don't feel so good. Do you want me to get you something?"

Faith opened her mouth as if to speak, but nothing came out except a small bubble of saliva.

Elizabeth dropped to her knees beside the bed. "Faith? Are you all right?"

The head moved jerkily on the pillow, and the dark eyes grew wider as Faith tried again to speak. This time, a drop of spittle formed at the corner of her mouth and traced a slow line down her chin.

"Faith?" Elizabeth said more sharply. She quickly put her hands out, checking for fever, checking for pulse. Faith's skin was cold to the touch, her heartbeat sluggish. "Damn it, I wish you could tell me what happened."

A wound? A rash? What? Elizabeth unbuttoned the front of the dress, in case Faith was having trouble breathing, then dropped her hands to the skirt to tug the whole thing off. But the skirt was damp, as if Faith had run through those same muddy pockets of water that Shiloh had not been unlucky enough to fall into. When Elizabeth lifted her hands, they came away smeared with blood.

"Sweet Jovah singing," Elizabeth whispered, and ripped the entire dress from Faith's thin body. Blood everywhere, invisible on the black gown but staining the white petticoat, the white sheets. What—what? A miscarriage, an eruption of the bowels? Elizabeth could see no wound, no external sign of damage. This must be a malady grown from within, hard to locate, harder still to treat.

"I'll be right back," she said fiercely to the still form on the bed, and dashed from the room, leaving red fingerprints on the wood frame of the door. "Ruth! Shiloh! Marah!" she called, running up and down the hall and pounding on doors. Heads popped out into the hallway and everyone asked the same jumbled question.

"Somebody go get Mary," Elizabeth panted. "Faith is dying."

CHAPTER TWENTY-TWO

At first, the color in his Kiss was so faint that Obadiah could convince himself it was not there. A streak of sunlight, a rogue refraction in the crystal, nothing more significant. And, indeed, in some lights, the twist and flare of opal fire disappeared entirely. He was sure he was imagining it, late at night or in complete darkness, when the Kiss set its sweet and gentle glow against his arm.

He would have liked to get somebody else's opinion on this. Oh, he knew the tales that the young girls told, about how their Kisses would light the first time they laid eyes on their true lovers. And he knew that Gabriel and Rachel, Nathan and Maga, would admit (the women more readily than the men) that their Kisses had indeed performed pyrotechnics when they were first drawn together. Indeed, Nathan had told him once that he had begun to favor long-sleeved shirts whenever he and Maga were in formal company, because his Kiss still had a tendency to spark and glitter when his wife was nearby, and he didn't think such a thing was quite appropriate for a man of his standing.

But Obadiah had not heard of a Kiss turning ecstatic at random, when lover was far from beloved, when days or weeks might pass before the two were reunited. What would cause a Kiss to ignite on so little fuel, and to burn on without replenishment or renewal? That was what Obadiah would have liked to find out. But he couldn't think of whom to ask. Maga? Rachel? Oh, no. He had not even told them he had fallen in love, and he certainly wasn't prepared to detail for them the situation of his heart. Nathan was not much of one for confidences, and Obadiah, though friendly with all the other angels at Cedar Hills, didn't really feel close enough to any of them to initiate this discussion.

He thought about flying up to Mount Sinai, to pose the question to the oracle there. *Why would my Kiss suddenly produce a faint light, that time does not extinguish and circumstances do not warrant?* The Kiss was, of course, Jovah's most direct link with all his subjects, and it was possible the god was trying to send a message of some sort to Obadiah. In which case the oracle, who communicated with the god on a regular basis, would be the person to ask.

But Obadiah did not fly to Mount Sinai to make inquiries of the wise man. He didn't even make the much shorter trip to Mount Egypt to confer with the oracle there. He was not prepared yet to ask the question aloud. He was not prepared yet to learn the answer.

That it had something to do with Rebekah he had no doubt. Every time he saw her during the next few weeks—which was not as often as he would have liked—the flames in the Kiss grew stronger, steadier, less apt to flicker out. Not necessarily while he was in her presence, but later, as he lay solitary and miserable in Cedar Hills, he would notice that the colors of the Kiss burned at a brighter intensity. At this rate, he reflected, if he continued to see Rebekah for another year, the Kiss would eventually catch fire in his arm, explode in a frenzy of passion, and send Obadiah himself up in a tower of rapturous flame.

He resigned himself to this fate, because he could not imagine *not* continuing to see Rebekah—for another year, another ten years, the rest of his life.

Though in his heart, he knew that the affair would someday come to an end—soon, perhaps, maybe even sooner than her wedding. He could not think about it. He didn't even like to talk about it with Rebekah, and he found himself quickly changing the subject any time she brought up the name of her betrothed or the approaching date of her marriage. He was trying to concentrate only on the joy at hand, and not the rue to follow, though he found that harder to do with each passing week. Strange. In the past it had always been so simple for him to embrace the daily pleasures and disengage from the melancholy regrets. He had found it so easy to be happy that people commented always on his good nature and his ready smile. Now, his days were so rich that at times he felt his very blood was saturated with sensation, but he would not call himself happy.

Except for those few hours in Rebekah's arms, and then he was as content as a man could ever be.

Ever since their adventure on the roof, they had adopted a new system that worked extraordinarily well and that had the advantage, besides, of calming some of Obadiah's fears for Rebekah's safety. When he arrived in Breven, he would leave a feather on the skylight that looked into the fabric room of Hector's house. On the days that Rebekah saw that signal in place, she would climb to the roof at night, where he would be waiting for her. He would scoop her up in his arms and fling himself into the star-spattered night, so giddy at the chance to hold her again that he felt as unsteady and euphoric as he had felt so long ago when he had first been learning how to fly.

Rebekah loved these aerial journeys high above the shadowed architecture of Breven. Some mortals, Obadiah knew, were petrified at the great height or unexpected speed of an angel flight, and would agree to be carried through the air only if there was no other alternative, but Rebekah could not get enough of such experiences. One night, Obadiah spent hours aloft with Rebekah in his arms, flying low over the rippled, mysterious expanse of the ocean. The moonless night was lit by uncountable acres of stars, scattered across the sky by Jovah's careless, profligate hand. The sky was so dense with stars that they seemed in danger of spilling from the heavens into the sea—and the sea itself seemed so black and so endless that it appeared it could contain every one of those surplus coins of light.

Obadiah flew so low to the water that he could feel its scent and moisture rise up to him on tricky, salt-laced breezes, so far from the shore at last that they lost the lights of Breven entirely. This far from land, there was almost no sound at all—no lapping of waves against the rocky beaches, no cry of night birds, no interplay of human voices. It was possible to imagine that they were alone in the universe, first man, first woman, in the undifferentiated ether of space, that Jovah had not yet considered how to mold the world into continents and oceans and how to wrap its terrain with breathable air. They were suspended in some primeval fluid, the god's unborn children, awaiting his signal to emerge into a world fashioned especially for them.

Obadiah knew what that world would hold, if he was the one designing it. Much of what he was holding in his arms right now.

They did not speak at all during that long, slow flight, and it was only because they could sense the unwelcome arrival of dawn that they turned back at last for the shore. They returned to the roof of Hector's house and parted with a kiss and very few words. They had not made it to the hotel at all that night, yet there was no sense of loss or lack. What they had shared was profound enough to feed even their hungry souls.

Besides, there was still tomorrow night. Obadiah would come back for Rebekah then.

At times Obadiah believed his relationship with the Jansai Uriah would last as long and be, ultimately, even more frustrating than his relationship with Rebekah. Since he had resumed his regular visits with the Jansai chieftain two weeks ago, they had made no progress at all on negotiations.

"Let us begin by acknowledging that we speak in good faith," Uriah said each time they began serious discussions. He would nod to a corner of the tent, where he kept a most interesting display in a tall wooden frame: a contraband firestick. He had allowed Obadiah to handle it—finding an empty Breven alley and producing a rather frightening bolt of fire from the metal barrel—but he would not let Obadiah take the weapon back to Cedar Hills. And he would not disclose where he had gotten it or what tactics he had used to force the firestick's owner into relinquishing it. Obadiah could not even be certain that this was the weapon that had brought him down.

But he always responded, "Indeed, I have complete confidence in you."

"And I in you."

"So let us begin."

"Let us talk about the Edori," Uriah would say next.

"The Edori are a closed subject," Obadiah always replied, and that would be the end of it. Wine would be called for and food would be brought in, but all negotiations would be over.

"Can't we start with some other concessions and work our way back to the Edori?" Obadiah asked the day after his flight over the ocean with Rebekah. "Can't we see if there might be *something* we can agree on?"

Uriah shrugged and sipped from his wine. "What's the point? We can hammer out a contract that pleases us on every detail, but once we get to the question of the Edori, we will again fail to find agreement. And the whole of the contract will be void."

"You only play this game," Obadiah said, "because winter is upon us and most of your caravans are off the road. There is no urgency for you now, for there are no crops to haul and no produce to barter in the northern markets."

Uriah laughed. "Yes, exactly! And you play the game for the same reason. But who will be more worried when spring comes, tell me that? The Jansai, who are lazy men who would prefer to sit around in their tents all day sleeping, or the far-flung residents of the three provinces, who are waiting for the Jansai caravans to arrive?"

"Very well, then," Obadiah said with a sleepy smile. "Let us talk about the Edori."

"Ha!" said Uriah, and poured the angel another glass of wine.

"Let us ask ourselves if the Edori, who wander as far if not quite as purposefully as the Jansai, might become traders in their own right," Obadiah said pleasantly. "If the Jansai are not to bring produce and trade goods from Monteverde to Luminaux, well, then, perhaps the Edori shall provide that service for us."

Uriah's face blackened into a scowl. "The Edori are so unreliable that you would not get this summer's harvest till sometime late next winter, and you and all your merchant friends would starve or go broke awaiting their arrival."

Obadiah shrugged. "I am not so sure. I think we might find a few enterprising Edori who like the idea of a life a little more structured and who wouldn't mind striking a blow at their old enemies while they were about their new ventures."

"You would never pursue such a foolhardy plan," Uriah said, his breath sounding heavy and damaged in his lungs.

"Such a plan is already being considered in angel holds and Edori camps across Samaria," Obadiah said mildly. "Indeed, I find myself wondering if you won't find yourself with a few eager Edori competitors even if you do take to the roads again this spring—as, of course, we hope you do."

Not much to Obadiah's surprise, Uriah chose to cut short the conversation a few minutes later, adding an ominous observation that he thought his business associates would be happy to know the angel did not plan to be in Breven again any time soon. Obadiah nodded at the warning, bade a pleasant good-bye, and retreated to his hotel room.

"I won't be back for a while, love," he told Rebekah that night. "The volatile Uriah must have time to think over some unpleasant things I've said to him, and I won't be welcome here for a few weeks at least."

"Then I won't expect you," she said, as always seeming to be much more serene about the prospect of a long separation than he was. "But it has been so good to see you these two days."

"I might come back anyway. Some night when he's unlikely to know I'm in town. Look for me."

"I always do."

Nathan laughed out loud when Obadiah reported his most recent conversation with the Jansai leader. "Edori merchant peddlers— that's very good," he approved. "Surely Uriah didn't believe you?"

"He's a jealous and suspicious man. Of course he didn't believe me, but he couldn't quite get the idea out of his head once I'd introduced it. I think he might be more amenable to discussion when he sees me next."

"Which won't be for a while," Nathan said.

"Oh, I don't know," Obadiah said casually. "I might go back next week to see how my poisonous suggestion has eaten away at his confidence."

"I don't think you should," Nathan said. "Wait until he sends for you again. Let him know that if he doesn't want to deal, we don't need to deal. We're looking at other options. I don't think you should go back to Breven for a long time."

And that was the worst sentence of all.

But Obadiah didn't despair all at once. Who knew, Uriah might send for him right away, having been made so angry by Obadiah's careless comments that he couldn't stand the uncertainty of the future. And even if Uriah failed to summon him back, well, Obadiah had dropped into Breven uninvited before. All it took was a carefully planned late-night arrival and some discretion during the daytime. Even an angel could be invisible, even in Breven, if that was the prime consideration.

Still, he hated to disregard one of Nathan's outright injunctions, at least immediately, so he resigned himself to at least a fortnight of longing and loneliness. He accepted every dinner invitation issued by Nathan and Magdalena, a fellow dorm mate, or the most chance-met acquaintance. He was willing to fly messages to Semorrah, perform weather intercessions over the Plain of Sharon, pray for plague medicines over small towns on the very southern tip of the Galilee River. Anything to keep busy. Anything to distract his memory and redirect the energies of his body.

Oddly, the first person who seemed to notice something was wrong with him was the person he had considered, at the moment, to be too self-involved to pay attention to anyone else: Magdalena. She was still suffering from migraines and megrims, and terrors that would wake her in the middle of the night.

"But I feel calmer when you're around me," the dark-haired angel said with a tremulous smile that she no doubt hoped looked brave. "You make me feel more hopeful just by being in the room."

He laughed. "I would have thought, perhaps, Nathan?"

"Nathan makes me feel strong," she said. "Like I can endure whatever might come, for his sake as well as my own. But you make me think that—whatever comes—it might not be terrible."

"I do think the god has ordained this baby," Obadiah said.

"The priests would tell you he ordains all babies," she said a little playfully.

"That would be good," he agreed. "That would mean the god welcomes all children into the world. Which is what Rachel and her Edori friends would tell us anyway. And perhaps they are right."

Magdalena sighed. "As long as he welcomes this child," she said, "then I will be happy."

"So what can I do to keep you cheerful until that day arrives?" he asked. "Tell you amusing stories? Accompany you down to one of the new cafes for pastries and hot tea?"

She tilted her head to one side. "You can tell me stories, but I doubt they will be amusing," she said.

He affected offense. "Are you saying that my stories are monotonous and full of woe?"

"I'm saying that you don't seem very cheerful yourself these days. Like something powerful is weighing on your heart. I wish you would tell me what it is. You have been so good to me these last few months that I would like a chance to be good to you in turn."

He was so surprised at her perceptiveness that he did not think to deny the charge immediately. "Thank you, lovely, but I don't think there's anything you can do to make things better."

She inspected him. "Then there is something."

He shrugged. "We all have cares from time to time."

"You're not ill, surely? You would tell me that."

He laughed. "What, and have you call down healers from all over Samaria to poke and prod at me? You're the last person I'd tell. But of course I'm not sick."

"And your family—your mother?"

"Everyone is fine. Maga, let's forget it."

"I can't imagine that you'd be disappointed in love," she said with a smile.

He opened his mouth to make some jesting remark but found himself wordless. The silence ran on too long for him to be able to frame a plausible denial.

"Obadiah?" she said wonderingly. "You've fallen in love? With a lady who has *rejected* you? I find that to be—completely impossible to believe."

"She has not rejected me," he said in a low voice. "She is just—there is—her circumstances do not permit—"

Now Maga looked even more astonished. "You've fallen in love with a married woman? Oh, Obadiah."

"That's not exactly it—" Though it would be soon enough. "She's betrothed," he amended.

"But surely—for an angel—for *you!*—she would give up this other man, who must be in every way your inferior—"

He had to laugh. "You can't know that."

"I know you, and I would choose you over anyone. Except Nathan, of course." She stopped, eyeing him with some misgiving, for she had instantly thought of the only other angel she held in as high esteem as her husband. "It's not—you're not still sighing over Rachel, are you? Oh, Obadiah—"

"No, it's not Rachel," he said in a testy voice. Had he had any idea how many people were aware of his infatuation with the angelica, he would have thrown himself in the ocean to drown a year ago. "I cannot believe you would even say that to me."

"Then, who?"

"Maga, please—"

"Is she someone you met in Breven? Is that why you have spent so much time there?"

"No," he said, for it wasn't a lie. "I didn't meet her in Breven."

"But she lives there? Or very near," Maga guessed. "You go there so often with such cheerfulness there can be no other explanation."

He found a tiny smile. "Yes, upon occasion, when I go to treat with Uriah, I have seen—I have met with—this lady. But I don't— there is—and of course I have always discharged my duty first!"

"Yes, of course, no one would ever doubt that," Maga said absently. "Is she lowborn, Obadiah? A farmer's daughter, perhaps? I know you think I'm a dreadful snob, but I'm not, truly I'm not. I would welcome anyone you loved. We all would."

"Maga, I cannot explain the circumstances to you," he said firmly. "I don't even want to talk about this anymore."

"You could bring her to Cedar Hills for a visit."

"Maga!"

"I would be very gracious," she assured him. "And I would tell her all your sterling qualities. I would make you sound so wonderful that she would think I was in love with you myself."

"Yes, that would be certain to make her trust me."

"Have you sung for her? She won't be able to resist you if you've sung for her."

"She has heard my voice once or twice," he said stiffly.

"I cannot believe that she is not secretly in love with you, no matter what she says to your face."

Obadiah was silent a moment. "Yes," he said, "I believe she is in love with me as well. But she is afraid to give up the life she knows for the life she might find with me. I don't blame her for that, but some days it fills me with despair."

Maga leaned forward and put a hand on his arm. "Bring her to Cedar Hills," she said warmly. "We will find a way to keep her. Of all the angels in the three holds, you are the one I would least want to see despairing. We will take this recalcitrant girl and prove to her that you are her ideal lover."

"If she ever comes to Cedar Hills," he said, "she will stay for a lifetime. But I do not know that she will ever make the journey, Maga. I do not believe we will ever see her here."

The second person to notice Obadiah was out of sorts was a virtual stranger, and she made the comment the day following his rather unsettling interview with Magdalena. It was a fine day, chilly but flooded with sun, and he was sitting outside on one of the many benches scattered throughout the city. This one was backless, to accommodate angel wings, and faced a pretty fountain of Luminaux design. The water had been turned off in deference to the cold, but Obadiah studied the graceful bronze shapes of three singing angels and thought that the artist had perfectly caught the expression of raptness that many singers felt upon hitting a particularly beautiful note. He could not remember if, in warmer days, water dripped from their feathers or spouted from their lips, but he thought this might detract from the overall impression somewhat. All in all, he was just as glad to be viewing the sculpture in unadorned winter.

"Angelo?" came a hesitant voice a little to one side of him. The speaker was female and deferential; he knew that if he did not acknowledge her, she would hurry on her way. He was tempted, but his essential good nature won out. He turned on the bench to get a look at whoever had addressed him.

It was a woman with thick chestnut hair and an uncertain smile, and everything from her clothes to her posture screamed "angel-seeker." But her face was teasingly familiar and it was not in him to be rude, so he smiled back at her. "Hello," he said neutrally.

"I'm sorry, I didn't mean to interrupt. It's just that I saw you sitting here and I wondered how you've been doing since you got wounded—"

"Elizabeth!" he exclaimed, memory locking in place. Yes, yes, she had bound his hurts and checked on his progress and even helped him on with his clothes, and she had shown him true kindness at a time when he really needed it. "How are you! It's been weeks since you were so good to me."

Her smile strengthened, lighting her face and turning her into a pretty girl. "You remembered my name," she said, and then blushed, as if mortified at making such a girlish remark.

"Yes. Of course. Here, sit beside me and tell me how you've been doing. I haven't seen you at the dorm lately, have I? Of course, I've been gone a lot myself."

Looking awed and grateful, she perched on the bench beside him, as far from him as the seat would allow. She clearly did not want to appear encroaching. "No, I've left the laundry room. I've become an apprentice to the healer Mary—the one who wrapped your wounds—and I've learned a great deal. I'll never go back to working in kitchens and laundry rooms again."

"Well, good for you!" he exclaimed and meant it. "So now you can heal cuts and bruises on your own, and deliver babies, and administer potions. You're the one I should call on next time I get careless and have a hole torn in my wing, I suppose?"

She laughed. "Well, no, not quite yet. I can *help* at the birthings and the broken bones, but I'd want Mary around to guide me if anyone was truly sick or hurt. But I hope you won't get shot down from the sky again any time soon!"

He laughed. "No, I hope not, too."

"And you're all better? All healed?"

He flexed his wings behind him, bringing the one so close to her back that it brushed her hair. He could see her tremble a little with delight, and had to restrain himself from doing it again, just to preen. Well, it was a fine thing, now and then, to know your very existence made someone else quiver with sensation. "All healed," he said. "No scar remains."

"I'll tell Mary," she said.

"So both of us have nothing but glad tidings this day."

"Yes," she said earnestly. "For I got the best news this morning."

"And what was that?"

"A friend of mine was so sick. She almost died. I'm the one who found her, but Mary was the one who saved her. Although until this morning we weren't sure that she would live."

"How awful," he said with easy sympathy. "What happened to her? She fell ill?"

Elizabeth hesitated. "She took—there was—she accidentally drank too much of a healing potion, and it nearly killed her," she said at last. "It was my fault, really. I'm the one who gave her the potion. Although I did warn her—" She broke off and looked away a moment before resuming. "Anyway, she's better now. And Mary told me I learned an important lesson about the misuse of drugs and the frailness of human beings. But I would rather not have learned the lesson. Or, at least, not learned it on Faith."

"That is the only way we ever learn lessons," Obadiah said gently. "When they are applied to the people we love. I'm sorry you've been sad. It's been a strange winter for heartache."

She lifted her eyes to his face, and the expression on her own face was suddenly wise. "You've been sad, too," she said. "You never looked like this, even when you had a fever."

He was caught off guard. "Didn't I? Then I must look completely dreadful now, since never in my life have I felt so wretched as I did back when I was injured."

She shook her head. "Not dreadful. Sad," she said again.

"I guess I am a little melancholy," he said. "It will pass."

She hesitated again. "If there is—if you wanted—if you were lonely and simply wanted to talk—or something—I've gotten much better at listening than I used to be," she said.

Sweet Jovah singing, an angel-seeker to her core, and yet the offer of comfort seemed so sincere that he was actually moved. "I thank you for your kindness yet again," he said very gently. "It is good to know that there is somewhere I could turn if I needed solace.

That will be a bright thought to take home with me on a dreary day."

His words pleased her almost as much, he thought, as his body might have if he had brought her back with him and taken her to bed. She was not yet accustomed to thinking of herself as good-hearted or generous, he could tell that; she had not had enough experience thinking of anyone except herself. He could only guess at the life that had led her to Cedar Hills, hoping to better herself in the most drastic way possible, and that was not a life that had admitted of too many altruistic or generous impulses. But he had hope for this girl. She seemed to have strength, loyalty, and a sense of purpose. She might yet make a good life for herself and extend her charity to others.

"I think you're sad because someone doesn't love you," Elizabeth said then, proving once again that every thought in his head was completely visible for anyone who glanced in his direction. "All I can say is, she does love you."

"You can't know that," he said.

She smiled. "Anybody would."

So that little interlude was just as unnerving as the one with Magdalena, though it left Obadiah feeling curiously heartened, as though the apprentice physician really had developed some healing skills, and not just in making the body whole again. Or perhaps he was just pleased to know that someone found him attractive and exceptional, worthy of love. Flattery always led to an improvement in mood.

Still, he realized he must work on his expressions and his attitude or risk having all his acquaintances approach him with words of sympathy and concern. He found, not entirely to his surprise, that if he spent his time with men, he was wholly safe from these intimate little conversations about his feelings, and so for the next few days, he kept company that was almost exclusively male. He couldn't refuse, though, when Maga sent a note inviting him to dinner one night, even though it was with some trepidation that he read she was planning a "surprise" for him. A bevy of eligible Manadavvi girls, perhaps, imported specifically to distract him from his woeful love life, or one of the oracles brought in to discuss theology and to remind him that there were matters beside the heart that could occupy a man all his days.

But it was worse than all his speculations. At the door to Nathan and Maga's suite, he was met by an apparition: Rachel, dressed in gold and looking magnificent. She had obviously stationed herself outside the main room in order to snag him before he went in to join the general party, and because she was Rachel, everyone had let her do exactly as she wished.

"So," she said, kissing him on the cheek and then standing back to survey him. "Maga tells me you've fallen in love with a completely unsuitable woman. You have to tell me everything."

CHAPTER TWENTY-THREE

Rebekah could not even remember the first time she'd noticed the fugitive colors loitering in her Kiss. When she tried to cast her mind back, it seemed like they had always been there, traces of ice and opal hovering just below the edge of noticing, but she knew that wasn't true. A week or so ago, as she was standing naked in the water room, yes, there had been a flicker of color in her Kiss then; and a week before that, as she turned over in the middle of the night, she had noticed a faint glow nestled in the crystal's white heart. And each time she had thought, "Yes, there's that color again," so neither episode was the first time, but she couldn't remember the first time.

It seemed important to remember. It seemed important to understand at least one of the strange things that was happening to her.

She had become moody and a little withdrawn in the past few weeks, missing Obadiah so much that it terrified her. Unless she was dealing with her mother, she had always been relatively even-tempered, willing to do her share of work or deal with the most unlikable members of the household. But these days she didn't want to talk to anyone, not her mother, not Jordan, not Hepzibah, not Martha when she came to visit. She wanted to sit alone in her room, and think about Obadiah, and cry.

Since this was scarcely possible in a house that contained twelve other women, even a large house, she found herself crying mostly at night. Lying on her mat, curled up in a ball, sobbing. At times, her weeping would grow to such a frenzied pitch that it was almost hysteria; she could not think what to do to make herself stop. She would push herself to her feet and pace the floor, still torn by racking sobs, wringing her hands together or flattening them against her cheeks in stark despair. Some nights, this went on for hours. When she finally lay back on her bed, she would be too tense to fall asleep; she would stare up at the dark ceiling, unable to close her eyes. It would be well past midnight before she would sleep, and she often woke up every hour or two until dawn, after which she could not sleep again.

Needless to say, she looked wretched in the morning—pale, pinched, and exhausted—and this added to her desire not to leave her room. When she did emerge, someone would always ask her if she had fallen ill. "I was coughing all night" had become her standard response. When she'd been a child, she had suffered from lung troubles, and she knew a few other women who regularly had trouble breathing in the green spring months. Still, it did not seem like a very satisfactory answer, particularly in the heart of winter, but no one questioned her too closely. Not her mother, who was too focused on her youngest son, or Hepzibah, who did not want to know the answers.

She could not understand the crying any more than she could explain away the colors in her Kiss. Yes, she missed Obadiah; not a minute of her day went by when he did not perch like a persistent songbird at the edges of her conscious thought. But she had missed him before and not skipped to the brink of sanity this way. Had not felt so dreary, so hopeless, so utterly ruined. She wanted more than anything to see him again, but she could not imagine how even that would help, because he would just go away again, leaving her more starved and desperate than before. Better to plan to never see him again, to recover now, this one time, from her strange dependence on him, than to experience this misery over and over again every time he was gone from her.

But the thought of never seeing him again sent her into an even worse spiral of depression, so she could not entertain that thought for long.

The other thought—the whispering of some treacherous, sinful demon—was that she would leave with him the next time he returned. Leave behind Breven and her family and her life, and spend the rest of her days with the angel.

It was not an option she had seriously considered before, no matter how often Obadiah had suggested it. He had seemed to her, he still seemed to her, an aberration in the course of her existence, a chapter she would look back on in awe and wonder years after it had closed. Although she could not imagine the relationship ending, in her heart she could not imagine it continuing, months and months, years and years, for the whole span of her days. It was a special gift, a hallowed time, a precious, sun-warmed bracket of days, but this time with Obadiah could not go on forever.

Unless she left. Unless she ran away with him, allowed him to carry her on some moonless night over the folded golden miles of the desert. Unless she returned with him to Cedar Hills to be his bride or his friend or his forgotten lover, discarded once the thrill of secrecy was gone. She had never been able to see her way clear to it. She had never been willing to sacrifice everything she knew for a world of uncertain terrors and the love of a man with whom she had nothing in common. She did not know how she would exist in that world if he put her aside.

But she could scarcely exist in this world without him.

So she wept, and she worried, and she watched the rainbow in her Kiss, and she wondered.

"You look like dried cow dung too brittle to throw on the fire," Martha greeted her. It was three weeks since Rebekah's last assignation with Obadiah, and Jerusha had sent her to Uncle Ezra's house because "I need a day when I don't have to look at that pout on your face." On the whole, Rebekah preferred Martha's assessment to her mother's. It had been a relief, actually, to throw a veil over her face and walk beside Jordan to her uncle's house, knowing that for those two miles, no one was looking at her expression and finding it unacceptable.

"That's about how I feel," Rebekah agreed. "Dried, cracked, fragile, and useless."

"So you haven't heard from the angel."

Rebekah shook her head.

"But you will. Everything you've told me about him—he'll be back. He warned you that it would be a while before he could return."

"I know. It's just that—I feel so awful. I feel so awful that I'm not even sure that seeing him again would make me feel good."

Martha smiled at that. "Oh, it would. It will. When he comes back, you'll forget all this."

"And when he leaves again?"

Martha shrugged. "You'll grieve again. That's the life of an illicit lover."

"And when will you see Chesed again?" Rebekah asked.

Martha sighed. "Not for another week at least. Maybe two or three weeks. They're back in Gaza, and then they head down the western coastline, trying to make new contacts."

"I can't think of any cities along the western coast. Certainly no place big enough to have a trading center."

"I know! That's what I told him! But he said there are mining communities west of the Corinnis that are beginning to accumulate some wealth and—and 'social status,' he said. The women are looking for luxuries. Anyway, his father wants to make the trek, and of course Chesed must go along. So it will be a few weeks."

Rebekah flopped over on her mat. They were sitting alone up in Martha's room because it was too cold to stay in the garden for long, and Martha's unpleasant aunt was in the fabric room. "Remember when 'a few weeks' didn't sound so long?" she asked. "You would be on the road to Velora for a few weeks. The trip to Windy Point would take a few weeks. It didn't matter. There was nothing to make you hurry back to Breven, nothing except a harvest festival or a spring feast to particularly look forward to. Now, 'a few weeks' sounds like a lifetime sentence. It is too long to live out."

"But I know something that might pass the time a little," Martha said. "If you'll come."

"What is it?"

"My father is taking my mother and my aunts out to the southern edge. Where the reskel grows. Aunt Rhesa says this is the best time to harvest the roots, once the leaves have all shriveled up in the winter cold. We'll only be gone a day or two, and it will be good to get away from—" Martha gestured at the walls. "This house and everybody in it."

Rebekah sat up, alarm sparkling through her. "But what if he comes while I'm gone? What if he only comes for a day, and I'm out in the desert with you, and I don't get to see him?"

Martha shrugged. "What if he comes tonight while you're here?"

Now Rebekah stood and started pacing. "I know. I thought of that. I didn't want to come for that very reason. But I thought—I thought I might throw myself from the roof if I sat in that house one more day. And I'll be back tomorrow night. And when he comes to Breven, he's usually here for a day or two. I will only miss him one night, I won't miss him completely—"

"You'll have to show him where my house is. Next time you see him," Martha said. "So he can drop feathers in my garden as well as yours, in case you happen to be staying with me. I'd like a collection of angel feathers, I have to admit. I'll sew them to the edge of my winter cape and look quite elegant."

Rebekah smiled at the nonsense. "I did show him your house once, when we were flying over Breven. But I don't know that he'd think to look for me here. So I don't think I can go on this expedition of yours."

"Oh, but you really should," Martha wheedled. "Just for two days! I think you'll be better if you get out of the house, into some fresh air and sunshine—"

"It's *cold* outside! We just came in from the garden!"

"Yes, but we'll have a fire at the campsite, and it'll just be us, just family, so we can all sit around the fire at night. And you know how beautiful and pure the desert smells in winter—like every grain of sand has been washed by hand and the sky has been laundered by Jovah—"

Rebekah actually laughed at Martha's poetry. "And I know what it's like to wake up with frost on my cheeks and icicles in my eyelashes."

"But it's not *that* cold. Not yet. And we'll only be out for a night."

"But what if Obadiah comes?"

"I'll ask my father," Martha said. "He'll know if the angel is planning a visit to Uriah any time soon."

"And won't your father wonder what you know about angels?"

"I'll say Eph told me all about his visit. He did, too. My father likes it when I ask him questions about politics and business. He thinks it means I'll be a smart wife for some merchant."

"But sometimes Obadiah comes to Breven without telling Uriah that he's going to be here. Sometimes he comes just to see me."

"Well, then, we'll—I know! We'll stop at your house on the way out of town. Say you have to have—something. A special shawl or a new pair of shoes. You run in, you check to see if Obadiah has left you any signals the night before. If he hasn't, you're free to come with us. We'll only be gone one night. If he has, well, then you suddenly find yourself too sick to travel. Everyone will be irritated with you, but they'll forget it as soon as we've been on the road for two hours."

"I could do that," Rebekah said, thinking it over. She still might forgo one precious night with Obadiah, but she would not miss him entirely. He would not send her messages and grow frantic when she did not reply. It would not be a catastrophe.

And it was true. She was desperate to get out of the house—this house, her own house, any collection of stone and spitefulness—wild to smell the fresh-scented desert air and run across the corrugated surface of the sand. She would feel better after a short trip, in Martha's cheerful company, distracted from her constant, nagging worries.

"All right," she said. "I'll go. When do we leave?"

Martha squealed and gave her a quick hug. "Tomorrow morning. We'd better let your mother know you're coming with us."

Jerusha heartily approving of any plan that kept her daughter out of her sight for another day or two, Rebekah set out the next morning with Martha, Martha's mother, two of her aunts, Ephram, and Uncle Ezra. After the quick detour at Hector's house—where there were no angel mementos—they were on their way, outside of the city limits only an hour or two after dawn. There were enough of them that they had brought two wagons, the older women riding in one with Ezra, and Martha and Rebekah being driven by Ephram. Everyone in the younger trio was in high spirits, and Ephram kept them laughing by telling them about the antics of some of his friends. Then Martha and Ephram began to imitate the behavior of some of their more unlikable relatives on their mother's side, and followed that up with hilarious stories from their childhood. Rebekah contributed a few tales of Jordan's mishaps as a baby, and the time her mother had mistaken hellsbane for dera leaves, causing Jordan to produce vile green excrement for two days straight. It hadn't been funny then; it was enormously entertaining now.

It was a little after noon when they arrived at their destination, a stretch of southern desert that existed in a long, shallow bowl. Something about its placement—low enough to be close to the underlying aquifer or to escape some of the harsher winds of summer—made it ideal terrain for the reskel bushes that were so scarce in the rest of the territory around Breven. Here, they could be found by the dozens, covered with smoky blue blossoms during the spring months and with waxy green leaves in the summer. Now they were just shriveled little collections of cold-looking branches, but they still ran their roots deep into the soil under the sand, and it was those roots that Rhesa and the other women were determined to dig up.

The men made camp while the women went straight for their treasure, fanning out around the perimeter of the campsite. It was chilly, but the sun was bright overhead; the day had a somewhat festive air. All the women had pulled off their veils as soon as they were outside of the city, and now they strolled through the winter sands with a heady sense of freedom, the sun on their faces, their hair loose in the wind.

"Oh, this is wonderful, this is *heaven*." Martha declared as she and Rebekah knelt beside a reskel bush and began to dig. "I feel like I'm breathing for the first time in weeks."

"Are you going to use that trowel? Hand it over."

"Aren't you glad you came?" Martha demanded, passing her the digging tool.

"Yes," Rebekah said. "It could be ten degrees warmer and I'd be happier, but this feels—" She couldn't find the word, so she just shrugged and kept on digging.

Martha sat back on her heels and seemed oblivious to the fact that they had come here to do work. "I wish we could just leave," she said suddenly. "Take the wagon all the way to—Semorrah, maybe. Gaza, even!"

"Oh, I wonder why you thought of Gaza," Rebekah said with affectionate scorn.

"He's probably not even there anymore. Just to go. Just to see it. It's been so long since I've been on the road. My father has taken Ephram with him everywhere since last fall, but I haven't traveled at all."

"I haven't been out since—" Rebekah fell silent.

"Since the time you met Obadiah," Martha supplied.

"Yes. Maybe that's what's been bothering me. I've been in the house too long."

Martha dropped her body down onto the sand, propping herself up on one elbow. "If you ask him, will Hector take you on his next trip?"

"Not unless my mother goes, and maybe not even then. I think my mother would be just as happy to be gone on a long journey and leave me behind."

"Well, I'll ask my father," Martha said. "Next time he travels. If he'll take you and me with him."

Rebekah continued to dig around the root base of the reskel. A few inches below the level of sand, the loose dirt became sticky and dense, hard to cleave apart with the little trowel. It was clear Martha wasn't going to help at all. "Well, we'll see," she said.

"Don't you want to go?"

"Not if—" Rebekah shrugged. "Not if I'd miss Obadiah."

Martha made a grunting sound. "Right. Well. Next time your angel is here, tell him you want to travel. Tell him when you might be gone. Let him know you're not going to just sit around on rooftops waiting for him to reappear."

Rebekah grinned briefly. "I suppose that's how you phrase it to Chesed."

"Oh, I speak my mind to him, never doubt it."

Rebekah had dug deep enough now to free some of the roots, fat as her finger but long as a whiplash. "How much can I take from a plant without killing it?" she asked.

"Two pieces, I think," Martha said. "Maybe three."

"Let's be safe. I'll take two."

As soon as she had harvested two of the long, stalklike roots, Rebekah patted all the soil back in place and then smoothed sand all around the base of the bush. "All right," she said. "Next one."

They worked at a leisurely pace for the next few hours, Martha only occasionally deigning to do any of the actual digging. Rebekah didn't mind. She actually enjoyed the pull on her muscles, the cramp in her hand, the ache developing in her back from bending over too long. It was good to move and labor, to stretch and strive. She liked the sense of accomplishment she felt when she had completed her task at one station and came to her feet, reaching her arms high over her head and forcing each bone and muscle to realign. She liked the drag of the sand against her feet as she walked between shrubs, liked the insistent prying of the wind at her uncovered face. She liked feeling stresses on her body instead of her soul.

"I'm hungry," Martha said as they finished up their task. Early dark had descended on the desert, hurrying as if afraid of arriving late. "Do you think anyone's made dinner yet?"

"No," said Rebekah. "I think the men are sleeping beside the wagons, and the women are still out gathering roots."

"Then let's go back to the campfire and start cooking."

The meal was delicious, and the dinner hour passed pleasantly. The women chattered about inconsequential things, and Ezra added a comment or two as the mood struck him. He was a big, rather fierce man with hard, strong features, and Rebekah did not really like him—until the setting was intimate and relaxed like this one. Then he seemed at ease and willing to be amused. He treated his wife and children with affection, teased his sisters, and made a few clumsy jokes with Rebekah about her upcoming wedding.

"Pretty soon now," he said to her. "Isaac will be getting a good look at that sharp little face of yours—not to mention the other treasures under your robes."

"Ezra," Aunt Rhesa reprimanded in a faint voice.

"A couple months," Rebekah said serenely.

"Well, I hope your mother's taught you all the secrets a girl needs to know! A man likes a wife with a certain set of skills."

"*Ezra,*" Aunt Rhesa said even more strongly.

Rebekah thought for a moment of all the skills Ezra might be referring to and how she had acquired them. She couldn't even allow herself to look in Martha's direction.

"I hope he won't be disappointed," she said, keeping her expression modest but allowing a little lilt to creep into her voice.

Ezra loosed a crack of laughter. "And I'll wager he won't be! Your mother has kept two husbands quite happy. I imagine her daughter will be well prepared for her own role."

"There's some pie left. Would anybody like some?" Martha's mother said, obviously trying to change the subject.

"Oh, pie—I'll have it," Ephram said quickly, and the topic was turned. "More bread, too, if there's any left."

After they'd cleaned up the dinner mess, they all sat around the fire for another hour just to enjoy its warmth. At first they exchanged desultory conversation, long silences intervening between the words, and then Aunt Rhesa began to sing. It was a slow lullaby, a song Rebekah had sung a hundred times to Jordan and to Jonah, and they all joined in a few notes into it. Ezra had a fine voice—he had performed with the Jansai more than once at the Gloria—so they let him sing the next melody all by himself when he swung into a new song. Once he was done, Aunt Rhesa offered a lighter piece, a call-and-response song, and they all warbled back her melody lines, occasionally managing a fairly respectable three-part harmony. The Jansai were not the singers that the rest of the people of Samaria claimed to be. They offered their prayers to Jovah, and they attended the Gloria, and they accorded music a certain careless respect, but they did not make it the center and focus of their lives.

As Rebekah had heard the angels did. But then, everything the angels did was different from the Jansai way. There could not be two peoples on the planet so different in outlook.

"Well, I think it's bedtime for these old bones," Martha's mother said, coming to her feet with a muffled groan. "Ezra, where have you decided everyone should sleep?"

"I thought all you girls would want to stay close to the fire," he said, seeming to have forgotten that two of the "girls" were at least five years older than he was. "It'll be a chilly night. Eph and I will take the wagons."

"Rebekah and I wanted one of the wagons," Martha said. "We won't be cold. We brought extra blankets."

"You just want to stay awake all night and whisper," her mother said with a sniff.

"That's right," Martha replied, grinning. "But why should we disturb you by whispering around the fire?"

Ezra was nodding. "You two take the smaller wagon. Eph and I will take the one I drove. Does anyone need anything else for the night?"

There was a quick little scurry as everyone took one last opportunity to go off for a private moment before bedtime, and then it was another ten or fifteen minutes before they were all actually settled down for the night. Rebekah found that it was cold indeed once she and Martha had stepped any distance from the fire, huddling down into the bed of the wagon and burrowing under a pile of five blankets. She shrieked as Martha sat up a moment to rearrange the covers, causing a whippet of cold air to dart in across her shoulders.

"Lie *down*. I'm *freezing*," she hissed, and Martha giggled and snuggled back under the quilts.

"There, I'm getting warmer already," Martha whispered. "Isn't this better than lying by the fire?"

"Not yet it isn't," Rebekah grumbled, but she could already feel the heat of her body getting trapped by the down and cotton of the blankets and warming up the whole makeshift bed.

Martha took a long breath. "Can't you just smell the starlight?"

"Starlight doesn't have a smell."

"It does. Breathe deeper."

"All right. It smells lovely. I'm going to sleep."

Martha laughed and was silent for a few moments. Rebekah turned over, trying to find a more comfortable spot on the hard wood of the wagon.

"That's funny," Martha said.

"What's funny?" Rebekah said in a resigned voice.

"Your Kiss. Look at it."

Rebekah didn't bother to look, just pulled the cover up higher over her shoulder so that the crystal didn't show. "What about it?"

Martha was sitting up, leaning over her. "Let me see that again. Is it—doesn't it have a kind of peculiar glow?"

"I don't know. Maybe."

"*Maybe?* Your Kiss is lighting up at night and you haven't said anything to me?"

"It's just this faint little light. I don't know why it does that. I don't think it means anything."

"Let me see again."

So Rebekah pulled her arm out from under the covers and let Martha examine the crystal in her arm. "Is it hot? Does it hurt?"

"No and no."

"When did this start?"

"I don't know. I just noticed it one day and it's been like that ever since."

"Does it have anything to do with Obadiah?"

"How could it possibly?"

"I don't know. But that would be very romantic."

Rebekah yawned and buried her arm back under the quilts. "I don't think it means anything," she said again. "Anyway, I'm too tired to talk about it anymore. I just want to go to sleep."

"I'm not tired at all."

"That's because you didn't do any work all day! I did!"

Martha laughed. "All right. You go to sleep, then. I'm just going to lie here a while and think."

"Good night, then."

"Good night."

Unbelievably for her, Martha didn't say another word, just lay there quietly. Rebekah let her eyes close and her body relax as she grew warmer and more comfortable. She didn't really expect to fall asleep right away, but the combination of sun, fresh air, and exercise had tired her more than she realized. After only a few fuzzy moments of conscious thought, she gave in to exhaustion and fell immediately into formless dreaming.

She might have slept straight through till noon the next day, except that Martha woke her the next morning while most of the rest of the camp was still sleeping. "Damnation and isolation," Martha's voice came in a furious whisper. "Corpses, crows, and curses."

"What is it?" Rebekah asked sleepily, turning to her side to face her cousin and fighting to open her eyes. "Did you get bitten by something in the middle of the night?"

"No! I started my monthly bleeding. I didn't bring anything with me. I wasn't expecting—and my mother won't have anything."

Rebekah yawned and pushed herself up on one elbow. "I brought an old hallis with me, since I figured we'd be tramping through the sand and getting everything filthy. You can rip it up and make cloths from it. I don't need it."

"Are you sure? What a waste of good material."

"Better than ruining your clothes."

"And we're nowhere near water and I've made a mess—"

"There's a gallon in the wagon. We'll tear up my hallis and you can clean yourself up—"

"I don't know why this never happens to you," Martha grumbled. "All right, show me where this hallis is."

The words struck Rebekah dumb. Silently, she climbed out of the warm covers and, shivering, dug through her pack of belongings till she'd located the ancient and tattered undergarment. Silently, she helped Martha rip the fabric into reasonable portions and watched the blond girl hurry off toward a windbreak of bushes where she could strip down in privacy and clean herself up. Still silent, and now both frozen and terrified, she slipped back under the covers and lay there trembling, realizing she would never be warm again.

When, in fact, had her own monthly bleeding last occurred? Not for weeks now—not for months. She had never paid much attention to her cycles, which had always been erratic and hard to predict; she had just learned to deal with each episode as it occurred. But she was thinking furiously now. If she had not had her bleeding this month, or the last month, or the month before that—

Sweet Jovah singing like a mournful angel of death. She was carrying Obadiah's child.

CHAPTER TWENTY-FOUR

The pregnant woman screamed again, squeezing down on Elizabeth's hand with a pressure that almost broke the bones, and then subsided into a quiet, moaning pant. Elizabeth didn't even ask; she used her free hand to toss through her satchel and dig out two more tablets of pain-reducing medicine. "Here, take these," she said, holding the pills to the woman's mouth.

"I don't—want to—faint," the woman gasped.

"You won't," Elizabeth promised. "But I think you'll feel better."

Mary glanced up from her position between the woman's legs. "Soon now," she said.

"Is my baby going to be all right?" the woman managed, between huffs of breath.

"I think so. I see its head, that's a good sign. We just need a little more effort from you—and some patience—"

"It hurts." The woman sighed.

"Yes," Mary said. "Unfortunately, that's the way of it."

And this child fighting for entrance into the world was not even angelic, Elizabeth reflected. Although Elizabeth had yet to actually witness an angel birth, she had formed a pretty fair idea of the difficulties an angel child could cause to its mother even before it was brought into the world. Just a week ago, she and Mary had been called to the bedside of Magdalena, who was suffering severe pains and terrified that her child was trying to arrive too early.

Elizabeth had never seen any angel look so desperate and pale, her skin whiter than her wings, her slender hands too shaky to hold a glass of water to her lips. Mary had commanded Elizabeth to mix a variety of herbs while the healer massaged the angel's stomach and tried to feel for the size and placement of the tiny life inside. The potion Elizabeth had eventually fed to the angel had caused Magdalena to fall into a drugged sleep—and, Mary had predicted, would halt the early labor pains as well.

"But she must take some of this medicine every four hours for the next two weeks," Mary had told the golden-haired woman who had appeared to be the angel's private nurse. "And if the pains resume, you must call for me right away."

The golden-haired woman had nodded. "Do you have something that will take away her nausea? Everything she eats makes her sick. But she has to eat, or the baby—" The woman gestured.

"Corvine works best for that," Mary said regretfully. "But I don't have any."

"Oh, yes, the Edori use corvine for stomach upsets," the other woman replied. "I'll see if any of the clans are in town and ask if I can buy some from them."

Which had seemed like such an odd thing to say that Elizabeth had paused in the repacking of her satchel to give the other woman a long, curious stare. She was mortal, and remarkable in looks only because of that hair, but there was something about her that rivaled the self-assured arrogance of the angels. Not a nurse after all, Elizabeth decided. A Manadavvi, perhaps. A friend of Nathan's wife, come to aid her in her time of need, and willing to take drastic measures to make sure Magdalena was cared for.

"If you find any Edori willing to sell their herbs, send them over to me," Mary had replied. "I prefer the Edori medicines much of the time."

The golden-haired woman had smiled. "So often," she had said, "everything about the Edori ways is to be preferred."

Later that same day, a courier had arrived at Mary's suites with a selection of powdered herbs in various pouches and canisters. Mary had exclaimed greedily over the new riches and carefully explained to Elizabeth which potions were to be used in which situations. In fact, Elizabeth had already fed one of the powdered herbs to their current patient, though it wasn't clear that the medicine had had much effect. The two big white tablets, however, seemed to have tamed some of her pain, for she now lay more quietly on her bed.

"How much longer now?" the woman asked in a voice that was almost a whisper.

"Soon," Mary said again. Elizabeth, who had now attended more than a dozen births, figured they had another hour to go.

There was a commotion outside the room and the sound of urgent voices raised, most of them male. Elizabeth knew one voice belonged to this woman's husband, but the others were unfamiliar. They all sounded angry.

A minute later, there was a knock on the bedroom door, and the husband himself came into the room, giving his wife one wretched, compassionate look. "I'm sorry," he said, addressing the healer. "There are men outside. They say there's been an accident, and they need your help."

"I can't possibly leave her," Mary said sharply.

"That's what I told them. But they say a man has been severely hurt, and he could be dying."

Mary looked over at Elizabeth, who felt her stomach do a giddy flip. "It's up to you," Mary said. "You can bind a cut and set a bone. Do you feel up to going on your own?"

"I don't know, I—" Elizabeth stammered.

"What about my wife?" the man demanded.

"You'll just have to help me," Mary said. "I'll tell you what to do."

"What if I can't help this man?" Elizabeth said.

"You'll do him more good than a bunch of fool-headed men who would just stand around and watch him bleed," Mary said roundly. "If you fail, you fail, but at least you'll have tried to save him."

Elizabeth felt stupid and nervous, unsure of herself and clumsy. She glanced around the room as if looking for an excuse to stay, and her eyes came to rest on the face of the patient on the bed.

"Go to him," the woman panted. "I'll be—fine. I would feel so dreadful if—someone died . . . because of me."

Elizabeth felt her lips tighten and her stomach curl into a small ball. She stood up. "I have to wash my hands," she said. "Tell them I'll be right there."

Three men had been injured at the construction site on the west edge of town, but only one of them was in severe straits. He was not only unconscious and probably suffering from a concussion as well, but he had an open wound that sliced from his neck across his chest and down to his hip, which was shattered. Elizabeth could not believe he had not already bled to death. Gazing down at him, she felt her own blood retreat in her veins, leaving her hands cold and her brain too numb to function.

"Those two over there—broken bones, that's all, we know how to set those, but Henry—you've got to do something," said the man who had brought her down here at a run so hard she was still struggling to regain her breath. "He's going to die."

"He might," Elizabeth said in a small voice. "Somebody bring me a bucket of water. And somebody else set some water on to boil. I'll do what I can."

She knelt beside him where he had been laid on a blanket that had been thrown down in the middle of a muddy street. This was her makeshift sickroom. Someone here had known enough to stanch the blood and put pressure on the wounds, but the cloth across his chest was still leaking with fresh blood. She could lather him with manna root paste to slow the bleeding and force tablets down his throat to prevent infection, but she was not sure she could sew up a wound that stretched so far and went so deep—not sure she could do it in time, not sure she could do it at all. So far the only cut she had sewed up on her own had been a small one on a little girl's finger. She didn't have a clue what to do about the shattered hipbone. She would start with the wound and hope that, by the time she was done, Mary would have arrived to finish the job.

"Somebody will have to help me," she said in a small voice. "I need a pair of hands to peel back the cloth slowly and hold the edges of the wound together."

It seemed like hours that Elizabeth labored over Henry's broken body, moving as painstakingly but efficiently as she could. His breathing was ragged and uneven, and every now and then it seemed to stop for the space of a beat or two. Elizabeth had forced a mixture of painkillers and anti-infection drugs down his throat before she began working on his wound, but she was not sure he was awake enough to feel any of her ministrations anyway. He didn't grunt or cry out whenever her needle entered his skin; he didn't move or jerk away from the sting of salve along his open sore. He just continued that heavy, clumsy breathing, in, out, pause, pause, in, out, pause. . . .

Once she was past the tricky veins of the neck, Elizabeth felt more sure of herself, though the blood trickled out in sluggish, regular spurts as she worked her way across his chest. She was so cold; her fingers could not feel the oversize needle, trembled every time she tried to insert new thread through the eye. Someone brought her hot liquid and held it to her lips, since she did not want to touch anything with her bloody fingers. Someone else—or maybe the same person—brought a blanket and wrapped it around her where she knelt on the rocky dirt, looping it through her arms and tying it around her back so that she received some warmth without having the edges fall in her way. The third time she paused to rethread her needle, someone caught her hand.

"Here," said a voice that she almost recognized. "Put these on."

"These" were a pair of small cotton gloves, not entirely clean, from which the fingertips had been clipped away. They were too big for her, but she gratefully slipped her frozen hands inside. "Thank you," she said, sparing a moment to glance up at her thoughtful assistant.

It was the Edori Rufus. Whom she had not seen in more than three months.

"What else can I get you?" he asked gravely. "How can I help?"

For a moment her mind was completely blank. "Something else hot to drink, thank you," she said. "Soup, if there's any to be had. I don't want to get faint."

"I'll be right back."

She wanted to stare after him, wanted to call, "Wait! How have you been? I've thought about you." But the troubled breathing of her patient called her back to her situation, and she quickly bent over his wounded chest again. Broken ribs, too, no doubt, but there wasn't much she could do about them. She silently recited the list of imperatives that Mary had taught her on her very first week on the job: *breathing, bleeding, bones, burns.* He was breathing; she was taking care of the bleeding. He had no burns, and his bones could wait. She took another stitch.

It was close to sunset by the time Mary arrived, looking exhausted but capable. Rufus and two of his fellow workers had strung a few lanterns above Elizabeth's head so that she wouldn't have to work in darkness, though she still had to be careful to hold her head so that its shadow did not fall in her way. The cold had gotten even sharper as a wind had arisen. Now Elizabeth couldn't feel any part of her body: not her knees and ankles where she knelt on the ground, not her icy fingers, not her frozen nose.

"Let me see, let me see," Mary said briskly, and Elizabeth was never so glad to turn responsibility over to another human being. "Hmm—yes, very good. Has he spoken? Has he thrown up?"

Elizabeth shook her head and quickly rattled off the drugs she'd administered and the steps she'd taken. "But I don't know how to set his hipbone, and I'm sure he's got some broken ribs," she finished up.

"Well, you did an excellent job sewing up the wound," Mary said. She had knelt beside Elizabeth on the dirt road, but now she glanced up and around. "We can't leave him outside in the middle of the street. We have to get him to a house, or at least a bed. Somewhere he can stay a good week or two. He's going to have to be immobilized."

"We were afraid to move him," someone said.

"Right, you did the right thing for the moment, but now he's going to have to be taken someplace safer," Mary said. "How far is his house?"

There followed a short discussion about possible sickbeds, with the construction crew quickly deciding that their foreman's office was the closest and most logical location. "But I don't know how we can move him without killing him," one of the men added.

"I'll get a door," Rufus said. "It'll be flat and sturdy. We'll pull the blanket over onto that. Four of us can carry him once he's on it."

"Is he ready to be moved?" Mary asked Elizabeth, who was setting the final stitches as close as she dared to the smashed hip.

"I've done what I can," Elizabeth said, sitting back on her heels. She used the back of her wrist to push the hair out of her eyes. She wanted to curl up in a ball and fall asleep, right here in the middle of the road. "How's the baby?"

"Just fine," Mary said, permitting herself a small smile. "Little girl, quite perfect. The mother is sleeping. The baby is *not* sleeping, and so her father is getting a chance to learn how to calm her."

"I wish you'd been here," Elizabeth said.

"It doesn't look like you needed me," Mary said. "But the man told us three people had been hurt. Where are the others?"

Elizabeth rose tiredly to her feet. "I can look at them now, if you can take care of Henry."

Mary nodded, all her attention back on the unconscious man. "You do that," she said. "I'll finish up here."

There wasn't much Elizabeth could do for the other two injured men, for other hands had cleaned their wounds and applied rough medicine. But she checked the splints anyway, offered drugs to stop pain and infection, and asked after any symptoms of dizziness or fever. One of the men, a thin, evil-looking fellow, cursed venomously the whole time she looked him over, furious at the prospect of missing work and losing pay, and blaming someone named Joe for carelessness on the job. His fellow sufferer just looked tired and morose, accustomed to more and worse setbacks than this.

"If you have any pain or bleeding or any red marks streaking up your arm, come look for Mary or me," Elizabeth instructed the second man.

"It's just a bone," he said wearily.

"A broken bone can kill you if you're not careful," she said.

The thin man had been listening to their conversation. "Then I'll just have to kill Joe first," he said.

"Or find a job that better suits your good temper," Elizabeth said without pausing to think about it. There was a short silence, and then the second patient burst out laughing. The thin angry man jumped to his feet and stalked away.

"That's better than any number of drugs," said the tired man, suddenly cheerful. "Thank you for your help."

"You're welcome," she replied.

After he left, levering himself to his feet and cradling his wrapped arm against his chest, Elizabeth repacked her bag with slow, deliberate movements. She was so exhausted she wasn't sure she could stand up, and the thought of making the long walk back to the dorm was almost overwhelming. Her eyes were not focusing properly; her mind kept flashing her images of the long, ugly gash in Henry's chest, the sharp bits of bone protruding from the destroyed hip. Neither Henry nor Mary was to be seen in the street, so Elizabeth assumed the other workers had carted the patient off to some protected place where Mary was doing what she could to set the bone.

Elizabeth should go help her. She should push herself to her feet and ask one of the construction workers where the healer and her patient had gone. She should go stand at Henry's bedside and closely watch Mary's ministrations, so that next time she was alone with someone so drastically injured, she would not feel foolish and helpless and terrified.

Instead, she leaned over and vomited into a ditch at the side of the road.

There was nothing she hated more than throwing up. She hesitated a moment, and then vomited again.

"Maybe it was the soup I brought you, but I think it was the sight of Henry's blood pumping out of his heart," said a soft, burred voice behind her, and a hand was laid comfortingly upon her shoulder. She knew even before she looked that it was Rufus. "You haven't been at the healing profession so long that you're used to sights like that."

"I'm sorry," she whispered, wiping at her mouth and hating the taste on her tongue. She was mortified that he had seen her.

"Sorry? For being sick? That's a silly thing to say. Here. I think a little water might improve things."

He handed her a jug of water but nothing to pour it into. She cupped her hand and managed to take a few swallows. The water tasted sweet, a welcome contrast to the acrid residue in her mouth.

"Thank you," she said. "I didn't realize—I haven't done that before."

"Now let's see if you're able to stand up," he said, a trace of humor in his voice. "You look worn down to sinew. A mighty frail state for a girl who's going about saving lives."

She climbed to her feet and found herself a bit steadier than she'd expected. "Where's Mary?" she asked. "She might need me."

"Mary sent me out here to tell you to go on home."

Elizabeth regarded him with suspicion. His face was smooth and dark, the face of any Edori man; the silky black hair had been cut recently, leaving the broad cheekbones and brown eyes completely exposed to view. Yet she found it hard to read his expression. "You might just be saying that," she said, her voice half-accusing, "because you think I look so weak."

He grinned. "And I would say it, too, for just that reason, except she really did tell me to send you home. She said, 'I've got things well in hand here. Tell that girl to go home and sleep.' "

"I think I'm too stunned to sleep," Elizabeth said.

Rufus nodded. "Oh, and I forgot! She said, 'And if Elizabeth says she doesn't feel like sleeping yet, well, Rufus, you just take her back to town and make sure she gets a good dinner.' "

In spite of herself, Elizabeth giggled. "Now, that I know you made up."

"I did," he admitted. "But doesn't it sound like a good idea? You've just lost your lunch and breakfast."

"I don't think I could eat," she said. "But I'd like some hot tea."

"I know just the place," he said.

They sat in a cozy little cafe not far from the center of town and talked for the next two hours. After the hot tea, Elizabeth decided her stomach was calm enough to chance a little bread; and after the bread, she believed she would try some soup. Rufus ate more heartily but paused every few bites to ask her how she was feeling. He didn't order any wine, which made her grateful. David's constant indulgence in wine and other spirits had made Elizabeth begin to lose her taste for alcohol.

Not that she had seen David for three weeks or more.

"So how's the healing business going?" Rufus asked. "You seem to have become adept in a short time."

Elizabeth made a face. "There's so much I don't know. I feel like I've learned amazing things—and then every day something happens, and I don't know how to deal with it. It makes me feel stupid."

"Not stupid," he said quickly. "But young enough to have a lot to learn."

"I don't feel so young, either," she grumbled.

He grinned. "Well, but younger than Mary, who must be fifty, wouldn't you guess? Do you think she learned everything in one winter? I would suppose it took her a good twenty years to become the healer she is now. And even she is probably still learning."

"I love the work," she said. "But there are so many things that can go wrong." She looked up at him, her face serious. His own face looking back at her readied itself for solemn news. "I've seen two people die," she said in a quiet voice. "Though we did everything we could. And I saw someone almost die—a friend of mine."

"And you hadn't seen people die before?"

She nodded vehemently. "Yes! My mother and one of the hands on my cousin's farm. But they weren't—I wasn't trying to save them. I didn't know that I might be able to. Now I think, if I do everything right, why *shouldn't* I be able to save everyone? So it frightens me to think I might do something wrong."

"Though everyone will die sooner or later, and not all the work of the best healer in Samaria will be able to save them," he said gently. "Yovah gathers up the old souls to make room for the new ones. That is the way the cycle goes."

"Yes, but—" She shook her head. She was not thinking clearly enough to get into a debate on religion and the miracle of existence. "Yes, but they shouldn't die because my skills failed," she said.

He nodded gravely. "And this friend of yours? What happened to her? For it's clear she was one you did save."

Elizabeth was silent a moment, long enough for the Edori to guess that the story was not a simple one. "Or clear that I almost killed her," she said at last. "I gave her some herbs, and she took too many, and her body started bleeding, and she almost died." She looked up at him. "I did tell her. I did warn her. But I didn't speak strongly enough. I was irresponsible."

"Or she was," he said. "What did she want so badly from these drugs? Sleep? A release from pain?" He half-smiled and made a motion with his hand. "Those brilliant, crazy, waking dreams that you can distill from the lossala plant?"

"Fertility," Elizabeth said. "She was in love with an angel boy, and he was on the point of leaving. She thought—if she had one last try—these herbs would increase her chances of conceiving his child. But instead—" She hesitated a long moment, remembering Faith's bitter sobs that day they had conferred in Mary's office. Faith had not blamed Elizabeth, not once, but Elizabeth felt as guilty as a murderess. "Instead, the drugs have burned out her womb, and she will never bear children for anyone, angel or mortal. She believes her life is ruined. I am so happy that she is alive, but she is so sad that sometimes I'm not sure she can go on."

Rufus made no reply for so long that Elizabeth had to look up at him to try to gauge his reaction. He, too, looked sad, but he did not exhibit Faith's level of wild grief, just a certain wistfulness at the way the world was ordered.

"I understand the desire for children—that is a deep need among the Edori, to bear children and raise them with great joy—but this obsession with bearing angel children—" He shook his head. "I cannot comprehend it."

"It's just that—"

"A child is a gift from Yovah," he interrupted, his voice gaining passion as he spoke. "Every child. Can you imagine a greater miracle—a new life, set in your arms by a god who trusts you? One day there is nothing, just you and your small circle of friends. The next day there is another living creature, created from *you*, from desire and divinity. That thought doesn't stop your heart with wonder? That realization does not make you shiver where you sit?"

Elizabeth stared at him, struck dumb.

"Among the Edori, every new birth is celebrated. The whole tribe rejoices, and when the clans come together at the Gathering, it is with pride and delight that the elders stand up and recite the names

of every new child born to their tents. But among the mortals—"
Rufus made another gesture with his hand, an angry one, brushing
debris from an invisible surface. "Children are thrown away every
day. In Semorrah, in Castelana, there are beggars in the streets—
cripples and blind boys and girls who are missing an arm—these
were left behind by parents who decided an imperfect child was not
pleasing. How can such things happen? But that is not the worst of
it. Women who care only for angel babies will abandon infants who
are born without wings. Will leave them in the streets or the alleys or
the roads outside of town to die of exposure and starvation. So they
can seduce another angel lover and try again for a better child."

He stopped, his generous mouth pinched tight, his dark eyes even
darker with a long-held fury. "But why am I saying this to you?" he
said, his voice quieter. "It is for just such a child that you made your
way to Cedar Hills."

She was racked by emotions so deep and conflicting that for a
moment she could not answer him. She wanted to lie—she wanted to
explain—she wanted to say something that would make him admire
her, or at least forgive her, and she could not think why that mattered. She scarcely even knew this man. But she could not let him
leave this table thinking so badly of her, classing her with the worst
of women, the worst of human beings. And he looked like he was
ready to surge to his feet at any second and stalk away.

"Yes," she said in a small voice. "But that is no longer why I
stay."

It was enough; it kept him in place, anyway. "I came because I—
because it had been so long since I had anything of value. Since I had
been anyone who mattered," she said, her voice quavering but determined. She had never really thought how to put this into words. All
the women she knew understood this instinctively. "If you bear an
angel child, everybody loves you. I just wanted to be loved. I wanted
to do something to be loved *for*."

"People love you for who you are, not the angels you produce,"
Rufus snapped. But he was listening.

She nodded. "People love you for who you are if you are worth
loving," she said in a soft voice. "And I don't think I was. What did
I do, what did I know, that mattered to anyone?"

"But you could have done anything!" he exclaimed. "Taught children or constructed buildings or written music or merely determined to be a kind person—"

"Or become a healer," she said steadily. "Yes. I understand that now. Don't hate me because I didn't know it before."

He grew suddenly quite calm but intense; his gaze was fixed on her with both sternness and speculation. "So you no longer chase angels like a child chasing after butterflies?"

She gave a tiny smile. "I only ever chased one angel. And I haven't seen him for weeks now."

Rufus shrugged. "There are plenty of other angels in Cedar Hills. And other holds across the three provinces."

"Having seen the—the *rigors* of childbirth, I am a little less eager to experience it for myself," she said. "And from the stories I've been told, delivering an angel child is even more dangerous. If I fell in love with an angel and he fell in love with me? Oh, then I would happily try to bear his child. But as it stands right now—" She spread her hands palm up over the table. "I have other goals."

"Falling in love with an angel is probably no better than falling in love with any man," Rufus said rather gruffly.

Elizabeth could not stop a peal of laughter. "You think not? I don't know. I've never fallen all the way in love with anyone. I suppose the experience could be just as fine if you fell in love with a farmer or a merchant or a miner."

"Or an Edori," he said.

"Or even an Edori," she said.

"But you would have to make the experiment to be sure."

"You're the only Edori I know," she said.

He gave her such a look then—part mischief, part shyness—that she ducked her head and snatched up her water glass just to provide herself with a distraction. He might have been planning to say something, but she rushed into speech before he could. "And you're not a typical Edori, I think," she said. "You haven't lived among your people since you were a child."

Whatever else he might have planned to say was blown away in a regretful sigh. "That's true," he acknowledged. "I haven't been to the Gathering in thirteen years."

"That's the second time you've mentioned that," she said. "What is the Gathering?"

His face lit up. "Only the most important event to occur on Samarian soil every year."

"That would be the Gloria," she said primly.

He laughed. "Or so the angels would have us believe! No, the Gathering is far more significant, to my way of thinking. It's when all the clans come together for a few days to one great campsite, and renew old friendships and forge fresh ones, and sing their histories to each other, and celebrate the births and mourn the deaths. It is a time for connection and rejoicing. It is a time to remember what it truly means to be an Edori."

"And when is this held?"

"Just as winter is grudgingly giving way to spring, about a month before the Gloria that the angels brag of so often."

She grinned. Samaria would not endure without the annual observance of the Gloria; it was something the god demanded of his people, to come together once a year to honor him and prove their harmony with each other. This Gathering might be a delightful event, but it could not eclipse the Gloria in true importance.

"Where is it held? On the Plain of Sharon, like the Gloria?"

"Certainly not," he said, affecting horror. "To go to the same spot, year after year, like habitual creatures with no sense of adventure? The Edori would not do such a thing. They are wanderers with souls that cannot stay still. We choose a different place every year."

"So where is the event to be this year?" she asked patiently. She had heard Mary and Tola complain about the difficulty of getting a clear answer from an Edori, and she was just now beginning to realize what they might have meant.

He waved a hand, apparently meant to indicate a northeasterly direction. "On the coastline just above the northern edge of the desert."

She was not good with geography. "Show me."

So he spilled salt on the table and used his finger to draw a map: the eastern coast, the ragged oval of the desert, the long spine of mountains stretching down from the Caitanas. He placed an olive on the right-hand side of his composition. "Breven," he said. A fruit seed was laid an inch above it, indicating a distance of many miles. "The Gathering."

She studied it. "That's a good five-day trip from here," she guessed.

He nodded. "And that's assuming your horses are sound and the weather holds true."

"So are you going? It's only a few weeks away."

He didn't answer.

"You're not going," she said. "Why not?"

He shrugged. His fingers swept lightly through the granules of salt, erasing the mountains and the cities. "I have a job, and I've grown fond of the money. To be gone two weeks when a man is counting on you—that's not very responsible."

"Well, but if you told him you were leaving and that you'd like to return to him when you got back—"

Rufus shrugged again. "He'd probably allow it. He's a thoughtful man. All the workers like him."

"So?"

"So?" he mocked.

"So what are your other reasons for not going?"

"Oh, it's a long trip and I haven't traveled so far on my own since I was—well, ever, really. I was young when I was taken from the people. I can make a fire and find water and catch game, of course, but I don't want to travel so far alone."

"There are other Edori in Cedar Hills," Elizabeth said. "I'll bet some of them are going to the Gathering."

A small smile lit behind the dark eyes, warming them considerably. "Yes, you're right about that as well."

"So? Other reasons?"

"It's been a long time since I was among my people," he said softly. "All those from my own tribe are dead."

"You told me all Edori are clan."

He nodded. "Yes, but would there be any among the other tribes to recognize me? To call out my name and invite me to sleep in their tents? It would be a hard thing to travel so far looking for kin and then find none but strangers."

"So you're afraid to go," she said.

He gave her another tiny smile. "It sounds harsh put in just that way."

"Afraid to be turned away. Afraid not to be welcomed by the people who should love you."

"Ironic, isn't it?" he said. "Just the situation you described a little earlier this evening."

"Oh, not just the same," she assured him. "If I had thought there was anyone in the three provinces who might—might *possibly*, had the barest *chance* of welcoming me—I would have run to that city so fast you would not have been able to see me for the cloud of dust I raised. But there was no one who wanted to take me in."

"Your cousin."

"Take me in and love me," she amended.

"I might go next year," he said.

"What will be different next year?"

He laughed. "The Gathering will be longer than a few weeks away and I'll have more time to think about it!"

"I think you should go now," she said.

"And be gone from you for two whole weeks?" he said, his voice light. "It would seem too long."

"I don't think you should include me in any of your future calculations," she said sternly, but she could not keep the smile from playing around her mouth.

"Oh, but I do," he said, laughing at her. "And I don't think there's going to be much I can do about that."

When they were finally bored with sitting at the table, they paid their bill and headed back outside. The air was bitter now, a frigid wind blowing straight down from the Heldoras, and the night sky was frosty with stars. Two steps from the cafe door and suddenly Elizabeth felt all her weariness rush back and lodge itself in her feet, her lungs, her eyes.

"I had so much fun tonight," she told Rufus. "But I have to go home now. I'm so tired."

"And I'm the scoundrel for keeping you out so late when I knew you scarcely had the strength to stand," he said remorsefully. "Come on. I'll take you home."

"Oh, don't bother, I walk alone all the time in Cedar Hills."

"I'll take you home," he repeated, and put an arm around her shoulder. "It's not that I worry about the danger to your person, it's that I'd like the last five minutes of your conversation."

She yawned and then laughed. "I don't think my conversation will repay you very well right now. I can hardly think."

"Your company, then."

So they walked in silence, briskly because of the cold, though Elizabeth was too tired to really hurry. She was both glad and sorry when the boardinghouse came into view.

"This is me. That's my window there. See it? With the blue curtains. I wonder if Faith is still awake."

"If she is, you'll have a great deal to tell her about the details of your day."

She smiled up at him. Outside at night, his dark face was even harder to read. "It was good to see you again, Rufus."

"So, then, dinner tomorrow night?" he asked casually.

She had to laugh. "Do you think I have *every* night free for dinner with you?"

"I didn't ask for every night. Tonight and tomorrow," he protested. "It's true that tomorrow I might ask for the night after that—but I might not. You never know."

"Tomorrow night will be fine."

Dark as it was, she could see the smile appear on his face and quickly vanish. "Till then," he said, and bent to kiss her on her cheek. He waited until she stepped inside the door and shut it behind her.

For a moment she stood there, back to the door, hand to her face, feeling astonishment tingle along her veins. She could not remember the last man who had given her a salute so tender, so undemanding. Her father, perhaps, when she was a very little girl. She could not even remember the last time she had kissed a man on the mouth when she was not planning on immediately going to bed with him. She wasn't sure she'd realized such a thing was possible—affection—or how greedily she might snatch up such a treasure once it was offered.

She moved slowly through the hall and common rooms, absent-mindedly greeting the few people she passed, and just as slowly climbed the stairs. She was not sure how much she would tell Faith. She might have to think over all the events of the evening, of the day, before she would be able to share them.

CHAPTER TWENTY-FIVE

There was never a moment's privacy to tell Martha what had happened. On the trip back from gathering reskel roots, Martha's mother insisted that the younger girls ride with her.

"I never get a chance to talk to you, Rebekah, and soon you'll be leaving us," the older woman complained. "Sit here beside me and tell me about your wedding."

There was nothing Rebekah was less interested in discussing at this moment than her wedding. "I have not really been consulted on most of the details. You'd be better off to ask my mother," Rebekah heard herself say. Her voice sounded a little thin, but that might be the effect of the desert air, so icy this morning that you could almost snap the willful little breezes between your fingers. Almost anyone would assume she was behaving quite normally.

"Tell me about your dress, then. What color are you wearing? How will you style your hair? Do you plan to marry in the morning? I prefer afternoon ceremonies myself. Otherwise there's so much time to sit around all day, worrying about what comes with the night."

"I don't think Rebekah's too worried about her wedding night, Mother," Martha said, sneaking a sidelong look at her cousin.

"No, I'm sure Jerusha has prepared you well enough for that," the older woman said. "But it's just that, after the meal is eaten and the toasts are drunk and everybody goes away, it's just so awkward to sit around staring at your new husband and just *wondering*. Better to get it over with right away, that's what I say. We'll plan Martha's wedding for very late in the afternoon, I promise you that."

"And is Martha getting married any time soon?" Rebekah asked politely.

Ezra, sitting on the driver's seat and only half-listening, gave a snort of laughter at that. "She'll be married soon enough, don't you be worried about her," he said. "I have a couple of husbands in mind."

"I think I'm only allowed one," Martha said.

Her father laughed again. "I'm going to choose the best one of the lot. But I'm still looking them over."

So the whole interminable drive had gone, Martha's mother asking prying questions in her whining voice, Ezra offering the occasional bluff counterpoint, and Rebekah and Martha supplying silly or serious responses as the occasion seemed to require. The entire time, Rebekah felt detached and unreal, numb with disbelief, but braced for the pounce of terror that was sure to come.

She had to get home. She had to think. She had to consult calendars and count days. She simply had to be wrong.

"I need to talk to you," she whispered to Martha as the wagon halted in front of Hector's house and Ezra alighted to pull down Rebekah's traveling bag. She was speaking through her veil and she could not clearly see Martha's face, but even with these baffles, Martha could catch the urgency in her tone.

"I'll see if I can come over tomorrow," she said.

Her mother caught this exchange. "Not tomorrow! Your father's cousins are coming. How can you have forgotten? They'll be here four or five days, and you'll have to help me keep them entertained."

"As soon as you can, then," Rebekah said, giving Martha's hand a hard little squeeze.

Martha nodded. "As soon as I can."

Once inside the welcome warmth of the house, Rebekah wanted nothing so much as a chance to run to her room and then stand there, shrieking out silent screams of panic and desperation. But Jordan spotted her at the door and darted over to see how the trip had gone, and then Jerusha stopped her in the hall to see how much reskel root she'd brought back for Hector's kitchen. And then her mother thrust Jonah in her arms and said, "Jovah's bones, he's done nothing but scream for two days running. Take him, keep him, leave him in the garden for the birds to eat up, I don't care. I have a headache, and I'm going to lie down."

Jerusha disappeared down the hall in a swirl of robes. Rebekah stood unmoving for a moment, staring down into Jonah's moody face. It would be only a moment, she knew, before he started squirming and kicking and demanding to be set free, wailing at the top of his lungs to reinforce his demands.

"You are the very last creature I want to deal with right now," she said in a voice so low even he might not have heard it. "I am not feeling so fond of babies at the moment. If I could, I swear by Jovah's ears, I would find a way to make you disappear."

She held him to her as she ascended the stair, clasping him more tightly as he began to writhe and whimper. But after all, she loved Jonah. He was not the baby she truly wished to make disappear.

Once they were safely in her room, she set him down and let him scamper on hands and knees through the furnishings. She kept a pile of toys in one corner, collected expressly for him, and he headed straight there, yodeling out his incomprehensible language. Rebekah sat on her mattress, her legs folded under her, her arms crossed over her chest and her hands wrapped around her throat, and tried to think.

Not last month. No. Not the month before that. Jovah's bones, she was at least two months pregnant. Possibly almost three. This explained everything: the lingering nausea, the emotional outbursts, even the changing contours of her body, which she and Martha had noticed the last time they were trying on clothes.

She glanced down at the Kiss in her arm, sparkling with a visible fervor. Could this, too, be attributed to the presence of the child in her womb? When had she first noticed it? When had she realized that it, like the baby inside her, was growing stronger day by day? It was said that the god caused the Kiss to flame when lovers came together for the first time. Maybe its incendiary joy now was a reflection of the god's delight at the creation of a new life, a silent, exquisite promise to

Rebekah about how much she would love the child she was carrying inside.

But she would not love it. She would not even have it. There were ways, there were drugs, Jansai women knew all sorts of methods to keep an unwanted child from coming. She searched her mind, trying to recall every whispered, half-overheard conversation among the married women who were tired of producing a baby every year, ruining their bodies and sapping their strength. Certain herbs were abortificants; certain readily available ingredients could be combined to produce the desired effect.

"Beb-be-be-be," Jonah cooed, crawling over. He gripped the fabric over her folded knees and pulled himself shakily to a standing position. "Po-po."

She swung him into her arms and carried him across the room to the chaos of his playthings in the corner. "I don't want to play with you. I want to sit and think," she said, but she dropped to the floor and crossed her legs, and set him down beside her.

"Heh," he said, picking up a carved wooden horse that Hector had brought back from some journey. It had wheeled feet and a rather nasty expression on its long face.

"Horse," she said, and pushed it back and forth on the floor for him. Then she did much the same thing with a handful of brightly painted wooden balls. Then back to pushing the horse. Tedious beyond description.

Martha would know the secret recipe for getting rid of a child. Martha had been wrong about the chances of a mortal girl becoming pregnant with an angel's child, but a practical piece of information like this would be part of Martha's basic store of knowledge. Hepzibah probably knew the formula as well, and might help Rebekah obtain the ingredients, but Rebekah shied away from that source of aid. Only if she was desperate. Only if there was no other course.

"Bah!" Jonah shouted, so she rolled the balls in his direction again.

The question was, had she waited too long? How much poison would it require to discourage this parasite, unhook its tiny fingers from their tenuous hold, wash it out of her body? She had heard awful tales, adolescent gossip, about this woman or that who had tried to force a miscarriage and badly miscalculated, bled to death on some unwatched bed as she made her try in secret. Rebekah could hardly go down the hall to the water room and expect to find a day of privacy. Someone would notice if she lay there for three or four straight hours, bleeding away an inner life. That would be just as bad as trying to carry the child to term; that would mark her for just as much guilt.

Martha would know. Or Hepzibah. One of them would help her.

"Bah!" Jonah cried again. Her hands had been too slow on the small painted spheres. She pushed them his way again.

She didn't know how she would tell Obadiah. They had never discussed the concept of children. Jonah's name came up from time to time but was never followed with, "So do you see children in your future? How many would you like to raise?" She didn't even know how angels organized themselves into family units or whether or not angels as a race were particularly fond of children. And who knew how Obadiah the individual felt about the idea of babies of his own? Would he be sad to think she might destroy a life that he had had some part in creating? Would he be horrified to learn of her carelessness, relieved that she had acted quickly enough to take all responsibility from him? And what if Martha had been in some way right? What if mortals really could not bear angel children? Was the child inside her anathema to her own life?

There was a frightening thought.

Jonah babbled at her again, and when she did not respond correctly, began crying in mingled fury and despair. Even when Rebekah picked him up to rock him, he could not be comforted. It never ceased to amaze her how quickly his moods could change, from sunny to stormy and back again in the space of minutes. "Are you hungry?" she asked, because usually food would satisfy him, no matter what else had sparked his misery. "Would you like some cheese? Some bread?"

He didn't answer intelligibly, of course, but his cries did abate. So she carried him downstairs and rummaged up snacks for both of them. They had eaten twice on the road, but these days she was always hungry. Well, one more mystery explained.

Jerusha found them ten minutes later. "What have you been giving him? I hope he's still hungry at dinner."

Rebekah handed him over. "He's always hungry," she said.

Jerusha took a moment to smile down at her son's happy face, wiping a purple stain from his mouth with the edge of her sleeve. "Well, he's growing, isn't he? That's my Jonah, that's my big boy."

"I'm going to go up and sleep," Rebekah said.

Jerusha glanced up, and then her sharp gaze lingered on her daughter's face. "You look tired. Were you and Martha up all night talking in the wagon?"

"Pretty late."

"Well, I'll need your help tonight. Hector's cousin is coming over with his sisters and his daughter, so we'll have company at dinner."

"All right."

"And that one girl might stay a few days. What's her name? Sarah."

"How long? I want to go to Martha's in a day or two."

"You'll go to Martha's when your uncle has invited you."

"I'm always welcome there."

"Well, I need you here for a few days. You're always gone."

"Then maybe Martha can come here."

"We'll see what her father says."

Rebekah shrugged and turned toward the door. "You wear one of your nice jeskas tonight," Jerusha called after her. "I want you to look pretty for Hector's family."

Rebekah didn't even bother to respond, just continued on her way through the door, down the hall, and up the stairs to her own room. She fell asleep the minute she lay on the mattress.

When she woke a couple of hours later, she lay still for a few minutes, gauging time of day by the level of activity in the hall. She could hear Hepzibah arguing with her sister, and the younger girls giggling as they hurried down the hall. An hour before dinner, probably. The guests would be arriving soon. Time to get up.

Rebekah continued to lie there anyway, hands pressed against her belly. It felt smooth, slightly rounded, hardly changed at all. Maybe a little extra heat seeped through from the interior lining out to her palms; but maybe that was her imagination. She tried to picture the creature that coiled inside her, which she envisioned as the size of a worm, maybe, but with fully formed limbs and features.

How did it eat? How did it breathe? How had her body, all on its own and with no prompting from her, understood how to nurture and protect it, how to divert her consumed nutrients into its frail blood and bones? What would it look like, if it came to term? Like Jonah, with his beautiful, expressive face? Like Rebekah, with her pointed, watchful one? Like Obadiah, blond and laughing?

I cannot kill this baby, Rebekah realized, flattening her hand with some pressure across her stomach. *What am I going to do?*

The meal was rich and well prepared, but the dinner hour itself was overlong and dull. Rebekah sat with her stepcousins and the daughters of their guests and did not make much effort to be sociable. This would reflect badly on her mother, if the girls complained to their own mothers about Rebekah's behavior, but she did not much care. She answered questions when addressed, tried to speak politely, and did not slurp at her food. Otherwise, she made no effort at all.

"So, Rebekah. How are plans coming for your wedding?" Sarah asked. "My father has said I will be allowed to come."

"It will be nice to have you there," Rebekah said politely.

"Is the dress ready? What color are you wearing?"

"Sage and varieties of green," Rebekah said. "No, it's not finished yet. Asa had two other weddings to sew for this winter. She's supposed to come back—next week? The week after? My mother has made all the arrangements."

"It must be exciting to be married," Sarah said.

I will never know, Rebekah wanted to respond. She didn't see how she could keep Obadiah's baby and still marry Isaac. She was pretty sure Isaac was clever enough to know that if he married a girl and she had a baby a few months later, the baby had not been fathered by him. Therefore, she had to find a way to avoid getting married. She hadn't yet worked out how to do this. She also hadn't figured out how she would explain bearing a child when she was unmarried.

She hadn't figured out anything.

"What food will you be serving? Will you have Manadavvi wines? My father says Manadavvi wines are the best, and that's all he'll serve at *my* wedding," Sarah said.

"Are you planning to wed soon?" Anything to change the subject.

Sarah tossed her head. "Oh, my father is looking into it. It has to be just the right man, you know, from just the right house. He thinks it's a pity that your brother is so young."

"Jonah?" Rebekah exclaimed before she could stop and think.

"No, silly. Jordan. He's only three years younger than I am, but way too young to marry. My father doesn't want to wait that long."

For the first time that evening, Rebekah gave some serious consideration to Sarah's smug, narrow face. The girl had fine, dark skin and startlingly green eyes; she was not unattractive. But she was selfish and stupid and she didn't know when to simply sit there and be quiet, and she certainly wasn't good enough to marry *Jordan.* "No, I'm sure your father is right. You shouldn't wait for my brother to come of age," Rebekah said, trying to keep her voice neutral. "There must be someone much better who's ready to be married."

"You're the lucky one," Sarah said enviously. "My father says Isaac's a strong, handsome man—smart, too. My father says he'll be rich as Uriah someday. The best catch in the city, my father says."

You can have him, Rebekah thought. *I'm sure he'll be happy to have you and your empty womb.* "I know your father won't stop searching until he finds someone just as good as Isaac," Rebekah said. "If I were you, I wouldn't worry at all."

So the evening was wearisome, but it finally ended. The next day was slow and boring, as Aunt Hepzibah snagged Rebekah at the breakfast table and demanded her help in the fabric room.

"I'm stitching away all on your behalf, you might as well help me out," the old woman said in her scratchy, irascible voice. "For you'll need table linens and bed linens and nightclothes, and I've made a good start, but there's more to do."

She may as well sew as sit and fret. Someone would use these tablecloths and bedsheets, even though Rebekah herself would need no dowry. "All right," Rebekah said and followed her upstairs.

The fabric room was sunny and cheerful, the overhead skylight admitting a fountain of white winter sunlight, and the work was mindless enough. Rebekah made precise hems in four sets of sheets, working slowly but competently, and paid little attention to the conversations going on around her. Hepzibah gossiped with old Aunt Gabbatha, and two of the younger girls sat in a corner and whispered about mysterious but, apparently, very funny events. Rebekah ignored them all and continued stitching.

She would have to get word to Obadiah. He might know what to do. But she had no idea when Obadiah would be back in Breven. Someday—she held on to that belief more tightly than her cramped fingers clutched the thin needle. He would return for her when he could.

She just hoped she had figured everything out by then.

The next two days passed with a similar monotony, though Rebekah continued to be amazed at how calm she was. Every morning when she woke, her first thought was, *Sweet god of the desert, I'm pregnant.* Every night when she lay on her mat to sleep, she thought, *When I wake up tomorrow, my baby will be one day older, one day closer to being born.* She believed these things absolutely. She rubbed her hand across her smooth stomach every morning, trying to note any sensible changes, reminding herself of the terrifying miracle occurring inside. But she still didn't really believe it. It was impossible that such a thing could be true.

The colors in her Kiss made no pretense of bashfulness anymore; they glittered night and day with a manic frenzy. She had to wear her darkest jeskas to cover up its pulsing light, and she was very careful to be alone in the water room before she stripped for a bath. Quickly in, quickly clean, quickly dressed again, before someone stepped inside and stopped dead in amazement.

She didn't know what would happen once she was discovered, as sooner or later she would be. Something else she hadn't figured out. She hoped to have a plan in place before that disaster occurred.

She spent the third day, all day, watching Jonah, an activity that made her seriously rethink how badly she wanted to have a baby of her own. "You were never this much trouble when you were little," she told Jordan that evening, when he came to the kitchen looking for her. "You didn't scream and cry until you got everything your own way."

He grinned. "I think you probably just don't remember. You

were only six when I was Jonah's age. You were probably even more trouble than I was."

"If I had been more trouble than Jonah, our mother would have left me on the side of the road."

"Maybe you'll be lucky. Maybe she'll leave Jonah at the side of the road someday."

Rebekah sighed. "No, she loves him too much. More than she ever loved either of us. And even I love him most days. But other days he reminds me too much of Hector."

Jordan laughed but took a quick look around to make sure none of Hector's sisters was sitting close enough to hear. "I'm going over to Uncle Ezra's tomorrow," he said. "Eph and I are going to spend a day down in the markets."

The news erased some of Rebekah's exhaustion. "Ask if Martha can come visit, will you? Or if I can go over there. I'm so bored."

He nodded. "Sure. When?"

"Tomorrow. The day after. Any day. I thought they were having company this week, though."

"They are. Ezra's cousin and his family. That's why we're going to the market tomorrow. Eph wants to show his little cousin some of the gaming stalls."

"They don't live in Breven?"

Jordan shook his head. It was rare, but a few Jansai had taken up residence in some of the other major cities of Samaria, all of them major trading centers where they could buy and sell. "Up by Monteverde, I think. Somewhere in Gaza. They came in with a merchant caravan."

Rebekah thought of Chesed, but there must be hundreds of caravans that originated in Gaza and made the trek across the entire country. "How long will they be here? I really need to see Martha."

Jordan grinned again. "I don't know. I'll ask that, too, while I'm there. Anything else I can do for you?"

"Take Jonah with you?" she said hopefully. "He's just the right age to learn to gamble."

Jordan laughed. "Then our mother would leave *me* at the side of the road. But I'll be home before nightfall. I'll come find you and tell you what we did."

"Sounds good," she said. "Enjoy the day."

Her own day passed pleasantly enough, even though she had Jonah in her care again while Jerusha lay low with a headache. The weather was unexpectedly fine: cold, but not bitter, with a mightily shining sun to make even the wind seem friendly. Rebekah kept Jonah in the garden most of the day, letting him crawl and dig and chase winter insects until he was so tired he couldn't keep his small head upright on his thin neck. She carried him in and placed him in his crib beside Jerusha's bed.

"How's your head?" she asked when her mother stirred.

"Better. If he starts screaming—"

"I'll come check on him again in half an hour."

She stopped for a snack in the kitchen—always hungry, always feeding her own baby—and then headed back to the garden. She couldn't stand to waste the sunshine, rare enough in this season of sullen clouds. She brought a blanket with her and wrapped it around her shoulders as she sat on the stone bench, face upturned, eyes closed, completely relaxed for the first time this whole day.

Jordan found her about twenty minutes later, bursting through the women's gate with such haste and clumsiness that Rebekah opened her eyes in surprise. His face was pale and his eyes were wild, and the premonition of disaster pushed her unsteadily to her feet. The blanket fell behind her to the bench.

"Jordan, what's wrong?" she demanded, putting up a hand to his shoulder as if to offer him strength or assistance.

His face looked riven; she had never seen the happy-go-lucky boy so shocked and seared. Had he seen a murder today on the streets of Breven? "Bekah," he whispered. "Bekah, they've taken Martha."

She felt her whole body go cold in one wave of horror. "Who— who's taken—taken her *where?*"

But she knew.

"We were—we were in the market. I told you. Eph and his little cousin Shem and me. And we were at the gaming stalls all morning, but then Eph wanted to show Shem the merchandise booths, and Shem said he wanted us to meet the others in his caravan, and we didn't care about those people, who would, they're Manadavvi, but Ephram was trying to be nice to him, Shem's a little guy—"

"Martha," Rebekah said, her mouth so dry she could scarcely speak.

Jordan nodded. "So we got there—to this booth—all these Mana-davvi wagons lined up in back and their sleeping tents set up, and Shem was having us meet everyone they'd traveled with. And he kept saying, 'Chesed, where's Chesed? You have to meet him, he's the best.' And somebody laughed and said, 'Where *is* Chesed? Back in the tent with that girl of his, I'll wager.' And so someone went back to roust him out, and you could hear a man laughing, and you could hear a woman laughing, and in a few minutes this Manadavvi man came out of the tent. And right behind him—right behind him—"

"Martha," Rebekah whispered again.

"And her veil was off and she was smiling and she was tugging on her jeska, like maybe she had had it off—"

"Sweet lord of the desert," Rebekah said.

"And Eph—and Eph saw her—and she saw Eph—and they just stared at each other. And Shem, he was so happy, saying, 'This is my friend Chesed, he lets me hold the reins when we're driving, he lets me sample the grapes and the bread,' and everyone else was silent, just staring. And we were in the middle of the market, there were hundreds of people around, some merchants from other provinces but mostly Jansai, and all of a sudden, Eph lets out this *yell*."

Rebekah closed her eyes. She could picture it, the brightly col-ored stalls, the milling crowds, the Luminauzi and Manadavvi in their booths selling goods, the colorful Jansai buying and selling and laughing, hundreds of Jansai, all of them men—

"He yelled, *'Kirosa! Kirosa!'* over and over again, and at first I couldn't think what it meant—"

"Broken," Rebekah said. It was the feminine form of the word. "Broken girl."

Jordan nodded. "And it must have been—it was like a signal—all these Jansai men came dashing to our booth, leaping over stalls and wagons, like they were running to help, like they were coming over to help put out a fire. And Chesed and his family—they were star-tled, they didn't know what was happening at first, and then they realized—all these Jansai, all these men, they were coming for Martha. So they tried to protect her, push her back into their tent, but Eph had grabbed her, and some men I didn't know, and they were pulling her out into the market. And Chesed was trying to come after her, he was screaming and yelling, but his own people were holding him back. Shem was crying—I don't know, *I* might have been crying—and Eph had his face up in Martha's face and he was howling at her, calling her names—I've never heard a man say such things out loud—and she was just—she was sobbing. She was on her knees, she was begging him, I think she was begging him to let her stay with the Manadavvi. But he—but he *hit* her, he hit her over and over again, and the other men were holding her arms, holding her so she couldn't get away—"

"Sweet god," Rebekah murmured. She couldn't hear any more of this. But she had to. She had to hear every single word, every horrifying detail. "Sweet Jovah."

" 'Someone find my father!' Eph shouted, and half a dozen people ran off. A couple of the Manadavvi, older men, came forward and tried to reason with Ephram, but he shoved them away, and then there were more Jansai pushing them away. I don't know what happened to Chesed—I didn't see him again—but pretty soon Uncle Ezra was there. 'What's this? What's this?' he was yelling, and then he saw Martha, and then he—I can't explain it. It was like he became even taller and darker, like he was full of anger, except he got so quiet—"

Rebekah had seen Ezra in a state of righteous rage before. "Like Jovah," she said, "just before he throws a thunderbolt."

"Yes! That was exactly it! And he started tossing orders at people—'Samuel, get a wagon and some horses. Joseph, food and water for two days.' And Martha started *shrieking* at the top of her lungs—'No, no, no, no!'—and I still didn't know what was going on, I—and then Eph looked at his father and said, 'Can I come in the wagon?' and Ezra said, 'You can drive it.' And then I thought—then I realized—"

"They took her out to the desert," Rebekah said, her lips so stiff they could barely shape the words. "To leave her."

Jordan nodded. "It was awful. Standing there waiting for the wagon to come. Martha sobbing and Shem crying and Eph every once in a while remembering to hit Martha and Ezra just standing there looking grim—and it took forever. And then the wagon came and they threw her into it and maybe ten men climbed in the back with her—men I didn't know, I don't know if they were friends of Ezra's or just people who happened to be in the marketplace—and Eph and Uncle Ezra climbed onto the seat in front. And Eph looked at me and he said—he said, 'Come with us. We'll be back by tomorrow night.' And I said, 'No, I have to get home, I have to tell the others.' And Eph looked like he wanted to argue, but Ezra said, 'No, that's good. We need a witness to tell the true story. Jordan, you go on home and tell Hector what tragedy has happened here today.' And they drove off. They drove away."

There was a moment's silence. Rebekah had finally forced herself to open her eyes, but Jordan couldn't meet her gaze anyway. He was standing before her, his head turned away, his hands—his whole body—shaking like a sick old woman's. She realized for the first time that he was taller than she was, though he was still slim and eager and childlike in so many ways. Not a true Jansai man, not yet. Not one of them.

"What did you do then?" she asked, her voice oddly calm.

"I took Shem back to Ezra's house, and I told Ezra's cousin what had happened. Shem was sick, throwing up on the side of the road as we came back. Ezra's cousin—he started swearing, and then he sort of pushed me out the gate. I guess—I guess he's going to tell Martha's mother—"

Rebekah nodded. "Have you told Hector yet?"

He shook his head. "No, I—I just wanted to—I just wanted to find you, I wanted you to hear it from me before—I wanted you to—"

He couldn't complete a sentence. His trembling grew more pronounced, and then he started crying. Rebekah put her arms around him and drew him down to the stone bench where she had been sitting. He sobbed and sobbed, making no attempt to hide the shameful emotion, clinging to her as he had never clung to their mother, even when he was little. She shushed him, stroked his hair, talked to him in the same soothing tones she used with Jonah, but she knew there was no comfort. She knew there was no way to make him whole again.

"What will—what will they do to her?" he hiccuped, his face still against her shoulder. "Will they stone her to death? Why did they need the wagon? Why will they be gone till tomorrow night?"

Almost, she didn't want to tell him. But someone else would—Ephram or Ezra or Hector, or one of those jeering Jansai boys who imagined themselves men already. "They'll drive far enough out in the desert that she can't find her way home," Rebekah said quietly. "They'll leave her there with no food or water. They might stone her, or kick her, or hurt her in some way, but they won't kill her outright. And they'll drive away, leaving her to wander in the desert for however many days it takes her to die of thirst or exposure. It's cold now, of course. It might not take her very long."

He raised his head to stare at her, horror breaking through the blotchy red and the streaks of tears. He looked like he, not Martha, had been pummeled by men in the marketplace. "But she'll—but—but Bekah—"

She pushed the hair away from his forehead. She was so calm. Her hands weren't even shaking. "I know," she said quietly. "She will die, Jordan. They will leave her to die. Our uncle and our cousin and their friends have taken Martha in the desert to die."

His face crumpled, and he started sobbing again. Rebekah held him as tightly as she could, rocking him as she would rock Jonah, and wondered how she could be so composed, so detached. She could picture it, every detail Jordan had described, and those she could not stop herself from imagining. It was too warm tonight; Martha would survive this first day in the open. But tomorrow might be colder—and, perhaps, if Jovah was kind, it was already colder out in the desert, closer to the Caitanas, than it was here on the very edge of the sea. Maybe those frigid winds would blow down from the mountains this very evening, wrap their chill, kind arms around Martha's tense body, and carry her off to sleep and death. That was the best to hope for.

Rebekah prayed for ice.

"She's dead," Jordan was sobbing into her jeska. "Martha's dead."

Yes, Rebekah thought, suddenly realizing why she was so serene. *And I will be soon.*

CHAPTER TWENTY-SIX

There was never any denying Rachel. If she wanted to know something, you might as well tell her right away, because she would not stop harassing you until you told her every detail, answered every question. Obadiah had tried evasiveness before. It had never worked.

But he was determined not to tell her about Rebekah. So instead, because he was not good at fabricating lies, he told her about Zoe.

"So where did you meet this woman?" Rachel asked him.

"In Breven."

"In Breven! No one meets women there."

"I'm unique, then."

"Under what circumstances did you meet her?"

"There's a hotel. She helps her family run it."

Rachel raised her eyebrows. It was three days after her arrival, three days after the lavish dinner party thrown in her honor, and Rachel had only waited so long to grill him because she had been preoccupied with Magdalena, who had gone into early labor. But Maga had stabilized, though she seemed to require a great deal of rest, and Rachel had taken the opportunity to hunt Obadiah down.

"You became friendly with a Jansai woman in a Breven hotel?"

"Ah. She's not Jansai," he said. "She's Manadavvi."

"Well, you could have made that clear earlier!"

"Pardon me, Rachel, but what I could have made clear earlier is that I don't really want to be discussing my romantic life."

She grinned. A happy marriage and enormous responsibilities had not really tamed the defiant child in her. There would be something of the street urchin about Rachel till the day she died. This despite the fact that she wore her golden hair pinned back with sapphire clips and dressed in the finest Luminauzi silks. "Who cares what you really want," she said. "I want to determine if this woman is good enough for you."

"Let's talk about something else," he interposed. "How's Gabriel? Is he disappointed with me? I've made so little progress on this Jansai issue."

"Actually, he seems quite pleased with you. He's never managed to get Uriah to agree to see him on two consecutive visits, and all of the Jansai hate him without reservation. Well, he hates them, too. Well, so do I. Who doesn't? So you've done better than he hoped."

"We haven't reached any resolution."

"I say, let's call down thunderbolts and destroy the whole city of Breven," said Rachel, always the extremist. "That would solve everything."

"But realistically, how many Samarian landmarks can Gabriel annihilate during his tenure as Archangel?" he teased. "First, Mount Galo—"

"That was not Gabriel's fault!"

"Then, Windy Point—"

"It deserved to come down."

"And now Breven? After a while, the people in Semorrah and Castelana and Luminaux will start to wonder if they are next on the Archangel's list."

"Well, I wouldn't mind seeing Semorrah go up in flames, but I suppose I'm the only one," Rachel grumbled. "But no one would miss Breven."

Obadiah thought of the bright markets, the rowdy street festivals, the difficult, obstructive men, the silent, secretive women. "I would miss Breven," he said softly.

Rachel shook her head impatiently. "Oh, we'd make sure your

innkeeper's daughter was safely out before Gabriel prayed for lightning."

"No, I'd miss the whole city, I think," Obadiah said. "There are many things about the way it is run that I find hard to understand—appalling, even—but there is a great deal of energy and beauty in the Jansai culture. It is very fierce, very pure. Exotic. The whole time I'm in that city I feel like I could be on a different world altogether. I would miss it if it was gone."

Rachel was watching him with that predatory intentness she brought to anything that interested her. "You lied to me," she said.

He showed surprise. "About what?"

"That girl you love. She's no Manadavvi. She's a Jansai."

He could not think of a facile answer quick enough, and his silence betrayed him. "How is that possible?" Rachel asked wonderingly. "That you could *meet* a Jansai woman, and often enough to come to love her? How have you managed that? Even you?"

"The story is too long, and I don't want to tell it."

"How does it end?" she asked. "Or has it ended already?"

"Jovah, I hope not," he said.

"When will you see her again?"

"As soon as I can get back to Breven. But Nathan has interdicted the trip, and I think Gabriel supports him."

Rachel was unimpressed. "Go back," she said. "Right now. Tomorrow. If you really love this girl, don't wait another day. Bring her back to Cedar Hills with you."

"She's afraid to leave her family—everyone she knows. She says she won't have any friends in Cedar Hills."

Rachel gave him that radiant smile, always irresistible. Even now, it warmed him through from eyebrow to wing tip. "I'll be her friend," she said. "And when the angelica is your friend, you are never lonely."

"You hate Jansai," he retorted.

"Even if I hate her, I will love her for your sake," she said. "I would bring down Breven for you. I would spare it for you, too. There's nothing I wouldn't do for someone you loved."

"If I can convince her to come—"

"Don't ask her. Just bring her."

"Oh, yes, like such coercion always worked so well with you."

She smiled again, mischief in every line of her face. "But perhaps she is more tractable than I am," she said. "Anybody would be."

In fact, it was another two days before he could leave for Breven. He wanted to check on Maga, who was pale but determinedly cheerful when he finally saw her, and he accepted a few nearby commissions from Nathan. But finally, early one chilly and overcast morning, he set out for the desert city, arriving well after full dark.

Uriah would not welcome him at this juncture, so there was no need to advertise his presence. He made one brief stop, landing silently on the rooftop of a certain well-maintained mansion, and left a signal behind on the skylight: a colorful scarf weighted in place with a flat stone. Anyone working in the room below might glance up and see the strange bounty blown in by a playful wind; only one woman in the house would recognize it for the message it was.

Then he checked into the Hotel Verde, flashing his bracelets at the Manadavvi clerk who was stationed at the registration desk. Zoe was nowhere in sight and this young man—not her brother, Obadiah thought—did not seem inclined to gossip. Indeed, he looked quite grim. Obadiah asked no questions, just showed himself to his room.

Unreasonable to expect Rebekah to get his signal and be able to join him that very night, but he could not help himself: He felt an incandescent excitement shimmering through him, lighting the interior surfaces of his bones, shining a candle inside the cathedral of his heart. He was nervous, actually, pacing the room like a young boy preparing to meet his first lover, rehearsing what to say. But there were only a few words, after all. *I've missed you so much. I'm so glad to see you again. I love you.*

He ate hastily, showered even more quickly, and headed back out into the night. He flew low enough over the city that he would spot Rebekah if, by some miracle, she had found his message and was already on her way. But there were very few people abroad at this hour, and most of them were walking in groups or riding in horse-drawn wagons. No fugitive girl flitting down the unlit back streets, heading for an illicit tryst. Indeed, the whole city seemed deserted, as if it had been visited by tragedy and no one wanted to stray far from home.

Obadiah arrived at Hector's house and set his feet quietly on the roof, wings outstretched to take his weight so that no untoward sound clattered down to the sleeping inhabitants. A few steps over to find the right vantage point, and then he gracefully folded himself into a seated position, right in front of the trapdoor. He would find himself in an embarrassing predicament if anyone else lifted that door and stepped onto the roof, whether for legitimate or unauthorized purposes. He didn't know how he would explain away his presence, since voyeurism would be almost as unpalatable as the truth. He just had to hope that everyone else in the household was asleep or engaged elsewhere, and he settled himself in to wait.

It was a cold night, growing steadily colder as he sat there, but Obadiah rather enjoyed the chill. He was dressed in his flying leathers, and the air on Hector's roof was no more frigid than the air at high altitudes, and considerably less windy. He leaned back on his elbows to survey the sky, gaudy with constellations. If he reached out his hands, he was sure he could swipe his fingers through the stars, come away with diamonds between his fingertips.

The hours passed, and Rebekah did not emerge from the winter stairwell. Obadiah had eventually lain flat on his back, wings spread carelessly across the roof, hands clasped under his head, and given himself up to waiting. But by the time midnight was an hour gone, he was fairly certain Rebekah would not be coming. He pushed himself to his feet, shook his head to focus his thoughts, and drove his wings down hard to make the stationary takeoff. He was back in his room a few minutes later, and sleeping shortly after that.

The next day he didn't rise till noon. He had no incentive to get up earlier: There was little he could do till evening, and he did not especially want to show himself around the city. Angels rarely had the luxury of completely unstructured time—particularly lately, when angels were in such short supply—so he hardly knew what to do with himself. He leafed through a novel that some other guest had left in the room, and he spent about an hour quietly practicing vocalizing exercises, but he didn't really feel free to sing aloud, since he didn't want to disturb any of his neighbors.

Not until dinnertime did he leave his room, heading downstairs to the hotel restaurant. He was pleased to see Zoe stationed at the registration desk, and he crossed through the atrium to greet her.

"Angelo," she said, showing a certain faint pleasure at seeing him. "When did you arrive?"

"Last night, late. You weren't around."

"How long will you be staying?"

"I'm not sure. A day or two. Depending on—" He shrugged.

Zoe glanced quickly around the lobby, but no one was near enough to overhear. "I'm not sure your friend will be able to get away to meet with you," she said, keeping her voice low. "There has been such a disaster here."

He felt his heart immediately bound with worry. "What?"

Zoe, he noticed suddenly, looked as tense and unhappy as the young man who had watched the desk the night before. "Five days ago. There was a Jansai girl who apparently had taken a Manadavvi lover. No one I knew. His family ran a freighting caravan out of Monteverde country. Apparently they were here every few weeks, and somehow this girl had come to know him. And all the usual circumstances unfolded."

"Yes," he said, for he knew about those circumstances.

"And five days ago, she went to see him during the day, and they were in a tent behind one of the booths in the market square. And—how could the god allow such a dreadful mischance?—that same day her brother and some of her cousins went strolling through the market, and they came to this very booth—"

"They found her."

Zoe nodded. She looked both sad and infinitely angry. "They found her. They dragged her screaming from her lover's arms. The whole market came alive with Jansai men, running over to beat this one poor girl—this girl they didn't even *know*, whose face they had never seen in their *lives*—came over to make sure that their barbaric form of justice could be served on her. Well, of course, the Manadavvi did what they could to save her—my brother has talked to the men of the caravan, you can imagine how distraught they are—but there were too many Jansai. They dragged her off."

He could hardly bear to ask the words. What happened to this nameless Jansai girl could happen to any other disobedient woman. "Dragged her off where?"

Zoe stared at him, both sorrowful and implacable. It was strange to see such conflicting emotions on one still, serene face. "Off to the desert, so my brother says. Where they left her to die."

Obadiah recoiled as if he'd been slapped. "But she—certainly they—you mean, they gave her food and water, so that if she is lucky, and encounters some other merchant caravan—"

Zoe shook her head and said nothing.

Obadiah began pacing. "Sweet Jovah, sweet lord of the heavens," he muttered. "Then, if they will treat one girl this way—"

"I'm afraid your friend could be in some danger," Zoe said.

"Yes! Great danger! She always was, and I knew it, but somehow I managed to convince myself—" He shook his head and paced some more. "I must get her out of Breven."

"I don't think you'll accomplish that any time soon. My brother says there have been no women on the streets these past few days, not even the poor women from the tent circle, who come in from time to time to buy produce. Not even going from house to house under the protection of their men. He says he thinks every Jansai woman in the city has been confined to her house—locked inside—probably guarded more closely than ever before. I don't think your friend will make it out tonight."

Obadiah stopped his striding and stood before Zoe's desk. "I would not even want her to make the attempt," he said bleakly.

But Rebekah would not have to go far. Just up the stairs. Just to the roof. He would carry her to safety if she could just make it those few steps.

"I'm sorry," Zoe said. "I wish there was something I could do to help you."

He nodded. "I will stay a day or two anyway," he said. "Just in case she—just to see what might happen."

"We are always happy to have you in our establishment, angelo," she said formally.

He nodded. "Thank you for the information. It is horrifying, but it comforts me a little to know what her circumstances are, and that if she does not come to me, it will not be because she does not want to."

Zoe allowed herself to smile. "If I were you, I would not permit myself any doubt."

He made his way to the restaurant, suddenly stripped of all appetite, but he forced himself to eat anyway. He did not know how quickly or violently he might be forced into action, and he wanted to keep himself fit and fed against the possibility of sudden flight. It was possible—quite possible—that the house doors and garden gates were guarded at Hector's house, but that no one had thought to post sentries in all the interior corridors. How much ground did she have to cover, anyway—perhaps a hallway or two, a couple of stairwells? If she could just win free to the roof! Even if her stepfather was chasing after her madly, even if the whole mansion was roused to fury, she would be safe if she could just get close enough to be swept up in the angel's arms.

That would cause an incident between races, to be sure. That would send Uriah into a screaming fit of rage, would obliterate any progress Obadiah had made in negotiations with the Jansai. Gabriel would be furious—but then again, Gabriel would understand. The Archangel had a deep and abiding intolerance for injustice, fueled even more by Rachel's passionate hatred of slavery in any form. Gabriel also had some conception of what it meant to behave irrationally for love.

So Obadiah ate a reasonable dinner and returned to his room to await nightfall. He had not brought much with him—a shoulder bag that carried a few personal items and changes of clothes—and he would take this with him tonight when he left for his rooftop vigil. If Rebekah joined him, he would scoop her up and carry her off, flying as far as his strength would take them before the dawn arrived. That meant bringing water and at least a little food as well. He repacked his bag to add the necessary items.

Back out once the night was relatively advanced and the streets were almost empty of strays. Back to the house where his love lay sleeping—or fretting or scheming, wondering how to get in touch with him. The scarf on the windowpane was undisturbed, so at least no one other than Rebekah had come up here to investigate its appearance. *Look what the wind blew all the way to our rooftop . . . how funny. And this little rock, landing right on top of the fabric. You never know what next the god will send your way.*

As he had the night before, Obadiah settled himself comfortably, relaxed enough to endure a long wait, alert enough to spring to sudden action. He toyed with the idea of leaving one of his feathers behind, alongside the scarf, to reinforce his message, to underscore his longing. But he decided not to press his luck. He did not know what conversations had been occurring between these walls, what scraps of detail sharp eyes might have noticed. Rebekah knew the signal; she would answer it if she could.

But she did not.

Again, Obadiah lingered until dawn was almost upon him, until he ran the very real risk of being observed by a neighbor or a curious passer-by. He flowed to his feet and took off, low, over the rooftops and alleyways of wealthy Breven. He was stiff and even a little cold from the long, fruitless wait, but not even a little discouraged. He would return tomorrow night, and the night after that, hoping for a glimpse of Rebekah.

Obadiah slept most of the day, emerging in late afternoon when hunger chased him from his room. Zoe was not at the desk when he went into the dining room, but when he emerged an hour later, she was there. She waved him over.

"This arrived for you a little earlier today," she said, and handed him a folded note. It was not sealed, meaning anyone—even Zoe—could have read it, and for a moment Obadiah was afraid to scan its contents.

"Who knows I'm here?" he asked. "Who brought it?"

She shook her head. "I didn't see the messenger. My brother said it was a young Jansai boy—fourteen or fifteen—who looked very ill at ease. He just handed it to my brother and said, 'This is for Zoe.'"

"For you!" Obadiah exclaimed, and turned the paper over. *Zoe* was written on the front in a slanted, painstaking script.

"I read it because it was addressed to me," she said quietly, "but I am certain it was meant for you."

Obadiah's mind was racing, trying to puzzle this out. From Rebekah, of course, but who had she found to deliver it and what tale had she told? Her younger brother Jordan seemed the likeliest courier, but Obadiah could not imagine how she had explained to him that she had a friend among the Manadavvi. He unfolded the paper and quickly read the carefully composed words.

Dearest Zoe:

By now you must have heard about the terrible tragedy that has befallen my cousin Martha, who was discovered wickedly consorting with a Manadavvi man . . . .

Obadiah looked up at Zoe, so stunned that for a moment his vision went blank and he did not clearly see her face. "Sweet Jovah singing," he whispered. "Her cousin—"

"I know," Zoe said.

Obadiah dropped his eyes to the page again but it was a moment before he could take in the rest of the words.

. . . I am sure you must be worried about me, since you have had no word from me in so long. I just wanted to write to tell you that I will not be able to see you for some time—days, certainly, and weeks perhaps. My stepfather and my uncles are understandably upset. They are taking all precautions to make sure that their beloved women are safe. I have given myself over wholly to their care and do not expect to leave my own house any time soon, for any reason.

So you must not worry when you do not see me! I am well, though I wish very much to visit with you again, as soon as possible. How I wish we could fly away somewhere, to one of those cities you have told me about, and see all the marvels of the world.

Give my affection to all of our common friends. I do not think I will be able to write again, but I think of you often.

The letter was signed with a single looping "R."

Obadiah looked over at Zoe again, his heart pounding. Rebekah was alive, she was safe, but she was not completely out of danger. And, unless he totally mistook the sense and meaning of her words, this missive held a delicate promise.

"She is willing to leave Breven and come with me to Cedar Hills," he said, almost not even aware that he spoke aloud.

Zoe nodded. "I think she would be wise to do so."

"But she cannot get free just now. There is no point to me camping out here another night."

"We are happy to accommodate you, but I think you're right. There is nothing you can do at the moment. She's safe."

"For now," Obadiah answered.

CHAPTER TWENTY-SEVEN

"I've been thinking about the Gathering," Rufus said.

"Good. You've decided to go," Elizabeth said with an encouraging nod. They were having dinner at a very small, very new cafe on the west edge of town. Half-built structures loomed all around, skeletons of houses and shops, and the smells of lumber and tar mingled rather pleasantly with the scents of cooked meat and baking bread. Rufus had commented the other day that neither of them would save a cent if they spent all their money eating out, but it hadn't stopped them from making plans for the next night and the night after that.

"I've decided I'll go," he said, "if you'll come with me."

"Me! I don't belong there. I'm not Edori."

"The Edori are always happy to receive strangers. They say strangers are just friends they haven't met yet."

"Well, maybe that's true in the general run of things, but I'm sure they feel differently during the Gathering."

"No, you're wrong. If you come as the guest of an Edori, they'll welcome you. They'd welcome you if you simply wandered in off the desert. You should come with me."

"I know you're nervous about going alone—"

"Oh, I won't be going alone. There are three other Edori who have decided to make the trek from Cedar Hills to the Gathering.

But I want your company. Two weeks on the road with you. There's nothing we won't know about each other by then."

He gave her a wicked grin—or what, among the Edori, passed for wicked. Elizabeth had long since concluded that if all Edori were like this one, there was no malice or cruelty in any of them; the worst they could conjure up was mischievousness.

"Maybe I already know you as well as I'd like," she said.

"Maybe I'm the one who's still trying to dig deeper. Surely there's a core of sweetness somewhere in this girl, buried under all the spite and bile?"

"Dig right through to the bone," she invited. "No sweetness here."

"So I think you should come with me," he said.

"I thought you'd found a few others to travel with."

"I did. But I want you to come along, too."

"Rufus, I—"

"Please," he wheedled. "It won't seem so strange if you come."

"You need to go to the Gathering so you can find the people you lost," she said. "Find out if they're the way you remember. Find out if that's where you really belong. You can't do that if I'm there with you, distracting you, pulling you back."

"If you're not there with me, that will be an even greater distraction," he said. "I won't be able to focus on the people, what with all the time I'll be spending missing you."

"Rufus, you know I can't go."

"Why? Is it the travel or the company you can't abide?"

"I don't mind the travel, and I suppose I can endure your company for a while, but I can't possibly be gone for two weeks or more. Mary needs me."

"You could ask her. She might be able to spare you for a little while. She might have a friend who can help out in your place."

"There's no chance she would have a friend that good." Elizabeth sighed. "But I'll ask."

"And if she says yes? Will you come with me?"

She looked at him, at his dark, smiling face, lit just now with hope and affection. It astonished her, sometimes, how quickly he had become attached to her, how genuine his emotion was. He only had to see her walking in his direction, separated from him still by the span of the road or the width of the room, to be wakened to a dazzling smile. Even from the same distance, that look on his face would flush her with warmth and pleasure. Even before he touched her, she felt cradled in his love.

They had not yet slept together. Elizabeth wasn't entirely certain why this was so, for Rufus could have no illusions about her purity and could not be worried that she was unwilling or shy. She thought—she really thought—he wanted to be surer of himself, surer of the two of them as a couple, committed to some future that envisioned them together, before indulging in the act of love. She had never operated from such reasoning before. She had always thought that offering the act of sex would result in her partner offering the gift of love. It had not occurred to her that the exchange could be postponed or reversed.

"Yes," she said finally. "If Mary says I can go, I will come with you to the Gathering. But, Rufus, don't get your hopes up. I can't believe she would be able to spare me for so long."

As it happened, Mary could spare Elizabeth for twice that long. "Diana's back in town for the month!" Mary greeted her the next morning. "Starting to show a little around the belly, but not due for another four months yet. I didn't realize how much I'd missed her until she showed up at my door last night. *With* her young man in tow, though I have to admit he still doesn't impress me that much."

"I don't suppose she'd be interested in working with you for a couple of weeks," Elizabeth said pessimistically. "To earn a few extra dollars."

Mary gave her a sharp look. "Now how did you know that? She didn't say it in so many words, but it's clear to anyone with two eyes that she's the one holding that household together. She said, 'Mary, if you need an extra pair of hands while I'm here, I'll be happy to help out as much as you like.' "

How rare that Jovah juxtaposed one individual's set of desires so neatly with another's! Elizabeth was suddenly flooded with an excitement she had not allowed herself to feel when Rufus first made his proposal. "Then—but only if you're agreeable to it—I'd like to take a couple of weeks off. And go on a trip. I said no, because I didn't think you could spare me, but if you *can,* and you're *willing*—"

Mary was instantly intrigued. "A trip? With that Edori man you've been seeing? I like him, I must say."

"Yes, with Rufus. To the Gathering. I feel a little awkward going someplace like that among so many strangers—"

"To the Gathering! Oh, I don't think that's something you should miss. I've heard tales of it from time to time and always wished someone would invite me. Go, go. Diana will be delighted to hear she can earn two full weeks' salary. She's not as steady as you are, never was, but she's a good-hearted girl. I'll be happy to have her."

And as simply as that, the matter was settled.

Rufus was as excited as a boy when she told him that night she would be able to join him. He insisted they sit down instantly and plan what they needed to bring—clothes, food, and camping gear— and got out a map to show her their proposed route.

"Looks pretty close to the desert," she observed.

He nodded. "And Paul says that sometimes, in late winter when the storms blow off the mountain, it's actually easier to travel through the desert than to try to stay on fertile land. He knows the locations of a half a dozen waterholes scattered around the sand, so we shouldn't have to carry all our water with us. But some. You never know what to expect when you're traveling through the desert."

"And you think it will take us five days to get there?"

"And five days back. And we'll camp four days with the people. My foreman has agreed to my absence for so long."

"And I could be gone even longer and not fret for Mary's sake."

He smiled at her happily. "Then it's all settled. Paul and Jed and Silas would like to leave in two days' time, early in the morning."

Elizabeth shook her head a little, still not quite believing. "I've never camped out," she said. "Until I was sixteen, I never stayed in anything but the most luxurious accommodations. Then we moved to the small house, but it was a pretty place with two water rooms and a garden out back. Then I moved to James's house and was told to be happy that I had my own room, even though it was tiny. Then I came to Tola's, and I share my room with someone else—but at least it's still a room! Walls around me and a roof over my head, and a water room down the hall. *Now* I take one step farther down into obliteration, sleeping in a tent on the side of the road. What's next for me, I wonder?"

Rufus grinned. "We throw away the tent and let you sleep on the ground under the stars."

"I wouldn't be surprised!"

"Oh, and did I mention that the five of us will all be sleeping in the *same* tent?" he said casually.

She stared at him, and he broke into a laugh. "Joking," he added. "But the Edori do, you know. Sleep many and many to a tent. When we arrive at the Gathering, we'll be invited—I think we'll be invited—to join some family or some clan and sleep in a tent with five or ten others. But I thought you might not like that so much, so I thought we should have a tent of our own."

"Yes, you're quite right! A few yards of material between me and no privacy is all that I really require, but I do require that!"

"So I think we've got everything we need," he said. "Two days from now. Better start packing."

Faith was sad to see Elizabeth leave, even for so short a time. She sat cross-legged on her bed, brown hair piled haphazardly on her head, and watched Elizabeth sort through her clothes.

"Will you be warm enough?" Faith asked. "It's so cold now at night. And you'll be heading north."

"I guess we'll have a fire most nights. And sleep two together in the tent. And bring plenty of blankets! But it will be cold," Elizabeth agreed.

"So do you think—on the trip—you and Rufus—"

Elizabeth shrugged. "I don't know. How private is a tent, anyway, when you've got three men sleeping just a few feet away? I'm assuming we'll just go on as we are for a while longer."

"Maybe that's best," Faith said softly.

Elizabeth folded a sweater, bulky and soft and bought for quite a dear sum at one of the new Cedar Hills shops. "Maybe it is."

Faith was doing better these days, though she was imbued with an air of haunted fragility that made everyone treat her with extraordinary tenderness. She had nearly died almost five weeks ago—nearly died, and when she learned the costs, wished she had. Elizabeth couldn't count the number of nights she'd woken up to the sound of Faith's bitter, muffled weeping. To never be able to bear any child at all, even a mortal baby, was a blow so severe that it had seemed Faith would not recover from it. Certainly the fact would shape her course and personality for the rest of her life.

Her angel lover had left only days after Faith's dreadful episode. He had come by several times to see her, refusing to leave the city until he had been assured that she would live. Elizabeth gave him great credit for that. He had even written a few times from Monteverde, hasty, brief messages about the coldness of the weather and how much he missed her. But these letters were growing scarcer and scarcer, and no one, least of all Faith, expected to see Jason hovering around Tola's door any time in the near future, looking for the beloved but barren girl.

"Why do they have it in the dead of winter?" Faith asked suddenly. "It seems like a strange time to make people travel all over the country."

"I think the Edori travel all over the country all the time anyway, so it doesn't matter to them if it's summer or winter," Elizabeth said. "Anyway, I think that's why they do it—to hasten spring. You know, to remind Jovah that winter has been long enough, time to send the sunshine again."

Faith smiled weakly. "I don't think Jovah needs reminding."

"No, I suppose it's really the rest of us who need reminding. Winter can't last forever, after all."

Though it had seemed like it might. Between Faith's illness and the coughs and aches of half the residents of Cedar Hills, it had seemed the longest winter Elizabeth had ever endured. Even now, she thought, standing on Tola's front porch and gazing at a dismal gray sky, winter didn't seem any too likely to loosen its grip just because the Edori chanted a few rhymes and pronounced spring in the offing. It would be a cold trip to the Gathering and a cold trip back, and they would be lucky if they didn't wake up some morning to find their tents covered in snow.

"Elizabeth!" It was Rufus, hurrying down the narrow lane to

fetch her. "We don't think the wagon will fit down the alley. Come on, I'll carry your bag."

He stooped to grab the long leather strap and swing it over his shoulder, then paused to give her a quick kiss on the mouth. He looked different somehow, buoyant; it took her a moment to come up with the word *joyous*. "Are you excited?" he asked.

She couldn't help laughing at him. "I certainly am."

In a few moments she was settled into the wagon and they were on their way out of town. Rufus, Elizabeth, and a thin Edori man named Paul were seated in the back of the open wagon, among the luggage and the camping gear; Jed and Silas were on the seat up front.

"Do you drive?" Paul asked Elizabeth. "You can have a turn handling the horses if you'd like."

"Umm, no, thank you. I can't drive or ride."

Silas turned around from the seat. "You can still have a turn sitting up front," he said. "More comfortable than it is back there, though not truly comfortable even so."

"How far will we travel today?" she asked.

Silas laughed. "As far as we make it."

That seemed like an odd answer, until Elizabeth had spent one full day with the Edori. And then it seemed—well—typical. The Edori were not much for planning, for setting an agenda and following it. They liked to accept the gifts of the day, to pause when they got hungry, or pull to the side of the road when they saw an interesting sight ahead. They didn't mind being asked to take a privacy break, even if they'd just lost an hour eating lunch. They didn't seem worried about whether or not they'd find a proper campsite come nightfall. They seemed to harbor no anxiety at all—or even what Elizabeth would call a sense of purpose. Before the day was out, she found herself astonished that the whole race could organize itself sufficiently to plan something as synchronized as the Gathering. Based on her experience with these four members of the tribe, she would have said such a feat was impossible.

There were differences among them, of course. Rufus and Paul called themselves "city Edori," a term that she quickly translated to mean "former slave." They were a little more focused, moved a little more quickly to set out a meal or solve a problem. Silas and Jed, middle-aged men who now lived in Cedar Hills, had grown up among their clans and merely drifted into urban life through a series of unplanned chances. They had never missed a Gathering, even when they lived on one side of the continent and it was scheduled to take place on the other. Then again, they had meandered to every single one of these events with all the randomness of a summer bee making its way through the most alluring of gardens. Or so Elizabeth, after a day in their company, surmised.

Though she was not convinced they'd covered enough ground to permit themselves the reward of stopping for the night, nonetheless she was happy when Paul pulled up at a likely place along the roadside. "Here's water and a little break from the wind," he said, indicating a small stream and a tumble of rocks. "Or do you want to go farther?"

Silas glanced up at the sky. "Getting on toward dark," he said. "Time for camp."

With more efficiency than Elizabeth would have expected, they unhitched the horses, built a fire, and pitched the two tents. Soon enough they were all gathered gratefully around the bright warmth of the fire, eating an assortment of dried fruits and meat. Talk was low and easy, though from time to time all conversation lapsed and a comfortable silence settled over them. Elizabeth could not stop yawning, though she mentally chided herself. What had she done that was so taxing, after all? Nothing—merely sat in the wagon and been jounced along the road all day. Still, she was as tired as if she'd worked beside Mary for twelve straight hours, delivering babies and seeing out the dead.

"A prayer for Yovah," Jed said softly, and lifted up a tenor voice in a simple song. Elizabeth could not understand the words, though the syllables were melodic and sweet. Paul and Silas joined in, Paul on the tenor line and Silas adding harmony, and Elizabeth felt her heart twist. Such a simple thing—music before a campfire on a frosty winter night—and yet there was something primeval about it. So men had sung for centuries, since they first made their homes on Samaria, so men had sung, perhaps, back on that home world that the first settlers had left behind. How many years, how many voices raised to the listening god? She had a swift, peculiar vision of herself, or women just like her, sitting at uncounted campfires down the long march of time. It took her out of her own body, made her feel adrift and untethered—yet, at the same time, the thought made her feel anchored to her past and her history as she never had before. Just an instant, while the image lingered in her mind; then it faded, and she was herself, sitting before the dying flames, and starting to shiver.

"Bedtime for all of us, I think," Rufus said. "On our way early in the morning."

"Cold will wake us," Silas said with a grin. "We won't be lingering all that long."

It was a matter of minutes before the fire was banked, last-minute trips were taken out beyond the firelight, and all of them had ducked inside their respective tents. Now was the time for some awkwardness, Elizabeth felt, as she and Rufus found very little room to maneuver under their own low canopy.

"Did you dress in a couple of layers, as I told you to?" Rufus asked. She nodded. "Good. Then you can strip down to your underthings and crawl into the blanket."

"I don't want to take anything off," she said helplessly. "I'm too cold. But I can't sleep in this dress—"

"Quick, undress and slip inside," he said, pulling off his own outer shirt and trousers. Underneath, on both top and bottom, he wore what looked like heavy flannel clothing in a neutral gray. He kept his socks on, she noticed. "I'll be right beside you. We'll warm each other up quick enough."

She took a deep breath and divested herself of her traveling clothes, then scrambled under the covers as fast as she could. Rufus was beside her almost instantly, but it still took a few moments for the heat of his body to do anything to dissipate the chill. She felt herself being shaken by violent tremors, deep and uncontrollable. Rufus put his arms around her and drew her closer.

"Soft city girl," he said in a teasing voice, but the tone was kind. "Never far from a fire or the comforts of home."

"I used to—sleep in a cold room—at James's," she said through chattering teeth. "Because—Angeletta—didn't want to—waste a fire on me. But still! Inside the house—it was never—quite as cold—as it is here."

His hands clasped themselves over hers. She marveled that he could have such reserves of heat in his body that it could be pumped even to the outlying regions of his fingers. She could feel some warmth beginning to seep through to her from his body, folded over hers. Her back was beginning to thaw, where it was pressed against his torso; his arms, wrapped around hers, were creating a small firestorm in her heart.

"Wait till the morning," he murmured. "All cozy in here, all freezing outside. You won't want to get up, even to meet your basic needs. You'll just want to burrow down under the covers with me."

"I'll never—be warm—even by morning," she said. "I think my nose—has frozen off."

He reached a hand out to test her assertion, then quickly pulled his arm back under the blankets to recover his hold on her fingers. "Nope. Still there. Mighty cold, though."

"Have any Edori ever frozen to death?"

"Not in any story I ever heard. That's because they sleep all tumbled together, as I told you. All that body warmth. It defeats winter." He stirred, as if moved by a sudden thought. "Say! We could join the others in their tent. That would warm us up quick enough."

"No," she said, even though she was sure he was joking. "No. I'm warmer now. I want to stay here, just with you."

Silence a moment, and then he leaned in from behind her and kissed her cheek. "Yes," he whispered, "and I want to stay with you. This trip. When we're back in Cedar Hills. After that. All those days."

She would have turned then, to kiss him or to ask him what he meant or just to talk it through—for it was what she wanted as well—but he tightened his arms and held her in place. "Sleep now," he said. "Travel in the morning. Plenty of time later to settle everything else."

Part of her still wanted to clarify everything, to lay out plans and commitments, but another part of her was able to shrug and acquiesce. This was the Edori way, she realized, to know what you wanted and pursue it, perhaps with great determination, but without impatience. To enjoy the event as it unfolded, whether it was a journey to see a friend or the impossibly slow, impossibly wonderful act of falling in love. She wondered, if this man had carried a Kiss in his arm, if it would be lighting with fire at this moment. She thought that, if she could summon the energy to sit up in bed and roll back her sleeve, she might see her own Kiss sending up shy signals of light. She was too tired to make the effort. She closed her eyes and snuggled even closer to him. In minutes, she was asleep.

They were on the road three more days and nights, the rest of their trip going pretty much as the first day had. It was almost midday of the fifth day before Silas, at the reins, lifted his head and appeared to be listening to the gossip of the wind.

"Do you hear that?" he said, grinning at his companions. "The drums."

Indeed, when Elizabeth strained forward she could catch the faint sound, a low, broken rhythm that might be the heartbeat of the earth itself. They were too far away from the source to be able to catch every stroke and hammer, just the teasing intermittent suggestion of bass percussion.

"How much farther?" she asked.

Silas clucked to the horses. "We'll be there within the hour."

And sure enough, before that hour had passed, they had arrived at the bright, chaotic scene of the Gathering. Hundreds of tents were laid out in no discernible order around a double ring of campfires; a makeshift corral held a thousand horses. The scene was alive with figures bending over fires, clustered before tents, hurrying down the hill with water buckets in hands; the world seemed made over in the Edori image. The very air smelled like a feast. And the drums never stopped their insistent, exultant pounding.

"The Gathering," Rufus said, standing up in the wagon as it came to a halt. Elizabeth thought his voice sounded half reverent and half fearful as he surveyed the scene, the site of so many of his longings.

"Let's see if anyone is prepared to take us in," she said, and swung herself out of the wagon.

The men had barely climbed down when a smiling woman approached them with her hands outstretched. She was in her early thirties, perhaps, with the lustrous black hair and dark skin that marked all of the Edori, and she looked at once placid and joyful. Though Elizabeth could hardly credit it, she appeared to have been appointed by a foresighted Edori committee to make sure any late-comers were welcomed to the assembly.

"Hello to this group of stragglers! We are so glad to have you among us! You did not ride in with a clan. Do you have a tribe to go to, or would you like to pitch your tents beside those of my family? We would be happy to take you in."

Just like that, Elizabeth thought. *Welcome indeed.*

"I'm off to the Cashitas," Silas said, "and my friend with me."

"I'm looking for the Barcerras," Jed said.

"Excellent! They are both camped down that way. You see the big brown tent? Just beyond that," the woman said, pointing. Her attention came back to the other two wayfarers, her gaze resting briefly on Elizabeth's pale skin. No reason to think Elizabeth had any clan connections here.

"I arrive without a tribe to go to," Rufus said, speaking more stiffly than Elizabeth had ever heard him. He was always so relaxed, so composed; but here, where it mattered most to him to be accepted, he was clearly uneasy. "My family is all gone."

The woman nodded, compassion quickly overcoming the open happiness on her face. "There are more than a few of the people who have been lost in the past fifteen years," she said softly. "We mourn all of their names. The clan that you belonged to?"

"The Kalessas," he said in a tight voice. "I am Rufus sia a Kalessa."

"I have not seen one of them in more than ten years," the greeter said sorrowfully. Then her face changed subtly, lightened again to what Elizabeth guessed was its more habitual expression. "But you—a Kalessa returned to us! This is good news indeed!"

Rufus bowed his head a little. "I have not been—free—to come to a Gathering in some time," he said in a quiet voice. "I have forgotten much of the Edori ways. But I thought—even without my clan—if I came to the Gathering—"

"But you have a clan! You will be a Chieven!" she interrupted. "I am Naomi of the Chievens, and I say you will sleep in our tents, eat from our cook pots, and sing beside us at the great fire. Welcome, Rufus sia a Kalessa." And she stepped forward to kiss him on the cheek.

He closed his eyes and took that kiss as if it grounded his spirit back into his body after years of aimless travel. Elizabeth found she had stopped breathing for a moment, so painful was it to watch his hope warring with his fear, and now her lungs labored extra quickly to make up for her short loss of oxygen. She was still catching her breath when Naomi turned that warm smile on her.

"And you?" she asked. "Is there a clan you are looking for?"

"His. Rufus's. I'm traveling with him," Elizabeth said, tripping over the stupid words. "That is, I don't mean to intrude—"

"You, too, are greatly welcome," Naomi said, coming forward to kiss Elizabeth as well. "Blessed is Yovah, that he brings together so many for us to love! What name do you go by, or should I simply address you as Rufus's?"

A smile went along with that, and Elizabeth found herself liking this woman a great deal. *Just like that.* "Elizabeth."

"Rufus and Elizabeth, come with me. We will find you a tent among the Chievens."

The Chievens, it turned out, comprised ten tents, all filled to bursting with Edori of every age and size. Naomi introduced them to two or three dozen people, and Elizabeth smiled and accepted hugs or other signs of affection, but she knew in the first three minutes that she wouldn't be able to keep any of these people straight. Rufus seemed to be having no trouble, though. He gripped hands and offered embraces and seemed to grow both calmer and more excited with every exchange. It was as if he was feeding on the Edori lifeblood, renewing himself after a long starvation, and the most casual contact, the most quickly spoken word, acted on him like an infusion.

He is among his people now, Elizabeth thought. *He may never leave them again.*

Just as well, perhaps, that she had not, the other night, forced that conversation about what their future together might hold. Hers, she was very sure, lay back at Cedar Hills or somewhere that constituted civilization. His might very well lie with the Chievens or the Cashitas or the Barcerras or any of these other tribes. Once having rediscovered his spiritual family, she thought, Rufus might never be willing to leave them behind again.

She squared her shoulders. Well, she would deal with that day when the day arrived. She knew enough Edori philosophy by now to resign herself to that.

"Now, Luke and I have no extra room in our tent, but Anna and Eber, perhaps—there are only six of them—they could squeeze in two more."

Rufus looked over at Elizabeth with a laugh in his eyes. She thought it might be the first time he'd remembered her existence since they walked into the camp. "Thank you kindly, a generous offer, but my *allali* girl is more comfortable alone in a tent with me—and even then she thinks the accommodations close."

Naomi laughed and Elizabeth smiled, though she felt certain *allali* was not a compliment, and she hoped she didn't seem rude. "Yes, and young lovers need their privacy, and two to a tent is the only way to ensure that," Naomi said gaily. "But you will eat with us, surely? You won't insist on your own campfire?"

"We will take every scrap of food from your very hands," Rufus promised. "Though you must put us to work as well. We are not here to lie about and watch others do all the labor."

"No, and I have no patience with such poor, lazy creatures," Naomi said with mock sternness. "Very well then! Pitch your tent here, and when you are done, come find me—I'm right there, see?—and we shall decide just what needs to be done."

And just like that, they were among the Chievens.

They had scarcely laid their bundles on the ground and begun to untie the canvas when two teenage boys materialized from nowhere. "My aunt says we have to help you put up your tent," one of them said, and they practically took it from Rufus's hands. In minutes, the tent was situated, their blankets were unrolled, and Rufus had gone off with the boys on some kind of hunting expedition. Elizabeth went in search of Naomi.

"Not half an hour in the camp, and I've been abandoned," she announced when she found Naomi standing over a cauldron, cooking something that smelled delicious. "Tell me what I can do to help."

Naomi looked over and smiled. "Can you cook? Bake?"

Elizabeth nodded. "I used to work in a farm kitchen, making meals for all the hands. Just tell me how many I'm feeding and where the ingredients are, and I can get started."

"I can see you'll be very handy to have around!" Naomi exclaimed. "In that box there—see?—yes, the stone container is the one with the yeast. If you'll get started on the bread—"

The next hour passed in a haze of work, talk, and contentment. Either all the Edori loved everyone with a warmth that was inexhaustible, or Naomi must have been the most popular woman in camp, because hundreds of people dropped by to speak with her. She offered advice, took messages, loaned tools, related news, complimented babies, and generally seemed to be the nerve center of the collective Edori soul. More than one person seemed to approach this campsite to ask specifically whether someone named Raheli sia a Manderra would be attending the Gathering this year; they all went away disappointed.

"Who's Raheli?" Elizabeth finally asked when the two of them were alone again.

"Oh, she is practically my sister!" Naomi said. "We grew up together in the Manderra tribe, but then she was lost for so many years—but two years ago she returned to us, and you can imagine the rejoicing."

"She was—taken? Like Rufus?"

Naomi nodded. The Edori woman was chopping dried vegetables and feeding them slowly into a simmering pot. "I heard nothing of her for years. Everyone said she was dead, but I knew she was not. I knew it. And then, two years ago at the Gathering, there she was. I have not been so happy since the day my first daughter was born."

"But she's not coming this year?"

"No, her friend is going into a difficult labor, and Raheli is afraid to leave her. Well, *that* I can understand. I almost couldn't bear to let Luke's sister out of my sight when I was pregnant. She had had five children herself, so I was sure she could help me through my own birthing! But Raheli is no midwife, I assure you, and so I think it a little funny that her friend is so sure she cannot survive this event without her. But Raheli is a very fierce friend, and she would not leave behind anyone who needed her. I do admire her for that. But I miss her!"

"Well, maybe she'll come to the Gathering next year, and you can see her then."

Naomi stirred, tasted, and stirred again. "Oh, I'll see her much sooner than that. The whole clan will travel to the Plain of Sharon to hear her sing at the Gloria."

"Sing at—your Edori friend sings at the Gloria? With the angels?"

"Well, anyone can sing at the Gloria once the angels are done with their part, you know," Naomi said. "Though it is true that not many Edori attend from year to year. More of us go now that Raheli leads the singing."

Elizabeth felt as though she had somersaulted backward. "Your friend Raheli—is Rachel? Is the *angelica?*"

Naomi beamed. "Yes, angelica, that's what they call her. I'm not very good with titles. The Edori don't care much for such things."

"And she—who is her pregnant friend, then?"

"That lovely woman who is married to Gabriel's brother. Why can't I remember her name? I met her once—"

"Magdalena?" Elizabeth said in a strangled voice. She was remembering the outspoken, golden-haired woman who had seemed so protective of the angel, wretched with early labor pains. *Fierce* was not a bad word to describe her.

"Yes, that's her! They're very close. So naturally Raheli could not leave her at a time like this."

"No," Elizabeth said, hoping she had not said anything snippy or overfamiliar during her brief conversation with the angelica. "Of course not."

Naomi smiled over at her. "May I tell you again how happy we are to have you among us? I am so glad you accompanied your friend."

Elizabeth shook away thoughts of angels and their consorts to concentrate on a topic she was more familiar with. "He wanted so desperately to come, but he was unsure of his welcome. I think he brought me more as a hedge against rejection than as a companion of his days."

Naomi sighed a little and started peeling an onion. "So many of them . . . last year and this year . . . all the people who were snatched up by Jansai during the time of Raphael's reign, they are making their way back to us. But they are hurt and afraid and unsure of their welcome, and it breaks my heart to see them limping into camp with such hope and terror in their eyes." She gave Elizabeth one quick, straight look. "Not limping with their feet, you understand. Limping with their souls."

Elizabeth nodded. Yes. She had understood.

"And some of them—you can see them heal, as soon as they cross into the camp. You can see their heartbeats readjust to the sound of the drums. One or two of them—it makes me cry to recount the story, can you see the water in my eyes?—they have found clan members among the other tribes. An uncle or a sister who escaped the Jansai depredations and who came to rest with another clan. And to see them reunite with someone they loved when they thought everyone they loved was dead—it breaks your heart at the same time as it lifts you up. I would wish for such a thing for your Rufus. But I have not heard of any of the Kalessas coming back to us last year or this."

"Maybe next year," Elizabeth said hopefully. "Maybe when he— or she—gets his courage up. It took Rufus weeks and weeks to be sure that he could come."

"Yes, that's what I hope," Naomi agreed. "That every year more of them will come back to us, freed from their masters and free in their hearts as well. And maybe Yovah has spared a dozen of the Kalessas. The god has been so good for so long."

Naomi paused, as if briefly overcome by emotion, and Elizabeth turned her attention back to her dough. Punching down first this loaf, then that one. She would be able to feed fifty people on bread alone.

"So who's going to eat all this food?" she asked presently. "Surely there's enough here to feed the whole camp, but I thought I saw everyone else cooking and baking as well."

"Oh, yes!" Naomi said, her voice bright again, her normal voice. "But today and tomorrow we cook enough for two days so that everything is ready on Feast Day and there is nothing to do but listen to the singing."

"And that's what you do for a whole day? Sing?"

"Well, every clan takes its turn, of course. One of the clan elders gets up to relate the events of the past year—where the tribe traveled, what it discovered, which woman left to follow a man in another clan, what babies were born, who died—oh, the whole history of the year. Thus we learn in one long day what has happened to all our people."

"I would think it would be hard to remember all that."

"Really? I admit, I forget bits and pieces of what the other elders have told us, but there are some who can recite the stories of every clan for the past twenty or thirty years. Luke can tell you everything he has heard since he was a boy. He knows where the Barcerras wintered five years ago and how many women of the Lohoras have followed the Corderra clan. He has a splendid memory."

"Luke is your husband?"

Naomi laughed. "I chose to leave my clan and follow him, yes, but the Edori don't take husbands and wives. Which is why it is so funny to me that Raheli has married the angel Gabriel—though, don't mistake me, I admire Gabriel greatly, and I could not have picked out a better mate for Raheli if I had sat down and interviewed every angel, Edori, and *allali* in the three provinces. But to *marry* him! Well, it is a strange idea to me."

"Then how do you know you have found the right man if you don't marry him? How do you know he will stay with you?"

Naomi shrugged. "How do you know these things if you do speak words in a ceremony? No words will bind you if your heart sets you free. I cannot imagine my life without Luke. I believe he will be with me always. That is binding enough for me."

Elizabeth was not so sure this doctrine worked for her. She had dreamed for so long of being cherished and protected by a powerful man that she could not imagine blithely accepting the prospect of a long-term future dictated only by the whims of affection. She wondered how Rufus felt about this Edori concept. She was not sure she wanted to ask him.

It was almost as if Naomi had read her mind. "So tell me a little bit about Rufus and yourself," she said. "Where did you take up with an Edori man? In some city, I suppose. He called you an *allali* girl."

Elizabeth laughed. "I'm afraid to ask what that means."

"Oh, nothing too terrible! City dweller—except that—well, Edori don't have a high opinion of people who live in cities. You understand. We cannot stand to be trapped very long in one place."

"Yes, I guess I am an *allali* at that," Elizabeth said. "I've lived in

Semorrah and a few other places. For the last few months in Cedar Hills."

"And that's where you met Rufus?"

Elizabeth nodded. "He's working with the men who are putting up new buildings. The city is growing every day."

"And you think he plans to stay in Cedar Hills?"

Elizabeth returned her attention to her dough, punching down a loaf that had just risen sufficiently. "I don't know. I think he's a little lost. Displaced. I think he might—having come to the Gathering—decide it's time to live among his people again. Having been apart from them for so many years."

Naomi was silent a moment. "I would wish for that," she said. "I will offer him a place in my clan, in my tent, before he leaves. But I don't think he'll take it. He's a halfling now—part Edori, part something else. So few of the people who were taken from us by Jansai have come to live with us now that they've been freed. They come to the Gathering, yes, they travel with us for a few weeks or a few months, but our life is not their life anymore. Part of them wants other things. Your Rufus is probably that way, too—pulled in two directions at once." She smiled over at Elizabeth. "And, of course, he will not want to leave *you*."

Elizabeth smiled, trying to hide her embarrassment. "Oh, I don't know that he will make all his calculations around me."

Naomi made a *tsk!* sound of disbelief. "You! He cannot take his eyes off you! He carried you with him how many hundred miles so he did not have to spend a night away from your body!"

This was plain speaking indeed—another Edori trait—but Elizabeth felt it almost a relief to confess the truth. "I'm not so sure—that is, as for my body—well, we have not—not yet—"

"You have not yet made love?" Naomi demanded. "Oh, now, that's a sin. A beautiful girl like you and a man as handsome as Rufus? Such gifts are not to be wasted. We must work to remedy that."

"Well, but I—and it was such a long trip—I feel so dirty with dust from the road and no chance to get really clean—"

Naomi lay down her spoon and called for one of her daughters. A small, shy, smiling girl, maybe eight years old, emerged from

Naomi's tent. "You watch the cook pots for me," Naomi instructed. "Elizabeth and I will be gone for a little while."

"Gone where?" Elizabeth asked as Naomi took her arm and pulled her away from the fire.

"To the water tents. You didn't know we had such things set up? No, it never occurs to a man to talk about luxuries. Do you have soap with you? Scent?"

"Soap, yes, a little, but scent? No."

Naomi *tsked* again. "And clean clothes? Something soft and beautiful? With your hair, I would think you wear a lot of rich colors? A lot of greens? I have a lovely dress, not exactly a dress, a wrap that hangs about me like a robe. Very soft, very pretty—girlish, you know what I mean."

"Feminine," Elizabeth supplied.

"Exactly! And some perfume—I bought it in Luminaux, it smells like flowers on a summer night. Do you have pins for your hair? Anything that sparkles? Glitter in your hair will draw a man's eyes to your face, did you know that? Yes, I assure you, it is true."

Helpless and fascinated, Elizabeth followed Naomi inside her tent, where the Edori woman tossed through a trunk to find the items she wanted. Then she followed Naomi through the entire campsite—though they paused hundreds of times to exchange greetings or gossip with others that they passed—to a long row of tents set up on the very perimeter. All of these tents straddled a small stream that meandered around the camp and southward. Each of the tents appeared to be floorless, unlike the sleeping tents set up inside the camp.

"Normally, we do not go to such trouble, but the Gathering is special. Everyone wants to be clean for the god! So we have the water tents here—the *necessary* tents, as some people call them—so you don't have to wander out to the bushes in the middle of the night. And then we have bathing tents here, one for the men, one for the women. See?"

Naomi pulled back a flap of one of the long, low structures, and they stepped inside. It was quite an unexpected scene, filled with steam and scented with woodsmoke. A substantial fire burned on one bank of the stream, its smoke vented through a hole in the tent roof; over it hung a massive cauldron of water. Half a dozen naked Edori women lounged about on stools or on mats spread upon the ground on either side of the creek. They were drying their hair or smoothing cream into their skin. All of them looked up when the other two women entered, then smiled and returned to their preoccupations.

"See?" Naomi said again, gesturing. "Hot water to bathe with. And it is nice and warm in here, so you can take your time scrubbing your body. You can get much cleaner than you can hopping into a mountain river in the middle of the winter."

"You can get your *hair* clean," one of the other women said.

"And you will feel much better than you would have believed possible," Naomi assured her. "Come. Let's get you out of your travel clothes."

And Elizabeth, who was not used to stripping down in front of strangers, allowed Naomi to help her out of her dress and her underthings and position her on the rocky bank so the wash water would fall most naturally into the river. Fire or no, it was still chilly standing naked on the edge of the stream, waiting to be doused with water, and Elizabeth shivered a little. But the idea of being truly clean and dressed in pretty clothes held her feet in place, and she gasped with delight when the first bucket of warm water splashed over her head.

Dinner that night was a lively communal affair as all the Chievens gathered around Naomi's cook-fire and engaged in banter and discussion. Everyone wanted to hear Rufus's story, though he told it haltingly: the massacre of the Kalessas, followed by the misery of slavery and the aimlessness of freedom. Elizabeth listened closely to see if there were any details she could pick up, any more clues. She thought she understood him; she wanted to know if she had missed or misinterpreted any signals.

Her own story was demanded next, and supplied, and then conversation became more general. The men talked about the day's hunt, the children chimed in with tales of their own adventures, the women shared glances of amusement and recounted some of their own stories. Elizabeth could not tell which child belonged to which parent, since the children seemed to turn with equal affection to every adult in the circle. Naomi's daughters sat with women who were situated across the fire, and Naomi herself held on her lap two small boys who hadn't been in the camp during the daylight hours. Elizabeth wasn't even sure if these children belonged to the Chievens or had wandered over from some other clan and been accepted with the impartial welcome that seemed to be extended to every wayfarer who stumbled in this direction. It made her, briefly, long to be small enough and incautious enough to be able to seek sanctuary at any likely haven, sure of affection. She thought it must be a wonderful thing to be an Edori child.

Unless your tribe was ravaged and annihilated, of course. Unless you were ripped from safety and serenity and thrust into a life of captivity. She understood a little of what it was like to go from security to privation, but she had not lived at either edge of the extremes, as Rufus had. She was not sure she would have emerged half as assured as he had.

Though the wounds were there, she knew.

She was not sitting next to Rufus during dinner, though she was not sure how that had happened. She thought perhaps Naomi had engineered the seating arrangements, placing Elizabeth between a good-looking Edori man of about her own age and an older woman with grizzled gray hair and a radiant smile. Elizabeth was getting a fair idea of Naomi's thinking process by now, and she could read the Edori's intent: Show off Elizabeth's youth and beauty by placing her next to a grandmother, awake a spark of Rufus's jealousy by seating her next to a handsome man. She wasn't sure it was working, though. Rufus seemed perfectly happy chatting with Luke and one of the other Chievens as he sat across the fire from Elizabeth. He did look over at her and smile from time to time, but he seemed neither alarmed at her chance for flirtation nor struck by her alluring appearance. Elizabeth smoothed the soft blue folds of her borrowed gown and smothered a sigh.

The meal was good, and everyone made a point of complimenting the bread once Naomi let it be known that Elizabeth had prepared it. Once the food was cleared away, the singing began. Some of the songs Elizabeth recognized—lullabies and ballads—though some of them were offered in the Edori tongue, and she knew only the melody, not the words. Most were unfamiliar to her, some plaintive, some joyous, all of them with the power to shift her mood within a few measures. Naomi, who had the loveliest voice of the clan, sang a duet with Luke, and then harmonized in a trio with two other women. Everyone applauded and called out praise when the song ended, but Naomi shook her head.

"I miss Raheli's voice," she said with a sigh, coming over to sit beside Elizabeth. "Have you ever heard her? The god himself grows mute and bedazzled when Raheli sings."

"Perhaps I'll be at the Gloria someday, and hear her then," Elizabeth said politely, sure this was quite unlikely.

"Do you sing? Let us hear your voice," Naomi urged.

Elizabeth felt a small current of alarm glow through her. "Me? No. I never—I don't sing."

"Come. One piece? A love song?" Naomi said, letting her eyes dart toward Rufus and then back again.

"I—really, I can't. No treat to hear me."

"You can join the general voices," said the old woman now sitting on the other side of Naomi. "We will all sing a good night prayer to Yovah, and you can sing along then."

Elizabeth nodded numbly. "If I know the song."

"Oh, everybody knows this song," Naomi said, and launched into the first verse. It was an old melody, a simple one, sung by children in every city in Samaria, and apparently every child in the tents and wagons of the Edori as well. Elizabeth did not understand the Edori words, but she obligingly sang along in the language she knew, hearing her own rusty, untrained voice blending agreeably with the Edori voices around her. Angeletta had told her once that she sang like a screech owl on a disappointing night, and Elizabeth had never sung in public again. But here, at this camp, with these people, she didn't mind participating in the universal chorus, adding her imperfect notes to the great swell of supplication and thanks. No one could hear her, except perhaps the god; and though he treasured a beautiful melody above all things, he cherished any faithful heart that lifted up a song in prayer. Or so the priests had always said. Elizabeth sang a little more loudly.

That was the last event of the day. People were on their feet even as the final amens sounded, yawning through the last note and wishing each other sweet dreams. The old woman was once again complimenting Elizabeth on her baking when Rufus materialized at her side, smiling in the firelight and taking her chilly hand in his.

"Time to rest after a very long day," he said, tugging her in the direction of their tent. "I am sleepy if you are not."

Elizabeth could not help herself. She glanced quickly at Naomi, who was standing close enough to listen, and who responded with a quick nod of encouragement. "I am ready to go to our tent," Elizabeth responded. "A long day indeed!"

In a few minutes they were ensconced inside, hearing all around them the sounds of the Chievens settling in for the night. It was completely dark inside and much colder than it had been sitting before the fire, shoulder to shoulder with others, and for a moment, Elizabeth felt both lost and despondent. What was the point of wearing a dreamy blue dress and placing pins in her hair if she was just going to shiver on a blanket in an unlit tent? Who would notice her finery, who would be moved to passion by her arts?

Rufus was on his knees, maneuvering around the tent poles, but it was hard to get lost in such a small space; he fetched up against her immediately. She felt his arms slip about her, chasing away some of the cold. "Ah, I thought I caught a sweet aroma when I pulled you away from the fire," he murmured into her hair. "What is that scent? It makes me think of springtime."

She smiled in the dark. "Something Naomi lent me."

His fingers ran lightly over the soft folds of the wrap. "And this? This lovely outfit you are wearing? I don't remember seeing it at any time while we were on the road."

"Another gift from Naomi. A loan."

"And is there any reason this Edori clanswoman would have for lavishing exotic perfumes and sumptuous fabrics on a *allali* woman who has just happened by for a visit? Jewels in your hair, even. What could she mean to accomplish with such decorations?"

Elizabeth could feel her lips bow into a smile. "I don't know. Perhaps she felt sorry for me, bedraggled and grim from my travels. Perhaps she thought she might make me beautiful to catch the eye of an

Edori clansman. There are one or two handsome men among the Chievens, I noticed."

His hand now was combing through her hair, pulling out the glittering pins one by one. "Did you now? And do you have extensive experience with Edori lovers?"

"I do not," she said primly. "I don't know if they're joyous or solemn, faithful or faithless, whether they boast about their conquests or keep every secret whispered to them in the dark."

"Joyous," he said, leaning in to kiss her on the cheek. Her skin warmed under his lips. "Faithful. Keeping every secret."

She turned in his embrace, putting her arms around his neck and drawing him close enough so that she could whisper her next words against his mouth. "I would take an Edori to bed, then," she said. "I would learn what such a lover is like."

"So little choice," he said. "Only one Edori in the tent."

"Then I would make love to him."

"There is much still to be decided between us," he said, but his arms tightened around her back, and she felt the pace of his heartbeat quicken.

She laughed softly, her breath mingling with his, and then she pressed her mouth to his in a long kiss. "This will help us decide," she said at last. "Let me take off this gorgeous blue gown."

CHAPTER TWENTY-EIGHT

Everything was so simple once Rebekah decided what she must do.

She had to leave Breven. She had to go to Cedar Hills with the angel.

She had no choice; she could see that now. All her worries about leaving behind her family, entering into a new life surrounded by strangers—none of those mattered when measured against the likelihood of losing her life. She could go with Obadiah and transform herself completely, or she could stay in Breven and die.

And her baby would die.

She was astonished at the fierceness of her determination to protect the life inside her. She had always known she would have fought to the death to save Jordan from harm, and Jonah had such a hold on her heart that she could not imagine what it would be like to leave him, but even these emotions paled before the intensity of her love for her unborn child. She schemed for this child; it figured in every calculation. Every night she dreamed about a baby who was fair and serene and watched her with dark, unreadable eyes. So strong were her tactile impressions of holding and nursing this child that when she woke in the mornings, her arms empty, she was assailed by a sense of ungovernable loss. She had not known it was possible to love—love so *much*—something invisible, intangible, alive only in imagination.

Yet the mound of her belly grew more rounded every day, and the Kiss in her arm pulsed with a dangerous fire. Not so intangible after all.

She must leave Breven as soon as possible, before she was discovered. Long before her marriage. She thought there was a good chance she could conceal her pregnancy until very late in her term if she carefully chose her jeskas and ensured as much privacy as possible when using the water room. So, although it was imperative that she leave Breven, it was not urgent. Not yet. She still had time.

The knowledge that she was truly going to leave her family, her home, every single familiar detail of her life, at times overwhelmed her with a grief so great that only an even greater corresponding fear kept her resolution intact. She did not know how quickly the angel might return and how swiftly she might be able to plot her escape, so she could not gauge how much time she had left among the people and the things she loved. Her days were invested with melancholy as she did her routine chores. She might never sit in the garden again in the winter sunlight, watching Jonah crawl between the bare, spindly bushes. She might never again linger at the communal dinner table, listening to the old women gossip and the young women whisper. She might never hear Jordan boasting about some horse he had mastered, though Hector told him he was not strong enough to hold such a brutish animal. She might never endure another public scold from her mother and then late in the day receive, not an apology, but a kiss on the cheek or a gentle "thanks." She might never know if her mother loved her. So often she had been sure Jerusha did not, but when Rebekah was far away, lost to her forever, would Jerusha weep into her pillow until Hector begged her for silence?

She would never know that, either.

It was impossible to guess when Obadiah might reappear. She had taken pains to make him think she was safe, so he would not haunt the streets of Breven, looking for her, drawing more attention than would be good for either of them. But that plan might have been miscalculated, since she had no way of letting him know her situation would soon be desperate. She did not think she could convince Jordan to deliver a second missive to the Hotel Verde, since he had been so reluctant to carry the first. She had had to explain over and over again how she had met Zoe at the house of one of Martha's cousins, how she was a nervous and fretful girl, prone to imagining the worst.

"She will have heard what happened to Martha," she said. "And she will be crazy with grief and worry over me."

"What do we care what a Manadavvi girl worries about?"

"Please. She's a friend. I have no other way to reach her."

In the end he had consented when she allowed him to read the letter—so carefully composed, so full of hidden messages!—and agreed that he could toss it away and disavow it if by some chance it seemed too dangerous to deliver. This had not kept her from pouncing on him the instant he returned and demanding to know if he had put the letter in Zoe's hands.

"No, of course I did not! I gave it to some man inside the hotel. He looked Manadavvi—her brother, perhaps."

"But you told him it was for Zoe? He knew?"

"Her name was on the paper."

"But you told him?"

"I told him."

And she was fairly certain the letter had been forwarded to Obadiah, for there were no more signals dropped on her roof or in her garden in the next few days. But he would be back. She knew him well enough by now to be sure of that.

She spent a great deal of time imagining what their next meeting would be like. What would she say first? "I want to leave Breven to be with you" or "I'm carrying your child." What would his reaction be to either of these statements? She had no doubt, none at all, that Obadiah was an honorable enough man to see her to safety even if he no longer loved her, even if he was horrified or repulsed by the news of her pregnancy. But he might be rendered speechless by the miracle, might be struck dumb and senseless by joy. She rather thought Obadiah was that kind instead.

How to meet him to share this news was another one of her preoccupations. It was not clear when the extreme measures of security would be lifted from Hector's house—indeed, from all the wealthier houses of Breven. The men no longer slept in their beds; they slept on the floor before the kitchen door, on the landings between stairwells, anyplace that might conceivably be considered an exit. There was no way to steal from the house by night.

Rebekah could not help imagining scenes of great daring and boldness. She pictured herself charging down the steps in the middle of the day, sprinting through the garden with Hector and his brothers in full pursuit, dashing down the street at a flat-out run as her Jansai relatives grew ever closer—and then being snatched up by an angel swooping down from the hard bright sky. The trouble with this scenario, of course, was that Obadiah would have to know in advance just exactly when she would require him to be swooping.

More likely, she thought, was that he would leave some token on the skylight and she would find a way to creep up the back stairs by night. Perhaps it would be Jordan guarding the upper floor on the night she wanted to escape, and he would let her pass without even a question. Perhaps it would be one of Hector's brothers, both of them big men who liked to drink, and who might sleep soundly even on the rough floor of the hallway. Perhaps they would be easy to step over and leave behind.

Now and then she thought about a third course, as risky as the others. She would sneak from the house in her boy's guise—night or day, whenever the opportunity arose—and make her way to the Hotel Verde. There she would wait, hidden and sheltered in one of the opulent rooms, until Obadiah could be sent for. There was little risk that the Jansai would track her down there, and so she could wait in relative safety for however long it took Obadiah to arrive. No one would think to look for her in such a haven; no one would have any reason to suspect she had any association with the Manadavvi.

Except Jordan.

Once that thought occurred to her, she turned it over and over in her mind. She could not believe Jordan would betray her, would lead Hector and his family to her hiding place, knowing what would befall her at their hands. He had been so distraught over Martha's expulsion that she could not believe he would engineer her own. And yet, Ephram was the one who had denounced his sister, and he had been greatly lauded among the Jansai for his quick and ruthless action. Jordan might be hungry for some honor of his own.

No. Not Jordan. Not that sweet, funny, generous, happy boy.

But still she made no plans to don boy's clothes and creep out into the street. She would wait until she knew the angel was in town. Her escape would be much more certain then.

Even though she would rather not have, Rebekah accepted Hali's help in finishing up her bridal trousseau. The companionship was pressed on her by Jerusha, who claimed Hector's niece would be a good, steadying influence on Rebekah, who had "seemed so flighty these past few weeks I honestly don't understand how you make it through the day."

"I'm just fine. I don't know what you're talking about."

"You're jumpy as a child before a festival, looking around you all the time as though you expect something strange or marvelous to be leaping out at you from the corners."

That was a fairly accurate assessment, Rebekah had to admit, though she was surprised that her mother had noticed. "There's a lot happening," was all she said. "Martha—and my wedding—"

"Don't you talk about Martha," Jerusha hissed, looking around quickly to see if anyone had overheard. They were sitting together in the fabric room, and Jerusha had just expressed her impatience with the endless task of hemming linens. Her eyes had fallen on Hali, sitting demurely across the room, hands busy with some mending and expression indicating that she was listening patiently to Hepzibah's harangue. "Martha is dead, do you hear me? They went back a week ago and found her bones. If you even mention her name, you could be dead, too."

Rebekah raised her eyes briefly to her mother's face, her own expression so stark and level that Jerusha actually recoiled. *I could be dead for crimes more appalling than speaking my cousin's name,* she thought. "I know that Martha is dead," was all she said.

It took Jerusha a moment to recover from the strangeness in Rebekah's expression. When she did speak again, her voice was a little strained. "So. You will make new friends. Martha was always a wild one. But Hali. She's a good girl. Quiet. She never does anything to make her mother worry."

"I don't like Hali."

Jerusha slapped her none too gently on the fingers. "Don't say things like that! You'll have her help you with your dowry. You girls should be friends. That would make your father happy."

She didn't even waste breath saying, *He's not my father.* "I don't care who does the sewing," she said instead, too tired to argue anymore. "If Hali is willing, let her help."

So Jerusha invited Hali to join Rebekah, and then she casually decided to "leave you young girls alone to talk." Hali barely noticed.

"Oh, I love the fabric you've chosen for your sheets," she exclaimed, running her fingers over the smooth, fine cloth. "This is for your wedding night? It's from Luminaux, isn't it?"

"My mother picked the fabric," Rebekah said.

"And the jeskas you're to wear for your first year! I want to be a married woman so I can wear fabrics so beautiful. Did you embroider all the hems in gold?"

"Three of them. Two I embroidered in silver for feast days."

"How long will you live in Simon's place? How long before Isaac has his own house? I would not want to live alone in a house, just my husband and me. Will you bring some of Isaac's sisters with you?"

"I think it will be a while before he can manage a household of his own. We might live with Simon for years."

"Or perhaps Simon will *die,* and Isaac will take over his father's house! That would be excellent, would it not? His house is very big."

"It would not be so excellent for Simon, I suppose."

"No, but you know what I mean! He will have to die sometime."

So the conversation went, for the next two dreary hours—and the next two dreary days. It was the bitter tail end of winter, just weeks before shy spring was due to arrive, but the weather was colder and windier than it had been all season. As if winter could not bear to release her bony, hateful grip on this southern land, as if she wanted to prove that an old lady's whims were more powerful than a young girl's fertility. So they had all stayed indoors for three interminable days. There were no feasts coming up, so no need to spend hours in the kitchen, baking; none of the men were planning journeys in the next few weeks, so there was no rush to mend the tents or put their clothing in order. Nothing to do but work on Rebekah's trousseau.

"When I am married I will have only sons," Hali said to Rebekah on the third day. The two girls sat in the middle of the room, surrounded by piles and piles of fine cloth. Hepzibah and her sisters were gathered in one corner, working on household projects and grumbling about something Hector had done. "Five of them."

Rebekah knew a little about the unpredictability of pregnancy, and she couldn't let this pass. "I'm not sure you are allowed the ordering of such things," she said. "When you will have children, or how many. Or what kind."

"Yes, but I don't *want* any daughters," Hali said earnestly. "It's the sons who will look after you when you're old, and take you into their homes. A daughter would have to ask her husband if you could take up space in his house, and you would have to be very meek and do everything he told you to do. But your own sons would still have to listen to you and show you honor."

"I would be happy to have either a son or a daughter," Rebekah said softly. *If I can survive long enough to bear the child.*

"But I'd like to travel first. If I marry a merchant, you know, he'll most likely take me on trips to Semorrah and Castelana and the Manadavvi holdings. So I don't want to have children right away."

Rebekah couldn't help smiling at that. "Oh," she said, "I don't think I'll be able to wait very long to have my first child."

They had been at work for at least two hours by this time. Rebekah could not keep herself from glancing up toward the skylight every once in a while, wondering what she might see there: a patch of winter-gray sky, droplets of rain, a single broad feather.

"Why do you do that all the time?" Hali exclaimed when Rebekah raised her eyes once more to the glass pane. "There's nothing to see up there!"

A shudder of fear, as if the other girl could actually piece together Rebekah's impossible story, and then Rebekah smiled. "I keep thinking the weather might change," she explained. "That I'll see sunshine through the window, not clouds. I want to go out in the garden."

Hali shivered. "Even if the sun comes out, it will be too cold to walk in the garden today. Didn't you hear Hepzibah moaning about her dera bushes? Covered in frost this morning. They'll likely die. My father says the temperature tonight may drop lower than it has all season."

Rebekah sighed. "Isn't it spring yet?" she asked sadly. "Isn't it time for everything to change?"

Hali laughed. "This is Breven," she said. "Nothing ever changes."

A bustle at the door made them look up, hopeful for new company: cousins from across town allowed to come visit for the afternoon, or even neighbors from the other side of the street, with news or fresh pastries. But it was only Jerusha and Asa bearing folded sheaves of cloth and discussing an ill-considered dress that Uriah's wife had worn to some event years ago.

"She still thinks it's a shade that flatters her," Asa said with a snort. "Hair that color, and she chooses to wear red! I can't do anything with her. Praise the god she never had daughters so she could pass on her poor taste in fashion."

"I hope you'll tell me," Jerusha said, "if I ever make such a mistake."

"You," Asa said fondly. "You could be a merchant yourself, you've such an eye for color and quality."

Rebekah glanced over at them and then let her eyes drift upward a moment. (Nothing to be seen in the skylight, not even sky, just a coil of somber clouds.) She had just returned her attention to her work when Jerusha called her over.

"Rebekah! Come see. Asa has almost finished your wedding dress."

Hali jumped up, more excited than Rebekah, and the bride herself came slowly to her feet. "Oh, you must try it on right now," Hali said. "I want to see it."

"I'm sure it's just fine," Rebekah said listlessly.

Jerusha motioned imperiously. "Come here! We have to check the fit, Asa says."

The old seamstress was carefully unrolling the cloth in her hand and shaking it out. Yes, this was the soft, sage-colored fabric that Rebekah remembered Jerusha making such a fuss over, and the almost sheer golden sheath that would lie against her skin. She had no desire to try it on, to parade around this room before the other women, pretending she was excited about her upcoming wedding day.

Sweet Jovah singing, she had no desire to undress before these women, show off the ripening curves of her body. Rebekah's disinterest was replaced by a rising sense of alarm. She stopped a few yards away from her mother.

"I can try it on some other day," she said, trying for her usual surly tone.

Jerusha would have slapped her if Rebekah had been standing close enough. "Don't be troublesome! Asa is here now, and she's a very busy woman, and you'll try on your wedding dress as she says."

Asa cackled with laughter. "Not so eager for the dress, or not so eager for the day?" the old woman wondered.

"Isaac is a fine boy," Jerusha said. "She's lucky to marry him."

"I don't want to try on the dress," Rebekah said.

Jerusha strode over to grab her by the arm and drag her the few feet to Asa's side. "There was never a girl as difficult as you!" she exclaimed. "Off with your jeska, yes, and your hallis, too. No pretense of modesty, now, just do what you're told."

Hali crowded behind her, cooing over the craftsmanship of the design. Rebekah slowly disrobed, taking pains to hold each layer of clothing close to her body as she pulled it off, covering her breasts and her stomach as well as she could. Let them think she was embarrassed by her nakedness as long as they didn't notice her condition. She turned her back to Hepzibah and her sisters, watching with great interest and amusement from across the room.

Asa threw the translucent yellow sheath over her head and tugged it into place over her shoulders and hips. "That's—hmm, tighter than I expected. Have you gained weight, girl?"

Jerusha laughed. "Who doesn't, in the winter? I eat and eat, hungry all the time."

"Well, I can let out the side seams a little. But the overdress—" And Asa threw this over her head. "The fit must be perfect."

It was then that Rebekah remembered how closely tailored the bridal dress was, so much different from the loose-fitting jeskas. She half-turned toward her mother, a look of panic flitting across her face, trying to think of what she might say. Yes, she'd gained weight—*eating and eating the whole winter through*—*hungry all the time*—

Asa had dropped to her knees to close the front buttons of the dress where the design cinched in at the waist. She grunted in surprise as the edges would not come together, tugging as if to loosen an errant fold of cloth.

Rebekah kept her eyes on her mother, conveying she knew not what message of supplication and alarm. Jerusha, at first distracted by something Hali was saying to her, gradually turned away from the other girl's chatter, her face showing puzzlement, her eyes fixed on her daughter.

"What?" Jerusha asked, shaking her head as if to say she could not comprehend.

Asa tugged some more. "Now *this* was not a mismeasurement!" the old woman said. "Twice I tied the string around your waist, and your waist was nowhere near this size."

Rebekah said nothing, just continued staring at her mother. Jerusha's eyebrows drew down and concern sharpened her cheekbones.

"Oh, it's so pretty," Hali breathed, moving around to view the gown from the back. Rebekah could feel the girl standing behind her, blocking her exit, choking off her escape. She stared at her mother.

Asa clambered to her feet. "Then let us check the bustline, see if there's trouble there."

Jerusha's face blanched. Her eyes darkened with sudden terrible knowledge, and her lips formed an unspoken word.

There was nothing she could say.

Asa had pulled her string from her pocket and wrapped it around Rebekah's breasts. "Look at this!" the seamstress exclaimed. "Two—no, three inches bigger! In a few short months! How do you expect me . . ."

Her voice trailed off. Now Asa gazed at Rebekah with as much stupefaction as Jerusha, as Hali, as Hepzibah and the old women who had slowly crept forward. Even from across the room, they had been able to sense tragedy unfolding, and now they stood, a semi circle of them, between Rebekah and the door.

Rebekah continued to gaze at her mother. Jerusha did not say a word.

"Wicked girl!" Asa shrieked, startling them all. She pointed at Rebekah with the fingers of both hands and backed away as if fearful of contamination. "Wicked, dreadful woman! Impure! *Kirosa!*"

Hepzibah and her sisters began to gasp and mutter, and Hali let out a long, shrill wail of confusion. "What is it? Aunt Jerusha, what has happened?" Hali cried.

Jerusha did not answer, did not move. She kept her eyes on her daughter and began to mouth a silent, desperate prayer.

"She is *pregnant!*" Asa said fiercely. "Breasts and belly swollen up so that she won't fit into her wedding gown. *Pregnant!* And you, pretending you were virginal, pure enough to be a bride!"

Without warning, Asa darted forward and hit Rebekah hard across the face. Rebekah jerked away, but not before the blow landed, jarring her head to one side and making her step backward to keep her balance. A chorus of outrage from the old sisters then, and Hepzibah darted between Rebekah and the seamstress.

"We don't need you to chide our young women," Hepzibah said sternly. "We will deal with her ourselves."

For a moment, Rebekah saw hope flare in her mother's eyes, though she still said nothing aloud, either to condemn or succor. She was helpless here, completely without power; she could not save Rebekah if the men turned against her, could not save herself if her own carelessness was blamed for Rebekah's fall.

"It is time you left this house and didn't think of carrying secrets into other houses," Gabbatha added in her quavery voice.

"Secrets!" Asa exclaimed. "You think to shield her, this—this— abomination? She must be cast forth into the desert! She must be stoned from the streets of Breven!"

"She must be dealt with by the men of her own family," Hepzibah said firmly.

A mistake. "Uncle Hector!" Hali screamed, running for the door before any of them could think to grab her. *"Uncle Hector!"*

"Ha!" Asa said in satisfaction, and Jerusha seemed to crumple where she stood, but the old aunts moved with sudden swift purpose.

"You—to my room," Hepzibah said to her youngest sister. "I have money there under my mat. Meet us in the garden. Gabbatha, watch the door and don't let this one leave."

"I will leave if I want! You can't hold me here!" Asa cried.

"You," Hepzibah said, turning to Rebekah. "Do you have someplace to go? Your lover's house?"

Rebekah shook her head, then nodded. "Not his house—somewhere—"

"Then when you meet my sister in the garden, you take my money, you run there—*run!*—through the streets. Here, put on your jeska, cover your face with my veil. Let anyone who sees you assume you are a poor woman from the outer tents."

"Rebekah . . ." Jerusha whispered. She was on her knees, clawing at the air as if it would give her a handhold, something with which to pull herself to her feet.

Hepzibah spun around and shoved Jerusha back to the floor. "Say nothing!" she spat out. "Not a word! You share her fate if you try to save her."

"Rebekah . . ."

Hepzibah had ripped the bridal dress from Rebekah's body and flung the jeska over her head. Now she was yanking it none too gently in place. "Your shoes—good, they are thick and comfortable ones. I have a waterskin over by my basket, you can take that with you—"

"She is wicked! *Kirosa!* She deserves to be thrown into the streets!"

"I will throw *you* in the streets, you foul-tongued old witch," Hepzibah said over her shoulder to Asa as she flew across the room. "If you say a word of this to anyone—a *word!*"

Rebekah was closest to the door, and so she was the first one to hear the commotion on the stairway, the upraised voices sounding the alarm. She looked at her mother, so small and misshapen in her pose on the floor that she looked like a melted candy representation of a woman. Jerusha caught the sounds next, and her head lifted, like a wild animal casting about for the source of danger.

"Rebekah," Jerusha whispered.

"I love you," Rebekah said out loud.

Men burst through the door, so many and so savage that Rebekah could not count or separate them. In the split second before they descended on her, a dark horde of vengeance, she recognized Hector and her uncle Ezra. Then hands grabbed for her and fingers tore at her clothes, her skin. Something was tossed over her head, a blanket, perhaps. She could hear women screaming and men cursing. Blows rained down on her through the blanket, hard punches that connected with her skull, her collarbone, her hip. Instinctively, she tried to curl her body over her stomach, protecting the fragile life within. Cords were whipped around her shoulders and her legs, then drawn tight, and she stumbled forward, unable to break her fall. Then she was wrenched into the air and carried out the door, her head and knees bumping painfully against the frame. Behind her, she could hear someone sobbing. She knew it was her mother.

The journey seemed to last for days. Rebekah lay on the bare plank bottom of the wagon, her head still covered with the blanket, her body still bound by ropes, jouncing miserably with every inch they traveled. It was, in a way, a relief to be blinded, to not be able to see the faces of the men who had abducted her. She did not want to know who was among them. Hector, yes; Ezra, yes, no surprise there. Ephram, perhaps. Isaac? Simon?

Jordan?

They had flung her into the wagon, still shouting, still aiming the occasional blow in her direction, still calling on the vengeance of Jovah to see this wicked, willful girl destroyed. Once they were in the streets of Breven, moving forward, the shouting and cursing continued, and Rebekah knew they made a slow parade through the streets of the city, howling out the news to all who were close enough to hear. *"Broken! Kirosa! Broken! Kirosa!"* She could hear footsteps running up, fresh voices raised in lament, new horses and carts being appropriated to join the caravan of shame. They would wind through Breven once, rallying such supporters as they could, then exit at the western edge of the city and head straight out toward the desert.

Where they would leave her.

Rebekah lay in the bottom of the cart, trying to summon panic, but all she felt was a blank numbness. Her body hurt all over, bruised and bleeding in places from the ferocity of the blows she had already sustained. More of that to come, no doubt, when they left her in the untracked sand. She could only hope they hit her hard enough, often enough, to strike her insensate, to let her fall into a peaceful unconsciousness that would allow her to ease into death.

But if I die, my baby will die.

The thought sent the first true spasm of fear through her body, caused her hands to clench at her sides and her eyes to widen, trying to see through the blackness of the cloth. There was no escape from this wagon, no way to prevent the punishment that was to come, but if she could endure it, if she could survive it . . . People had wandered in the desert before and lived. They had stumbled upon waterholes, come with impossible luck upon the caravans of strangers. There was food and water in the desert, if you knew where to look. There was shelter. It was winter now, and that was bad, she could die of exposure—but it was not summer, and that was good. She could last more than a day. If she had any water, even the smallest amount, she could last three days or more. If she was not crippled, if she was not bleeding too badly, she could walk toward safety, assuming she could determine in which direction safety lay. She would not have to lie there, broken and defeated, where they left her in the sand. She and her baby would not have to die.

Martha is dead. They went back and found her bones.

Rebekah's brief rush of courage faltered. If ever anyone had had the will to live, it had been Martha, and she had not survived her own exile. *They found her bones.* But perhaps Jerusha had just said that to frighten Rebekah, perhaps she had merely been trying to impress on Rebekah how grave her own plight could be. Perhaps it wasn't true, and Martha was alive somewhere, happy, reunited with her Manadavvi lover.

If she only had water.

So the journey went for the next hour, the next two hours, seemingly forever, as Rebekah wavered between resolution and despair. She thought she was calm—she thought she was prepared—but when the wagon stopped and she caught the barking commands of Hector's voice, she was washed with a sense of utter panic. Here! Now! She was to be left in the desert to die!

Rough hands wrapped around her arms and hauled her from the wagon, dragging her carelessly over the side so that her legs and shoulders banged against the wheels. Shouts and laughter and curses. She made no attempt to separate the sounds into words, the voices into individuals. She was put on her feet and then pushed forward, stumbling and unable to see where she was going. She fell and was yanked upright, thrust forward again. Three more times, till she was far enough from the wagons to satisfy them.

"Show us the whore's face!" someone cried. She thought it might be her uncle Ezra, but it was so hoarse she could not be sure. The cords were stripped from her body, and the blanket was whipped from her head with so much force that she was thrown off balance again, and she tripped to her knees in the soft sand.

"*Whore!*" the voice cried again, and a rock hit her on the shoulder with an angry force. "*Kirosa!* Impure!"

Other voices took up the chant. "*Kirosa!* Impure!" More rocks, a hailstorm of them, striking her cheek, her chest, her bent knees. She cowered before them, head bent low, cradling her hands over her stomach, afraid to try to crawl away lest such a show of spirit rouse their anger even more. One stone hit her in the soft place right before her left ear, and she felt the force of it ring through her skull. It pushed her over, it toppled her to the ground, and then they were crowding all around her, screaming at her, showering her with stones. Now that her head was on the sand, her gaze traveled upward, and she was able to see all their faces, contorted with rage and elation and a curious, mad sense of conviction. They were doing this terrible thing, and they believed they were right, they were justified, they were honorable. They were killing her, and they believed they had the sanction of the god.

Against her will, she trained her gaze on each of the separate faces, recognizing them even as their fury and zeal turned them wholly unfamiliar. Hector—his two brothers—Isaac, yes, but she didn't see Simon—Ezra—Ephram—

Jordan.

Jordan.

It was as if her body ceased to feel the pounding of the stones, as if her mind for a moment emptied of all other thought. She could see that Jordan had registered her gaze, that he knew she was staring at him. His face was ashen and his eyes were haunted, but his hands were not empty. As she stared at him, her bloodied mouth trying to shape the syllables of his name, he lifted his right hand, which held a good-sized rock of an impossible shade of granite blue. When he threw it, it struck her shoulder and bounced away.

She could not bear it. She could not look anymore, she could not think, she could not scheme. She closed her eyes and felt the continual strike and hammer of falling stones, but it was as if they no longer connected with her skin or jolted along her bones. Her mind refused to acknowledge her existence, and she whirled away into blackness.

The world was still black when Rebekah opened her eyes, but it was not an unrelieved starkness. Moonlight. Starlight. The ghostly reflected gold of the sand. These illuminated the outer world far more than any hope or determination could illuminate her interior landscape.

It was nighttime. The men were gone. She was not dead.

Her baby was not dead.

Crying out in pain as she did so, Rebekah pushed herself to a sitting position to try to assess her condition. They had not killed her—but then, they never killed the girls they drove out into the desert, for a quick death would have been too merciful. Exposure, thirst, starvation—these were the proper roads to death for an impure woman. They had not, she thought, even continued to stone her for very long after she had fainted. Every bone, every inch of skin, contained its own separate memory and bruise, but she was, in a way, surprised that she did not feel worse. She felt dreadful, she felt broken, she felt more terrible than she had ever imagined she could feel, but she could move, and she could think, and she could stand, and so she must push herself to her feet and begin to walk.

She was not dead, and so she must make herself live.

From her seated position, she tried to take stock of her situation.

They had not bothered to bind her hands and feet, and they had left her clothed, both conditions that would give her some slight advantage in the hours to come. They had also, inexplicably, left behind the blanket that had been thrown over her head. An oversight, she was sure, but another advantage to her. Her shoes were still on her feet. She would be able to walk.

If she could push herself upright, make herself stand. She was not sure that was possible.

It had to be possible.

She would walk at night, so that she did not freeze to death, and sleep by day, when the sun would lend her a faint additional warmth. Which direction to travel? That was the question. How far to the edge of the desert, how far to the nearest waterhole, how far to the nearest cluster of marrowroot bushes that could offer a slim, welcome sustenance?

She squinted up at the stars, trying to gauge her location by their positions, but she was not good at night craft. She recognized some of the major constellations but did not know if they were supposed to rise in the east or shift toward the north as the hours passed. The moon, she knew, made a smaller and smaller sweep over the western horizon as the winter gave way to spring, so that would be her guide of sorts; she would walk toward the moon.

When she could push herself to her feet.

She sat there a moment longer, trying to gather her strength, trying not to let herself be overcome by the sheer enormity of what had befallen her. Her stepfather, her uncle, her cousin, her brother—stoning her at the edge of the desert, leaving her to die—she could not think about it. She could not let her mind go there.

Her brother with his arm upraised, flinging an object at her—

Don't think about it.

Yet her mind could not release that picture, of Jordan with his arm lifted, a granite-blue stone in his hand. He had flung it at her and it had hit her on the shoulder, not hurting nearly as much as she had expected it to, as much as all the other stones had. Because she was so hurt already, so numbed, by the very fact of his condemnation—

Or because he had not actually thrown a rock.

She sat up a little straighter, looking about her at the great scattering of stones. So much ammunition for one wayward girl! They must have brought the stones with them; there weren't that many to be found in any square mile of the desert. Stones of all sizes, but most of them fist-sized, rough-edged, heavy, designed for maximum impact—

On the ground not six feet away from her she finally spotted the blue object that had come from Jordan's hand. The color was barely discernible here in the pale light, but she was sure it was the item that Jordan had thrown. She forced herself to her hands and knees and scrabbled through the sand to retrieve it. The instant her hand closed over it, she knew that Jordan had not tried to stone her. He had tried to save her.

The item consisted of cloth wrapped around something molded, smooth, and heavy. Fingers shaking, Rebekah untied the series of small knots holding the fabric in place and slowly unwrapped the contents. It was a small metal container with a cork stopper such as the Luminauzi used to carry water when they traveled.

Water.

Holding the container to her ear, Rebekah shook it slightly, enough to hear the liquid slosh inside. Her eyes closed, briefly shutting out the brittle starlight. *Water.* Jordan had bought her a day, maybe two. Bought her, possibly, her life.

She wanted to weep with joy and thankfulness and despair, all mixed together, but she could not waste the energy, could not spare the moisture from her body. Grunting as she did so, she pushed herself up to her knees and then to her feet, wavering a moment before she could catch her balance. Jovah's bones, there was not a vein in her body that had not exploded into a bruise, not a muscle that did not shriek with pain. On the side of her head where a rock had hit, an ache began a slow, insistent throbbing. She was not sure how long she could stand, let alone how much energy she would be able to summon for forward motion.

The blanket was clutched in her right hand, so she slowly wound it around her shoulders like a shawl. The water container was in her left. She rewrapped it in the blue cloth, then tied that around her waist so her hands were free. In case there was something she needed to pick up on her travels, in case she needed to use her hands to break her fall.

She turned her face toward the full moon, low on the horizon and polished as a silver coin. West. Moving as slowly as winter itself, she put out first her right foot and then her left, and began the long trek across the desert.

CHAPTER TWENTY-NINE

Elizabeth actually thought she was sorrier to leave the Edori camp than Rufus was. He had been relaxed and happy for their entire stay with the Chievens, helping the men gather food, lifting his voice in prayerful songs around the fire at night. During Feast Day, when all the Edori gathered around the central fire and took turns chanting out the stories of what had befallen them in the past year, Rufus took his turn singing before the assembled people. He told them his own story, simply and starkly, setting unrhymed words into a familiar children's melody. His voice had not faltered, and his face had been serene, but it was a recital that had left him much more drained and exhausted than he had wanted anyone to know. That night, he had wept in Elizabeth's arms as she had never expected any man to weep. She had kissed him and comforted him as she had never thought she would be able to comfort anyone, and she had held him until he had fallen asleep.

She had thought then, as she had thought every day of their stay at the Gathering, *He will not want to leave his people.* But he had woken the next day appearing cheerful and whole, filled with a restless energy that could not be contained by a tent or a campsite.

"Shall we wait until tomorrow to leave?" he asked, for that had been their plan all along. "Or would you like to start out for Cedar Hills this morning?"

Elizabeth was so surprised that she didn't know how to answer. "Today? But what do Paul and the others want to do?"

"I don't know. I'll ask them. Paul at least has work to get back to. He won't mind an early start."

But I will, she thought. She was already sad at the idea of leaving behind Naomi and the other Chievens, to know that she wouldn't see them again for another year—if ever. For who knew what the next year would bring? Would she still be with Rufus, would he care to go to the Gathering again, would sickness or some other calamity keep them from traveling, even if they planned to make the journey together? The world was filled with uncertainty; that Elizabeth knew for certain. She was depressed at the thought of leaving this much friendship and pleasure behind.

"Check with the others, then," she said. "We can leave if all of you want to go."

But Paul and Silas wanted to stay the additional day, and Jed, it turned out, did not want to leave at all. "I'm going to ride with the Barcerras for a while," he told them in an offhand voice as he stopped by the Chieven campfire that morning. "A month or two, at any rate. Maybe longer."

"And they'll be happy to have you," Naomi commented as she bustled by. "Another set of hands to do the work of the camp! Who wouldn't be happy?" She grinned at Elizabeth and Rufus. "You're welcome to travel with us, you know, as far and as long as you like."

"And do all the chores that you and your Luke are too lazy to do?" Rufus scoffed. "I'd rather be in Cedar Hills and earn my pay, thank you very much."

And that, as far as Elizabeth could tell, was that. "If you did want to stay with the Chievens for a while," she said to Rufus that night as they packed their belongings and made sure everything was ready for an early start, "I could travel back with the others."

He paused to kiss her. "Ah, it's true, then. I thought I saw you eyeing Silas, thinking he was a fine-looking man. You're hoping for a chance to be alone with him on the road."

She set her hands on her hips. "That is not true! I've had my fill of wastrel Edori men. Once I leave you behind, I'll settle for nothing less than a merchant or a shopkeeper. Someone who knows the value of hard work and a little extra money from time to time."

"Stingy, though, those commercial men. Saving every copper to invest in the next round of merchandise. You're better off with an honest laborer like me."

She didn't know how the conversation had devolved so quickly from serious to silly. "But if you wanted to stay with the Chievens—" she tried again.

He fastened the pocket of his traveling bag. "But I don't."

"But I don't know why," she said softly.

He looked over at her, his face no longer laughing. It was early evening and dark already, but they had brought in candle stubs so they had light by which to do their packing. "The things I want are no longer here with the people," he said.

She felt a brush of fear. "If it is me that keeps you in Cedar Hills—I don't want to be the cause of such a decision. Because if the decision is wrong, and I'm the reason you made it—"

He shook his head. "You're a part of it, maybe. No. The decision to turn *allali* is maybe one of the reasons I do love you. I'm not a true Edori anymore. This is not the life for me. There are too many people and too many privations. It is too close and too hard, do you understand?" He glanced around the tent once, but he was not seeing the interior of the canvas wall; he was looking around the entire campsite, the assembled mass of Edori. "I will want to come back every year for the Gathering," he went on. "Now that I have been reunited with my people, I will have to have them in my life again. They are the place where my heart comes from, and my heart will have to visit from time to time. But my heart has wandered too far away to stay with these people now."

She waited a moment to be positive he was done speaking. "If you're sure, then," she said.

He kissed her again. "I'm sure."

They left in the morning after many tearful hugs and promises to reunite. "We will come to Cedar Hills. This summer, maybe," Naomi said. Elizabeth replied, "We will come to the Gathering again. Every year." Both promises, though they might not be carried out, were entirely sincere.

For the first few hours of the return journey, Elizabeth sat in the back of the wagon with Silas and allowed herself to feel downcast. It was not often she cared for people enough to feel some sense of loss when they were gone from her. Clearly, she was the only one in the wagon who was sorry to go. Rufus and Paul sat on the front bench, talking with great animation about some building project under way in Cedar Hills, while in the back of the wagon, Silas slept. Only Elizabeth turned her gaze to the path behind them and felt morose.

She perked up a little as they stopped by a little stream for lunch, realizing she was hungry. She hadn't been much interested in food that morning, but now the bread and cheese revived her. Paul and Silas hunched together over a somewhat tattered map, arguing over the course they should follow for the rest of the day.

"Joseph said the road was nearly impassable yesterday. We must have just gotten through on our way north."

"But we'll lose time going through the desert," Silas said consideringly. "The sand creates a drag on the wheels."

"And we'll have to bring all our water and fuel with us for three days," Paul interjected.

Rufus shrugged. "Evils both ways," he said. "But we came in by the mountain road."

Even Elizabeth could read the Edori reasoning in that. *We came in by the mountain road, therefore, let us go home by some totally unfamiliar route. Who knows what treasures we might discover along the way?*

"The waterholes are marked on Joseph's map," Silas said.

Paul grunted. "And when could anyone ever navigate the desert by a map? Everything shifts every day."

"Not the waterholes."

"There's plenty of timber here," Rufus said, looking around. "And room in the wagon."

Paul shrugged. "Then let's start gathering wood."

So they spent another hour picking up and bundling branches and filling every spare container with water. The back of the wagon, never exactly luxurious, became even more cramped with the addition of the wood, so Elizabeth squeezed herself onto the driver's seat between Rufus and Paul. She had never traveled through sand before, and she was fascinated when they crossed into the vast, rippled, golden expanse of desert. It reminded her, in a way, of the southern grasslands by James's farm, baked blond by summer heat, extending for miles in all directions with an unvarying sameness that made the world seem very big and the girl in the center of it very small.

"How do we keep from getting lost?" she wondered.

Paul laughed. "We follow our course straight southwest."

"But how can you tell where that is?"

Rufus glanced down at her, amused. "Edori never lose their sense of direction. Always know which way they're going, which way they've been. Tie a blindfold around an Edori's eyes and spin him around, or throw him in the back of a slave caravan and travel for four days. He can tell you exactly where he is and how much ground he's covered."

Paul nodded. "Truth," he said.

Not, maybe, such a comforting skill to have in a time like that, Elizabeth thought, but it would come in handy as they crossed the desert now. "And how far to water?" she asked.

Paul laughed again. "Well, that depends on the reliability of the map. But don't worry. We've got enough to see us through."

Their pace was slower as they crossed the ridged dunes and shifting surface of the sand, but Elizabeth was comfortable wedged up against Rufus, and she was enjoying discovering what beauties the landscape offered. From time to time she spotted a thin, tan-colored animal streaking in front of them and disappearing into an invisible hole, and often enough to stop seeming like a miracle she saw bunched marrowroot bushes still clutching their wilted leaves. Rufus hopped out of the wagon once to pluck a few for her, offering them as a delicacy. She found the taste too strong and odd to say she liked it, but once she'd swallowed the chewed pulp, she liked the way her mouth felt, minty and clean.

"Next best thing to water when you're traveling," Rufus said.

"I'd rather have water," Paul said.

The day had been pleasantly sunny, though the air had been cool, while they traveled in daylight. The minute darkness fell, however, the temperature dropped rapidly. They made a quick camp, building a small fire and huddling around it, still not able to get completely warm. They ate well, since they had brought much more food with them than they could possibly eat, but they drank their water sparingly.

"Not a bad day's travel, though," Paul remarked. "Covered a lot of ground. We'll be out of the desert in a couple more days."

"And home in three," Silas said. "I'm ready."

They all slept together in the wagon for warmth, Elizabeth between Rufus and Paul, her head so close to a bundle of kindling that she could feel curious twigs reaching out spidery fingers to test her hair. She had seen enough this day to know that the desert was not the sere, empty landscape it appeared at first glance, so she was a little alarmed at the faint scuffles and skitters she could hear in the dark around the wagon. Night creatures, out to prowl. How big and how dangerous? The men slept around her, either oblivious or unafraid. She listened awhile longer to the sounds of tiny scuttling feet and decided they belonged to scavengers, not hunters, and allowed herself to relax. Morning came before she even realized she had surrendered to the night.

"Brr! No reason to linger here," Silas observed. "Let's eat and be on our way."

They were in motion again not an hour after they'd all woken up. Elizabeth found herself not quite so entranced with the beauties of the desert on their second day. The variations in landscape were so slight that she could not convince herself they had made any forward progress at all; they might be covering the same few miles in an endless loop, passing this stand of bushes, that small dip and rise, over and over as the hours crawled by. Surely not; surely they would come across their own wheel ruts with every circular pass and realize their error. She gazed behind them just to assure herself that their tracks were indeed visible for some distance, and was not comforted to see the slow drift of sand healing over all marks of their passage even while she watched.

Rufus glanced over at her and smiled. The two of them were sitting in the back of the wagon this day, traveling for the most part in a companionable silence. "Don't worry," he said, apparently reading her thoughts. "Once you've been in the desert for an hour, you feel like you've spent your whole life there. A three-day trip across the sand feels like a three-month trip across the whole world. But we're making good time. Better than on the road, maybe. Fewer distractions and no reason to stop."

She managed a dismal smile. "I do believe if I had to spend much time in this climate it would drive me mad."

He made a small gesture with his hands. "Explains the personality of the Jansai, perhaps."

She nodded, and turned her attention back to the passing scene.

If she had not been watching the view so intently, hoping to find some proof of change and distance, she would not have seen the shape huddled on the desert floor maybe thirty feet from the route the wagon was taking. At first she thought it was the abandoned detritus of a Jansai camp—a hunk of discarded rags—and then she wondered if it might be the carcass of some desert creature that she had not spotted so far, oddly covered in smooth white feathers. *It's about the size of a child,* she thought, turning her head to watch it as the wagon pulled by. *I wonder if it's prey or predator.*

And then the wagon moved even farther on, and she saw flesh and hair at the extreme end of the bundle of rags.

"Stop!" she shrieked, coming to her feet while the wagon still rocked on its way. "There's a person—somebody—stop the wagon!"

Paul hauled on the reins, calling out in confusion, but Elizabeth had placed her hand on the side and vaulted clumsily over while the rig was still in motion. She landed in a heap on the sand, then picked herself up and began running toward the collapsed figure. Behind her, she heard more shouts and questions as the men stared after her.

"Rufus! Bring my satchel!" she cried over her shoulder, lifting her skirts and trying to run faster. The sand pulled at her feet, making it hard to keep her balance. She could not generate any speed. Sweet Jovah singing, yes, that was a body, possibly a corpse—see the hair fanned out, dark against the gold of the sand, a woman, a young woman. "Bring water!" she added, still running, still panting.

In a matter of minutes, she had skidded to a stop beside the body and dropped to her knees. Sweet lord of the lost and lonely, it *was* a woman, so battered and bloody that her face almost could not be seen through the discoloration. Elizabeth checked instantly for a pulse, sure she would not find one, equally sure the woman could not have been

dead for long or she would have already served as feast for some of
these mysterious desert creatures. She was as astonished as she had ever
been when she felt, against her two fingers, a slow and constant beat.

"You're alive," Elizabeth whispered. "How did you manage that?"

Rufus was beside her that moment, crouching down and offering
up her medical kit. "Is she—can she be—"

"Yes," Elizabeth said. "Water first. Soak a cloth for me and we'll
squeeze some drops into her mouth."

Paul and Silas arrived seconds later, standing on either side of
the body and staring down at miracles. Elizabeth was ready to
be irritated with them for their helpless stupefaction, but it lasted
only a moment. "What can we do?" Silas asked quietly. "Can she be
moved?"

Elizabeth shook her head. "I don't think so. Not yet. Bring the
wagon over. Prepare to set up some kind of shelter over her. Blankets. A fire. Her skin is so cold."

"Is she in shock?" Paul asked.

"I don't know. Shock, exposure, dehydration, infection—any of
it, all of it. Rufus, can you take this pill—yes, this one—and grind it
up and mix it with the smallest amount of water you can use? We'll
get that down her throat to start with. I've got to check her body for
injuries. Paul, do we have any juice? Honey? Something with sugar.
Water and sugar, we've got to get sustenance inside of her."

Elizabeth talked as she methodically tested the woman's limbs
for breaks, pushing back the edges of the loose clothing to examine
the forearms, the biceps, then the long, thin legs. This woman was
battered everywhere, as if she had tumbled down a ravine for miles
or been trampled on by small hooved animals. No bones appeared to
be broken, although the skin was ripped and bloody in places, and
red marks of infection had begun to rim some of the rawest patches.

"What *happened* to this poor creature?" Elizabeth murmured
more to herself than to anyone who might be listening.

"Stoned," Rufus said quietly.

Her hands at the throat of the woman's clothing, Elizabeth stilled
and looked over at him. "What do you—*stoned?* By whom? Why?"

He shrugged. He was holding a wet cloth to the woman's mouth
and squeezing droplets of water between her cracked lips. "By the

men of her family. For some infraction. That's what the Jansai do."

She stared at him. "That can't be true," she said flatly.

"Ask her," he said, "if you can save her."

Shivering from a sensation that was not cold, Elizabeth slowly unfolded the front of the woman's tattered outfit to check for damage on the torso. There were no large swaths of blood on the fabric, so she wasn't really expecting wounds on the chest, but she had to make sure. The soft flesh over her bosom and rib cage was less marked than the rest of her body, as if she had crouched low or curled in a fetal position to protect her vital organs. No stab wounds to the heart or lungs, no scar across the major arteries, no gash in the slightly swollen belly—

"Sweet Jovah singing," Elizabeth whispered, her hands slack on the cool, flawed flash. "She's pregnant."

Rufus looked over at her sharply, then nodded. "That would do it," he said. "Guessing she's not a married woman, though she looks old enough. How far along is she?"

Elizabeth shook her head slowly, unable to fathom it. "I don't know. Three months—maybe four months. She might have been able to conceal her condition for that long. You probably can't tell when she's standing and wearing this loose gown."

"Can you save the baby?" he wanted to know.

"I don't know if I can save *her*," she answered sharply.

"Yes," he said. "You can."

The others arrived then with the wagon and went to work with economical efficiency, spreading a tarp over the injured woman and building a fire. Elizabeth felt so terrified and helpless that she almost couldn't imagine what to do next. Which of these drugs in her satchel might harm the baby in this woman's womb? She didn't know—she didn't know. But unless she forced healing medicines down her throat, the woman and her baby would both surely die. She must try. She must do something.

"Is she taking the water? The powdered tablets?" she asked Rufus.

"All of it. And a little honey. But I don't think she's conscious."

"I want to get her clean. And I want to move her to a blanket, off this sand. Can you help me lift her? Carefully—very carefully."

In a few moments, they had the woman lying on a clean tarp,

completely stripped and covered with another blanket. Working slowly and gently, Elizabeth freed one arm, wiped it clean of blood and sand and dirt, and smeared it with manna root salve. Then the other arm, then each leg, and then the front and back of the woman's body. Last, she washed the woman's battered face, with its exotic high cheekbones and determined, pointed chin. She combed out the matted dark hair, then tied it in a knot on the top of her head, just to keep it out of the way.

Strange—unbelievable—this woman had been abandoned in the desert to die, but she was wearing still a ransom in jewelry, four or five necklaces, dozens of gold bracelets, one silver bracelet, a few rings. Maybe not so strange, Elizabeth thought. People who didn't mind throwing away a life might not mind throwing away a fortune in gold and gems.

"I don't know," Elizabeth said when she was done, talking half to herself and half to her patient. "I don't know what else I can do for you."

"She looks better already," Rufus said in an encouraging voice. "A little color in her cheeks. Under the black and blue."

"I wish she'd wake up. Tell us her name, what happened to her."

"How long do you think she's been unconscious?"

She shook her head. "I don't know. Less than a day, I think. She's not completely dehydrated, so she's had water sometime in the last day or two."

"She wasn't covered with sand, so she hadn't lain here all that long," Paul added. He and Silas were standing over the three on the ground—like the others, feeling helpless and useless.

Elizabeth glanced up at him. "Yes. Right. So that means she was conscious, and even mobile, yesterday. That's good."

"What else can we do?" Silas asked.

She should have thought of this sooner. "Put up a plague flag," she said.

None of the men moved. "What's that?" Paul asked.

She was confused. It was as if someone had asked what the Gloria was. "A plague flag! It's what you put over your house or your camp when you want an angel to come down and pray for you."

The three Edori exchanged glances. "But what—"

She braced her hands on her knees, exasperated. "Haven't you—don't the Edori call on the angels for help?"

A small hoot of muffled laughter from Silas. "Never. What can the angels do for us?"

Not worth arguing about, certainly not now. "Well, I think they can help this poor girl. So let's put up a flag."

"But there's no plague here," Paul said helpfully.

"No! It doesn't have to be plague! It can be any emergency! It's just—that's just what they call it!"

"And what do we use for a flag?"

"*Anything!* A bright shirt, a small blanket, something that will whip in the wind and catch the attention of someone flying overhead. Find a tree or—well, there are no trees here—a pole, something, anything, as high as it can be. Just so—just so someone sees it."

The other two Edori went off to carry out this mission while Elizabeth and Rufus hovered over the injured girl. The most they could do for her now was get liquid in her body, Elizabeth reasoned, and wait for the drugs and the salve to take effect. So she dripped a little more water into the half-open mouth and watched the throat unconsciously clench and swallow.

"Can you make some broth?" she asked Rufus quietly. "We've got some sugar in her; now we need some salt. I can't give her too much, I don't want her to throw up, but just a little—"

"I'll make stew," he said, "but you'll have to eat some, too."

She looked up, startled. "What? Oh, I'm not hungry."

"But you'll eat some, too," he repeated steadily. "Because I predict you'll be bending over this girl for the rest of the day and most of the night, and you won't be thinking about yourself because you'll be thinking about her. So you'll have some, too."

She smiled and leaned in to kiss him. "Very well, then. You take care of me while I take care of her."

Which was a strange thing, she thought, as she continued dribbling moisture down the woman's throat. To have somebody care for her at all. She wondered who had been supposed to be watching over this girl and failed so miserably that she would end up pregnant and almost dead, lost in the Breven desert. By the god's own grace, Elizabeth's path had not been so brutal, hard though it had been. She felt a fierce surge of protectiveness and pity for this stranger fallen inadvertently under her care. *I will watch over you now,* she thought. *No more harm will come your way.*

By nightfall, the woman was no better, and no one had responded to their signal of distress. "How long does it usually take?" Silas wanted to know. "For an angel to drop by once you put up a flag?" He and Paul had lashed together their tent poles and forced this post into the sand. From its top hung one of Rufus's shirts, a rather woebegone scarlet, listlessly stirring in the light breeze.

"I don't know. A while, I imagine," Elizabeth answered. "How often do angels fly over the desert? Over this very spot?"

"Not so often, I would think," Rufus said. "What do we do if no one has arrived by daybreak?"

Elizabeth looked over at him. "I'm not sure she can travel."

Paul spread his hands. "Then we leave you here with the wagon and one of the horses, and one of us rides back to Cedar Hills with all speed."

"No. That will take too long," she said sharply.

"Two days, maybe three," Paul said. "Can she live that long?"

"I don't know," Elizabeth whispered.

"Maybe it's better to put her in the wagon and see how she stands the journey," Silas said.

Elizabeth wrapped her arms around her body, hugging herself as tightly as she could. "I don't know," she said again.

"Decide in the morning," Rufus suggested. "Maybe she'll be better by then, our sick one."

"We can't let the fire die," Elizabeth said.

"This is all the fuel we have," Silas said. "If we burn it all night, there will be none tomorrow."

Elizabeth tried to choke back a sob. Too many questions, all the answers wrong. How could she save this desert waif when circumstances were so desperate? "Just for tonight," she said, forcing herself to speak calmly. "In the morning, we'll know more."

"We'll take turns standing watch and tending the fire," Paul said.

"No need," Elizabeth replied. "I'll be awake with her. I'll feed the fire."

"You'll be watching her," Paul said gently. "We'll take turns guarding the fire."

Even so, the night was too cold for a woman so hurt to endure. Rufus lay down on one side of her, lending his considerable body heat, and Elizabeth pressed herself against the stranger's other side. She did doze from time to time, waking as the men stirred the fire or when the woman beside her made a whimpering sound in the night. Every time she woke, Elizabeth sat up and ministered to her patient, tilting water into her mouth, pasting a concoction of medicine onto her tongue. Quite late, sometime after midnight, Elizabeth got out the jar of manna root and reapplied that all over the woman's body. It did not have the systemic efficacy of the god's pills, but it would do its small bit to heal and soothe. And she had to do something.

Rufus was awake as she finished this task. "I'm sorry," she whispered. "Go back to sleep."

"How is she?" he asked.

"I can't tell. Still breathing. She doesn't seem as cold. She might be able to heal, even if we can't get her back to Cedar Hills, but we don't have enough fuel and supplies to stay out here as long as it would take."

"And there's another danger you're not aware of," he said gravely. "The men of her family may come back, looking for proof of her death."

Elizabeth was so shocked that for a moment she could not speak, and then so furious that she had to turn her head away. At the moment she wanted nothing so much as one of this woman's relatives to come close enough for her to claw his eyes out.

"How do you know so much about the Jansai and how they treat their women?" she asked at last.

"You forget," he said, his voice very dry. "I was a guest of the Jansai for a little while myself."

That drew her attention back to him, and she gazed at him wonderingly. Rufus and Paul. Imprisoned by Jansai, their family members murdered or sold into slavery. "You must hate her, then," she said. "And all her people. How can you help her? How can you not stomp on her face and leave her to die?"

A small motion of his shoulders. "She is not the one who harmed me. The Jansai women are not to blame for the actions of their men."

"But—"

"And if it had been a Jansai man, lying here in the desert, broken and bleeding," he interrupted, "I would not have left him here to die, either. Not I, not Paul. It is not the Edori way. We cannot willingly bring pain to another living soul, not our enemies, not anyone. It is one reason the Edori fell so easily to the Jansai raiders, because we could not believe anyone could mean us harm. We were always so sure that they recanted and felt remorse. We were always so sure they had changed their ways."

Elizabeth bent her gaze down to the face of the sufferer on the blanket. "People who can do things like this," she said, "are not capable of remorse."

"Yovah believes all souls can be saved, and he puts his Kiss in the arm of every Jansai man and woman," Rufus countered. "And you are here to tell me you know something Yovah does not? They can be saved. They can be converted. We have just not found the right words, we mortals, that is all."

His words reminded her. "Did you see her Kiss?" Elizabeth asked. "When I cleaned her body? It is glowing with the strangest light."

"Really?" he asked, true innocence in his voice. "And that's unusual?"

"Yes, it's—oh, you Edori and your strange beliefs and your 'Yovahs' and your no Kisses!" she hissed in exasperation. "They say—don't you remember, I told you once—that the Kiss in your arm will light with fire when you meet your true love. But I have never heard of a Kiss just sparkling with light for no reason at all."

"Unless one of us is her true love," Rufus said with a smile. "Paul, perhaps. Or even me!"

"I would think some other man has been before you with his own version of true love," Elizabeth said tartly. "But where is he now? Why didn't he protect her?"

"Perhaps he is close, then," Rufus suggested. "In a caravan camping nearby."

Elizabeth felt a spike of alarm. "With the members of her family, perhaps? Come looking for her body?"

"Perhaps. Perhaps he does not love her after all, but merely used her and now cannot forgive her for being so weak."

"Do you really think her family will seek her out here?"

He nodded. "I'm afraid I do."

"Then there's no other choice," she said. "We'll have to drive on in the morning. Covering her in the bottom of the wagon so that if any Jansai caravans come upon us, they will not see we carry her."

"Perhaps an angel will arrive before we have to break camp," Rufus said in a comforting voice.

Elizabeth felt her lips twist. "When did an angel ever appear when you most needed one? Never in my life."

But she wronged the whole divine race with that bitter belief. For in the morning, while they were still sipping hot tea and stamping some feeling into their cold toes, a shadow formed over the campfire and grew gradually larger. Elizabeth glanced up quickly, shot with sudden hope, to see the gorgeous, symmetrical wings fold down as an angel made a graceful landing a few yards from the wagon. He was a blond and white shape against the gold of the desert, all pristine, snowy feathers and curling yellow hair. He strode forward, a pleasant smile on his face, and spoke before Elizabeth could address him.

"What can I do to help?" the angel asked. "My name is Obadiah."

CHAPTER THIRTY

Flying harder and faster than he had ever flown. His wings making great scooping motions, gouging out the air before him, his whole body straining forward as if the very tension of his muscles could slice open the treacly air. The body in his arms still and almost weightless, the face against his chest showing no consciousness at all.

Dear Jovah, sweet Jovah, give him the strength to proceed without pause, to streak through the skies like some swift, mysterious comet. Let him not tire. Let him fly on and fly on.

He had spotted the plague flag early this morning, on his way back from a weather intercession as he planned to make a quick, unauthorized journey into Breven. He almost had not stopped. *Almost had not stopped.* He had flown on, past the small campsite, on toward the true heart and lodestone of his journey, but a sense of guilt and responsibility had made him swear and wheel around. There was little chance Rebekah would be able to see him, anyway, if he arrived in Breven this night. He might as well justify his existence by aiding these poor travelers, people who would be grateful for the attention of an angel.

And then—and then—

He had listened briefly to the rapid speech of the auburn-haired woman (familiar; did he know her?), registering only the words "Jansai" and "stoning" and "pregnant." His first thought had been that, impossibly, Rebekah's cousin had survived her expulsion from the city and had been found by strangers. His second thought had been that Rebekah would be joyous beyond measure at such news.

His third thought never took coherent form.

Rebekah.

He had not even paused to explain himself as he gathered up the frail, broken figure and swept himself to his feet. The other woman was still chattering, listing the drugs she had administered or the injuries she had catalogued, but Obadiah could not absorb any of her words. "I'll carry her to Cedar Hills," he said in a harsh voice, and took off without another word.

The men of her family had discovered her—found his bracelet in her room, or a feather, or some other small token he could not even remember dropping—or they had caught her, creeping from the house one night in the hopes of finding him secretly in the city. The thing he had most dreaded had come to pass, but he had not dreaded it enough; he had not realized the true nature of the punishment that might befall her. She had known—she had to have known—and after Martha's banishment could have had no doubt remaining about the fate meted out to disobedient Jansai women. That letter she had sent to Zoe—that had been brave indeed, reassuring and unalarming—she had made him believe she was in no danger, that all was well. And all along, she had known how madly she flirted with death, how she courted him almost as assiduously as Obadiah had courted her. Had he known, had he guessed how much danger she was in, he would have landed in her step-father's garden one day and stalked inside the house, ransacked the rooms until he found and rescued the woman he loved.

What had they discovered? How had she been betrayed?

It was only about an hour into his headlong flight that he remembered what the other woman had said: "We think they must have cast her out when they discovered that she was pregnant."

Pregnant.

Rebekah was carrying his baby? Rebekah was—great god of the limitless heavens—she had conceived his child, and she had not told him, and she had faced alone the great risk of discovery and censure. Why hadn't she told him? Didn't she trust him? Did she think he would reject her, reject the child? Or hadn't she known she was with child? It had been nearly six weeks since they had seen each other. Had she just realized her condition? Maybe, and maybe that, more than Martha's fate, had prompted her to write that letter to Zoe, with its veiled promise to come live with him in Cedar Hills. It had been a message, an invitation, and he had been too dull to read it. Or at any rate, too dense to understand its urgency.

"Rebekah," he whispered, but the wind of his passage carried the word away.

He flew on even faster.

He did not want to, but he had to stop several times to take care of his own basic needs and hers. It was not an easy thing to tilt water down the throat of a woman who appeared totally unconscious, but Obadiah was patient, coaxing the mouth open, stroking the throat, making sure a little liquid was swallowed, and then a little more. As for himself, he gulped down both food and water, less from any sense of appetite than from the knowledge that he had to fuel his body or fall from the sky far short of his destination. Though he felt no lack of strength or ability. He was sure he could fly from the edge of the desert to the heart of Cedar Hills on fear and adrenaline alone.

Flinging himself back into the air—fighting for altitude, for speed—rushing forward so fast that he felt he outraced the spin of the world itself. He had lost all sense of time and distance; he could not calculate how long he had been flying or how much longer it would take before he reached his destination. All he knew was that the woman in his arms was still alive, for he felt the faint warmth of her mouth turned against the skin of his body. While she lived, he would not falter, and he would not fail.

The sky changed from the spring blue of morning to the summer gold of noon, and he flew on. Sunset streaked its autumn colors over the western horizon, and he flew on. Night, with its panoply of winter stars, and Obadiah flew on without pausing.

It was near the dinner hour when Obadiah came upon the lights of Cedar Hills. He dropped toward the ground, hardly abating his pace at all, and landed at a flat-out run. He had targeted his precise spot and was only a few yards from the doorway of the main building, the one that housed Nathan and Magdalena's suite and so many of the functions of the hold. Many people were still out at this hour, both angels and mortals. A few stared at him or called out to him as he raced past them, up the path and through the door and up the first two flights of stairs to Nathan's doorway.

He did not have a hand free, so he kicked at the door with his foot, calling out as he did so. "Nathan! Maga! Let me in!"

He was not here to see either of them, of course. He was not even here hoping to find that woman, that healer, who had haunted the place since Maga began having her inconvenient contractions. He was here, though he could not have said why, to see the woman who flung open the door, looking imperious and impatient and very short of sleep.

"Rachel," he panted. "She's dying. Help me."

In a very short time, Rachel had organized everything. She had put Rebekah in her own bed, summoned the medic, cleared the suite of everyone but necessary personnel, and elicited the entire story from Obadiah. This was why he had come to her, he realized that now—because never, at any point in her tumultuous life, had Rachel been at a loss. Whereas he had been at the end of his own strength and invention. He had not known what to do next. But Rachel could always initiate the next action, no matter how drastic. She was never brought down by indecision.

And Rachel would not let harm come to anyone he loved. She had told him that once, and now she had the chance to prove it.

He would not leave the room where the healer labored over Rebekah's scarred body, though Rachel had drawn him to the far corner and bade him speak quietly. So he had recited the tale—as much of it as he knew or had pieced together—and she had nodded from time to time or asked a quick, pointed question.

"Did we get to her in time? Will she live?" he asked, over and over, but the healer was too busy to answer.

"Yes," Rachel said, every time he asked.

"But how do you know?"

"Because otherwise Yovah would not have led you to her side at all."

"But how could this have happened? How could I have let such things happen? How could Jovah?"

"It was the god's will, perhaps, that the two of you be brought together. Maybe to create this child she bears, maybe for some other purpose."

"But the god could not have wanted her to suffer so much! What kind of divine plan is that?"

"Everybody suffers," she said in a low voice. "Sometimes it is to no purpose. But this time, I believe, it is."

"Will she live?" he demanded.

"Yes," the angelica replied.

The door opened, and an angel stepped through, her wings folded forward over her shoulders as if to protect the item she carried. In the dim light of the sickroom, Obadiah needed a moment to identify Magdalena, cradling an infant in her arms.

"How is she?" Maga whispered.

But Obadiah was staring at her. "You—Maga—I have only been gone three days! Is that—"

Dire though the situation was, both women were smiling. "Yes," Maga said happily. "A boy. Perfect."

"An angel," Rachel said dryly. "The real reason she thinks he's so perfect."

"I did not say that!"

"But he has come too early," Obadiah said. "Has he not?"

"Earlier than he should have," Rachel conceded. "He is very small, but he seems quite healthy."

"And everything went smoothly?" Obadiah asked.

Maga grimaced as she came to sit beside them on a low stool. She did not sit entirely still, but rocked back and forth with a slow, absent motion, as if she could not help herself, as if she did not even notice. "I am assured that my labor and delivery were no worse than anybody else's, but sweet Jovah howling! It was painful. I thought I was dying. And you don't even want to hear about the blood."

"No," he said earnestly. "I don't."

"But I've recovered—mostly—and this little one is such a miracle of delight that I am trying to convince myself I don't remember any of my pain. Everyone tells me I'll soon forget it. Though I don't think so."

"Congratulations," he said. "I am so pleased and happy for both of you." And he leaned forward to drop a kiss on her cheek and then on the fuzzy dark head of the baby in her arms.

"Obadiah is to be a father soon," Rachel observed.

Maga smiled, a luminous expression in the dark. "So you said! Though I still cannot believe—" She shrugged. "Any of it."

"I am having trouble coming to grips with it all myself," he replied.

"And this Jansai woman? Is her child angelic?"

"That doesn't matter!" Rachel exclaimed.

"I was just asking."

Obadiah shook his head. "I don't know. I don't care. I don't even—Jovah hear me and understand—I don't even care if the baby lives or dies, so long as Rebekah lives. She is all that matters to me."

"She will live," Rachel said solemnly. "I swear to you."

Maga gave the angelica a doubtful glance, as if wondering how anyone could make such a promise, and then turned her attention back to Obadiah. "How did you meet her? How does this story go? And how could you not have said a word to me for all this time?"

So he began the story again, editing it a little this time. Maga nodded and tried not to look disbelieving, but he could see that the romance of the tale appealed to her less than it had to Rachel. She was roused to real horror, though, by the twin tales of Martha's exile and Rebekah's stoning.

"How can such things happen?" she murmured, shaking her dark head and drawing her son closer to her body. "How can anyone have the power to so abuse someone else, someone so powerless—"

"The Jansai have long been abusers," Obadiah said grimly, his gaze resting on Rachel. The angelica knew firsthand how ruthless the Jansai could be. "They have imprisoned and mistreated their women for centuries."

"I've sent for Gabriel," Rachel said.

Obadiah shook his head. He was starting to feel wearier than he ever had in his life, the strain on both body and heart finally making itself felt. "It is the Jansai way. There is nothing Gabriel can do."

"Oh yes," she said, her eyes smoldering with all the righteous triumph of a zealot who finally, finally, had a tool shaped to suit her vengeance. "Gabriel can do anything."

About an hour after she had arrived, the healer smoothed the sheet up to Rebekah's chin and came over to confer with the others in the room.

"How is she?" Obadiah demanded before the woman could speak. "Will she live?"

"Here, Mary, have a seat," Rachel said, drawing a chair over. Few mortals would sit in the presence of an angel unless invited, but Rachel had never had much patience with protocol. "How is she?"

Mary looked troubled. "I think the chances are very good that she will survive," she said. "Her bruises are extensive but not severe, and she has only a slight fever. And that is fading fast. She has suffered some dehydration, but, again, it's not severe. Whoever found her in the desert acted quickly to give her drugs and water, and it is to those people that she truly owes her life."

"She looked so familiar," Obadiah said. "That woman—"

Rachel was watching the healer. "And yet?" the angelica asked.

Mary shook her head. "I don't know. She hasn't regained consciousness. She hasn't spoken or indicated that she—that her mind is engaged. In times of great trauma, I have sometimes seen this. A person withdraws into himself, hides inside his own head, or so it seems. As if the pain he suffered was so great that he cannot bear the idea of opening his eyes and enduring it again. Pain of the body," she explained, "or pain of the heart."

"How can we get her back?" Obadiah asked.

"Sometimes it's just a matter of time—a few days—the body begins to heal and sends its signals of safety on to the brain. Sometimes it takes more, as if you have to push that person out of the closed door of his mind and into the crowded hallway of common life. Sometimes that requires that you talk to the sick person, draw him back to you by the power of your voice, by the memories you evoke. I have seen recoveries prompted by the scent of flowers brought into the room. You don't always know what will fire a person's desire to reenter the world. Or what will show him the way back. Sometimes I think it is not so much the will to return as the way. Someone like this woman, who has been hurt so deeply and gotten lost so completely inside herself, might not remember the path back out."

"Then what can I do?"

"For now, let her sleep. A day or two. I will be back as often as I can. Give her the medicines I leave with you. Make sure she takes in food and water. And talk to her. Remind her of who she is. Who you are. Reassure her that she is safe."

"What about her baby?" Magdalena asked, rocking her own.

"As far as I can tell, the baby is strong. If she lives, her child should live as well."

Rachel leaned over and took Obadiah's hand. "Then they will both survive," the angelica said.

Pain and darkness. Pain and darkness. Fear. Pain and darkness. *Terror.* Pain and darkness.

Color. Voices. Light. Nothing sensible, nothing tangible.

Pain and darkness.

Swirls of light and motion. A cool hand against the skin. Words, incomprehensible. The sounds of stress and worry. Tones of reassurance. Water held to the mouth, a chemical taste against the tongue.

Sleep. Nothing.

More light, more motion. Whispers, questions, emphatic replies. Nothing that made any sense.

Where was this place? Who were these people? A struggle to sit, to think, to remember, to care. Then a swift, indifferent submission. Too hard to try. No energy. No volition.

Darkness. Sleep. No thought, no remembrance. No self.

"Nothing? No word? No response? None at all?"

"I told you. Sometimes it takes days."

"It's been days!"

"Or longer."

"But she is better? Her body is better? And the baby?"

"She is healing. Just be patient."

"I do not have this much patience."
"There is nothing you can do."
"But I love her. . . ."

Words again, sentences that went on an on. Stories told, pictures painted of a world, a place that had no meaning. People that could not be remembered. Names, over and over, until they were just syllables, a collection of sounds, something a bird might chirp or a cricket might rasp out.

Rebekah . . . Rebekah . . . Rebekah . . .

Hands on her face, her forehead. Damp cloth against her skin. Again and again, the cup lifted to her mouth, the water eased down her throat, or the juice, or the broth. Trying, now and then truly trying, to open her eyes, to focus, to see who ministered to her, who repeated those meaningless words. But the strain was too great. The muscles went slack, the brain grew too lazy to try.

Obadiah . . . Obadiah . . . Obadiah . . .

Light and darkness, sound and silence. Nothing else.

"She's still no better?"
"Mary says she is almost healed. It is just—"
"She hasn't woken up."
"She's awake. I know she is. Her eyelids flutter and sometimes— sometimes—it seems as if she's focusing on me. Or trying to. And then she loses interest. As if it's not worth the effort. I don't know how to reach her. I don't know how to draw her back out."
"Maga is worried about you."
"I can't help that."
"I'm worried about you, too. I think you have to spend a day somewhere outside of this room."
"I'm not leaving her alone!"
"I'll stay with her."
"You? Of all the people I picture sitting at a sickbed—"
"Don't be rude. I can take care of her."
"I can't. I can't leave her."
"Gabriel's here."

"What can he do?"

"He wants to talk to you. Go visit with him. Then go spend some time somewhere else—alone, or with Nathan, or anywhere but here. You look dreadful."

"But I'm so worried."

"What can happen to her while I'm at her side? Now go."

Light, fading slowly from gold to gray. Silk against the fingertips, droplets of liquid against the lips. Simple pleasures, easy and undemanding. Luxurious. No pain, no fear.

A woman's voice. *Is it that you don't want to come back or that you don't know the way?* No sensible words. Drowsing, eyes half shut against the slanting sunlight. Dark soon, emptiness to follow. There was no difference.

And then there was a sound.

It caught her wandering attention, it burrowed into her brain. It made the disorganized cloud drifts of her mind cohere around a central point. A sound—a note—a melody.

Someone singing.

The voice moved gradually from the lowest register to a higher octave, gorgeous and insistent. No escaping it, nothing to do but follow after it, stumbling in the half-dark of consciousness. It crooned and beckoned, drawing her forward, luring her into a place of shape and substance. Just when she thought she had grown used to it, just when she thought she could fall back into her waking sleep, the voice sharpened, grew more importunate, coiled around her like an iridescent cord and yanked her on. She was climbing steps, flat, shallow golden stairs, tugged upward by that relentless song.

Now her breath grew labored and swift; now she was afraid, as if she approached a magical doorway at the head of that broad stair. The voice soared with ecstasy, a hummingbird of grace and delight, and Rebekah felt herself gaze after it, lift her hands toward it, want to follow it. Another step up, another, chasing that elusive, alluring creature, hearing that sublime invitation chanted into her ear.

Rebekah. My name is Rebekah.

Glorious now, that voice, exploding with trills and impossible leaps of melody. Intoxicating and irresistible, it summoned her on, and Rebekah ran after it, flung herself up those steps, and through that insubstantial door that closed off the world of dreams.

Gasping, she looked around. She was in a room of stone and windows. On a high bed such as she had never seen before. Staring straight into the face of a golden-haired stranger. Who did not look as if she had been singing, or talking, or doing anything except waiting for Rebekah's appearance through that ensorceled gate.

"I knew you were in there," the golden-haired woman said with a certain satisfaction. "Hello, Rebekah. I'm Rachel."

CHAPTER THIRTY-ONE

They arrived in Cedar Hills late in the afternoon in a sleeting rain. They had been miserable for the past thirty hours, making a cold, wet camp the night before, not even trying to build a fire in the downpour. They had not had a fire their last two nights in the desert, either, since they had burned all their fuel in an attempt to keep their battered patient alive. The trip back from the Gathering had been far less enjoyable and far more eventful than the trip out.

Nonetheless, the three Edori men remained cheerful, making jokes about the cold and the bad weather, and putting together edible meals despite the handicaps. It was Elizabeth who was tense and edgy, thrown into a near frenzy whenever something delayed them on the road. All she could think about was that girl, carried off so suddenly by the angel. All she could do was worry about her, and hope she had survived, and wonder if she would ever know the full story.

Faith would know. The women in the dorm knew every bit of gossip that pertained to any citizen of the town. Faith would know if the angel had arrived in time and if the girl had lived. That was why, when they arrived in the muddy streets of Cedar Hills, Elizabeth almost could not bear their slow progress down the crowded roadways. She wanted to leap from the wagon and dash down the alley to the dorm, pelting pedestrians with questions as she ran.

"Patience," Rufus counseled, laughing at her. "A few more minutes and you'll be home. Out of this rain very shortly."

"It's just—I want to know what happened to her."

"See? I am so certain that she is fine that I cannot bring myself to fret."

"Nothing makes you fret! You Edori—"

He shook his head and ruffled her damp hair. They had rigged a tarp over the back of the wagon, but it hadn't been particularly effective in keeping out the angled rain. "I would fret if you were hurt or missing. I would fret if I came by your door and you would not let me in. There are many things, most of them involving you, that would make me pace across my floor at night."

Elizabeth's face softened and she caught his hand in hers. "You can sleep well at night, then, because I'm not likely to turn you away—*or* go missing for any reason."

"So, see? I cannot be too concerned. Besides, I know our injured traveler has recovered nicely. You have the gift of healing in your hands. Yovah guided her when he put her in your path."

"Yes, but I want to be *sure,* you understand? I am so worried."

And he did understand; a kiss on her cheek signified that. It was another twenty minutes, though, before Paul pulled the wagon to the side of the road so that Rufus could haul Elizabeth's luggage from the back.

"I can carry it myself the rest of the way," she said, and he nodded and didn't try to hold her back. He merely kissed her again, promised to see her the following night, and let her run down the alley toward the dorm without another word of good-bye.

Once inside the door, Elizabeth hurried through the house, shaking her wet hair impatiently back from her eyes and wondering where she might locate Faith. It was still early enough in the day that the other girls could be at work—or in the parlor—or in the kitchen. Elizabeth poked her head into the various common rooms, made brief hellos to the residents who called out a welcome, promised to come back later and tell her stories, and headed up to her bedroom. If Faith wasn't there, Elizabeth would unpack her clothes and take a *real* bath in the water room and then pace up and down till her roommate returned. She could get stories from some of the other girls who lived here, but the best ones would be from Faith.

Who, most conveniently, was propped up in her bed, blanket drawn to her chin and a look of petulance on her face. Felled by a winter ailment, no doubt, and not very happy about it.

"Good, you're sick," Elizabeth said, striding into the room and dumping her possessions on the floor.

"Elizabeth!" Faith squealed, her face transformed. "You're back!"

Elizabeth came straight over to Faith's bed and made herself comfortable sitting at the patient's feet. "Tell me everything that's happened," she commanded.

"Magdalena had her baby. Angel. Boy. They're calling him Jeremiah after Nathan's father—"

"Tell me about that girl," Elizabeth interrupted. "The one that Obadiah brought back."

"I was just getting to that! She . . ." Faith's voice trailed off and she stared at Elizabeth. "How did you know about her?"

"We were the ones who found her in the desert. But she was unconscious—almost dead—I never even learned her name."

"Then you don't know about—sweet Jovah singing, you don't *know!*" Faith exclaimed, nearly bouncing in the bed. She seemed to have completely forgotten her illness, whatever it was. "The most romantic thing! That girl—her name is Rebekah—she's a Jansai—"

"Yes, we figured that out."

"And she'd been secretly meeting with Obadiah for *months.*"

Elizabeth stared at her.

Faith nodded emphatically. "Yes! Really! They were lovers! But he didn't know that she was pregnant—"

"With his—that girl is carrying an angel's child? That girl who almost died in the desert?"

"Yes! That girl who would have died except for you!"

Elizabeth just continued staring, unable to marshal her thoughts. If that were true—but how had it happened? What would have brought an angel and a Jansai together? How could they have met? How could they have courted? And, once having taken an angel for a lover, how had this girl gotten into a situation so desperate? And then, by what unimaginable stroke of coincidence, how had it been

Obadiah who responded to their plague flag, Obadiah who landed just in time to save his lover's life?

"What an impossible tale," Elizabeth said at last. "But has she survived? What's her condition?"

"I think it's still pretty serious. They say Obadiah won't leave her room and that Mary is there every day. Her body is healing but her mind—" Faith shook her head. "It hasn't recovered yet."

"But if her body heals—"

"Mary says she's sure eventually she'll come back to herself."

"And the baby?"

"The baby seems to be healthy. Of course, we don't know if it's an angel baby or not."

Elizabeth nodded. Of course they didn't. But given the other fantastical parts to this tale, Elizabeth was ready to bet that it was. She remembered the sight of that glowing Kiss on the Jansai woman's arm. The god was celebrating some aspect of this woman's life; why not the conception of an angel child?

"How strange," she said slowly, sinking back so her spine rested against the wall. "For so long I wanted to conceive my own angel baby. And now I know I never will. But I may have helped bring one into the world after all."

"You might," Faith argued. "You might still meet an angel who desires you—"

Elizabeth shook her head. "I don't think so. I don't think—I don't want to be with anybody but Rufus."

Faith clasped her hands together under her chin. "So it was good? Your time with Rufus? Did you—was it—all that time together—"

Elizabeth looked over at her and laughed. "Yes, we did. It was. He's wonderful. He's just—" She spread her hands, unable to explain. "It's so much different. It's never felt this way."

"Does he love you?"

"Oh, he loves me."

Faith sighed and sank back into her pillows. "You know, this just gives me hope. See, I met this man the other day—not an angel, and at first I didn't care to talk to him—but he was so funny. And then I saw him again the next day, and I really liked him—"

They talked for another hour, catching up. Shiloh was so sick with pregnancy nausea that she had convinced everyone her child was angelic, but Faith personally believed Shiloh was faking her symptoms. Ruth had had three dates with the angel Matthew but had said very little about them, leading Faith to suspect nothing of importance had occurred. The whole city was in a frenzy as the angels—and many of the residents of Cedar Hills—prepared to head north to the Plain of Sharon. The Gloria would be sung in a little over two weeks' time, and there was still much to be done to get ready.

They would have talked on past dinnertime except that Elizabeth was so grubby and so hungry. She hurried down the hall to take a bath and change her clothes. By the time she returned, Faith had decided she was well enough to join the others in the dining hall. Before leaving the room, they both spent a few minutes fixing their hair.

"But Obadiah," Faith said suddenly, her eyes meeting Elizabeth's in the mirror. "What did he say to you when he found you on the roadside, tending his lover?"

Elizabeth shook her head. "He scarcely even saw me. I'm not sure he even had time to register my face. The minute he recognized her—"

"You mean, he didn't realize it was you? But he *knows* you! You're a friend of his!"

"I'm not his friend. I've seen him from time to time, and he's been kind to me. I'm glad I could do something to help someone he loved. But—" She shook her head again. "We're not friends."

"I would be hurt," Faith said.

Elizabeth smiled. "No, you'd feel like I do. Lucky to have played even a small part in such an amazing story."

Three days later, they were all at breakfast when an urgent knock sounded on the door, and Tola's daughter ran to answer it. Elizabeth's first thought was that it was Mary, looking for Elizabeth's aid in some medical emergency. The healer's fill-in assistant had announced that she was going back to Gaza tomorrow, so Elizabeth had agreed to be ready to work as soon as Mary needed her. She had hoped for another day or two of rest, but that was perhaps greedy;

she had gotten more than she had bargained for already on this particular vacation.

Tola's daughter rushed into the dining room, her eyes wide with excitement. "Someone's come for you," she said to Elizabeth.

Elizabeth came quickly to her feet, swallowing the last of her juice. "I thought that might happen."

"It's an angel!"

A small murmur ran around the table at that, and all the other girls looked speculatively at Elizabeth. "Is it David?" Shiloh asked.

David had never come looking for Elizabeth before and was unlikely to start now. "I doubt it," Elizabeth said shortly. "Probably someone who needs a healer."

But she found, when she hurried down the hall and out the front door, that she had already done what healing she could for this particular angel. "Obadiah," she said blankly when she recognized the fair-haired visitor waiting for her on the street.

He put his hands on her shoulders and stared down at her, his face a mix of pleasure and earnestness and remorse. "Elizabeth," he said, pronouncing her name deliberately. "I am so sorry. It took me a week to remember who you were."

She smiled, feeling a great pleasure wash over her. She had not expected him to remember at all. "You had others to be thinking of at just that moment."

"So you've heard the story? I suppose there are no secrets in Cedar Hills."

"The woman is the one you love, and her baby is yours."

He nodded. "And you saved them. You saved them both."

"She's better, then? They'll be fine?"

"Rebekah is almost healed. There are a few places where the bruises look like they'll never go away. But she's well. She's happy. She's a little nervous—her life in Breven was nothing like the life she sees here—but I think she's happy. She is—and, Elizabeth, I owe her life to you. What can I do to thank you? What can I say?"

"You've already done it," she said. "Just by coming here."

His fingers tightened a moment on her bones. "For the rest of my life, anywhere I am, in any hold in Samaria, you will have a place. You will be welcomed and considered a friend."

What she had dreamed of for so long! Schemed of and sacrificed for! "I have a place somewhere else now," she said quietly. "But to believe you think of me as a friend would make me very happy."

He leaned in and took her in a careful, sweet embrace. She felt the brush of feathers along her back, against the skin of her neck. She could not help it; she shivered with the sheer physical delight of that delicate touch. "Come see her today," he said into her hair. "Come be a friend to both of us." He kissed the top of her head and stepped back, releasing her.

She was moved, but not so overcome that she couldn't smile up at him. "As soon as I can," she promised. "First I have to see if Mary needs me."

CHAPTER THIRTY-TWO

At first Obadiah said he would not go. He would not leave Rebekah. But Gabriel had turned those pure blue eyes on him and said, "You can rescue ten of her or twenty or a hundred, if you come with me." And, as always, there was no gainsaying Gabriel.

He wasn't sure how much to tell Rebekah, still frail and a little disoriented from her week of delirium and her physical ordeal. But Rachel, meddling as always, had been before him, smoothing the way or forcing his hand, it was hard to tell. Always hard to tell with Rachel.

"I hear you're going to Breven," Rebekah said to him, once he had greeted her with a kiss and interrogated her on her own health and the status of the baby. He came to see her maybe six times a day, and every time he asked her the same questions. She endured this with remarkable serenity, as she seemed to endure everything. She did not seem to be suffering at all.

"I—well, Gabriel wants me to go. I haven't decided yet if I will."

"What does he plan to do there?"

Obadiah shrugged. He was playing with Rebekah's fingers, so thin and fragile. She had lost weight and strength during her recovery period, and it would be a long time before she was sturdy again. She was trying to increase her physical durability by taking slow, extended journeys every day through the mazelike hallway of the building. Mary had not yet let her outside to try her balance on the open streets of Cedar Hills.

"Gabriel wants to meet with Uriah, I suppose," Obadiah said. "Express his outrage at what happened to you and to Martha. Bring the full disapproval of the Archangel to bear on the Jansai community. Not that the Jansai community will care, but Gabriel believes in the value of the deliberate gesture. So that everyone knows where he stands and what he will tolerate." He looked up from their entwined fingers and smiled at her. "I don't imagine his censure will change anything, though."

She smiled back, though even that did not alter the seriousness of her sharp, pointed face—even sharper and more keenly angled than before. "Could you do something for me while you're in Breven?"

She had never asked him for anything, not during their courtship, not since she had recovered her senses in Cedar Hills. "Of course! Anything!"

"Will you go to my stepfather's house and tell my family I'm alive?"

He stared at her a long time, trying to read the turmoil that must lie behind the composed face. "Your family members are the ones who tried to kill you."

She shook her head. "Not my mother. Not Jordan. If you could let them know."

He nodded and shrugged, trying to convey that it did not matter how unorthodox it would be—an angel approaching a Jansai house, and bearing such news—that he did not care what kind of chaos he might create with his arrival. "Certainly. I will tell them. Any other messages I can deliver?"

She smiled and leaned forward to kiss him, her mouth lingering against his. "That I am well, and happy, and cared for."

He returned the kiss with some enthusiasm but looked at her with rising doubt. "But—but are you?" he burst out. "You seem so—so ethereal, almost. So calm and so quiet. And after all you have been through. I have been so afraid for you. So worried that you would come back to me terrified and cowering, or not come back to me at all. And here you are—relaxed and tranquil—and I am so afraid. Of what horrors still lurk beneath that calm exterior. I am afraid that you are still stumbling and that I will not be able to catch you when you fall again."

She almost laughed at that. "Oh, Obadiah, you kind man," she said, and kissed him again. "I have been so afraid for so long that there is no more fear left in me. Well, yes, a little bit! I am afraid of what your angel friends think of me, and I am afraid to walk out on your strange streets with my face uncovered, and have everyone look at me, and know who I am, and know my story. I am afraid I won't be a good mother. I'm afraid someday you may no longer love me. I'm—"

"That at least won't happen," he interrupted.

"I'm afraid of all the small terrors that life holds. But only a little afraid. Worried about them. But not very much. My child and I almost died, and yet we have survived. The god wrapped his hands around us and kept us safe. After that, I don't think much of anything will frighten me too deeply. When Jovah puts his finger to your cheek and bids you live, you change a little, that's all."

He put his own finger to her cheek and traced the line of the bone. All healed now, the outer skin. All the bruises gone from the flesh. The bruises to the spirit would last far longer, he thought, than even she might realize. "Don't change too much," he teased. "For I was very fond of you the way you were."

She turned her head to plant a kiss upon his hand. "And I," she whispered against his palm, "am so very fond of you."

They set out around noon the next day, a battalion of angels, and advanced on Breven. They were accompanied by Ariel, down from Monteverde to visit her newborn nephew, and three of the other angels from Gaza. As well as half the angels of the Eyrie and all but two angels from Cedar Hills. The only time angels usually gathered in such numbers was to sing at the Gloria, and Obadiah had to admit it was an impressive sight. A flock of great feathered creatures flying swiftly and purposefully on a mission of justice.

They spent one night on the road and arrived in Breven around noon the next day. As they came closer to the city, Obadiah moved to the head of the phalanx to lead the way to Uriah's. Gabriel, with his majestic wingspan and absolutely unvarying focus on the goal, had led them this far, but Obadiah was the one who best understood the layout and politics of Breven. So he guided them to the gaudy red tent in the commercial district, where Uriah was most likely to be at this time of day, and came to a graceful landing. One by one, the other angels touched down behind him. Nearly seventy angels, wings spread out behind them, hands clasped before them, faces set and serious.

Gabriel nodded to Obadiah, and the two of them strode forward. Half a dozen of Uriah's disciples had rushed out of the tent as the angels began to arrive and now stood staring silently at the intruders. Merchants and their young sons, standing in the shelter of neighboring tents, watched and whispered among themselves. No one stepped up to challenge them. No one asked why they had come.

Obadiah held back the tent flap for Gabriel, and the Archangel stepped inside, ducking his head and folding back his wings to fit through the narrow slot. Obadiah followed, assessing the situation inside with a quick glance. Yes, there was Uriah, on his feet and looking both apprehensive and calculating. There were two of his sons and about ten of his cohorts. All on their feet, all staring. All wondering.

"Good afternoon, Uriah," Obadiah said quietly, nodding at the Jansai leader. "I believe you know the Archangel Gabriel."

Neither of the men stepped forward or offered to shake hands. "We're familiar with each other," Uriah said.

"Good. Then let's not waste time," Gabriel said. The Archangel looked like the very incarnation of divine justice, with his stark face, his black hair, and his icy blue eyes. Every line of his body bespoke righteous anger. "You and your fellow Jansai citizens have recently sent two women into the desert to die. You will stop this practice. While I am Archangel, it will not occur again."

There was a moment of silence and then a disbelieving laugh from Uriah. Around the tent, the other men uttered low growls of anger. "I don't believe it's within your purview to tell the Jansai how to observe their customs. By our laws, these women sinned—"

"I believe it's not only within my purview to tell you, but within my ability to enforce my directives," Gabriel interrupted coldly. "You will not again, while I am Archangel, send a woman into the desert to die."

"I don't think you—"

"There will be a place set up," Gabriel continued, "within the limits of Breven itself, where Jansai women can go when they are endangered. It will be a sanctuary, and once they are there, you cannot touch them. Any woman will be able to go there at any time. This news will be spread to every house and tent in Breven."

The muttering behind them grew louder, but Uriah only laughed. "And who will run this sanctuary for you? What Jansai woman would be so bold?"

"I will install a Manadavvi woman, or a mortal from one of the cities," Gabriel said. Obadiah had high hopes that Zoe would eagerly take this commission, but they had not paused to ask her. "Or a whole contingent of men and women whom I trust to run this place."

"You can pitch your own tent and run the place yourself, but no Jansai woman will use it," Uriah spat at him. "We will keep our women locked in our houses forever before we will bow to some ridiculous mandate from an angel—from *you*. There will be no sanctuaries. There will be no change in the Jansai laws. We will continue to run our lives and the lives of our families as we have for generations."

"You will do as I say," Gabriel said.

Now Uriah did take a step toward the Archangel, fury in every line of his portly body. "Or you will do what, Gabriel? Call down the god's thunderbolts on us—as you did at Windy Point, as you threatened to do when you last treated with Malachi? Or will you instead call down rainstorms, turn the sand of Breven into a wretched bog? That, too, you threatened in the past. Well, bring down your god's wrath. Make your fiery little speeches. The Jansai are not afraid of you. We will not do your bidding."

Gabriel shrugged, the motion causing his taut white wings to tremble and settle back. "Then your city will slowly die," he said in a flat, unemotional voice. "I will spread the word to the Harths and the Vashirs in Gaza: Do not trade with the Jansai. I will call a council of merchants in Semorrah and Castelana and every town along the Galilee River, and I will tell them: Do not trade with the Jansai. I will send angels to every farm and homestead in the three provinces. I will walk through the azure streets of the Blue City myself. I will raise my voice—and my voice can be heard across Samaria—and I will say one thing only: Do not trade with the Jansai. I will ruin you with commerce, Uriah, more slowly and more certainly than I could ruin you with weather. Don't think I will not do what I say."

Uriah's eyes snapped to Obadiah's. "He cannot mean any of this," Uriah grated out.

Obadiah spread his hands in a complicated, temporizing gesture. *We have been such good friends, you and I; I would spare you the bad news now if I could.* "I have known Gabriel forever," Obadiah said quietly. "He never promises what he is not willing to ensure."

"But he can't be serious!"

"I assure you, I am."

"I assure you, he is," Obadiah said with gentle regret. When he wanted to jump up and down, howl in satisfaction, point his fingers, and level all sorts of accusations at the men in the tent. But Gabriel had told him to continue to play the part of mediator, to act as if he would do what he could to see that reason prevailed. Gabriel might be righteous, but he was not rash; he liked to keep an ally or two in position. "I told you before, the angels are willing to see the Edori become the commercial conduit of the country. In the face of this fresh scandal—" Obadiah shrugged, his wings, like Gabriel's, fluttering with the motion. "The Archangel is more than ever determined to see such an alternate plan come to fruition. You do not have much to bargain with, I am afraid."

"But this is our life! Our culture! Our ways! We do not interfere with angel ways! We do not ride into the cities and proclaim their customs wrong—though we think them sinful and appalling. We do not attempt to force our beliefs on anyone outside of our own people—"

"The difference is, your own people are put to death for your beliefs," Gabriel said shortly. "Unacceptable."

Uriah was in a rage now, pacing closer to the angels and then farther away. The men in the tent had bunched together behind him and were muttering furiously among themselves. "Unacceptable? Tell me if *this* is unacceptable to you!" the Jansai leader shot at them, still pacing. "You think your god requires a member of every race to be present on the Plain of Sharon when you sing your precious Gloria. You think he will punish us all if you do not come together in harmony. Well, you have just knocked harmony from the world! There is discord now and forever between angels and Jansai! There will be no Jansai on that plain when you go to sing in a few weeks, and you will see then whether the god hears your voices! You will see then whom he strikes down!"

"There will be at least one Jansai present when we go to sing," Gabriel said with infinite calm.

"We will stay in Breven—every one," Uriah snarled.

"Oh no," Gabriel said. "Didn't I tell you? The woman Rebekah whom you expelled two weeks ago. She survived, and she is in the hands of the angels now. She will be happy to come sing with us and thank the god for her deliverance."

Uriah gaped, and the men behind him gawked. Gabriel added, "You have until tomorrow morning to think about my terms. We stay at the Hotel Verde, and we leave with the dawn."

The Archangel spun around with a whirl of white feathers and headed for the door of the tent. Then he paused, turned back, and fixed his gaze on an object to his left. "And I believe I will take that with me as I go," he announced. In three long strides he had crossed to the firestick Uriah kept in his tent, lifted it from its box, and stalked back to the doorway. "Thank you," he said, and walked out. Even stooping to duck through the canvas door did not detract from his dignity.

Obadiah paused to give the Jansai leader a sorrowful glance. "It is a new day, Uriah," he said. "Gabriel will not relent." And then he, too, slipped through the tent, narrowing his wings behind him so that he could ease through the constricted door.

Outside, he found Gabriel giving orders and dividing the host of angels into sections. "Every house," the Archangel was saying, carelessly leaning on the firestick as if it were a cane. "Every tent. I will go to the Hotel Verde and prepare them for company."

In minutes, the residential streets of Breven were alive with angels. They went in pairs from gate to gate, door to door, raising their beautiful voices and commanding the residents of each house to come forward.

"Bring us your women!" cried Daniel, Obadiah's partner in this enterprise, every time the homeowner threw open his door and stared out.

"What? I will not—*what?*" was the typical response as the blustery Jansai merchant and two or three of his sons stared at their angelic visitors.

"Then we will go to them," would be Daniel's response, and the two angels would brush past them and into the houses.

After they had entered three or four mansions, Obadiah's impressions became somewhat confused. There were similarities to each: the great dividing wall between the men's quarters and the women's, the smooth, heat-absorbing stone of the walls and floors, the lush rugs and tapestries and gorgeous baubles strewn carelessly about as arrogant symbols of wealth. In each house, there were crowds of young men and teenage boys, alarmed and questioning; there were one or two older men, angry but a little afraid.

And there were the women, a few of them shrieking, all of them covering their faces with hastily grabbed garments, shrinking back against the walls. They could be found in the kitchens, in the separate dining areas, and sometimes—because Obadiah and Daniel did not stop looking through the house until they had found a cluster of them—a few stories up in the sewing rooms. They all looked terrified, their big eyes darting around the room, glancing from their husbands' faces to the faces of the avenging angels.

"We have come to tell you of a new day in Breven," Daniel said to each audience. "No longer will you be forced to cower in your houses, subject to the whims of the men who are supposed to love you. The angels are setting up a place of safety in the city of Breven itself. Any woman, of any age, who wants to leave her husband's protection, or her brother's, or her father's, may come to this place and be free."

"Any woman who wants to leave now, with us, may do so," Obadiah always added in a quiet voice. "We will take you to Cedar Hills and give you tools to start your life over."

They had been in more houses than Obadiah could count—fifteen, twenty—before a young woman actually broke free of her mother's protective embrace and scrambled across the room toward them. "Take me," she begged, falling on her knees before Daniel. "Take me with you."

Her mother screamed and her father bullied his way forward,

face contorted with fury and fist upraised to strike. Daniel blocked his blow and shoved the man backward with so much force that he crashed into a table on the other side of the room.

"She comes with us," Daniel said, "and any other who so chooses."

It took hours for the troops of angels to canvass the city, moving slowly from the inner circles of wealth to the outer circles of poverty. Twice Obadiah and Daniel made visits to the Hotel Verde, flying low over the streets so that anyone who wished to look up could see that angels had invaded Breven and were present still. Each time they brought back with them a woman who had stepped forward and asked to be given shelter. Each time they found, back at the hotel, a growing cadre of rebel women who had similarly taken this remarkable chance. Not as many as Obadiah would have expected—frankly, he would have thought the whole gender would have risen up and fled the city limits—but a good number, thirty or forty. Enough to send the Jansai men fuming into the streets. To create a backlash, perhaps, to make conditions even worse for the women left behind.

But so many of them had stayed, wedded to their accustomed lives and the families they loved. Had she not been pregnant, Obadiah wondered, would Rebekah ever have chosen to abandon the life she knew for a terrifyingly unfamiliar place and people? He did not think so. He thought only great fear, and the fierce love she bore for her endangered child, had driven her out at the end—almost too late, even so. He had to wonder what compelling pressures these refugees were under, how dire their own lives had become, that they, like Rebekah, would make the bitter decision to break away.

"I think we have covered the city," Gabriel said, coming up to Obadiah as he surveyed the crowded atrium of the Hotel Verde. Zoe and her brother were bringing out pillows and blankets and helping the women create makeshift bedrooms by the pillars and plants. "Eva and Ariel are back from the outer tents. We have carried the word everywhere."

"And returned with quite a haul," Obadiah said.

Gabriel's glance flickered over the crowd. "We may find ourselves with one or two more before the night is ended," the Archangel predicted. "Women who were not willing to walk away while their whole families were watching may find a way to slip out under cover of darkness."

"And Zoe?" Obadiah asked. "Has she agreed to turn this hotel into a safe zone for Jansai women?"

A wintry smile lightened Gabriel's stern features. "The young lady was most willing," Gabriel said. "Her brother and father, however, would like to work out a system of monetary compensation. This hotel is a commercial establishment, after all, and cannot support a whole range of charitable endeavors."

Obadiah could not help smiling. "Jovah bless the Manadavvi and their mercenary hearts," he said. "But you have come to an agreement?"

"Not yet," Gabriel said, "but we will. I think I will leave a few angels here for a day or so yet, and we will probably need to have a permanent presence in Breven for a while. But I believe we have made our point and shaken Uriah to the core."

"He will agree to the terms," Obadiah said.

Gabriel shrugged, utterly indifferent. "He will have to."

Obadiah nodded. "Then, if you are done with me—"

Gabriel gave him a swift look of amusement. "Back to Cedar Hills tonight? You are that impatient?"

Obadiah shook his head. "No. I will leave with the rest of you in the morning. But I have another visit to make while I am here."

It was true night by the time Obadiah came to a hover above Hector's house. His first impulse was to go to the front door and pound on it, demanding admittance, as he had done all day. But then he spotted two figures below him in the sere inner garden. From the air they appeared to be two older women, sitting on a stone bench in the cold dark, their faces fairly well-illuminated by the light of a half moon. Obadiah wondered if they had come outside to discuss secrets in privacy, or if they were so weary of the echoes of trouble that still sounded inside this house that they sought an escape by sitting out in the chilly night air.

"Do not be afraid," he called out in a low voice, and drifted down to join them. Both women came to their feet as he touched down and folded his wings back, but neither of them looked alarmed. One of them automatically covered her face with her hand, so the stranger could not see it, but the other one looked too weary and too sad to make even that much effort.

"The angels have already been here," said the bare-faced woman in a tired voice. She looked old enough to be Rebekah's grandmother. One of Hector's aunts, perhaps. "You do not need to tell us again how the city of Breven is now flung open."

"No, I have other news," Obadiah said. "Bring the boy Jordan to me. I have a message."

"A message?" the old woman said sharply, and then turned to her companion. "Go get Jordan."

She hurried off, and Obadiah was left alone with the woman who had spoken. "It will do no good, you know," she said. "Rounding up women and pretending the Jansai must live as the rest of you do. For hundreds of years, the Jansai have followed their own laws and customs. No matter what your Gabriel manages to do while he is in charge, everything will change back the minute his laws are lifted. The Jansai traditions are stronger than the Archangel's will."

"Maybe," said Obadiah. "But there are thirty or so women who have chosen to come with us today, and their lives will be immeasurably altered—and the lives of their daughters and their sons. I think that is good enough for Gabriel."

The old woman shrugged. "Maybe I am too old and have seen too much," she said in a harsh voice. "I no longer believe in miracles."

Just then, the door to the house opened, and a young boy emerged, unaccompanied by the woman sent to fetch him. He looked to be about fifteen, his face sloped and angled just like Rebekah's, his expression solemn, his body tense.

"We have already been visited by angels today," the boy said quietly. "My stepfather has heard your conditions."

Obadiah wanted to brush the dark hair from the boy's eyes, to put his hands on the thin shoulders and transfer some of his own strength into that slim body. But he was a Jansai man, or would be soon, and not likely to welcome easy sympathy from an angel.

"Jordan," Obadiah said, "I have a message from your sister."

The boy stiffened, and the old woman cried out, then covered her mouth with her hand.

Obadiah continued. "She is alive, she is in Cedar Hills, and she is under my protection. I will care for her—and her baby—the rest of her life."

"*You?*" the old woman whispered. "An angel? It was *you?*"

Jordan's face was expressionless—not as if he hid fury, but as if he was too afraid to believe, in case the words weren't true. "She gave me two things to give to you," Obadiah went on, pulling the items from his vest pocket and offering them to the motionless boy. "This letter and this bracelet."

The letter was sealed, and Obadiah had no idea what words it contained. The bracelet was his own, a circlet of silver set with sapphires. It was meant for a man's wrist, Rebekah had explained, and Jordan knew how much she had loved it.

"She is—Rebekah is alive?" Jordan whispered, his fingers closing over both tokens.

Obadiah nodded. "You are to tell your mother as well."

"Praise the great good god," the old woman breathed, and began to cry. Jordan turned to her swiftly, as if to offer manly comfort, but Obadiah was not deceived. Even in the dark, he had seen the glitter of water in the boy's eyes. When Jordan bent over the old woman, murmuring something into her ear, a tear sparkled across his cheek and fell unnoticed onto the hard earth of the garden.

CHAPTER THIRTY-THREE

The driver clucked impatiently to his horses and tried to maneuver around the broken-down rig in his way. Not that he would get very far very fast even if he was able to pass the wreck. The streets of Cedar Hills were jammed with conveyances of every description—Edori carts, Manadavvi caravans, wagonloads of lumber, and grain and merchandise—all jostling together down the main avenues with a clamor of hooves and squeals and curses. His own course would take him through the completed central district and down to the warehouses on the far edge of town. He was beginning to wonder if he would not have been better off striking out across the unpaved grass and circling the city to its western edge. The horses might have foundered in the slashes of mud and patches of snow, but all in all, he didn't think he would have wasted so much time.

"Jovah's bones! Will you move out of the way?" some irate traveler called out behind him, but he merely shrugged and pointed to the obstacle in his path. Two laborers were grunting over the ruined wagon, trying to pull it to the side of the road, but it didn't look as if they'd make much progress very soon. He might be here for the rest of the hour.

The driver took advantage of his temporary pause to glance around the city and see what had changed in the months since he'd been here. There—that restaurant looked new—and surely that shop on the corner had just opened? He thought it had been covered in board and scaffolding last time he'd driven through. He might stable the horses and take a room for a day or two—plenty of new hotels to try out—and spend a little time browsing through the retail establishments. The god knew he got little chance to savor the luxuries of life when he was on the farm or on the road.

A cluster of young women walked by, laughing and talking, and he eyed them appreciatively. Not quite spring here, but they were all dressed in pale, fluttering dresses, made of the thinnest lace and gauze. Might be more to see in Cedar Hills than cafes and the newest fashionable clothing. That brown-haired girl, she looked like she'd offer a man an interesting time, or that tall blonde, or the one with the dark auburn hair framing a serious face.

Hold a moment. He knew that face—he knew that hair. He frowned, trying to remember, for he only had a few acquaintances in Cedar Hills, and none of them were quite so youthful. But even though she was half turned away from him, responding to something one of her companions had said, he had the clearest memory of her features, seen at a close and friendly distance.

And then he remembered. "Elizabeth!" he called out, standing up and waving to get her attention. "Elizabeth! Hey! Over here!"

At the sound of her name, she turned and scanned the traffic, trying to identify the man who would address her so rudely in public. She said something to the women with her and then crossed the road to speak to him.

"Yes?" she said, her voice neutral and the look on her face warning him that she didn't take solicitations from strangers.

But he was delighted to see her. "Elizabeth! It's me! Bennie! How are you? It's been months since I left you here!"

"Bennie—" she said, and then her face changed. She smiled up at him, turning into a much prettier girl than he remembered. Then again, she hadn't smiled much on their trip together. "Well, hello! I never thought to see you again. What brings you to Cedar Hills?"

He jerked a thumb over his shoulder, indicating his cargo in back. "Got a load to deliver. His lordship struck a deal to send hardwoods to the hold. All this building going on, I can't imagine there will be a tree left in Jordana by the time it's all over."

"So you're still working for James? How's everybody back at the farm?"

He grinned at her. " 'Bout as you'd expect. Such a ruckus there was when you didn't come back with me!"

"I'm sorry. Did you get in trouble? Doesn't look like they fired you."

"Well, your cousin was all set on letting me go, but his wife had a much more realistic view. She said, 'Elizabeth's a grown woman and well able to take care of herself. If she wanted to leave the safety of a good home for the uncertainty of life as a—' Well, you don't want to hear exactly what she specified there. Anyway, she said, 'That's entirely Elizabeth's decision. We certainly don't need to lose a good worker because of that silly girl's behavior.' "

"Sounds like Angeletta," Elizabeth observed. "I'm surprised she didn't offer you a bonus for getting rid of me."

Bennie grinned. "Who says she didn't? Anyway, they kept me on. I thought about moving on anyway, since the life doesn't quite suit me, but his lordship decided I should be his primary driver. And I like the travel just fine. So I'm staying. For a while, anyway."

"I'm glad to hear you're doing well."

"And you? Don't mind if I say that you look wonderful."

She laughed. "I don't mind at all. I feel wonderful. Life has been very good for me in Cedar Hills. Thank you for recommending Tola's for me. She's been very kind."

"So you found a place, found a job, all that?"

"Yes. I'm learning to become a healer, and I've made many good friends, and—oh, it's the best part! I've fallen in love."

"Did you now! So that angel thing worked out for you after all."

She shook her head. One of her friends, waiting impatiently across the road, called out Elizabeth's name, and she held up a hand to indicate that she'd only be another moment. "No. Turns out I didn't have much luck with angels. But I've found someone better."

"I didn't know there *was* anything better," he observed.

She laughed again. "Neither did I." Her friend called to her again. "I've got to go," she added. "It was good to run into you. If James asks, tell him you saw me and that I'm well and happy."

"And if he doesn't ask?"

"Then make sure you tell Angeletta."

Bennie was the one to laugh at that. With a quick wave, she made her good-bye, darting across the street just ahead of an oncoming vehicle. Bennie watched her go, saw her exchange a few animated words with the other women, and kept his eyes on them till they disappeared around one of the newly painted corners of Cedar Hills. No more time to dawdle or daydream, though; the wrecked rig in front of him had finally been dragged out of his way. He snapped the reins, and the horses started forward, picking their way past the ruined wagon. Yes, he thought he might stay in Cedar Hills for at least a day or two. Even if he never caught sight of Elizabeth again, there was so much to see in this freshly built town. It was a city of possibilities, after all.